P9-DCC-769

By Anne Perry
Published by The Ballantine Publishing Group:

Featuring Thomas and Charlotte Pitt:
THE CATER STREET HANGMAN
CALLANDER SQUARE
PARAGON WALK
RESURRECTION ROW
BLUEGATE FIELDS
RUTLAND PLACE
DEATH IN THE DEVIL'S ACRE
CARDINGTON CRESCENT
SILENCE IN HANOVER CLOSE
BETHLEHEM ROAD
HIGHGATE RISE
BELGRAVE SQUARE
FARRIERS' LANE
THE HYDE PARK HEADSMAN
TRAITORS GATE
PENTECOST ALLEY
ASHWORTH HALL
BRUNSWICK GARDENS
BEDFORD SQUARE

Featuring William Monk:
THE FACE OF A STRANGER
A DANGEROUS MOURNING
DEFEND AND BETRAY
A SUDDEN, FEARFUL DEATH
THE SINS OF THE WOLF
CAIN HIS BROTHER
WEIGHED IN THE BALANCE
THE SILENT CRY
A BREACH OF PROMISE
THE TWISTED ROOT

THE TWISTED ROOT

Anne Perry

BALLANTINE BOOKS • NEW YORK

A Ballantine Book
Published by The Ballantine Publishing Group
Copyright © 1999 by Anne Perry

www.randomhouse.com/BB/

Library of Congress Catalog Card Number: 00-104507

ISBN 0-8041-1936-8

Manufactured in the United States of America

First Mass Market Domestic Edition: September 2000

10 9 8 7 6 5 4 3 2 1

To June Anderson,
for her unfailing friendship

THE
TWISTED
ROOT

1

THE YOUNG MAN stood in the doorway, his face pale, his fingers clenched on his hat, twisting it around and around.

"Mr. William Monk, agent of enquiry?" he asked. He looked to be in his early twenties.

"Yes," Monk acknowledged, rising to his feet. "Come in, sir. How can I assist you?"

"Lucius Stourbridge." He held out his hand, coming farther into the room. He did not even glance at the two comfortable armchairs or the bowl of flowers pleasantly scenting the air. These had been Hester's idea. Monk had been perfectly happy with the sparse and serviceable appearance the rooms had presented before.

"How can I help you, Mr. Stourbridge?" Monk asked, indicating one of the chairs.

Lucius Stourbridge sat uncomfortably on the edge of it, looking as if he did so more because he had been instructed to than from any desire. He stared at Monk intently, his eyes filled with misery.

"I am betrothed to be married, Mr. Monk," he began. "My future wife is the most charming, generous and noble-minded person you could wish to meet." He glanced down, then up at Monk again quickly. The ghost of a smile crossed his face and vanished. "I am aware that my opinion is prejudiced, and I must sound naïve, but you will find that others

1

also regard her most highly, and my parents have a sincere affection for her."

"I don't doubt you, Mr. Stourbridge," Monk assured him, but he was uncomfortable with what he believed this young man would ask of him. Even when he most urgently needed work he only reluctantly accepted matrimonial cases. And having just returned from an extravagant three-week honeymoon in the Highlands of Scotland, this was rapidly becoming one of those times. He had an agreement with his friend and patron, Lady Callandra Daviot, that in return for informing her of his most interesting cases, and—where she wished—including her in the day-to-day process, she would replenish his funds, at least sufficiently for his survival. But he had no desire or intention that he should avail himself of her generosity any longer.

"What is it that troubles you, Mr. Stourbridge?" he asked.

Lucius looked utterly wretched. "Miriam—Mrs. Gardiner—has disappeared."

Monk was puzzled. "Mrs. Gardiner?"

Lucius shook himself impatiently. "Mrs. Gardiner is a widow. She is . . ." He hesitated, a mixture of irritation and embarrassment in his face. "She is a few years older than I. It is of no consequence."

If a young woman fled her betrothal it was a purely private matter. If there was no crime involved, and no reason to suppose illness, then whether she returned or not was her decision. Monk would not ordinarily have involved himself. However, his own happiness was so sharp he felt an uncharacteristic sympathy for the anguished young man who sat on the chair opposite him so obviously at his wits' end.

Monk could never before remember having felt that the world was so supremely right. Of course, this was midsummer 1860, and he had no memory, except in flashes, of anything at all before the coaching accident in 1856, from which he had woken in hospital with a mind completely blank. Even so, it was beyond his ability to imagine anything so complete as the well-being that filled him now.

After Hester had accepted his proposal of marriage he had been alternately elated and then beset by misgivings that such a step would destroy forever the unique trust they had built between them. Perhaps they could not satisfactorily be anything more than friends, colleagues in the fierce pursuit of justice. He had spent many bleak nights awake, cold with the fear of losing something which seemed more and more precious with every additional thought of no longer possessing it.

But as it happened, every fear had vanished like a shadow before the rising sun over the great sweeping hills they had walked together. Even though he had discovered in her all the warmth and passion he could have wished, she was still as perfectly willing and capable of quarreling with him as always, of being perverse, of laughing at him, and of making silly mistakes herself. Not a great deal had changed, except that now there was a physical intimacy of a sweetness he could not have dreamed, and it was the deeper for having been so long in the discovery.

So he did not dismiss Lucius Stourbridge as his better judgment might dictate.

"Perhaps you had better tell me precisely what happened," he said gently.

Lucius took a gulp of air. "Yes." Deliberately, he steadied himself. "Yes, of course. Naturally. I'm sorry, I seem to be a little incoherent. This has all struck me . . . very hard. I don't know what to think."

So much was quite apparent, and Monk with difficulty forbore from saying so. He was not naturally tolerant. "If you would begin by telling me when you last saw Miss—Mrs. Gardiner, that would be a place from which to proceed," he suggested.

"Of course," Lucius agreed. "We live in Cleveland Square, in Bayswater, not far from Kensington Gardens. We were having a small party in celebration of our forthcoming marriage. It was a beautiful day, and we were playing a game of

3

croquet, when quite suddenly, and for no apparent reason, Miriam—Mrs. Gardiner—became extremely distraught and rushed from the garden. I did not see her go, or I would have gone after her—to find out if she was ill or if I could help . . ."

"Is she often ill?" Monk asked curiously. Genuine invalids were one thing, but young women subject to fits of the vapors were creatures with whom he had no patience at all. And if he were to help this unfortunate young man, he must know as much of the truth as possible.

"No," Lucius said sharply. "She is of excellent health and most equable and sensible temperament."

Monk found himself flushing very slightly. If anyone had suggested Hester were the fainting sort he would have pointed out with asperity that she indisputably had more stomach for a fight, or a disaster, than they had themselves. As a nurse on the battlefields of the Crimea she had more than proved that true. But there was no need to apologize to Lucius Stourbridge. It had been a necessary question.

"Who saw her leave?" he asked calmly.

"My uncle, Aiden Campbell, who was staying with us at the time—indeed, he still is. And I believe my mother also, and one or two of the servants and other guests."

"And was she ill?"

"I don't know. That is the point, Mr. Monk! No one has seen her since. And that was three days ago."

"And those people who did see her," Monk said patiently, "what did they tell you? Surely she cannot simply have walked out of the garden into the street alone, without money or luggage, and disappeared?"

"Oh . . . no," Lucius corrected himself. "The coachman, Treadwell, is missing also, and, of course, one of the coaches."

"So it would appear that Treadwell took her somewhere," Monk concluded. "Since she left the croquet match of her own will, presumably she asked him to take her. What do you know of Treadwell?"

Lucius shrugged slightly, but his face was, if anything, even paler. "He has been with the family for three or four

4

years. I believe he is perfectly satisfactory. He is related to the cook—a nephew or something. You don't think he could have . . . harmed her?"

Monk had no idea, but there was no purpose in causing unnecessary distress. The young man was in a desperate enough state as it was.

"I think it far more likely he merely took her wherever she wished to go," he replied, and then realized his answer made no sense. If that were the case, Treadwell would have returned within hours. "But it does seem as if he may have taken your carriage for his own purposes." Other far darker thoughts came to his mind, but it was too soon to speak of them yet. There were many other simpler answers of everyday private tragedy which were more likely, the most probable being that Miriam Gardiner had simply changed her mind about the marriage but had lacked the courage to face young Lucius Stourbridge and tell him so.

Lucius leaned forward. "But do you believe Miriam is safe, Mr. Monk? If she is, why has she not contacted me?" His throat was so tight his words were half strangled. "I have done everything I can think of. I have spoken with every one of my friends she might have gone to. I have searched my mind for anything I could have said or done to cause her to mistrust me, and I can think of nothing. We were so close, Mr. Monk. I am as certain of that as of anything on earth. We were not only in love, but we were the best of friends. I could speak to her of anything, and she seemed to understand, indeed, to share my views and tastes in a way which made her at once the most exciting and yet the most comfortable person to be with." He colored faintly. "Perhaps that sounds absurd to you—"

"No," Monk said quickly, too quickly. He had spoken it from the heart, and he was not accustomed to revealing so much of himself, certainly not to a prospective client in a case he did not really want and which he believed impossible to see to a happy solution.

5

Lucius Stourbridge was gazing at him intensely, his wide, brown eyes deeply troubled.

"No," Monk repeated with less emphasis. "I am sure it is possible to feel such an affinity with someone." He hurried on, away from emotion to facts. "Perhaps you would tell me something of your family and the circumstances of your meeting Mrs. Gardiner."

"Yes, yes, of course." Lucius seemed relieved to have something definite to do. "My father is Major Harry Stourbridge. He is now retired from the army, but he served with great distinction in Africa, and particularly in Egypt. He spent much time there early in his career. In fact, he was there when I was born."

A faint smile touched his face. "I should like to go there someday myself. I have listened to him speak of it with the greatest pleasure." He dismissed the thought ruefully. "Our family comes from Yorkshire—the West Riding. That is where our land is. All entailed on the male line, of course, but most substantial. We go there occasionally, but my mother prefers to spend the season in town. I daresay most people do, especially women."

"Do you have brothers or sisters?" Monk interrupted.

"No. Regrettably, I am an only child."

Monk did not remark that Lucius would thus inherit this very considerable property, but it was evident in the young man's face that he, too, had taken the point, and his lips tightened, a faint flush marked his cheeks.

"My family has no objections to my marriage," the younger man said with a slight edge of defensiveness. He sat perfectly still in the chair, looking straight at Monk, his eyes unblinking. "My father and I are close. He is happy for my happiness, and indeed, he is fond of Miriam, Mrs. Gardiner, himself. He sees no fault in her character or her reputation. The fact that she has no dowry or property to bring to the marriage is immaterial. I shall have more than sufficient for our needs, and physical possessions are of no importance to me compared with the prospect of spending my life in the companionship of a woman of courage, virtue and good humor, and whom I love more than anyone else on earth." His voice cracked a little on the last few words, and the effort it cost him to keep his composure was apparent.

Monk felt the other man's distress with a reality far greater than he could have imagined even a few weeks before. In spite of his intention to concentrate entirely upon Lucius Stourbridge's situation, his mind re-created pictures of himself and Hester walking side by side along a quiet beach in the late-evening sunlight, the color blazing across the northern sky, shadowing the hills purple in the distance and filling the air with radiance. They had not needed to speak to each other, knowing wordlessly that they saw the same beauty and felt the same desire to keep it—and the knowledge that it was impossible. And yet the fact that they had shared it gave the moment a kind of immortality.

And there had been other times: laughter shared at the antics of a dog with a paper bag in the wind; the pleasure of a really good sandwich of fresh bread and cheese after a long walk, the climb to the top of a hill; the gasp of wonder at the view, and the relief at not having to go any farther.

If Lucius had had any such happiness in his life, and lost it for no reason he could understand, no wonder he was at his wits' end to find the answer. However ugly or shattering to his dreams the truth might be, he could not begin to heal until he knew it.

"Then I shall do all I can to discover what happened," Monk said aloud. "And if she is willing to return to you—"

"Thank you!" Lucius said eagerly, his face brightening. "Thank you, Mr. Monk! Cost will be no consideration, I promise you. I have more than sufficient means of my own, but my father is also determined to find out what has happened to Miriam. What may I do to assist you?"

"Tell me the story of your acquaintance, and all you know about Mrs. Gardiner," Monk replied with a sinking feeling inside him.

"Of course." Lucius's face softened, the strain eased out of it as if merely remembering their meeting were enough to fill him with happiness. "I had called upon a friend of mine who lived in Hampstead, and I was walking back across the Heath. It was about this time of year, and quite beautiful. There were several people around, children playing, an elderly couple quite close to me, just smiling together in the sun." He smiled to himself as he described it. "There was a small boy rolling a hoop, and a puppy chasing a stick. I stopped and watched the dog. It was so full of life, bounding along with its tail wagging, and returning the stick, immensely pleased with itself. I found I was laughing at it. It was a little while before I realized it was a young woman who was throwing the stick. Once it landed almost at my feet, and I picked it up and threw it back again, just for the pleasure of watching. Of course, she and I fell into conversation. It all happened so naturally. I asked her about the dog, and she told me it actually belonged to a friend of hers."

His eyes were far away, his memory sharp. "One subject of conversation led to another, and before I realized it I had been talking with her for nearly an hour. I made it my business to return the following day, and she was there again." He gave a very slight shrug of self-mockery. "I don't suppose for a moment she thought it was chance, nor did I feel any inclination to pretend. There was never that between us. She seemed to perceive what I meant as naturally as if she had had the same thoughts and feelings herself. We laughed at the same things, or found them beautiful, or sad. I have never felt so totally at ease with anyone as I did with her."

Monk tried to imagine it. It was certainly not as he had felt with Hester. Invigorated, tantalized, furious, amused, admiring, even awed, but not very often comfortable.

No—that was not entirely true. Now that he had at last acknowledged to himself that he loved her, and had stopped trying to force her into the mold of the kind of woman he used to imagine he wanted, but accepted her more or less as herself, he was comfortable more often than he was not.

8

And, of course, there had always been the times when they were engaged in the same cause. She had fought side by side with the courage and imagination, the compassion and tenacity, that he had seen in no other woman— no other person. Then it was a kind of companionship which even Lucius Stourbridge could not guess at.

"And so your friendship progressed," he said, going on to summarize what must have followed. "In time you invited her to meet your family, and they also found her most likable."

"Yes—indeed . . ." Lucius agreed. He was about to continue but Monk interrupted him. He needed the information that might help in his efforts to find the missing woman, although he held little hope the outcome would prove happy for Lucius, or indeed for any of them. A woman would not flee from her prospective husband and his house, and remain gone for the space of several days without sending word, unless there was a profound problem which she could see no way of solving.

"What do you know of Mrs. Gardiner's first husband?" Monk asked.

"I believe he was somewhat older than she," Lucius answered without hesitation. "A man in a moderate way of business, sufficient to leave her provided for, and with a good reputation and no doubt of money or of honor." He said it firmly, willing Monk to believe him and accept the value of such things.

Monk read within the omissions that the late Mr. Gardiner was also of a very much more ordinary background than Lucius Stourbridge, with his inherited lands and wealth, and his father's outstanding military career. He would like to have known Miriam Gardiner's personal background, whether she spoke and comported herself like a lady, whether she had the confidence to face the Stourbridge family or if she was secretly terrified of them. Was she afraid, every time she spoke, of betraying some inadequacy in herself? He could imagine it only too easily. He had been the country boy from

9

a Northumbrian fishing village, down in London trying to play the gentleman. Funny, he only remembered that now, thinking of Miriam Gardiner also trying to escape from an ordinary background and fit in with a different class of person. Every time she sat at the table had she also worried about using the wrong implement or making a foolish observation, of being ignorant of current events or of knowing no one? But he could not ask Lucius such things. If Lucius were capable of seeing the answer, he would not now be staring at Monk so earnestly, his dark eyes full of hope.

"I think I had better begin by visiting your home, Mr. Stourbridge," Monk said aloud. "I would like to see where the event happened which apparently distressed Mrs. Gardiner so much, and with your family's permission, speak to them, and to your servants, and learn whatever they are able to tell me."

"Of course!" Lucius shot to his feet. "Thank you, Mr. Monk. I am eternally grateful to you. I am sure if you can just find Miriam, and I could be certain that she is unhurt, then we shall overcome everything else." Shadows filled his face again as he realized how strong was the possibility that she was not all right. He could think of no reason otherwise why she would not have sent him some message. "When shall you be ready to depart?"

Monk felt rushed, and yet Lucius was right: the matter was urgent—in fact, they might already be too late. If he was going to attempt the job at all, he should do it immediately. He could leave a note for Hester, explaining that he had accepted a case and would return whenever he had made his first assessment of the situation. He could not tell her in person because she was at the hospital working with Callandra Daviot. Of course, it was in a purely voluntary way. He had refused absolutely to allow her to help to support them by earning her own living. The subject was still one of contention between them. No doubt she would return to it sooner or later.

10

For the moment Monk had a case himself, and he must make himself ready to go with Lucius Stourbridge.

The Stourbridge house in Cleveland Square in Bayswater was handsome in the effortless style of those to whom money is not of concern. Its beauty was restrained, and it had obviously been designed in an earlier and simpler age. Monk found it greatly pleasing and would have paused to admire it longer had not Lucius strode ahead of him to the front door and opened it without waiting for a footman or maid.

"Come in," he invited Monk, standing back and waving his hand as if to urge him to hurry.

Monk stepped inside, but was given no time to look around him at the hallway with its family portraits against the oak paneling. He was dimly aware of one picture dominating the others, a portrait of a horseman in the uniform of the Hussars at the time of Waterloo. Presumably he was some earlier Stourbridge, also of military distinction.

Lucius was walking rapidly across the dark tiled floor towards the farthest doorway. Monk followed after him, no more than glancing up at the finely plastered ceiling or the wide stairway.

Lucius knocked on the door and, after the slightest hesitation, turned the handle and opened it. Only then did he look back at Monk. "Please come in," he urged. "I am sure you will wish to meet my father, and perhaps compare with him all that I have told you." He stood aside, his face furrowed with anxiety, his body stiff. "Father, this is Mr. William Monk. He has agreed to help us."

Monk walked past Lucius into the room beyond. He had a brief impression of comfortable, well-used furniture, not there for effect but for the pleasure of the occupant, before his attention was taken by the man who stood up from one of the dark leather armchairs and came towards him. He was slender, and of little more than average height, but there was a vigor and grace in him which made him commanding. He

11

was of similar build to Lucius, but in no other way resembled him. He must have been in his fifties, but his fair hair was hardly touched with gray and his blue eyes were surrounded by fine lines, as if he had spent years narrowing them against a brilliant light.

"How do you do, Mr. Monk," he said immediately, offering his hand. "Harry Stourbridge. My son tells me you are a man who may be able to help us in our family misfortune. I am delighted you have agreed to try, and most grateful."

"How do you do, Major Stourbridge," Monk said with unaccustomed formality. He shook Stourbridge's hand, and looking at him a little more closely, saw the anxiety in the older man's face that courtesy could not hide. There was no sign of relief that Miriam Gardiner had gone. For whatever reasons, he was deeply troubled by her disappearance also. "I shall do my best," Monk promised, painfully aware of how little that might be.

"Sit down," Stourbridge said, indicating one of the other chairs. "Luncheon will be in an hour. Will you join us?"

"Thank you," Monk accepted. It would give him an opportunity to observe the family together and to form some opinion of their relationships—and perhaps how Miriam Gardiner might have fitted in as Lucius's wife. "But before that, sir, I should like to speak more confidentially to you. There are a number of questions I need to ask."

"Of course, of course," Stourbridge agreed, not sitting but moving restlessly about the room, in and out of the broad splashes of sunlight coming through the windows. "Lucius, perhaps if you were to call upon your mother?" It was a polite and fairly meaningless suggestion, intended to offer him an excuse to leave.

Lucius hesitated. He seemed to find it difficult to tear himself away from the only thing that mattered to him at the moment. His intelligence must have told him there were discussions better held in his absence, but he could not put his mind or his imagination to anything else.

"She has missed you," the elder Stourbridge prompted. "She will be pleased to hear that Mr. Monk is willing to assist us."

"Yes . . . yes, of course," Lucius agreed, glancing at Monk with the shadow of a smile, then going out and closing the door.

Harry Stourbridge turned to Monk, the sunlight bright on his face, catching the fine lines and showing more nakedly the tiredness around his eyes.

"Ask what you wish, Mr. Monk. I will do anything I can to find Miriam, and if she is in any kind of difficulty, to offer her all the help I can. As you can see, my son cares for her profoundly. I can imagine no one else who will make him as happy."

Monk found it impossible to doubt Major Stourbridge's sincerity, which placed upon him an even greater emotional burden. Why had Miriam Gardiner fled their house, their family, without a word of explanation? Had it been one sudden event or an accumulation of small things amounting to a whole too great for her? What could it be that she could not even offer these people who loved her some form of explanation?

And where was Treadwell the coachman?

Stourbridge was staring at Monk, waiting for him to begin.

But Monk was uncertain where to start. Harry Stourbridge was not what he had imagined, and he found himself unexpectedly sensitive to his feelings.

"What do you know of Mrs. Gardiner?" he asked, more brusquely than he had intended. Pity was of no use to Lucius or his father. He was here to address their problem, not wallow in emotions.

"You mean her family?" Stourbridge understood straightaway what Monk was thinking. "She never spoke of them. I imagine they were fairly ordinary. I believe they died when she was quite young. It was obviously a matter of sadness to her, and none of us pursued the subject."

"Someone will have cared for her while she was growing up," Monk pressed. He had no idea if it was a relevant point, but there were so few obvious avenues to follow.

"Of course," Stourbridge agreed, sitting down at last. "She was taken in by a Mrs. Anderson, who treated her with the greatest kindness. Indeed, she still visits her quite frequently. It was from Mrs. Anderson's home that she met Mr. Gardiner, when she was about seventeen, and married him two years later. He was considerably older than she." He crossed his legs, watching Monk anxiously. "I made enquiries myself, naturally. Lucius is my only son, and his happiness is of the greatest importance to me. But nothing I learned explains what has happened. Walter Gardiner was a quiet, modest man who married relatively late. He was nearly forty. But his reputation was excellent. He was rather shy, a trifle awkward in the company of women, and he worked extremely hard at his business—which, incidentally, was the selling of books. He made a modest success of it and left Miriam well provided for. By all accounts she was very happy with him. No one had an ill word to say for either of them."

"Did they have children?" Monk asked.

A shadow crossed Stourbridge's eyes. "No. Unfortunately not. That is a blessing that does not come to every marriage." He drew in his breath and let it out silently. "My wife and I have only the one child." There was a sharp memory of pain in his face, and Monk was very aware of it. It was a subject he himself had considered little. He had no title or estates to leave, and he had no memory of ever considering marriage, far less a family. He felt in no way incomplete without such a thing. But, then, Hester was not an ordinary woman. He had married her with no thought of the comfort of domestic life. She was not the one he would have chosen if he had. The thought made him smile unconsciously. One could not tell what the future might bring. He had already surprised himself by changing as radically as he had. Perhaps in a few years he would think of children. Now he was honest enough to

14

know that he would resent such other demands on Hester's time and emotion as a child would have to be.

Stourbridge was waiting for his attention.

"She is somewhat older than your son," Monk put in as tactfully as he could. "Exactly how much older is she?"

A flash of amusement crossed Stourbridge's face.

"Nine years," he replied. "If you are going to ask if she could give him an heir, the answer is that I do not know. Of course, we would like it if Lucius were to have a son, but it is not our main concern. There is no guarantee of such a thing, Mr. Monk, whomever one marries, and Miriam was never made to believe it was a condition of the marriage."

Monk did not argue, but he would judge for himself whether Mrs. Stourbridge shared her husband's feelings. So far his questions had elicited nothing in which he could see any reason for Miriam Gardiner to have left. He wished he had a clearer picture of her in his mind. Seen through the eyes of Lucius and Harry Stourbridge, she was the model of the ideal woman. Their image gave her no flesh and blood, and certainly no passions. Had they seen anything of the real woman beneath the surface they so much admired? Was it any use asking Harry Stourbridge anything further, except bare facts?

"Was this her first visit to this house?" Monk said suddenly.

Stourbridge looked slightly surprised.

"No, not at all. She had been here half a dozen times. If you are thinking we did not make her welcome, or that she felt overwhelmed or less than comfortable with the idea of living among us, you are mistaken, Mr. Monk."

"Would she have lived here, in this house?" Monk asked, envisioning a score of reasons why she might have found the prospect unendurable. Having been mistress of her own home, no matter how ordinary compared with this house, so close to Kensington Gardens, she might find the sheer loss of privacy insupportable. Hester would have! He could not imagine her spending the best part of her life under someone else's roof. When she had nursed privately, as she had since returning from the Crimea, she had always known that any position was temporary and that, whatever its difficulties, it would reach an end. And she'd had a measure of privacy, and of autonomy, in that the care of the patient was in her charge.

A whole new concept of imprisonment opened up to him.

Harry Stourbridge was smiling.

"No, Mr. Monk. I have properties in Yorkshire, and Lucius is very fond of life in the north. Miriam had visited there some months ago—I confess, when the weather was a good deal less clement—but she was charmed by the area and was looking forward to moving there and being mistress of her own household."

So fear of losing a certain freedom was not what had driven Miriam Gardiner away. Monk tried again. "Was there anything different about this visit, Major Stourbridge?"

"Not that I am aware, except that it was a trifle more celebratory." His face pinched with sadness and his voice dropped. "They were to be married in four weeks. They desired a quiet wedding, a family affair. Miriam did not wish large crowds or great expense. She thought it both unseemly and unnecessary. She loved Lucius very deeply, of that I have no doubt whatever." He looked bemused. "I don't know what has happened, Mr. Monk, but she did not leave because she ceased to love him or to know how profoundly he loves her."

It was pointless to argue. The belief in Stourbridge's voice was complete. It was going to be uniquely painful if facts proved him to be mistaken and Monk were to find himself in the position of having to tell him so. He should never have accepted this case. He could not imagine any happy solution.

"Tell me something of your coachman, James Treadwell," he asked instead.

Stourbridge's fair brows rose. "Treadwell? Yes, I see what you mean. A perfectly adequate coachman. Good driver, knows horses, but I admit he is not a man for whom I have any natural liking." He rested his elbows on the arms of his chair and made a steeple with his fingers. "I knew men like

16

him in the army. They can sit a horse like a centaur, wield a sword, ride over any terrain, but one cannot rely on them. Always put themselves first, not the regiment. Don't stand their ground when the battle's against them."

"But you kept him on?"

Stourbridge shrugged slightly. "You don't put a man out because you think you know his type. Could be wrong. I wouldn't have had him as a valet, but a coachman is a very different thing. Besides, he's a nephew of my cook, and she's a good woman. She's been with the family nearly thirty years. Started as a scullery maid when my own mother was still alive."

Monk understood. Like everything else, it was so easily appreciated, so very normal. It left him little more to ask, except for an account of the day itself on which Miriam Gardiner had fled.

"I can give you a guest list, if you wish," Stourbridge offered. "But it included no one Miriam had not met before—indeed, no one who was not a friend. Believe me, Mr. Monk, we have all searched our minds trying to think of anything that could have happened to cause her such distress, and we can think of nothing whatever. No one is aware of any quarrel, even any unfortunate or tactless remark." Instinctively, he glanced out of the window, then back at Monk again. "Miriam was standing alone. The rest of us were either playing croquet or watching, when quite suddenly she gasped, went as white as paper, stood frozen for a moment, then turned and stumbled away, almost falling, and ran towards the house." His voice cracked. "None of us has seen her since!"

Monk leaned forward. "You saw this?"

"No, not personally. I would have gone after her if I had." Stourbridge looked wretched, as if he blamed himself. "But it was described to me by several others, and always in those terms. Miriam was standing alone. No one spoke to her or in any other way approached her." He frowned, his eyes puzzled. "I have considered every possibility that common sense suggests, Mr. Monk. We have called you because we can think of nothing further."

Monk rose to his feet. "I shall do all I can, sir," he said with misgiving. When Lucius Stourbridge had first explained his case Monk had thought it an impossible one; now he was even more convinced. Whatever had happened to Miriam Gardiner, it arose from her own emotions, and they would probably never know what it was that had so suddenly precipitated her into flight. But even if they were to learn, it would bring no happiness to them. Monk began to feel an anger against this young woman who had gone so thoughtlessly far along the path which a little consideration would have told her she could not complete. She had hurt deeply at least two decent and honorable people, probably more.

Stourbridge stood also. "Whom would you like to speak with next, Mr. Monk?"

"Mrs. Stourbridge, if you please," Monk replied without hesitation. He knew from working with Hester that women observed each other in a way a man did not; they read expressions, understood what was left unsaid.

"Of course." Stourbridge led the way out into the hall. "She will be in her sitting room at this hour."

Monk followed him up the wide, curving staircase and this time had an opportunity to look more closely at the magnificently plastered ceiling and the carving on the newel post at the top of the banister.

Stourbridge crossed the landing. A long window looked over the smooth lawn, and Monk caught a glimpse of croquet hoops still set up. It looked peaceful in the sun, a place of quiet happiness, family games, and afternoon tea in the summer. Trees sheltered hydrangeas beyond, their last flowers dropping in a blaze of color onto the dark earth beneath.

Stourbridge knocked on the third door along, and at a murmur from inside, opened it, ushering Monk in.

"My dear, this is Mr. Monk," he introduced them. "He has promised to assist us in finding Miriam."

18

Mrs. Stourbridge was sitting on a large chintz-covered chair, a scrapbook of poetry and photographs spread open on the cherry-wood table beside her where she had apparently laid it when interrupted. Her resemblance to her son was clear even at a glance. She had the same dark eyes and slender line of cheek and throat. Her hair grew from her brow in the same broad sweep. If Lucius had indeed come to see her, as his father had suggested, he had not remained long. She looked at Monk with concern. "How do you do," she said gravely. "Please come in. Tell me how I can help my son."

Monk accepted and sat in the chair opposite her. It was more comfortable than its straight back would have suggested, and the bright, warm room would, in any other circumstances, have been restful. Now he was searching his mind for questions to ask this woman which could help him to understand what had driven Miriam Gardiner to such extraordinary flight.

Stourbridge excused himself and left them.

Verona Stourbridge looked at Monk steadily, waiting.

There was no time for skirting around the edges of meaning.

"Would you please describe Mrs. Gardiner for me?" he asked. He wanted a picture in his mind, not only to allow him to imagine her himself but to know how Mrs. Stourbridge saw her.

She looked surprised. "Where will you look, Mr. Monk? We have no idea where she could have gone. Obviously, we have already tried her home, and she has not returned there. Her housemaid had not heard from her since she left to come here."

"I would like a woman's view of her," he explained. "Rather less romantic, and perhaps more accurate."

"Oh. I see. Yes, of course." She leaned back. She was slender, probably in her mid-forties, and there was a natural elegance in the way she held her hands and in the sweep of her huge skirts over the chair. Looking at her face, Monk thought

19

her observation of Miriam Gardiner would be clear and unsentimental, perhaps the first that might offer some genuine insight into her character. He watched her attentively.

"She is of average height," Verona began, measuring her words. "Perhaps a trifle plumper than would be the choice for a young woman. I daresay my son has already told you she was at least nine years older than he?"

"At least?" he questioned. "You mean she admitted to nine but you personally think it might be more?"

She shrugged delicately without answering. "She has excellent hair, fair and thick and with a becoming natural wave," she continued. "Blue eyes, quite good complexion and teeth. Altogether a generous face indicating good nature and at least averagely good health. She dressed becomingly, but without extravagance. I should imagine well within a moderate income."

"She sounds a paragon of virtues, Mrs. Stourbridge," Monk remarked a little dryly. "I do not yet see a woman of flesh and blood—indeed, a real woman at all—merely a recital of admirable qualities."

Her eyebrows rose sharply. She stared at him with chill, then as he stared back, gradually she relaxed.

"I see," she conceded. "Of course. You asked me what she looked like. She was most pleasing. Her character was also agreeable, but she was not incapable of independent thought. You are asking me if she had faults? Of course. She was stubborn at times. She had some strange and unsuitable views on certain social issues. She was overfamiliar with the servants, which caused difficulties now and then. I think she had much to learn in the running of a house of the size and standard my son would have required." She kept her eyes steadily on Monk's. "Very possibly, she would not have been our first choice of wife for him. There are many more suitable young women of our acquaintance, but we were not unhappy with her, Mr. Monk, nor could she have imagined that we were."

"Not even if she failed to give him an heir?" It was an intrusive and intimate question, and a subject upon which emo-

20

tions were often deep. Women had been abandoned because of it throughout history.

She looked a little pale, but her hands did not tighten in her lap.

"Of course, anyone would wish an heir, but if you accept a person, then you must do so wholeheartedly. It is not something she could help. If I thought she would have deliberately denied him, then I would blame her for it, but one thing I am perfectly sure of, and that is that she loved him. I do not know where she has gone, or why, Mr. Monk. I would give a great deal for you to be able to find her and bring her back to us, unharmed and as gentle and loving as she was before."

Monk could not doubt her. The emotion in her voice betrayed a depth of distress he could feel, in spite of the fact they had met only moments before and he knew nothing of her beyond the little that was obvious.

"I will do all I can, Mrs. Stourbridge," he promised. "I believe you did not see her leave the croquet party?"

"No. I was speaking to Mrs. Washburne and my attention was engaged. She is not an easy woman."

"Was Mrs. Gardiner apprehensive before the party?"

"Not at all. She was extremely happy." There was no shadow in her face.

"Did she know all the guests?"

"Yes. She and I made up the list together."

"Did anyone come who was uninvited? Perhaps a companion to one of the invited guests?"

"No."

"Was there any disagreement or unpleasantness, unwished-for attention?"

"No." She shook her head slightly, but her eyes did not leave his. "It was a most enjoyable day. The weather was perfect. No one spoiled it by inappropriate behavior. I have questioned all the servants, and no one saw or heard anything except the usual trivial talk. The worst that anyone knew of was a disagreement between Mr. Wall and the Reverend

Dabney over a croquet shot's being rather poor sportsmanship. It did not concern Miriam."

"She didn't play?"

She smiled very slightly, but there was no criticism in it.

"No. She said she preferred to watch. I think actually she never learned and did not like to admit it."

He changed the subject. "The coachman, Treadwell. He has not reappeared, and I am told no one knows what happened to him either."

Her face darkened. "That is true. Not entirely a satisfactory young man. We employed him because he is the nephew of the cook, who is a most loyal and excellent woman. We cannot choose our relatives."

"And, of course, your coach is still missing, too?"

"Indeed."

"I shall ask your groom for a description of it, and of Treadwell." That was a more hopeful line to pursue. "Was there a maid who particularly looked after Mrs. Gardiner while she stayed here?"

"Yes, Amelia. If you wish to speak with her I shall send for her."

"Thank you. And your cook as well. She may know something of Treadwell."

There was a knock on the door, and it opened before she had time to answer. The man who came in was tall and broad-shouldered, a trifle thick about the waist. His features were strong, and the family resemblance was marked.

"This is my brother, Mr. Monk," Mrs. Stourbridge said.

"You must be the agent of enquiry Lucius fetched in," the man said. He looked at Monk with gravity, and there was a note of sadness in his voice that could almost have been despair. "Aiden Campbell," he introduced himself, offering his hand. "I am afraid you are unlikely to have any success," Campbell continued, glancing at his sister in half apology, then back to Monk. "Mrs. Gardiner left of her own free will. In the little we know of the circumstances, that seems

22

unarguable. Possibly she was experiencing severe doubts which up to that moment she had managed to conceal. We may never know what suddenly caused her to realize her feelings." He frowned at Monk. "I am not convinced that seeking her will not lead to further unhappiness." He took a deep breath. "We, none of us, desire that. Please be very careful what you do, Mr. Monk. You may be led, in sincerity, to make discoveries we might be better not knowing. I hope you understand me?"

Monk understood very well. He shared the view. He wished now he had been wise enough to follow his original judgment and refuse the case when Lucius had first asked him.

"I am aware of the possibilities, Mr. Campbell," he answered quietly. "I share your opinion that I may not be able to find Mrs. Gardiner, and that if I do, she still might wish to stand by her decision. However, I have given my word to Mr. Stourbridge that I would look for her, and I will do so." Then, sensing the sharpness in Campbell's face, he added, "I have informed him of my opinion as to the chances of success, and I shall continue to be honest with him as to my progress or lack of it."

Campbell remained silent, pushing his hands into his pockets and staring at the floor.

"Aiden," Verona said gently. "I know you believe that she will not return and that only more disillusion and unhappiness will follow from seeking her, but neither Harry nor Lucius will accept that. They both feel compelled to do all they can to find out where she is, if she is unhurt, and why she left. Harry almost certainly for Lucius's sake, of course, but he is nonetheless resolved. I believe we should help them, rather than make them feel isolated and as if we do not understand."

Campbell raised his eyes and looked at her steadily. "Of course." He smiled, but the effort behind it was apparent to Monk. "Of course, my dear. You are perfectly right. It is something which must run its course. How can I assist you,

Mr. Monk? Let me take you to the stables and enquire after James Treadwell. He may be at the heart of this."

Monk accepted, thanking Verona and excusing himself. He followed Campbell down the stairs and out of the side door to the mews. The light was bright as he stepped outside. The smells of hay, horse sweat and the sharp sting of manure were strong in the closed heat of the yard. He heard a horse whinnying, and stamping its feet on the stones.

A ginger-haired boy with a brush in one hand looked up at him with curiosity.

"Answer Mr. Monk's questions, Billy," Campbell instructed. "He's come to help Major Stourbridge find Treadwell and the missing carriage."

"Yer in't never goin' ter see them again, I reckon," Billy replied, pulling his mouth into a grimace of disgust. "Carriage like that's worth a fair bit."

"You think he sold it and went off?" Monk asked.

Billy regarded him with contempt. " 'Course I do. Wot else? 'E lit outta 'ere like 'e were on fire! Nobody never told 'im ter. 'E never came back. If 'e din't flog it, w'y in't 'e 'ere?"

"Perhaps he met with an accident?" Monk suggested.

"That don't answer w'y 'e went in the first place." Billy stared at him defiantly. "Less 'e's dead, 'e should 'a told us wot 'appened, shouldn't 'e?"

"Unless he's too badly hurt," Monk continued the argument.

Billy's eyes narrowed. "You a friend of 'is, then?"

"I've never met him. I wanted your opinion, which obviously was not very high."

Billy hesitated. "Well—can't say as I like 'im," he hedged. "On the other 'and, can't say as I know anythink bad abaht 'im, neither. Just that he's gorn, like—which is bad enough."

"And Mrs. Gardiner?" Monk asked.

Billy let his breath out in a sigh. "She were a real nice lady, she were. If 'e done anythink to 'er, I 'ope as 'e's dead—an' 'orrible dead at that."

"Do you not think she went with him willingly?"

Billy glanced at Campbell, then at Monk, his face registering his incredulity. "Wot'd a lady like 'er be wantin' with a shifty article like 'im? 'Ceptin' to drive 'er abaht now an' then, as wot is 'is job!"

"Did she think he was a shifty article?"

Billy thought for a moment. "Well, p'haps she din't. A bit too nice for 'er own good, she were. Innocent, like, if yer know wot I mean?"

"Mrs. Gardiner was a trifle too familiar with the servants, Mr. Monk," Campbell clarified. "She may well have been unable to judge his character. I daresay no one told her Treadwell was employed largely because he was a relative to the cook, who is highly regarded." He smiled, biting his lip. "Good cooks are a blessing no household discards lightly, and she has been loyal to the family since before my sister's time." He looked around the stable towards the empty space where the carriage should have been. "The fact remains, Treadwell is gone, and so is a very valuable coach and pair, and all the harness."

"Has it been reported to the police?" Monk asked.

Campbell pushed his hands into his pockets, swaying a little onto his heels. "Not yet. Frankly, Mr. Monk, I think it unlikely my brother-in-law will do that. He makes a great show, for Lucius's sake, of believing that Mrs. Gardiner had not met some accident, or crisis, and all will be explained satisfactorily. I am afraid I gravely doubt it. I can think of no such circumstance which would satisfy the facts as we know them." He started to walk away from the stable across the yard and towards the garden, out of earshot of Billy and whoever else might be in the vicinity. Monk followed, and they were on the gravel path surrounding the lawn before Campbell continued.

"I very much fear that the answer may prove to be simply that Mrs. Gardiner, who was very charming and attractive in her manner, but nonetheless not of Lucius's background, realized that after the first flame of romance wore off she would never make him happy, or fit into his life. Rather than face explanations which would be distressing, and knowing that both Lucius and Major Stourbridge, as a matter of honor, would try to change her mind, she took the matter out of their hands, and simply fled."

He looked sideways at Monk, a slightly rueful sadness in his face. "It is an action not entirely without honor. In her own way, she has behaved the best. There is no doubt she is in love with Lucius. It was plain for anyone to see that they doted upon each other. They seemed to have an unusual communion of thought and taste, even of humor. But she is older than he, already a widow, and from a very . . . ordinary . . . background. This way it remains a grand romance. The memory of it will never be soured by its fading into the mundane realities. Think very carefully, Mr. Monk, before you precipitate a tragedy."

Monk stood in the late-morning sun in this peaceful garden full of birdsong, where perhaps such a selfless decision had been made. It seemed the most likely answer. A decision like that might be hysterical, perhaps, but then Miriam Gardiner was a woman giving up her most precious dream.

"I have already told Major Stourbridge that if I find Mrs. Gardiner I would not attempt to persuade her to return against her will," Monk answered. "Or report back to him anything beyond what she wished me to. That would not necessarily include her whereabouts."

Campbell did not reply for several minutes. Eventually, he looked up, regarding Monk carefully, as if making some judgment which mattered to him deeply.

"I trust you will behave with discretion and keep in mind that you are dealing with the deepest emotions, and men of a very high sense of honor."

"I will," Monk replied, wishing again Lucius Stourbridge had chosen some other person of whom to ask assistance, or that he had had the sense to follow his judgment, not his sentimentality, in accepting. Marriage seemed already to have robbed him of his wits!

26

"I imagine they will be serving luncheon," Campbell said, looking towards the house. "I assume you are staying?"

"I still have to speak to the servants," Monk answered grimly, walking across the gravel. "Even if I learn nothing."

2

H*ESTER SHIFTED* from foot to foot impatiently as she stood in the waiting room in the North London Hospital. The sun was hot and the closed air claustrophobic. She thought with longing of the green expanse of Hampstead Heath, only a few hundred yards away. But she was here with a purpose. There was a massive amount to do, and as always, too little time. Too many people were ill, confused by the medical system, if you could call it by so flattering a word, and frightened of authority.

Her desire was to improve the quality of nursing from the manual labor it usually was to a skilled and respected profession. Since Florence Nightingale's fame had spread after the Crimean War, the public in general regarded her as a heroine. She was second in popularity only to the Queen. But the popular vision of her was a sentimental image of a young woman wandering around a hospital with a lamp in her hand, mopping fevered brows and whispering words of comfort, rather than the reality Hester knew. She had nursed with Florence Nightingale and had experienced the despair, the unnecessary deaths brought on by disease and incompetence rather than the injuries of battle. She also knew Miss Nightingale's true heroism, the strength of her will to fight for better conditions, for the use of common sense in sanitation and efficiency in administration. Above all, she fought to make nursing an acceptable profession which would attract decent women and treat them with respect. Old-fashioned ideas must be got rid of, up-to-date methods must be used, and skills rewarded.

Now that Hester was no longer solely responsible for her own support, she could devote some of her time to this end. She had made it plain to Monk from the outset that she would never agree to sit at home and sew a fine seam and gossip with other women who had too little to do. He had offered no disagreement, knowing it was a condition of acceptance.

They had had certain differences, and would no doubt have more. She smiled now in the sun as she thought of them. It was not easy for either of them to make all the changes necessary to adapt to married life. Deeply as she loved him, sharing a bedroom— let alone a bed—with another person was a loss of privacy she found not as easy to overcome as she had imagined. She was not especially modest—nursing life had made that impossible—but she still reveled in the independence of having the window open or closed as she wished, of putting the light out when she chose, and of having as many or as few blankets over her as she liked. In the Crimea she had worked until she was exhausted. Then she had lain on her cot hunched up, shaking with cold, muscles too knotted up to sleep, and had to arise in the morning when she was still almost drunken with tiredness.

But to have the warmth, the gentleness, of someone beside her who she knew without question loved her, was greater than all the tiny inconveniences. They were only pinpricks. She knew Monk felt them, too. She had seen flashes of temper in his face, quickly smothered when he realized he was thinking only of himself. He was used to both privacy and independence as much as she was.

But Monk had less to forfeit than Hester. They were living in his rooms in Fitzroy Street. It made excellent sense, of course. She had only sufficient lodgings to house her belongings and to sleep in between the private nursing cases she had taken after being dismissed from hospital service for insubordination. He was developing a good practice as an agent of enquiry for private cases after his own dismissal from the police force—also for insubordination!

For him to have moved would have been unwise. People knew where to find him. The house was well situated, and the landlady had been delighted to allow them an extra room to make into a kitchen, and to give up having to cook and clean for Monk, a duty she had done only from necessity before, realizing he would probably starve if she didn't. She was very pleased to have both the additional rent and more time to devote to her increasingly demanding husband—and whatever other pursuits she enjoyed beyond Fitzroy Street.

So Hester was, with some difficulty, learning to become domestic and trying to do it with a modicum of grace.

Her real passion was still to reform nursing, as it had been ever since she had come home from the Crimea. Lady Callandra Daviot shared her feelings, which was why Hester was standing in the North London Hospital now waiting for Callandra to come and recount the success or failure of their latest attempt.

She heard the door opening and swung around. Callandra came in, her hair sticking out in tufts as if she had run her fingers through it, her face set tight and hard with anger. There was no need to ask if she had succeeded.

Callandra had dignity, courage and good humor, but not even her dearest friend would have said she was graceful. In spite of the best efforts of her maid, her clothes looked as if she paid no regard to them, merely picking up what first came to her hand when she opened the wardrobe door. Today it was a green skirt and a blue blouse. It was warm enough inside the hospital for her not to wear whatever jacket she had chosen.

"The man is a complete idiot!" she said furiously. "How can anyone see to diagnose what ails a person for any of a hundred diseases and still be blind as a bat to the facts before his face?"

"I don't know," Hester admitted. "But it happens frequently."

30

The door was still wide open behind Callandra. She turned on her heel and marched out again, leaving Hester to follow after her.

"How many hours are there in a day?" Callandra demanded over her shoulder.

"Twenty-four," Hester replied as they reached the end of the passage and went through the now-empty operating theater with its table in the center, benches for equipment, and the railed-off gallery on three sides for pupils and other interested parties to observe.

"Exactly," Callandra agreed. "And how much of that time can a surgeon be expected to care for his patient personally? One hour if the patient is important—less if he is not. Who cares for him the rest of the time?" She opened the farther door into the wide passageway that ran the length of the entire ground floor.

"The resident medicine officer—" Hester began.

"Apothecary!" Callandra said dismissively, waving her hand in the air.

Hester closed the door behind them. "They prefer to call them resident medicine officers now," she remarked. "And the nurses. I know your point. If we do not train nurses, and pay them properly, everyone else's efforts are largely wasted. The most brilliant of surgeons is still dependent upon the care we give his patients after he has treated them."

"I know that." Callandra hesitated, deciding whether to go right, towards the casualty room, or left, past the postmortem room to the eye department and the secretary's office and the boardroom. "You know that." She decided to go left. "Dr. Beck knows that." She spoke his name quite formally, as if they had not been friends for years—and not cared for each other far more than either dared say. "But Mr. Ordway is very well satisfied with things as they are! If it were up to him we'd still be wearing fig leaves and eating our food raw."

"Figs, presumably," Hester said dryly. "Or apples?"

Callandra shot her a sharp look. "Figs," she retorted with

31

absolute certainty. "He'd never have had the courage to take the apple!"

"Then we would not be wearing the fig leaves, either, heaven preserve us," Hester pointed out, hiding her smile.

"Marriage has made you decidedly immodest!" Callandra snapped, but there was satisfaction in her voice. She had long wished Hester's happiness, and had once or twice alluded to fears that her friend might become too wasp-tongued to allow herself the chance.

They reached the end of the corridor and Callandra turned right, towards the boardroom. She hesitated in her step so slightly that had Hester not felt the trepidation herself, she might not have noticed it at all.

Callandra knocked on the door.

"Come in!" the voice inside commanded.

Callandra pushed it open and went inside, Hester on her heels.

The man sitting at the large table was of stocky build, his hair receding from a broad brow, his features strong and stubborn. His was not a handsome face, but it had a certain distinction. He was extremely well dressed in a suit of pinstriped cloth which must have been very warm on this midsummer day. His white collar was high and stiff. A gold watch chain was draped across his broad chest.

The expression on his face tightened when he recognized Callandra. It positively flinched when he saw Hester behind her.

"Lady Callandra . . ." He half rose from his seat as a gesture of courtesy. She was not a nurse or an employee, however much of a thorn in his side she might be. "What can I do for you?" He nodded at Hester. "Miss Latterly."

"Mrs. Monk," Callandra corrected him with satisfaction.

His face flushed slightly and he gave a perfunctory nod towards Hester in mute apology. His hand brushed the papers in front of him, indicating how busy he was and that only politeness prevented him from pointing out the fact that they were interrupting him.

"Mr. Thorpe," Callandra began purposefully, "I have just spoken again with Mr. Ordway, to no avail. Nothing I can say seems to make him aware of the necessity for improving the conditions—"

"Lady Callandra," he cut across her wearily, his voice hard-edged. "We have already discussed this matter a number of times. As chairman of the governors of this hospital, I have a great many considerations to keep in mind when I make my decisions, and cost has to be high among them. I thought I had adequately explained that to you, but I perceive that my efforts were in vain." He drew breath to continue, but this time Callandra interrupted him.

"I understood you perfectly, Mr. Thorpe. I do not agree. All the money in the world is wasted if it is spent on operating upon a patient who is not adequately cared for afterwards. . . ."

"Lady Callandra . . ." He sighed heavily, his patience exceedingly thin. His hand moved noisily over the papers, rustling them together. "As many patients survive in this hospital as in most others, if not rather more. If you were as experienced in medicine as I am, you would realize that it is regrettably usual for a great number of patients to die after surgery. It is something that cannot be avoided. All the skill in the world cannot—"

Hester could endure it no longer.

"We are not talking about skill, Mr. Thorpe," she said firmly. "All that is required to ease at least some of the distress is common sense! Experience has shown that—"

Thorpe closed his eyes in exasperation. "Not Miss Nightingale again, Miss . . . Mrs. Monk." He jerked his hand sharply, scattering the papers over the desktop. "I have had enough letters from that woman to paper my walls! She has not the faintest ideas of the realities of life in England. She thinks because she did fine work in utterly different circumstances in a different country that she can come home again and reorganize the entire medical establishment according to her own ideas. She has delusions both as to the extent of her knowledge and the degree of her own importance."

33

"It's not about personal importance, Mr. Thorpe," Hester replied, staring straight at him. "Or about who gets the praise—at least, it shouldn't be. It is about whether a patient recovers or dies. That is what we are here for."

"That is what *I* am here for, madam," he said grimly. "What *you* are here for, I have no idea. Your friends would no doubt say it is from a devotion to the welfare of your fellow human beings in their suffering. Your detractors might take the view that it is to fill your otherwise empty time and to give yourself a feeling of importance you would not have in the merely domestic setting of running your own household."

Hester was furious. She knew perfectly well that losing her temper would also lose her the argument, and it was just possible that Thorpe knew that also. Personally, she didn't think he had the wit. Either way, she had no intention of catering to him.

"There are always people willing to detract with a spiteful remark," she answered with as good a smile as she could manage. "It is largely made from ignorance and meanness of spirit. I am sure you have more sense than to pay attention to them. I am here because I have some practical experience in nursing people after severe injury, whether caused by battle or surgery, and as a consequence have learned some methods that work rather better than those currently practiced here at home."

"You may imagine so." Thorpe looked at her icily. His light brown eyes were large but a trifle deep-set. His lashes would have been the envy of many a woman.

Hester raised her brows very high. "Is it not better that the patient lives than that he dies?"

Thorpe half rose from his chair, his face pink. "Do not be flippant with me, madam! I would remind you that you have no medical training whatsoever. You are unlearned and totally ignorant, and as a woman, unsuited to the rigors of medical science. Just because you have been of use abroad to soldiers in the extremity of their injuries while fighting for Queen and country, do not imitate the unfortunate Miss Nightingale in

34

imagining that you have some sort of role to teach the rest of us how we should behave."

Hester was quite well aware of Florence Nightingale's nature, far more so than Fermin Thorpe, who knew her only through her voluminous correspondence to everyone even remotely concerned with hospital administration. Hester knew Miss Nightingale's courage, her capacity for work and her spirit which fired the labor and sacrifice of this; and also her inexhaustible nagging and obsession with detail, her high-handed manner and the overwrought emotions which drained her almost to the point of collapse. She would certainly outlast Fermin Thorpe and his like—by sheer attrition, if nothing else.

Experience of the Crimea, of its hardships and its rare victories, above all of its spirit, calmed the retort that came to her tongue.

"I am sure Miss Nightingale believes she is sharing the reward of experiences you have been unable to have for yourself," she said with curdling sweetness, "having remained here in England. She has not realized that her efforts are not welcome."

Thorpe flushed scarlet. "I'm sure she means well," he replied in a tone he presumably intended to be placating, although it came through his teeth. "She simply does not realize that what was true in Sebastopol is not necessarily true in London."

Hester took a deep breath. "Having been in both places, she may imagine that, as far as the healing of injury is concerned, it is exactly the same. I suffer from that illusion myself."

Thorpe's lips narrowed to a knife-thin line.

"I have made my decision, madam. The women who work in this establishment are quite adequate to our needs, and they are rewarded in accordance with their skills and their diligence. We will use our very limited financial resources to pay for that which best serves the patients' needs—namely, skilled surgeons and physicians who are trained, qualified and experienced. Your assistance in keeping good order in the hospital, in offering encouragement and some advice on the moral welfare of the patients, is much appreciated. Indeed," he added meaningfully, "it would be greatly missed were you no longer to come. I am sure the other hospital governors will agree with me wholeheartedly. Good day."

There was nothing to do but reply as civilly as possible and retreat.

"I suppose that man has a redeeming virtue, but so far I have failed to find it," Callandra said as soon as they were outside in the corridor and beyond overhearing.

"He's punctual," Hester said dryly. "He's clean," she went on after a minute's additional thought.

They walked hastily back towards the surgeons' rooms, passing an elderly nurse, her shoulders stooping with the weight of the buckets she carried in each hand. Her face was puffy, her eyes red-rimmed. "And sober," Hester added.

"Those are not virtues," Callandra said bitterly. "They are accidents of breeding and circumstance. He has the opportunity to be clean and no temptation to be inebriated, except with his own importance. And that is of sufficient potency that after it alcohol would be redundant."

They passed the apothecary's rooms. Callandra hesitated as if to say something, then apparently changed her mind and hurried on.

Kristian Beck came out of the operating theater, but he had his coat on and his shirt cuffs were clean, so apparently he had not been performing surgery. His face lit when he recognized Callandra, then he saw her expression.

"Nothing?" he said, more an answer than a question. He was of barely average height. His hair was receding a little above his temples, but his mouth had a remarkable passion and sensitivity to it, and his voice had a timbre of great beauty. Hester was aware that his friendship with Callandra was more profound than merely the trust of people who have the same compassion and the same anger, and the will to fight

36

for the same goals. How personal it was she had not asked. Kristian was married, though she had never heard him speak of his wife. Now he was regarding Callandra earnestly, listening to her recount their conversation with Thorpe. He looked tired. Hester knew he had almost certainly been at the hospital all night, seeing some patient through a crisis and snatching a few hours' sleep as he could. There were shadows around his eyes and his skin had very little color.

"He won't even listen," Callandra said. She had been weary the moment before, and angry with Thorpe and with herself. Now suddenly her voice was gentler, and she made the effort to hide her sense of hopelessness. "I am not at all sure I approached him in the best way. . . ."

Kristian smiled. "I imagine not," he said with mild humor, full of ruefulness and affection. "Mr. Thorpe has not been blessed with a sense of humor. He has nothing with which to soften the blows of reality."

"It was my fault," Hester said quietly. "I am afraid I was sarcastic. He provokes the worst in me—and I let him. We shall have to try again from a different angle. I cannot think of one yet." She looked at Kristian and forced herself to smile. "He actually suggested that we should busy ourselves with discipline in the hospital and being of comfort to the patients." She gritted her teeth. "Perhaps I should go and say something uplifting?" Her intention was to leave Kristian and Callandra alone for one of the few moments they had together, even if they were only able to discuss the supply of bandages or domestic details of nurses' boarding allowances, and who should be permitted to leave the premises to purchase food.

Callandra did not look at her. They knew each other too well for the necessity of words, and it was far too delicate a matter to speak of. Perhaps she was also self-conscious. So much was known, and so little said.

Kristian's mouth curled in acknowledgment of the absurdity of it. Hospital discipline was a shambles where the nurses were concerned, and yet rigidly enforced upon the patients. Patients who misbehaved, used obscene or blasphemous language, fraternized with patients of the opposite sex, or generally conducted themselves in an unseemly fashion, could be deprived of food for one meal or more. Alcohol was banned. Smoking and gaming incurred discharge altogether, regardless of whether the person in question was healed of his or her illness.

For nurses, drunkenness was a different matter. Part of their wages was paid in porter, and they were largely the type of person of whom no better was expected. What other sort of woman scrubs, sweeps, stokes fires, and carries slops? And who but a maniac would allow such women to assist in the skilled science of medicine?

Hester marched off, actually to the apothecary's store, leaving Callandra alone in the corridor with Kristian.

"Have you heard from Miss Nightingale?" Kristian asked, turning to walk slowly back towards the surgeons' area of rooms.

"It is very difficult," Callandra replied, trying to choose her words with care. The entire country had a burning respect for Florence Nightingale. She was the perfect heroine. Artists painted pictures of her bending over the sick and injured heroes of the recent war in the Crimea, her gentle features suffused with compassion, lit by the golden glow of a candle. Callandra knew the reality had been very different. There was no sentimentality there, no murmured words of peace and devotion. Miss Nightingale was as much a fighter as any of the soldiers, and a better tactician than most, certainly better than the grossly incompetent generals who had led them into the slaughter. She was also erratic, emotional, hypochondriacal, and of inexhaustible passion and courage, a highly uncomfortable creature of contradictions. Callandra was not always sure that Hester appreciated quite what a difficult woman Florence Nightingale was. Her loyalty sometimes blinded her. But that was Hester's nature, and they had both been more than glad of it in the past.

Kristian glanced at Callandra questioningly. He knew little of the realities of the Crimea. He was from Prague, in the Austrian principality of Bohemia. One could still hear the slight accent in his speech, perfect as his English was. He used few idioms, although after this many years he understood them easily enough. But he was dedicated entirely to his own profession in its immediacy. The patients he was treating now were his whole thought and aim: the woman with the badly broken leg, the old man with the growth on his jaw, the boy with a shoulder broken by the kick of a horse (he was afraid the wound would become gangrenous), the old man with kidney stones, an agonizing complaint.

Thank God for the marvelous new ability to anesthetize patients for the duration of surgery. It meant speed was no longer the most important thing. One could afford to take minutes to perform an operation, not seconds. One could use care, even consider alternatives, think and look instead of being so hideously conscious of pain that ending it quickly was always at the front of the mind and driving the hands.

"Oh, she's perfectly right," Callandra explained, referring back to Florence Nightingale again. "Everything she commands should be done, and some of it would cost nothing at all, except a change of mind."

"For some, the most expensive thing of all," he replied, the smile rueful and on his lips, not in his eyes. "I think Mr. Thorpe is one of them. I fear he will break before he will bend."

She sensed a new difficulty he had not yet mentioned. "What makes you believe that?" she asked.

Even walking as slowly as they were, they had reached the end of the corridor and the doorway to the surgeons' rooms. He opened it and stood back for her as two medical students, deep in conversation, passed by them on their way to the front door. They nodded to him in deference, barely glancing at her.

She went into the waiting room and he came after her. There were already half a dozen patients. He smiled at them, then went across to his consulting room and she followed. When they were inside he answered her.

"Any suggestion he accepts is going to have to come from someone he regards as an equal," he replied with a slight shrug.

Kristian Beck was, in every way, intellectually and morally Thorpe's superior, but it would be pointless for her to say so, and embarrassing. It would be far too personal. It would betray her own feelings, which had never been spoken. There was trust, a deep and passionate understanding of values, of commitment to what was good. She would never have a truer friend in these things, not even Hester. But what was personal, intimate, was a different matter. She knew her own emotions. She loved him more than she had loved anyone else, even her husband when he had been alive. Certainly, she had cared for her husband. It had been a good marriage; youth and nature had lent it fire in the beginning, and mutual interest and kindness had kept it companionable. But for Kristian Beck she felt a hunger of the spirit which was new to her, a fluttering inside, both a fear and a certainty, which was constantly disturbing.

She had no idea if his feelings for her were more than the deepest friendship, the warmth and trust that came from the knowledge of a person's character in times of hardship. They had seen each other exhausted in mind and body, drained almost beyond bearing when they had fought the typhus outbreak in the hospital in Limehouse. A part of their inner strength had been laid bare by the horror of it, the endless days and nights that had melted into one another, sorrow over the deaths they had struggled so hard to prevent, the supreme victory when someone had survived. And, of course, there was the danger of infection. They were not immune to it themselves.

Kristian was waiting for her to make some response, standing in the sun, which made splashes of brightness through the long windows onto the worn, wooden floor. Time was short, as it always seemed to be between them. There were people waiting—frightened, ill people, dependent upon their help. But they were also dependent upon being adequately nursed after surgery. Their survival might hang on such simple things as the circulation of air around the ward, the cleanliness of bandages, the concentration and sobriety of the nurse who watched over them. The depth of the nurse's knowledge and the fact that someone listened to what she reported might be the difference between recovery or death.

"I wish he wasn't such a fool!" Callandra said with sudden anger. "It doesn't matter a jot who you are, all that matters is if you are right. What is he so afraid of?"

"Change," he said quietly. "Loss of power, not being able to understand." He did not move as another man might have, looking at the papers on his desk, tidying this or that, checking on instruments set out ready to use. He had a quality of stillness. She thought again with a hollow loneliness how little she knew of him outside hospital walls. She knew roughly where he lived, but not exactly. She knew of his wife, although he had seldom spoken of her. Why not? It would have been so natural. One could not help but think of those one loved.

A sudden coldness gripped her. Was it because he knew how she felt and did not wish to hurt her? The color must be burning up her face even as she stood there.

Or was it an unhappiness in him, a pain he did not wish to touch, far less to share? And did she even want to know?

Would she want him to say aloud that he loved her? It could break forever the ease of friendship they had now. And what would take its place? A love that was forever held in check by the existence of his wife? And would she want him to betray that? She knew without even having to waste time on the thought that such a thing would destroy the man she believed he was.

Nothing could be sweeter than to hear him say he loved her. And nothing could be more dangerous, more threatening to the sweetness of what they now had.

Was she being a coward, leaving him alone when he most

needed to share, to be understood? Or being discreet when he most needed her silence?

Or was friendship all he wanted? He had a wife—perhaps all he needed here, in this separate life from the personal, was an ally.

"There are still medicines missing," she said, changing the subject radically.

He drew in his breath. "Have you told Thorpe?"

"No!" It was the last thing she intended to do. "No," she repeated more calmly. "It's almost certainly one of the nurses. I'd rather find out who myself and put a stop to it before he ever has to know."

He frowned. "What sort of medicines?"

"All sorts, but particularly morphine, quinine, laudanum, Dutch liquid and several mercurial preparations."

He looked down, his face troubled. "It sounds as if she's selling them. Dutch liquid is one of the best local anesthetics I know. No one could be addicted to all those or need them for herself." He moved towards the door. "I've got to start seeing patients. I'll never get through them all. Have you any idea who it is?"

"No," she said unhappily. It was the truth. She had thought about it hard, but she barely knew the names of all the women who fetched and carried and went about the drudgery of keeping the hospital clean and warm, the linen washed and ironed and the bandages rolled, let alone their personal lives or their characters. All her attention had been on trying to improve their conditions collectively.

"Have you asked Hester?" he said.

Her hand was on the doorknob.

"I don't think she knows either," she replied.

His face relaxed very slightly in a smile—humor, not happiness. "She's rather a good detective, though," he pointed out.

Callandra did not need to tell Hester that medicines were missing, she was already unhappily aware of it. However, it was not at the forefront of her mind as she left Callandra and

42

Kristian and went to the patients' waiting room. She resented bitterly Fermin Thorpe's admonition to her to go and offer comfort to the troubled and moral guidance to the nurses, although both were tasks she fully believed in and intended to carry out. It was their limitations she objected to, not their nature.

She passed one of the nurses, a comfortable woman of almost fifty, pleasant-faced, gray-brown hair always falling out of its pins, a little like Callandra's. Had their backgrounds not been so different the resemblance might have been more apparent. This woman could barely read or write, not much more than her name and a few familiar words of her trade, but she was intelligent and quick to learn a new task, and Hester had frequently seen her actually tending to patients when she knew there were no doctors anywhere near. She seemed to have an aptitude for it, an instinctive understanding of how to ease distress, lower a fever, or whether someone should eat or not. Her name was Cleo Anderson.

She lowered her eyes now as Hester passed her, as if she wished to avoid attracting attention. Hester was sorry. She would have liked to encourage her, even with a glance.

There were some patients in the waiting room already, five women and two men. All but one of them were elderly, their eyes watchful in unfamiliar surroundings, afraid of what would happen to them, of what they could be told was wrong, of the pain of treatment, and of the cost. Their clothes were worn thin. Here and there a clean shirt showed under a faded coat.

Some of their treatment was free, but they still had to pay for food while they were in hospital, and then, after they left, for medicine as well if it was necessary.

She chose the most wretched looking of the patients and went over to him.

He peered up at her, his eyes full of fear. Her bearing suggested authority to him, and he thought he was about to be chastised, although he had no idea what for.

"What's your name?" she enquired with a smile.

He gulped. " 'Arry Jackson, ma'am."

"Is this your first time here, Mr. Jackson?" She spoke quietly, so only those closest to him would overhear.

"Yes, ma'am," he mumbled, looking away. "I wouldn't 'a come, but our Lil said as I 'ad ter. Always fussin', she is. She's a real good girl. Said as they'd find the money some'ow." He lifted his head, defiantly now. "An' she will, ma'am. Yer won't be done short, wotever!"

"I'm sure," she agreed softly. "But it wasn't money I was concerned about."

A spasm of pain shot through him, and for a moment he gasped for breath. She did not need Mr. Thorpe's medical training to see the ravages of disease in his gaunt body. He almost certainly had consumption, and probably pleurisy as well, considering the way he held his hand over his chest. He looked considerably over sixty, but he might not actually have been more than fifty. There would be little the physician could do for him. He needed rest, food, clean air and someone to care for him. Morphine would help the pain, and sherry in water was an excellent restorative. They were probably all impossibly expensive for him. His clothes—and even more, his manner—spoke of extreme poverty.

He looked at her with disbelief.

She made up her mind. "I'll speak to Dr. Warner and see if you shouldn't stay here a few days—" She stopped at the alarm in his face. "Rest is what you need."

"I got a bed!" he protested.

"Of course. But you need quiet, and someone who has time to look after you."

His eyes widened. "Not one o' them nurses!" The thought obviously filled him with dread.

She struggled for an argument to persuade him, but all that came to her lips were lies, and she knew it. Many of the nurses were kindly enough, but they were ignorant and often hard-pressed by poverty and unhappiness themselves.

"I'll be here," she said instead. She had placed herself in a position where she had to say something.

"Wot are yer, then?" His curiosity got the better of his awe.

"I'm a nurse," she answered rashly, and with a touch of pride. "I was out in the Crimea."

He looked at her with amazement. The word was still magic.

"Was yer?" His eyes filled with hope, and she felt guilty for how simply she'd done it, and with so little consideration of what she could fulfill. If only they could persuade Thorpe to see how much it mattered that all nurses should inspire this trust, not in miracles but in competence, gentleness and sobriety.

But how could they, when they were given no training and it was so blatantly apparent that the doctors had little but contempt for them? The anger inside her was rock hard; unconsciously her body clenched.

Harry Jackson was still staring at her. She must talk to him, reassure him. No one could heal his illness. Like half of the people in this room, he was long past that kind of help, but she could comfort his fear, and for a time at least alleviate his pain.

The physician came to the door and called the first patient. He looked frustrated and tired in a clean frock coat and trousers that were a little wrinkled at the knees. He also knew he could do little that was of real help.

Hester moved to another patient and talked with him, listening to his tales of family, home, the difficulties of trying to make ends meet, let alone to pay for medicine, when you were too sick to work.

A nurse walked through the room carrying an empty pail, its metal handle clinking against the rings that held it. The woman was stout, dark, about forty. She did not look to either side of her as she passed the waiting people. She hiccuped as she went out of the far door. She was in a world of her own, exhausted by hard physical labor, lifting, bending, carrying, scrubbing. Mealtimes and, more important, drink times would be the highlights of her day. Then she could share the odd joke with the other women, and the brief euphoria of alcohol which shut out reality.

It was all a long way from the dream of a sweet-faced woman with a lamp in her hand who would murmur words of hope and miraculously save the dying.

And that too was a long way from the passionate, tireless, short-tempered, vulnerable woman who sat in her house passing out orders, pleas and advice—almost all of it good—and being stoically ignored by men like Fermin Thorpe.

It was six o'clock before the last patient had been seen. Hester had managed to persuade the physician to admit Harry Jackson for a few days, and she savored that small victory. She was consequently smiling as she tidied the waiting room.

The door opened, and she was pleased to see Callandra, who now looked even more disheveled than usual. Her skirt was crumpled, her blouse open at the neck in the heat, and she had obviously been working, because her sleeves were rolled up and stained with splashes of water and blood. Her hair was coming out of its pins in all directions. It needed taking down, brushing, and doing again.

Absentmindedly, Callandra pulled out a pin, caught up a bunch of hair and replaced it all, making the whole effect worse.

She closed the door and glanced around to make sure the room was empty and all other doors were closed also.

"He's gone," Hester assured her.

Callandra rubbed the back of her hand across her brow.

"There's more medicine gone today," she said wearily. "I checked it this morning, and again now. It's not a lot, but I'm quite sure."

Hester should not have been surprised, but she felt a cold grip inside her close tighter. It was systematic. Someone was taking medicines every day or two and had been doing so for a long time, perhaps months, possibly even years. A certain amount of error or theft was expected, but not of this order.

"Does Mr. Thorpe know yet?" she asked quietly.

"Not about this," Callandra replied. "It's getting worse."

For a wild moment Hester actually entertained the idea that the thefts could be used to pressure Fermin Thorpe into seeing the necessity for training and paying better nurses. Then she realized that disclosure of the problem would only end in a full-scale investigation, possibly involving the police, and all the present staff, innocent and guilty alike, would suffer, possibly even be dismissed. In all probability not one would be able to prove her honesty, still less her sobriety. The whole hospital would grind to a standstill, and no good would be achieved at all.

"He's going to find out soon," Callandra said, interrupting Hester's thoughts. "They'll have to be replaced."

"Have we any idea who it is?" Hester struggled for something tangible to pursue. "We've got twenty-eight women here doing one thing or another. All of them are hard up, very few of them can read or write more than a few words, some not that much. Half of them live in the hospital, the other half come and go at all hours."

"But the apothecary's rooms are locked," Hester pointed out. "Are they stealing the keys? Or do you suppose they can pick the lock?"

"Pick the lock," Callandra said without hesitation. "Or sneak in and out when he's got his back turned. He's as careful as he can be."

"But he knows there are losses?"

"Oh, yes. He doesn't like Thorpe any more than we do. Well, not much. He'll not report it till he has to. He knows what chaos it will be. But he can't carry on hiding it much longer."

There was a knock on the door. Callandra opened it, and Cleo stood there, a look of polite enquiry on her face. "Yer 'ungry, love?" she said cheerfully. "There's a nice bit o' cold beef an' pickle goin' if yer fancy it. An' fresh bread. A glass o' porter?"

Hester had not realized it, but at mention of the food she was aware of how long it had been since she last ate, or sat

47

down comfortably, without the need to find words to comfort a frightened, inarticulate old man or woman, powerless as she was to give any real help.

"Yes," she accepted quickly. "Please."

Cleo jerked her hand to the right. "Along there, love, same as usual." She withdrew, and they heard her feet clattering away on the hard floor.

They went together up to the staff room and sat at one of the plain wood tables. All around them other women were eating with relish, and the porter glasses were lifted even more often than the forks. There was a little cheerful conversation in between mouthfuls, or during. They overheard many snatches.

" . . . dead 'e were, in a week, poor devil. But wot can yer 'spect, eh? 'Ad no choice but ter cut 'im open. Went bad, it did. Seen it comin'."

"Yeah. Well, 'appens, don' it? 'Ere, 'ave another glass o' porter."

"Fanks. I'm that tired I need summink ter keep me eyes open. I gorn an' popped that 'at, like yer told me. Got one and tenpence fer it. Bastard. I'd 'a thought 'e'd 'a given me two bob. Still, it'll do the rent, like."

"Your Edie still alive, is she?"

"Poor ol' sod, yeah. Coughin' 'er 'eart up, she is. Forty-six, lookin' like ninety."

"Yer gonner get 'er up 'ere, then, ter see the doc?"

"Not likely! 'Oo's gonner pay fer it? I can't, an' Lizzie in't got nuffink. Fred's mean as muck. Makin' shillin's, 'e is, at the fish market most days, but drinks more'n 'alf of it."

"Tell me! My Bert's the same. Still, knocked seven bells outta Joe Pake t'other day, and got 'isself locked up fer a while. Good riddance, I say. Yer got any more o' that pickle? I'm that 'ungry. Ta."

Hester had heard a hundred conversations like it, the small details of life for the women who were entrusted with the care of frightened and ignorant people after the surgeon's knife

48

had done its best to remove the cause of their pain and the long road to recovery lay ahead of them.

"Perhaps if I got figures together?" Hester said softly, as much to herself as to Callandra. "I could prove to Thorpe the practical results of having women with some degree of training!" She kept her voice low, not to be overheard. "Women with an intelligence and an aptitude for it, like Cleo Anderson. I know it would cost more, as he would be the first to point out, but it would be richly rewarded. Money's only the excuse, I'm sure of that." She was reaching for reasons, arguments, the weakness in his armor. "If he thought he would get the credit . . . if his hospital were to have greater success than any other . . ."

Callandra looked up from her bread and pickle. "I've tried that." A heavy bunch of hair fell out of its pins, and she poked it back, leaving the ends sticking out. "I thought I'd catch his vanity. Nothing he'd like better than to outdo Dr. Gilman at Guy's Hospital. But he hasn't the courage to try anything he isn't sure of. If he spent money, and there were no results, soon enough . . ." She left the rest unsaid. They had been around and around these arguments, or ones like them, so many times. It was all a matter of convincing Thorpe of something he did not want to know.

"I suppose it's back to writing more letters," Hester said wearily, taking another slice of bread.

Callandra nodded, her mouth full. She swallowed. "How's William?"

"Bored," Hester said with a smile. "Longing for a case to stretch his wits."

When Hester arrived home at Fitzroy Street it was a little after seven o'clock that evening. Monk had already returned and was waiting for her. There were faint lines of tiredness in his face, but nothing disguised his pleasure in seeing her. She still found it extraordinary; it brought a strange quickening of the heart and tightness in the stomach to remember that she belonged here now, in his rooms, that when night came she would not stand up and say good-bye, uncertain when she would see him again. There was no more pretending between them, no more defense of their separateness. They might go to the bedroom one at a time, but underlying everything was the certainty that they would both be there, together, all night, and waken together in the morning. She did not even realize she was smiling as she thought of it, but the warmth was always in her mind, like sunshine on a landscape, lighting everything.

She kissed him now when he rose to greet her, feeling his arms close around her. The gentleness of his touch perhaps surprised him more than her.

"What's for dinner?" was the first thing he said after he let her go.

It had not crossed her mind that she would need to cook for him. She had eaten at the hospital as a matter of habit. The food was there. She was thinking of the missing medicines and Thorpe's stubbornness.

There was food in their small kitchen, of course, but it would require preparing and cooking. Even so, it would not take more than three quarters of an hour at most. She could not bear the thought of eating again so soon.

But she could not possibly tell him. To have forgotten about him was inexcusable.

She turned away, thinking frantically. "There's cold mutton. Would you like it with vegetables? And there's cake."

"Yes," he agreed without enthusiasm. Had he expected her to be a good cook? Surely he knew her better than that? Did he imagine marriage was somehow going to transform her magically into a housekeeping sort of woman? Perhaps he did.

All she wanted to do was sit down and take her boots off. Tonight was her own fault, but the specter of years of nights like this was appalling, coming home from whatever she had been doing, been fighting for—or against—and having to start thinking of shopping for food, bargaining with tradesmen, making lists of everything she needed, peeling, chopping, boiling, baking, clearing away. And then laundry, ironing, sweeping! She swallowed hard, emotions fighting each other inside her. She loved him, liked him, at times loathed him, admired him, despised him ... a hundred things, but always she was tied to him by bonds so strong they crowded out everything else.

"What did you do today?" she asked aloud. What was racing through her head was the possibility of acquiring a servant, a woman to come in and do the basic chores she herself was so ill-equipped to handle. How much would it cost? Could they afford it? She had sworn she was not going to go back to nursing in other people's houses, as she had done until their marriage. Her smile widened as she remembered the day.

Automatically, she washed her hands, filled the pan with cold water and set it on the small stove to boil, then reached for potatoes, carrots, onions and cabbage.

Their wedding day had been typical of late spring: glittering sunshine gold on wet pavements, the scent of lilacs in the air, the sound of birdsong and the jingle of harness, horses' hooves on the cobbles, church bells. Excitement had fluttered in her chest so fiercely she could hardly breathe. Inside, the church was cool. A flurry of wind had blown her skirt around her.

She could see the rows of pews now in her mind's eye, the floor leading to the altar worn uneven by thousands of feet down the centuries. The stained glass of the windows shone like jewels thrown up against the sun. She had no idea what the pictures were. All she had seen after that had been Monk's stiff shoulders and his dark head, then his face as he could not resist turning towards her.

He was leaning against the door lintel talking to her now, and she had not heard what he had said.

"I'm sorry," she apologized. "I was thinking about the dinner. What did you say?" Why had she not told him what she was really thinking? Too sentimental. It would embarrass him.

51

"Lucius Stourbridge," he repeated very clearly. "His bride-to-be left the party in the middle of a croquet game and has not been seen since. That was three days ago."

She stopped scraping the carrots and turned to look at him.

"Left how? Didn't anybody go after her?"

"They thought at first she'd been taken ill." He told her the story as he had heard it.

She tried to imagine herself in Miriam Gardiner's place. What could have been in her mind as she ran from the garden? Why? It was easy enough to think of a moment's panic at the thought of the change in her life she was committing herself to and things that would be irrevocable once she had walked down the aisle of the church and made her vows before God—and the congregation. But you overcame such things. You came back with an apology and made some excuse about feeling faint.

Or if you really had changed your mind, you said so, perhaps with hideous embarrassment, guilt, fear. But you did not simply disappear.

"What is it?" he asked, looking at her face. "Have you thought of something?"

She remembered the carrots and started working again, although the longer it took to prepare dinner the more chance there was she could force herself to eat again. Her fingers moved more slowly.

"I suppose there wasn't someone else?" she asked. The pan was coming to the boil, little bubbles beginning to rise from the bottom and burst. She should hurry with the potatoes and put on a second pan for the cabbage. If she chopped it fiercely it would not take long.

He said nothing for a few moments. "I suppose it's the only answer," he concluded. "Treadwell must be involved somehow, or why didn't he come back?"

"He saw his chance to steal the coach, and he just took it," she suggested, putting the potatoes and carrots into the pan, a little salt in it, then the lid on. "William?"

"What?"

52

How should she approach this without either inviting him to tell her to give up working at the hospital on one hand, or on the other, implying that she expected a higher standard of living than he was able to offer her?

"Are you going to take the case?"

"I already told you that. I wish I hadn't, but I gave my word."

"Why do you regret it?" She kept her eyes on the knife, her fingers and the cabbage.

"Because there's nothing I could find out that would bring anything but tragedy to them," he replied a little tartly.

She did not speak for a few minutes, busying herself with getting out the mutton first and carving slices off it and then replacing it in the pantry. She found the last of the pickles—she should have purchased more—and set the table.

"Do you think . . ." she began.

He was watching her as if seeing her performing those domestic duties gave him pleasure. Was it she, or simply the warmth of belonging, particularly after the unique isolation of his years without memory, the comforts of the past which did not exist for him, except in shadows, and the fear of what he would find?

"Do I think what?" he asked. "Your pan is boiling!"

"Thank you." She eased the lid a little. It was time to put the cabbage in as well.

"Hester!"

"Yes?"

"You used to be the most straightforward woman I ever knew. Now you are tacking and jibbing like . . ."

She pushed past him. "Please don't stand in the doorway. I can't move around you."

He stepped aside. "What do you think made Miriam Gardiner change her mind so suddenly?"

Fear, she thought. Sudden overwhelming knowledge of what promises she was making. Her life, her fortunes for good or ill, her name, her obedience, perhaps most of all her body, would belong to someone else. Perhaps in that moment,

53

as she had stood in the sunlight in the garden, it had all been too much. Forever! Till death do us part. You have to love someone very much indeed, overwhelmingly . . . you have to trust him in a deep, fierce and certain way that lies even closer to the heart than thought, in order to do that. "William, do you think we could afford to have a woman in during the day, to cook for us and purchase food and so on? So that we could spend together the time we have, and be sure of a proper meal?" She did not look at him. She stood with body tight, waiting for his response. The words were said.

There was silence except for the bubbling of the water and the jiggling of the pan lid. She moved it a little farther off and the steam plumed out.

She wished she knew what he was thinking. Money? Or principle? Would someone else be an intrusion? Hardly. Everyone had servants. Money. They had already discussed that. He had accepted Callandra's help earlier on as a matter of necessity. Now it was different. He would never permit anyone else to support his wife. They had battled over her independence already. She had won. It was an unspoken condition of happiness. It was the only thing in which he had been prepared to give ground. It was probably the surest gauge of his love for her. The memory of it filled her with warmth.

"It's not important," she said impulsively. "I . . ." Then she did not know what else to say without spoiling it. Over-explanation always did.

"There's no room for anyone to live in," he said thoughtfully. "She would have to come every day."

She found herself smiling, a little skip of pleasure inside her. "Oh, of course. Perhaps just afternoons."

"Is that sufficient?" He was generous now, possibly even rash. One never knew what cases he would have in the future.

"Oh, certainly," she agreed. She took a skewer and tested the potatoes. Not ready yet. "Could she have discovered something about Lucius that made the thought of marrying him intolerable?" she asked. "Or about his family, perhaps?"

"Not that instant," he answered. "No one was standing

anywhere near her, far less speaking to her. It was just a garden croquet match, full of social chatter, very open, quite public. She couldn't have surprised him with another woman, if that's what you are thinking. And there was certainly no quarrel. Nor was it a question of being overwhelmed or feeling a stranger. She had been there many times before and already knew everyone present. She helped compile the guest list."

She said nothing.

"I want your thoughts," he prompted. "You are a woman. Do you understand her?"

Should she tell him the truth? Would he be hurt? She had learned that he was far more vulnerable than his hard exterior showed. He had courage, anger, wit. He was not easily wounded, he felt too fiercely and too completely for others to sway him. He knew what he believed. It was part of what drew her to him, and infuriated her, sometimes even frightened her.

But since they had been married she had learned the tenderness underneath. It was seldom in his words, but it was in his touch, the way his fingers moved over her body as if even in moments of greatest passion he never forgot her heart and her spirit inside the flesh. She was never less than herself to him. For that, she would always love him, hold back no portion of herself in fear or reserve.

But she could not have known that before. Miriam Gardiner could not know that. She turned around to face him.

"We don't know what her first marriage was like, not truly," she said, meeting his eyes. "Not when the doors were closed and they were alone together. Perhaps there were things in that which made her suddenly afraid of committing herself irrevocably again."

His gray eyes searched hers. She saw the question in them, the flicker of uncertainty.

"You cannot know beforehand how well or ill it will be," she said very quietly. "One can be hurt." She did not say "Or be repulsed, exhausted, feel used or soiled," but she knew he understood it. "Perhaps they knew each other very little in that regard," she said aloud. Then, in case he should imagine she had the slightest doubt or fear herself, she put her arms around his neck and, brushing her fingers gently over his ears and into his hair, kissed his mouth.

His response spoiled the dinner and sealed his determination to begin looking for a woman to take over domestic duties from now on.

3

M‍ONK LEFT HOME early the following morning. It was long before he felt like leaving, but if he were to have any success in helping Lucius Stourbridge, he must find out what had happened to James Treadwell and the carriage. Then he would have a far better chance of tracing some clue or indication where Miriam had gone, perhaps even why. He surprised himself when he realized how much he dreaded the answer.

It was now four days since her disappearance, and getting more difficult to follow her path with each hour that passed. He took a hansom to Bayswater and began by seeking the local tradesmen who would have been around at the hour of the afternoon when Miriam fled.

He was lucky to find almost immediately a gardener who had seen the carriage and knew both the livery and the horses, a distinctive bay and a brown, ill-matched for color but perfect for height and pace.

"Aye," he said, nodding vigorously, a trowel in his hand. "Aye, it passed me going at a fair lick. Din't see who were in it, mind. Wondered at the time. Knew as they 'ad a party on. See'd all the carriages comin'. Thought as someone were took ill, mebbe. That wot 'appened?"

"We don't know," Monk replied. He would not tell anyone the Stourbridge tragedy, but it would be public knowledge soon enough, unless he managed not only to find Miriam but to persuade her to return as well, and he held no real hope of that. "Did you see which way they went?"

The gardener looked puzzled.

"The coachman seems to have stolen the coach and horses," Monk explained.

The gardener's eyes widened. "Arrr." He sighed, shaking his head. "Never heard that. What a thing. What's the world coming to?" He lifted his hand, trowel extended. "Went 'round that corner there. I never saw'd 'im after that. Road goes north. If 'e'd wanted to go to town, 'e'd 'a gone t'other way. Less traffic. Weren't nobody after 'im. Got clean away, I s'pose."

Monk agreed, thanked him, and followed the way he had indicated, walking smartly to see if he could find the next sighting.

He had to cast around several times, and walked miles in the dusty heat, but eventually, footsore and exhausted, he got as far as Hampstead Heath, and then the trail petered out. By this time it was dusk and he was more than ready to find a hansom and go home. The idea held more charm than it had a month or two ago, when it would have been merely a matter of taking his boots off his aching feet and waiting for his landlady to bring his supper. Now the hansom could not move rapidly enough for him, and he sat upright watching the streets and traffic pass.

The next morning, Monk went early to the Hampstead police station. When he had been a policeman himself he could have demanded assistance as a matter of course. Now he had to ask for favors. It was a hard difference to stomach. Perhaps he had not always used authority well. That was a conclusion he had been forced to reach when his loss of memory had shown him snatches of his life through the eyes of others. It was unpleasant, and unexpectedly wounding, to discover how many people had been afraid of him, partly because of his superior skills, but far too often due to his cutting

58

tongue. Anything he was given today would be a courtesy. He was a member of the public, no more.

Except, of course, if he had had occasion to come here in the past and they remembered him with unkindness. That thought made him hesitate in his step as he turned the corner of the street for the last hundred yards to the station doors. He had no idea whether they would know him or not. He felt the same stab of anxiety, guilt and anticipation that he had had ever since the accident and his realization of the kind of man he had been, and still was very often. Something in him had softened, but the hard tongue was still there, the sharp wit, the anger at stupidity, laziness, cowardice—above all, at hypocrisy.

He took a deep breath and went up the steps and in through the door.

The duty sergeant looked up, pleased to see someone to break his morning. He hated writing ledgers, though it was better than idleness—just.

" 'Mornin', sir. Lovely day, in't it? Wot can I do for you?"

"Good morning, Sergeant," Monk replied, searching the man's pleasant face for recognition and feeling a tentative hope when it was not there. He had already decided how he was going to approach the subject. "I am looking into a matter for a friend who is young, and at the present too distressed to take it up himself."

"I'm sorry, sir. What matter would that be? Robbery, is it?" the sergeant enquired helpfully, leaning forward a little over the counter.

"Yes," Monk agreed with a rueful smile and a slight shrug. "But not what you might expect. Rather more to it than that—something of a mystery." He lowered his voice. "And I fear a possible tragedy as well, although I am hoping that it is not so."

The sergeant was intrigued. This promised to occupy his whole day, maybe longer.

"Oh, yes sir. What, exactly, was stolen?"

"A coach and horses," Monk answered. "Good pair to

drive, a bay and a brown, very well matched for height and pace. And the coach was excellent, too."

The sergeant looked puzzled. "You sure as it's stole, sir? Not mebbe a member o' the family got a bit irresponsible, like, and took it out? Young men will race, sir, bad as it is— an' dangerous, too."

"Quite sure." Monk nodded. "I am afraid it was five days ago now and it is still missing. Not only that, but the driver who took it has not come back, and neither has the young lady who was betrothed to my friend. Naturally, we fear some harm has befallen her, or she would have contacted a member of the family."

The sergeant's face was full of foreboding. "Oh, dear. That don't sound good, sir, I must say."

Monk wondered if he was thinking that Miriam had run off with Treadwell. It was not impossible. Monk would have formed a better judgment on that if he had seen either of them, but from the description he had of Treadwell from the other Stourbridge servants, the coachman did not seem a man likely to have attracted a charming and gentle widow who had the prospect of marrying into an excellent family and becoming the wife of a man with whom, by all accounts, she was deeply in love. Certainly, Lucius Stourbridge loved her.

"No, it doesn't," Monk said aloud. "I have traced the carriage as far as the edge of Hampstead Heath, but then I lost it. If it has been seen anywhere around this area, it would help me greatly to know it."

" 'Course," the sergeant agreed, nodding. "We got a good 'ospital 'ere. Mebbe she was took ill sudden, like. They'd 'a taken 'er in. Very charitable, they are. Or mebbe she 'ad a sudden breakdown in 'er mind, like young women can 'ave, sometimes?"

"I shall certainly enquire at the hospital," Monk agreed, although the sergeant had to be speaking about the hospital where Hester was, and he had already asked her if there had been any such young woman either seen or admitted. In either case, unless she were unconscious, why had she not made some effort to contact the Stourbridge family? "But I must also look further for the coach," he went on. "That may lead me to where she is. And in truth, the theft of the coach is the only aspect of the matter which breaches the law."

" 'Course," the sergeant said sagely. " 'Course. Sergeant Robb is very busy at the moment. Got a murder, 'e 'as. Poor feller beaten over the 'ead and left on the path outside some woman's 'ouse. But 'e in't gorn out yet today. I know that for a fact. An' I'm sure as 'e'll spare yer a few minutes, like."

"Thank you very much," Monk accepted. "I shan't hold him up for long."

"You wait there, sir, an' I'll tell 'im as yer 'ere." And the sergeant lumbered dutifully out of sight. He returned, followed by a slender young man with a good-humored face and dark, intelligent eyes. He looked harassed, and it was obvious he was sparing Monk time only to be civil and because the desk sergeant had committed him to it. Little of his mind was on the subject.

"Good morning, sir," he said pleasantly. "Sergeant Trebbins says you are acting on behalf of a friend who has had a coach stolen, seemingly by his fiancée. I am afraid if they have chosen to . . . elope . . . it is probably ill advised, and certainly less than honorable, but it is not a crime. The matter of stealing a coach and pair, of course, we can look into, if you have reason to believe they came this way."

"I do. I have followed the sightings of the coach as far as the edge of the Heath."

"Was that yesterday, sir?"

"No. I'm afraid it was five days ago." Monk felt foolish as he said it, and he was ready for disinterest, and even contempt, in the young man's eyes. Instead he saw his whole body stiffen and heard a sharp intake of breath.

"Could you describe the driver of this coach, sir, and the coach itself? Possibly the horses, even?"

Monk's pulse quickened. "You've seen them?" Then instantly he regretted the unprofessionalism of such a betrayal of emotion. But it was too late to withdraw it. Comment would only make it more obvious.

Robb's face was guarded. "I don't know, sir. Could you describe them for me?" He could not keep the edge from his voice, the sharpness of needing to know.

Monk told him every detail of the coach: the color, style, dimensions, maker's name. He said that the horses were a brown and a bay, no white markings, fifteen hands and fifteen-one, respectively, and seven and nine years old.

Robb looked very grave. "And the driver?" he said softly.

The knot tightened in Monk's stomach. "Average height, brown hair, blue eyes, muscular build. At the time he was last seen he was wearing livery." He knew even before he had finished speaking that Robb knew much about it, and none of it was good.

Robb pressed his lips together hard a moment before speaking.

"I'm sorry, sir, but I think I may have found your coach and horses . . . and your driver. I don't know anything about the young lady. Would you come inside with me, sir?"

The desk sergeant's face fell as he realized he was going to be excluded from the rest of the story.

Monk remembered to thank him, something he would not have done even a short while ago. The man nodded, but Monk's gesture did not solve his disappointment.

Robb led Monk to a tiny office piled with papers. Monk felt a jolt of familiarity, as if he had been carried back in time to the early days of his own career. He still did not know how long ago that was.

Robb took a pile of books off the guest chair and dropped them on the floor. There was no room on the already precariously piled table.

"Sit down, sir," he offered. He had not yet asked Monk's name. He sat in the other chair. He was a young man in whom good manners were so schooled they came without thought.

"William Monk," Monk introduced himself, and was idioti-

62

cally relieved to see no sign of recognition in the other man's face. The name meant nothing to him.

"I'm sorry, Mr. Monk," Robb apologized. "But at the moment I am investigating a murder of a man who answers fairly well to the description you have just given me. What is worse, I'm afraid, is that about half a mile away we found a coach and two horses which are almost certainly the ones you are missing. The coach is exactly as you say, and the horses are a brown and a bay, well matched, about fifteen hands or so." He tightened his lips again. "And the dead man was dressed in livery."

Monk swallowed. "When did you find him?"

"Five days ago," Robb replied, meeting Monk's eyes gravely. "I'm sorry."

"And he was murdered? You are sure?"

"Yes. The police surgeon can't see any way he could have come by those injuries by accident."

"Fallen off the box?" Monk suggested. Treadwell would certainly not have been the first coachman to be a little drunk or careless and topple off the driving seat, striking his head against an uneven cobblestone or the edge of the curb. Many a man had fallen under his own wheels, and even been trampled by vehicles behind him unable to stop in time.

Robb shook his head, his eyes not leaving Monk's face. "If he'd fallen off the box his clothes would show it. You can't land on the road hard enough for injuries like that and leave no mark on the shoulders and back of your coat, no threads torn or pulled, no stains of mud or manure. Even though the streets are pretty dry now, there's always something. Even his breeches would have been scuffed differently if he'd rolled."

"Differently?" Monk said quickly. "What do you mean? In what way were they scuffed?"

"All on the knees, as if he'd crawled quite a distance some time before he died."

"Trying to escape?" Monk asked.

Robb chewed his lip. "Don't know. It wasn't a fight. He was only struck the one blow."

Monk was startled. "One blow killed him? Then he crawled before he was struck? Why?"

"Not necessarily." Robb shook his head again. "Doctor says he bled inside his head. Could have been alive for quite a while and crawled a distance, knowing he was hurt but not how bad, and that he was dying."

"Then could he have fallen forward and caught himself one severe blow on an angle of the box? Or even been down and kicked by one of the horses?"

"Doctor said he was struck from behind." Robb swung his arms out to his right and brought them sideways and forward hard. "Like that . . . when he was standing up. Caught him on the side of the head. Not a lot of blood—but lethal."

"Couldn't have been a kick?" Monk clung to the last hope.

"No. Indentation was nothing like a horse's hoof. A long, rounded object like a crowbar or pole. Wasn't a corner of the box, either."

"I see." Monk took a deep breath. "Have you any idea who it was that killed him? Or why?" He added the last as an afterthought.

"Not yet," Robb admitted. He looked totally puzzled, and Monk had a swift impression that he was finding the case overwhelming. Already the fear of failure loomed in his sight. "He was hardly worth robbing. The only thing of value he had was the coach and horses, and they didn't take them."

"A personal enemy," Monk concluded. The thought troubled him even more, for reasons Robb could not know. Where was Miriam Gardiner? Had she been there at the time of the murder? If so, she was either a witness or an accomplice—or else she, too, was dead. If she had not been there, then where had Treadwell left her, and why? At her will, or not?

How much should he tell Robb? If he were to serve Miriam's interests, perhaps nothing at all—not yet, anyway.

"May I see the body?" he asked.

"Of course." Robb rose to his feet. Identification might help. At the least it would make him feel as if he were achieving something. He would know who his victim was.

Monk thanked him and followed as he went out of his tiny office, back down the stairs and into the street, where there was a stir of air in the hot day, even if it smelled of horses and household smoke and dry gutters. The morgue was close enough to walk to, and Robb strode out, leading the way. He jammed his hands into his pockets and stared downwards, not speaking. It was not possible to know his thoughts. Monk judged him to be still in his late twenties. Perhaps he had not seen many deaths. This could be his first murder. He would be overawed by it, afraid of failure, disturbed by the immediacy of violence which was suddenly and uniquely his responsibility to deal with, an injustice he must resolve.

Monk walked beside him, keeping pace for pace, but he did not interrupt the silence. Carriages passed them moving swiftly, harnesses bright in the sun, horses' hooves loud. The breeze was very light, only whispering through the leaves of the trees at the end of the street by the Heath. The smell of the air over the stretch of grass was clean and sweet. Somebody was playing a barrel organ.

The morgue was a handsome building, as if the architect had intended it as some kind of memorial to the dead, however temporarily there.

Robb tensed his shoulders and increased his pace, as if determined not to show any distaste for it or hesitation in his duty. Monk followed him up the steps and in through the door. The familiar odor caught in his throat. Every morgue smelled like this, cloyingly sweet with an underlying sourness, leaving a taste at the back of the mouth. No amount of scrubbing in the world removed the knowledge of death.

The attendant came out and asked politely if he could help them. He spoke with a slight lisp, and peered at Robb for a moment before he recognized him.

"You'll be for your coachman again," he said with a shake of his head. "Can't tell you any more."

They followed him into the tiled room, which echoed their footsteps. It held a dampness from running water, and the sting of disinfectant. Beyond was the icehouse where it was

65

necessary to keep the bodies they could not bury within a day or two. It had been five days since this particular one had been found.

"No need to bring him out," Robb said abruptly. "We'll see him in there. It's just that this gentleman might be able to tell us who he is."

The icehouse was extremely cold. The chill of it made them gasp involuntarily, but neither complained. Monk was glad of it. He had known less efficient morgues than this.

He lifted the sheet. The body was that of a well-fed man in his thirties. He was muscular, especially in the upper torso and across his shoulders. His skin was very white until it came to his hands and neck and face, which had been darkened by sun and wind. He had brownish hair, sharp features, and was blemished by a huge bruise covering his right temple, as if someone who hated him had struck him extremely hard, just once.

Monk looked at him carefully for several minutes, but he could find no other marks at all, except one old scar on the leg, long since healed over, and a number of minor cuts and scrapes on his hands, some as old as the scar on the leg. It was what he would expect from a man who worked with horses and drove a coach for his living. There were fresh bruises and breaks on the skin on his knees and on the palms of his hands.

He studied the face last, but with the eyes closed and the animation gone in death, it was hard to make any judgment of what he had looked like beyond the mere physical facts. His features were strong, a trifle sharp, his lips narrow, his brow wide. Intelligence and charm could have made him attractive; ill temper or a streak of greed or cruelty could equally have made him ugly. So much lay in the expression, now gone.

Was this James Treadwell? Only someone from the Stourbridge household could tell him beyond doubt.

"Do you want to see the clothes?" Robb asked, watching his face.

"Please."

But they told him no more than Robb himself had. There was only one likely conclusion: the man had been standing upright when someone had hit him a powerful blow which had sent him forward onto his knees, possibly even stunned him senseless for a while. The knees of his breeches were stained and torn, as if he had crawled a considerable distance. It was difficult to be certain of anything about the person who had delivered the blow. The weapon had not been found, but it must have been long, heavy and rounded, and swung with great force.

"Could a woman have done that, do you think?" Monk asked, then immediately wished he had not. He should not look for Robb to offer him the comfort that it could not have been Miriam. Why should she do such a thing? She could be a victim, too. They simply had not found her yet.

But if she was alive, where was she? If she was free to come forward, and was innocent, surely she would have?

And why had she left the Stourbridge house in the first place?

"May I see the coat?" he requested, looking at Robb before he answered.

"Of course," Robb replied. He did not answer as to whether he thought a woman could have dealt the blow. It was a foolish question, and Monk knew it. A strong woman, angry or frightened enough, with a heavy object at hand could certainly have hit a man sufficiently hard to kill him, especially with a blow as accurate as this one.

They left the morgue and went out into the sun again, walking briskly along the pavement. Robb seemed to be in a hurry, glancing once or twice at his watch. It was apparently more than a simple desire to be away from the presence of death which urged him on.

Monk would have freed Robb from the necessity of showing him the carriage and horses if he felt he could overlook them, but they were the deciding factor whether to bring Harry or Lucius Stourbridge all the way to Hampstead and distress them with identifying the body. It would certainly cause them additional anguish.

Robb was going at such a pace he stepped out into the street almost under the wheels of a hansom, and Monk had to grasp him by the arm to stop him.

Robb flushed and apologized.

"Have you an appointment?" Monk enquired. "This is only a courtesy you are doing me. I can wait."

"The horses are in a stable about a mile away," Robb answered, watching the traffic for a break so they could cross. "It's not exactly an appointment . . ." The subject seemed to embarrass him.

A coach and four went by, ladies inside looking out, a flash of pastels and lace. It was followed by a brewer's dray, drawn by shire horses with braided manes and feathered feet, their flanks gleaming. They tossed their heads as if they knew how beautiful they were.

Monk and Robb seized the chance to cross behind them. On the farther side Robb drew in breath, looking straight ahead of him. "My grandfather is ill. I drop in to see him every so often, just to help. He's getting a little . . ." His features tightened and still he did not look at Monk. Strictly speaking, he was taking police time to go home in the middle of the day.

Monk smiled grimly. He had no happy memories of the police hierarchy. He knew his juniors had been afraid of him with just cause, which was painful to him now. He had seen it in their nervousness in his presence, the expectation of criticism, just or not, the not-well-enough-concealed dislike.

His own superior had been another matter. Runcorn was the only one he could recall, and between them there had been friendship once, long ago. But for years before the final quarrel which had led to Monk's dismissal there had been nothing but rivalry and bitterness.

He felt his own body tighten, but he could not help it.

"We'd better go and see him," he answered. "I'll get a pie or a sandwich and eat it while you do whatever you have to do for him. I'll tell you what I know about Treadwell. If this is him, it'll help."

Robb considered it only for a second before he accepted.

The old man lived in two rooms in a house about five minutes' swift walk from the police station. Inside, the house was shabby but clean, and Robb deliberately made no apology. What Monk thought did not matter to him. All his emotions and his attention were on the old man who sat hunched up in the one comfortable chair. His shoulders were wide but thin now, and bowed over as if his chest hurt when he breathed. His white hair was carefully combed, and he was shaved, but his face had no color and it cost him a great effort that his grandson should have brought a stranger into his sanctuary.

"How do you do, sir," Monk said gravely. "Thank you for permitting me to eat my pie in your house while I speak with Sergeant Robb about the case we are working on. It is very civil of you."

"Not at all," the old man said huskily, obliged to clear his throat even for so few words. "You are welcome." He looked at Robb anxiously.

Monk sat down and busied himself with the pie he had bought from a barrow on the way, keeping his eyes on it so as to not appear to be aware of Robb helping the old man through to the privy and back again, washing his hands for him and heating some soup on the stove in the corner which seemed to be burning even in the heat of midsummer, as if the old man felt cold all the time.

Monk began to talk, to mask the sounds of the old man's struggle to breathe and his difficulty swallowing the soup and the slices of bread Robb had buttered for him and was giving to him a little at a time. He had already thought clearly how much he would say of Lucius's request. For the time being he would leave out references to Miriam. It was a great deal less than the truth. He would be deliberately misleading Robb, but until he knew more himself, to speak of her would have

69

set Robb on her trail instantly, and that would not be in her interest—yet.

"Mr. Lucius Stourbridge told me Treadwell had taken the coach, without permission, in the middle of the afternoon of the day he was killed," he began. He took another mouthful of the pie. It was good, full of meat and onions, and he was hungry. When he had swallowed it he went on. "He lives with his parents in Bayswater."

"Is it his coach or theirs?" Robb asked, offering his grandfather another slice of bread and waiting anxiously while the old man had a fit of coughing, spitting up blood-streaked phlegm into a handkerchief. Robb automatically passed him a clean handkerchief—and a cup of water, which the old man sipped without speaking.

It was a good question, and to answer it Monk was forced to be devious.

"A family vehicle, not the best one." That was true if not the whole truth.

"Why you and not the police?" Robb asked.

Monk was prepared for that. "Because he hoped to recover it without the police being involved," he said smoothly. "Treadwell is the nephew of their cook, and he did not want any criminal proceedings."

Robb was very carefully measuring powder from a twist of paper, making certain he used no more than a third, and then rewrapping what was left and replacing it on the cabinet shelf. He returned to the table and mixed water into the dose he had prepared, then held the glass to the old man's lips.

Monk glanced at the shelf where the paper had been replaced and noticed several other containers: a glass jar with dried leaves, presumably for an infusion; a vial of syrup of some sort; and two jars with more paper twists of powder. So much medicine would cost a considerable amount. He recalled noticing Robb's frayed cuffs, carefully darned, the worn heels of his boots, an overstitched tear in the elbow of his jacket. He was taken by surprise with how hard compassion gripped him for the difficulty of it, for the pain, and then

70

felt a surge of joy for the love which inspired it. He found himself smiling.

Robb was wiping the old man's face gently. He then turned to his own meal of bread and soup, which was now rapidly getting cold.

"Do you know anything else about this Treadwell?" he asked, beginning to eat quickly. Perhaps he was hungry, more probably he was aware of the amount of time he had been away from police business.

"Apparently not entirely satisfactory," Monk replied, remembering what Harry Stourbridge had told him. "Only kept on because he is the cook's nephew. Many families will go to considerable lengths to keep a really good cook, especially if they entertain." He smiled slightly as he said it.

Robb glanced at him quickly. "And a scandal wouldn't help. I understand. But if this is your man, I'm afraid it can't be avoided." He frowned. "Doesn't throw any light on who killed him, though, does it? What was he doing here? Why didn't whoever killed him take the coach? It's a good one, and the horses are beauties."

"No idea," Monk admitted. "Every new fact only makes it harder to understand."

Robb nodded, then turned back to his grandfather. He made sure the old man was comfortable and could reach everything he would need before Robb could come home again, then he touched him gently, smiled, and took his leave.

The old man said nothing, but his gratitude was in his face. He seemed better now that he had had his meal and whatever medicine Robb had given him.

They walked the three quarters of a mile or so to the stable where the horses and the carriage were being housed. Robb explained to the groom in charge who Monk was.

Monk needed only to glance at the carriage to remove any doubt in his own mind that it was the Stourbridges'. He examined it to see if there were any marks on it, or anything left in the inside which might tell him of its last journey, but there

71

was nothing. It was a very well kept, cleaned, polished and oiled family coach. It had slight marks of wear and was about ten years old. The manufacturer was the one whose name Henry Stourbridge had given him. The description answered exactly.

The horses were also precisely as described.

"Where exactly were they found?" Monk asked again.

"Cannon Hall Road," Robb replied. "It's yours, isn't it?" That was barely a question. He knew the answer from Monk's face.

"And the body?"

"On the path to number five, Green Man Hill. It's a row of small houses close onto the Heath."

"And, of course, you've asked them about it." That, too, was a statement, not a question.

Robb shrugged. "Of course. No one is saying anything."

Monk was not surprised. Whether they did or not, few people admitted to knowing anything about a murder.

"I'll need the body identified formally," Robb said. "And I'll have to speak to Major Stourbridge, of course. Ask him all I can about Treadwell." He did not even bother to add "if it is him."

"I'll go to Cleveland Square and bring someone," Monk offered. He wanted to be the one to tell Harry and Lucius, and preferably to do it without Robb present. He could not avoid the sergeant's being there when they identified the body.

"Thank you," Robb accepted. "I'll be at the morgue at four."

Monk took a hansom back to Bayswater, and when the footman admitted him, he asked if he could speak to Major Stourbridge. He would prefer, if possible, to tell the major without Lucius's having to know until it was necessary. Perhaps it was also cowardice. He did not want to be the one to tell Lucius.

He was shown into the withdrawing room with French doors wide open onto the sunlit lawn. Harry Stourbridge was standing just inside, but Monk could see the figure of his wife in the garden beyond, her pale dress outlined against the vivid colors of the herbaceous border.

"You have news, Mr. Monk?" Stourbridge said almost before the footman had closed the door from the hall. He looked anxious. His face was drawn, and there were dark smudges under his eyes as if he had slept little. It would be cruel to stretch out the suspense. It was hard enough to have to kill the hope struggling in him as it was.

"I am sorry, it is not good," Monk said bluntly. He saw Harry Stourbridge's body stiffen and the last, faint touch of color drain from his skin. "I believe I have found your coach and horses," he continued. "And the body of a man I am almost certain is Treadwell. There is no sign whatever of Mrs. Gardiner."

"No sign of Miriam?" Stourbridge looked confused. He swallowed painfully. "Where was this, Mr. Monk? Do you know what happened to Treadwell, if it is he?"

"Hampstead, just off the Heath. I'm very sorry; it seems Treadwell was murdered."

Stourbridge's eyes widened. "Robbery?"

"Perhaps, but if so, what for? He wouldn't be carrying money, would he? Have you missed anything from the house?"

"No! No, of course not, or I should have told you. But why else would anyone attack and kill the poor man?"

"We don't know . . ."

"We?"

"The police at Hampstead. I traced the carriage that far, then went to ask them," Monk explained. "A young sergeant called Robb. He told me he was working on a murder and I realized from his description that it could be Treadwell. Also, the carriage and horses were found half a mile away, quite undamaged. I have looked at them, and from what you told me, they appear to be yours. I am afraid you will need to send someone to identify them—and the body—to be certain."

"Of course," Stourbridge agreed. "I will come myself." He

73

took a step forward across the bright, sunlit carpet. "But you have no idea about Miriam?"

"Not yet. I'm sorry."

Verona was walking towards them across the grass, her curiosity too powerful to allow her to remain apart.

Stourbridge squared his shoulders as she came in through the door.

"What is it?" she asked him, only glancing at Monk. "You know something." That was a conclusion, not a question. "Is it Miriam?"

Monk searched her expression for the slightest trace of relief, or false surprise, and saw none.

"Not yet," Stourbridge answered before Monk could. "But it appears he may have found Treadwell . . ."

"May?" She picked up the inference instantly, looking from her husband to Monk. "You did not approach him, speak with him? Why? What has happened?"

"He has met with misfortune," Stourbridge put in. "I am about to accompany Mr. Monk to see what else may be learned. I shall tell you, of course, when I return." There was finality in his voice, sufficient to tell her it was useless pressing any further questions now.

Monk's relief at not having to tell Lucius what he had discovered was short-lived. They were crossing the hall towards the front door when Lucius came down the stairs, his face pale, eyes wide.

"What have you found?" he demanded, fear sharp in his voice. "Is it Miriam? Where is she? What has happened to her?"

Stourbridge turned and put up his hands as if to take Lucius by the shoulders to steady him, but Lucius stepped back. His throat was too tight to allow him to speak, and he gulped air.

"I don't know anything about Mrs. Gardiner," Monk said quickly. "But I may have found Treadwell. I need someone to identify him before I can be certain."

Stourbridge put his hand on Lucius's arm. "There was

74

nothing to indicate that Miriam was with him," he said gently. "We don't know what happened or why. Stay here. I will do what is necessary. But be discreet. Until we are sure, there is no purpose in distressing Cook."

Lucius recalled with an effort that he was not the only one to be affected, even bereaved. He looked at Monk. "Treadwell is dead?"

"I think it is Treadwell," Monk replied. "But he was found alone, and the coach is empty and undamaged."

A fraction of the color returned to Lucius's cheeks. "I'm coming with you."

"There is no need . . ." Stourbridge began, then, seeing the determination in his son, and perhaps realizing it was easier to do something than simply to wait, he did not protest any further.

It was a miserable journey from Bayswater back to Hampstead. They took the Stourbridges' remaining carriage, driven now by the groom, and rode for the most part in silence, Lucius sitting upright with his back to the way they were going, his eyes wide and dark, consumed in his own fears. Stourbridge sat next to Monk, staring ahead but oblivious of the streets and the houses they were passing. Once or twice he made as if to say something, then changed his mind.

Monk concentrated on determining what he would tell Robb if the body proved to be Treadwell, and he had no real doubt that it was. It was also impossible to argue whether or not it was murder. The body, whosoever it was, had not come by such an injury by any mischance. To conceal such information as his flight with Miriam Gardiner, and the fact that she had gone without explanation and was still missing, would now be a crime. Also, it would suggest that they had some fear that she was implicated. Nothing they said afterwards would be believed unless it carried proof.

Not that either Harry or Lucius Stourbridge would be remotely likely to hide the truth. They were both far too passionately involved to conceal anything at all. Their first question to Robb would be regarding anything he would know

75

about Miriam. They were so convinced of her entire innocence in anything wrong beyond a breach of good manners that they would only think of how she might be implicated when it was too late.

How would Monk then explain to Robb his own silence about the other person in the carriage? He had not so far even mentioned her.

They jolted to a stop as traffic ahead of them thickened and jammed the streets. All around, drivers shouted impatiently. Horses stamped and whinnied, jingling harnesses.

Lucius sat rigid, still unspeaking.

Stourbridge clenched and unclenched his hands.

They moved forward again at last.

Monk would tell Robb as little as possible. All they knew for certain was that Miriam had left at the same moment as Treadwell. How far they had gone together was another matter. Should he warn Stourbridge and Lucius to say no more about Miriam than they had to?

He looked at their tense faces, each staring into space, consumed in their fears, and decided that any advice would only be overridden by emotion and probably do more harm than good. If they remembered it to begin with, then forgot, it would give the impression of dishonesty.

He kept silent also.

They reached the morgue at ten minutes past four. Robb was already there, pacing restlessly up and down, but he made no comment on the time as they alighted. They were all too eager to complete the business for which they had come to do more than acknowledge each other with the briefest courtesies and then follow Robb inside.

The morgue attendant drew the sheet back from the body, showing only the head.

Lucius drew in his breath sharply and seemed to sway a little on his feet.

Stourbridge let out a soft sigh. He was a soldier, and he must have seen death many times before, and usually of men he had known to a greater or lesser extent, but this was a

76

man of his own household, and murder was different from war. War was not an individual evil. Soldiers expected to kill and be killed. Frequently, they even respected their enemies. There was no hatred involved. The violence was huge and impersonal. It did not make the pain less, or the death or the bereavement less final, but death in war was mischance. This was different, a close, intended and covert evil, meant for this man alone.

"Is it your coachman, sir?" Robb asked, but he could not help being aware that the question was unnecessary. The recognition was in both their faces.

"Yes, it is," Stourbridge said quietly. "This is James Treadwell. Where did you find him?"

The morgue attendant drew back the sheet to cover the face.

"In the street, sir," Robb replied, leading them away from the table and back towards the door. "On the path to one of a row of houses on Green Man Hill, about half a mile or so from here." Robb was sympathetic, but the detective in him was paramount. "Are you aware of his knowing anyone in this area?"

"What?" Stourbridge looked up. "Oh . . . no, I don't think so. He is a nephew of our cook. I can ask her. I have no idea where he went on his days off."

"Was it one of his days off when he disappeared, sir?"

"No . . ."

"Did he have your permission to use your coach, sir?"

Stourbridge hesitated a moment before replying. He looked across at Lucius, then away again.

"No, he did not. I am afraid the circumstances of his leaving the house are somewhat mysterious, and not understood by any of us, Sergeant. We know when he left, but nothing more than that."

"You knew he had taken your coach," Robb pointed out. "But you did not report it to the police. It is a very handsome coach, sir, and exceptionally well matched horses. Worth a considerable amount."

"Major Stourbridge has already mentioned that Treadwell was related to his cook," Monk interrupted, "who is a long-standing servant of the family. He wished to avoid scandal, if possible. He hoped Treadwell would come to his senses and return . . . even with a reasonable explanation."

Lucius could bear it no longer. "My fiancée was with him!" he burst out. "Mrs. Miriam Gardiner. It was to find her that we employed Mr. Monk's services. Treadwell is beyond our help, poor soul, but where is Miriam? We should be turning all our skill and attention to searching for her! She may be hurt . . . in danger . . ." His voice was rising out of control as his imagination tortured him.

Robb looked startled for a moment, then his jaw hardened. He did not even glance at Monk. "Do I understand Mrs. Gardiner left your house in the carriage with Treadwell driving?" he demanded.

"We believe so," Stourbridge answered before Lucius could speak. "No one saw them go." He seemed to have appreciated something of the situation in spite of Monk's silence. "But we have not heard from her since, nor do we know what has happened to her. We are at our wits' end with worry."

"We must look for her!" Lucius cut across them. "Tread-well is dead and Miriam may be in danger. At the very least she must be in fear and distress. You must deploy every man you can to search for her!"

Robb stood still for a moment, surprise taking the words from him. Then slowly he turned to Monk, his eyes narrow and hard. "You omitted to mention that a young woman was a passenger in the carriage when Treadwell was murdered and that she has since disappeared. Why is that, Mr. Monk?"

Monk had foreseen the question, though there was no excuse that was satisfactory, and Robb would know that as well as he did.

"Mrs. Gardiner left with Treadwell," he replied with as honest a bearing as he could. "We have no idea when she left him. . . ."

78

Lucius was staring at him, his eyes wide and horrified.

"Sophistry!" Robb snapped.

"Reality!" Monk returned with equal harshness. "This was five days ago. If anything happened to Mrs. Gardiner we are far too late to affect it now, except by careful thought and consideration before we act." He was acutely conscious of Lucius and of Harry Stourbridge. Their emotions filled the air. "If she met with violence as well, she would have been found long before now." He did not glance at either of them but kept his eyes level on Robb. "If she was kidnapped, then a ransom will be asked for, and it has not so far. If she witnessed the murder, then she may well have run away, for her own safety, and we must be careful how we look for her, in case we bring upon her the very harm she fears." He drew in his breath. "And until Major Stourbridge identified the body as that of Treadwell, we did not know that it was anything more than a domestic misunderstanding between Mr. Stourbridge and Mrs. Gardiner."

Lucius stood appalled.

Stourbridge looked from one to the other of them. "We know now," he said grimly. "The question is what we are to do next."

"Discover all the facts that we can," Monk answered him. "And then deduce what we can from them."

Robb bit his lip, his face pale. He turned to Lucius. "You have no idea why Mrs. Gardiner left your home?"

"No, none at all," Lucius said quickly. "There was no quarrel, no incident at all which sparked it. Mrs. Gardiner was standing alone, watching the croquet match when, without warning or explanation, she simply left."

"With Treadwell?"

"She left in the carriage," Stourbridge corrected him. "She could hardly have driven it herself."

A flash of irritation crossed Robb's face and then disappeared, as if he had remembered their distress. "Had Mrs. Gardiner any previous acquaintance with Treadwell, perhaps through the cook?"

"No," Lucius said instantly. "She had met no one in the house before I first took her there."

"Where did you meet Mrs. Gardiner?"

"On Hampstead Heath. Why? It is natural enough that he should bring her back here. She lives on Lyndhurst Road."

Robb pursed his lips. "That is about three quarters of a mile from where the carriage was found, and rather more from where Treadwell's body was. I assume you have already been to her home to see if she was there?"

"Of course! No one has seen her since she left to come to Bayswater," Lucius answered. "It is the first place we looked. Please, tell us what you know of Treadwell's death, I beg you."

They were outside in the street again now. Lucius stood breathing deeply, as if trying to clear his lungs of the choking air of the morgue with its close smell of death. Even so, he did not take his eyes from Robb's face.

"We know nothing except that he was murdered," Robb replied. "We did not even know his name until you gave it to us, although from his clothes we assumed his occupation."

"Was there nothing found in the carriage?" Stourbridge asked with a frown. "No marks or stains to indicate where it had been? What about the horses? Are they hurt?"

"No, they were lost, confused, aware that something was wrong. There was nothing to indicate they had bolted. The harness was not broken. The reins were still tied to the bar, as if the driver had stopped, then climbed down rather than fallen. The carriage itself has no scratches or marks but those of ordinary use."

Stourbridge turned questioningly to Monk.

"There is nothing further you can do here now," Monk assured him. "Thank you for coming to identify Treadwell. Perhaps you had better return home and inform your family— and, of course, the cook. She is bound to be distressed. As soon as I learn anything more, I will tell you."

Lucius stood still. "The answer must be here!" he insisted desperately, loath to leave without something further accomplished.

Stourbridge touched his elbow. "Perhaps, but Mr. Monk will find it more easily if we do not hamper him."

Lucius did not move.

"Come," Stourbridge said gently. "We shall only make it more difficult."

Reluctantly, still half disbelieving, Lucius bade good-bye and permitted himself to be led away.

"You realize I shall have to find this woman?" Robb shoved his hands deep in his pockets, staring grimly at Monk. He looked guarded, careful, his shoulders hunched a little. "At best she may be witness to the murder, at worst a victim herself."

It was unarguable. Monk said nothing.

"Or she may be guilty herself," Robb went on. "That blow could have been struck by a woman, if she were frightened enough or angry enough. Perhaps you will now be frank and tell me what you know of this Mrs. Gardiner. Since Mr. Stourbridge seems to have hired you to find her, presumably you know a great deal more than you have so far told me."

There was no evading it now, and perhaps it was the only way to help Lucius Stourbridge. Whatever the truth was, one day he would have to face at least part of it. Some details might be kept from him, but not the essence. If Miriam Gardiner were involved in the murder of Treadwell, it would be public knowledge sooner or later. Monk could not protect him from that, even if she were no more than a witness. And unless Treadwell had set her down somewhere before he reached the Heath, that seemed an unavoidable conclusion. It was plain in Robb's face now as he looked grimly at Monk, ignoring the traffic passing by them and the people on foot having to walk around.

Monk told Robb the outline of his interview with Lucius Stourbridge and his visit to Bayswater. He gave no more detail than was necessary to be honest, and none of his own impressions, except that he had believed what he had been told so far.

Robb looked thoughtful, biting his lips. "And no one gave you any idea why Mrs. Gardiner should have run off in this way?"

"No."

"Where did Treadwell serve before Bayswater? Where was he born?"

Monk felt himself flush with annoyance. They were obvious questions, and he had not thought to ask them. It was a stupid oversight. He had concentrated on Miriam, thinking of Treadwell only as someone to drive the coach for her. It was instinctive to try to defend himself, but there was nothing to say which would not make his omission look worse.

"I don't know." The words were hollow, an open failure.

Robb was tactful. He even seemed faintly relieved.

"And about her?" he asked.

This time Monk could answer, and did as fully as he knew.

Robb thought for several moments before he spoke again.

"So a relationship between Mrs. Gardiner and this coachman is unlikely, but it is not impossible. It seems she turned to him to take her away from the Stourbridge house, at least." He looked at Monk nervously. "And you still have no idea why?"

"None."

Robb grunted. "I cannot stop you looking for her also, of course, and perhaps finding her before I do. But if she is involved in this crime, even as a witness, and you assist her, I shall charge you!" His young face was set, his lips tight.

"Of course," Monk agreed. "I would in your place." That was unquestionably true. He had a suspicion from what he had learned of himself and the past that Robb was being gentler with him than he had been with others. He smiled bleakly. "Thank you for your civility. I expect we'll meet again. Good day."

* * *

Monk arrived home at Fitzroy Street a little after seven and found dinner ready and Hester waiting for him. It was extremely satisfying. The house was clean and smelled faintly of lavender and polish. There were fresh flowers on the table, a white cloth with blue cross-stitch patterns on it, and crockery and silverware. Hester served cold game pie with crisp pastry and hot vegetables, then an egg custard with nutmeg grated over the top, and lastly cheese and crusty bread. There were even a few early strawberries to finish. He sat back with a feeling of immense well-being to watch Hester clear away the dishes, and was pleased to see her return some twenty-five minutes later ready to sit down and talk with him for the rest of the evening. He wanted to tell her about Treadwell, and about Robb and his grandfather.

"Did you find the coach yet?" she asked.

He leaned back in the chair, crossing his legs.

"Yes. And I found Treadwell also." He saw her eyes widen, then the knowledge came into her face that there was far more to what he said. She understood the tragedy before he put it into words. She did not ask him, but waited.

"I went to the local police station to see if they had seen the coach. The sergeant was occupied with a murder case, but he spared me a few minutes . . ." He knew she would leap to the conclusion before he told her.

"Treadwell!" She swallowed. "Not Miriam, too?" Her voice was strained with expectation of pain.

"No," he said quickly. "There's no sign of her at all. I would not have had to mention her, except that I brought Major Stourbridge to identify Treadwell, and Lucius insisted on coming as well. Of course, they had to ask Robb about her."

"Robb is the sergeant?"

"Yes." He described him for her, trying to bring to life in words both the gentleness he had seen in the young man and the determination, and a little of the edge of his nervousness, his need to succeed.

He saw in her face that he had caught her interest. She had understood that there was far more he had not yet told her.

"How was Treadwell killed?" she asked.

"With a blow over the head with something hard and heavy."

"Did he fight?"

"No. It was as if he was taken by surprise."

"Where was he found?" She was leaning forward now, her attention wholly absorbed.

"On the path of a small house on Green Man Hill, just off the Heath."

"That's close to the hospital," she said quietly. "One or two of our part-time nurses live around there."

"I doubt he was going to see a nurse," he said dryly, but it brought to mind his visit with Robb to the old man, and the poverty in which they lived. Robb's return home would be so different from his own, no wife with a fine meal ready and a quiet evening in the last of the sun. He would find a sick old man who needed caring for, washing, feeding, cleaning often, and who was always either in distress or close to it. Money must be scarce. The medicines alone would be expensive, and perhaps hard to come by.

"What?" she said softly, as if reading his thoughts, or at least his emotions.

He told her about his lunchtime visit, his feelings pouring through his words in a kind of release. He had not realized how much it had cost to contain them within himself, until now that he could share them with her with the certainty that she understood. He could sense her response as surely as if she had answered every sentence, although she did not interrupt at all. Only when he was finished did she speak.

"I'll go and see him. Perhaps the hospital can—"

He did not allow her to complete the words. "No, you won't!" He did not even know why he said it, except that he did not want Robb to think he had interfered, implying that he was not looking after the old man adequately. For someone else to go in unasked would be an intrusion.

Hester stiffened, the whole angle of her body changed.

"I beg your pardon?" Her voice was cool.

Now was the time to make sure she understood him and it was plain between them where the bounds of authority lay.

"You are not to interfere," he stated clearly. He did not explain why. His reasons were good, but that was not the point. If he explained now, she would require an explanation every time. "It would be inappropriate."

"Why?" she asked, her eyes bright and challenging.

He had not intended to allow an argument. In fact, this was precisely what he had meant to avoid.

"I am not going to discuss it," he replied. "I've told you, that is sufficient." He rose to his feet to signal the end of the matter. Robb would be offended. He might very easily feel Monk believed his care of his grandfather was not good enough. Or worse, he might feel some implied pressure because he was using police time to go home and attend to the old man.

Hester rose also. Her voice was low and very precise, each word spoken carefully. "Are you telling me whether I may or may not do what I believe to be right, William?"

"You may do anything that is right," he said with a tiny smile of relief, because she had offered him a route of escape. "Always. This is not right."

"You mean I may do what you believe to be right?" she challenged.

"You may," he agreed. "You do not have to. The choice is yours." And with that he went out into the office, leaving her in the middle of the floor, furious. It was not what he wanted at all, but it was a victory that mattered. There were any number of reasons why he must be master in his own home, for the happiness of both of them. When her temper cooled, she would appreciate that.

He sat in the room alone for over an hour, but she did not join him. At first he missed her, then he became irritated. She was childish. She could not expect to have her own way in everything.

But she always had! He remembered with considerable disquiet how she had governed her own life in the past, how

85

willful she had been. Even the hospital authorities could not tolerate her—and did not. She was opinionated in everything, and not loath to express these opinions even at the least-opportune moments—and with a wit which made them even more offensive to some. He had laughed when he had not been on the receiving end. It was less funny when he was.

Not that his own tongue was not equally sharp and every bit as well informed. That was one of the reasons she could accept marriage to him, because he was more than her equal—well, occasionally.

But she must not be allowed to sulk. That was unaccept-able. He stood up and went to find her. This could not continue.

She was sitting at the table writing. She looked up when he came in.

"Ah, good," she said with a smile. "You've come to tell me more about it. I thought you would. The kettle is on. Would you like a cup of tea? And there is cake as well."

He thought of the night to come, and lying beside her warm, slender body, either rigid and turned away from him or gentle and willing in his arms. More than that, deeper in his soul, he thought of all that they had shared that mattered above any petty battle of wills or convention of behavior. The issue could wait until another time. There would certainly be other battles, dozens of them, perhaps hundreds.

"Yes," he agreed, sitting down on the other chair. "Tea would be nice, thank you. And cake."

Obediently, with a little smile, she rose to make it.

4

IN THE MORNING, Monk left home to continue his search for Miriam Gardiner, only now there was the added difficulty that he must do so without at the same time leading Robb to her. He did not underestimate Robb's intelligence. He had already had the chastening experience of being outthought in conversation, and the memory still stung.

Horses were intelligent animals, and very much creatures of habit. If Treadwell had driven them to Hampstead before then, they were likely to have returned to the same place.

Accordingly, the still, summer morning at seven o'clock found Monk standing in the sun on Lyndhurst Road, studying its tidy house fronts with their neat gardens and whitened steps.

He knew Miriam's address from Lucius Stourbridge. Naturally, it was the first place he had enquired, but all his questions had elicited only blank ignorance and then growing alarm. That might still be where Robb would begin.

Monk stood with the lazy sun warming his shoulders and the early-morning sounds of kitchen doors opening and closing, the occasional whack of a broom handle beating a carpet. Errand boys' feet were loud on the cobbles, as was the uneven step of one of them who was carrying a heavy bucket of coal. The only thought crowding his mind was where had Miriam been when James Treadwell was murdered. Had she been present? If she had, had anyone else, or had she killed him herself? The surgeon had said it seemed a single, extremely heavy blow, but not impossible to have been inflicted by a woman, given that she had used the right weapon. And Tread-well had not died straightaway but crawled from wherever it had happened, presumably looking for help. Neither Robb nor the police surgeon had offered any suggestion as to where the crime had taken place, but it could not have been far away.

Had Miriam struck him once and then fled? Had she taken the coach, driving it herself? If so, why had she abandoned it in the street so close by?

Perhaps she had panicked and simply run, as the blind, in-stinctive thing to do. Possibly she was unused to horses and did not know how to drive.

Or had there been a third person there? Had Miriam wit-nessed the murder and fled, perhaps for her own survival? Or had she not been there at all?

He would learn nothing standing in the sun while the world woke up and busied itself around him. He walked forward and up the step to the nearest door. He knocked on it and the maid answered, looking startled and ready to tell any errant tradesman where his appropriate entrance was and not to be so impertinent as to come to the front. Then she saw Monk's face, and her eyes traveled down his smart coat to his pol-ished boots, and she changed her mind.

"Yes sir?" she said curiously, absentmindedly pushing her hand through her hair to tidy it out of her eyes. "Master's not up yet, I'm afraid." Then she realized that was a little too re-vealing. "I mean, 'e in't 'ad 'is breakfast yet."

Monk made himself smile at the girl. "I'm sure you can help me without disturbing the household. I'm afraid I am lost. I don't know the area very well. I am looking for a Mrs. Miriam Gardiner. I believe she lives somewhere near here." He knew perfectly well that she lived about five houses along, but he wanted to learn all he could from someone who almost certainly would have noticed her and heard all the below-stairs gossip. If indeed there had been some relationship between her and Treadwell, then they might have been less guarded here, away from Cleveland Square.

"Mrs. Gardiner? Oh, yeah," she said cheerfully. She came farther out onto the step and swung around, pointing. "Four doors up that way she lives. Or mebbe it's five, number eight. Just along there, any'ow. Yer can't miss it."

"Would you know if she is at home now?" he asked without moving.

"Cor luv yer, no I wouldn't. I in't seen 'er fer a week ner more. I 'eard as she were gettin' married again, an' good for 'er, I says."

"Would that be an elderly gentleman who lives about a mile from here?" Monk assumed an ingenuous air.

"Dunno, I'm sure," the girl replied. "Shouldn't 'a thought so, though. Comes in a right smart carriage, 'e does. Matched pair like nobody's business. Step fer step they goes, like they was machines."

"Same color?" Monk asked with interest.

"Color don't matter," she replied with ill-concealed impatience. "Size an' pace is wot makes 'em ride well."

"Know something about horses?" he observed.

"Me pa were a coachman," she said. "None better, if I says so as shouldn't."

He smiled at her quite genuinely. Something in her pride in her father pleased him. It was simple and without self-consciousness. "Seen them about quite often, I suppose? Was that coachman much good?"

"Fair," she replied with careful judgment. "Not near as good as me pa. Too 'eavy-'anded."

"Have you seen him lately? I'd like a word with him." He thought he had better give some reason for all the questions.

"I in't seen 'im fer a few days now." She shook her head as if it puzzled her. "But 'e's around 'ere often enough. I seen 'im in the High Street. I recognize them 'orses. Goin' towards the 'Eath."

"You mean not to Mrs. Gardiner's house?" he said with surprise. "To a public house, perhaps?"

"In't none up that way," she replied. " 'E must 'a know'd someone."

"Thank you! Thank you very much." He stepped back. "Good day."

She stood on the path smiling as he walked away, then went back into the house to continue with her far less interesting duties.

He was speaking to a gardener busy pulling weeds when he saw Robb turn the corner of the street and come towards him, frowning, deep in thought. His hands were in his pockets, and from the concentration in his face, Monk surmised he was mulling over something that caused him concern.

It was as well for Monk that he was, otherwise Robb would almost certainly have recognized him, and that was something he did not wish. Robb had to be searching for Miriam just as diligently as he was. Monk must find her first, even if only to give her time to prepare what she would say.

He thanked the gardener, turned on his heel and strode away as fast as he could without drawing undue attention to himself. He went down the first side street he came to.

Robb did not pass him. Damn! He must have stopped to speak to the same gardener. It was the obvious thing to do. Then the man would also tell him of seeing the carriage drive by regularly over the last year or more. And Robb would ask who it was that had just been talking to him, and the gardener would say that he had given him the same information. Even if Robb had not recognized the well-cut jacket and the square set of his shoulders, Robb would know it was Monk. Who else would it be?

What had James Treadwell been doing here other than collecting and returning Miriam to her home after visiting with Lucius Stourbridge? Had he relatives here? Was there a woman, or more than one? Or some form of business? Had it anything to do with Miriam, or not?

A vehicle like that would be remembered by anyone who knew horses. This was not an area with many stables or mews where they could be kept out of sight. Most people here used public transport, hansoms, or even omnibuses. Short journeys would be made on foot.

He spent the next three hours combing the neighborhood asking boot boys, errand boys, and a scullery maid about the houses. He stopped a man delivering coal for kitchen fires, which were kept burning to cook on, even on such a hot summer day, his face black, sweat trickling through the coal dust that caked his skin.

Twice more he only narrowly avoided running into Robb. He spoke to a boy selling newspapers and a man with a tray of ham sandwiches, from whom he purchased what was going to have to serve him for a late luncheon. Most of them were happy to admit they knew Miriam Gardiner, at least by sight, and smiled when they said it, as if the memory were pleasant.

But they knew that Treadwell had been murdered, and none of them wished to be associated with that, however loosely. Yes, they had seen him in the past, but no, not lately, certainly not on the night he had met his death. They gazed back at Monk with blank eyes and complete denial. He could only hope Robb met with the same.

The only thing left to do was move closer to where the body had been found and try again. It was a matter of searching for the kind of person who was in a position to observe the comings and goings, and who might feel free to speak of them without involving himself in something which could only be unpleasant. Servants caught gossiping were invariably in trouble. The advantage he had over Robb was that he was not police. But being a civilian also held disadvantages. He could only persuade; he could oblige nothing.

He walked slowly along the pavement in the sun. It was a pleasant neighborhood, with rows of small, respectable houses. Inside, the front parlors would be neat and stuffy, seldom used, filled with paintings and samplers with God-fearing messages on them, possibly a picture of the family posed self-consciously in their Sunday best. Life would be conducted mostly in the kitchen and bedrooms. Prayers would be said every morning and night. The generations would be listed in the family Bible, which was probably opened once a week. Sunday morning would be very sober indeed, although Saturday night might get a little tipsy—for the men anyway.

He tried to think what Treadwell would do when he got to Hampstead. Did he meet friends, perhaps a woman? Why not? It would certainly be very foolish for him to form a friendship with a woman in the Stourbridge house, or close enough for others to become aware of it. Backstairs gossip had ruined more than a few men in service.

Had he come to buy or to pay for something, or to settle or collect an old debt? Or had it been simply to escape his daily life of obedience to someone else? Here, for an hour or two, he would have been his own master.

Monk crossed the street, still strolling gently because he had reached no decision. A young woman passed him. She was wearing the starched uniform and simple dress of a nursemaid, and she had a little girl by the hand. Every now and again the child took a little skip, the ribbon in her hair bobbing, and the young woman smiled at her. Far away in the distance, probably on the Heath, a barrel organ played.

If Treadwell had come here he would not have left the carriage and horses standing unattended. Even if he had merely stopped for a drink, he would have had to leave them in some suitable place, such as an ostler's yard.

There was a shop across the road ahead of him. He was not more than a quarter of a mile from Miriam Gardiner's house. This would be an excellent place to start. He increased his pace. Now he had a specific purpose.

He opened the door, and a bell clanked rustily somewhere inside. An elderly gentleman appeared from behind a curtain and looked at Monk hopefully.

"Yes sir. Lovely day, in't it? What can I get for you, sir? Tea, candles, half a pound of mint humbugs perhaps?" He waved a hand at the general clutter around him which apparently held all these things and more. "Or a penny postcard? Ball of string, maybe you need, or sealing wax?"

"Ball of string and sealing wax sounds very useful," Monk

agreed. "And the humbugs would be excellent on such a warm day. Thank you."

The man nodded several times, satisfied, and began to find the articles named.

"Mrs. Gardiner said you would have almost anything I might want," Monk remarked, watching the man carefully.

"Oh, did she?" the man replied without looking up. "Now, there's a nice lady, if you like! Happy to see her marry again, and that's not a lie. Widowed too young, she was. Oh! There's the sealing wax." He held it up triumphantly. "It's a nice color, that is. Not too orange. Don't like it to be too orange. Red's better."

"I suppose you've known her a long time," Monk remarked casually, nodding back in approval of the shade of the wax.

"Bless you, only since she first came here as a girl, and that's not a lie," the man agreed. "Poor little thing!"

Monk stiffened. What should he say to encourage more confidences without showing his own ignorance or curiosity?

The man found the string and came up from his bending with a ball in each hand.

"There you are, sir," he said triumphantly, his face shining. "Which would you prefer? This is good string for parcels and the like, and the other's softer, better for tying up plants. Don't cut into the stems, you see?"

"I'll take both," Monk answered, his mind racing. "And two sticks of the sealing wax. As you say, it's a good color."

"Good! Good! And the mint humbugs. Never forget the mint humbugs!" He laid the string on the counter and disappeared below it again, presumably searching for more sealing wax. Monk hoped it was not the humbugs down in the dusty recesses.

"I hadn't realized she was so young when it happened," Monk observed, hoping he sounded more casual than he felt.

"Bless you, no more than twelve or thirteen, and that's not a lie," the man answered from his hands and knees where he was searching in the cupboards under the counter. He pulled out a huge box full of envelopes and linen paper. "Poor little creature. Terrible small she was. Not a soul in the world, so it seemed. Not then. But of course our Cleo took her in." He pulled out another box of assorted papers. Monk did not care in the slightest about the sealing wax, but he did not want to interrupt the flow. "Good woman, Cleo Anderson. Heart of gold, whatever anybody says," the man continued vehemently.

"Please don't go to trouble." Monk was abashed by the work he was causing, and he had what he wanted. "I don't need more wax, I merely liked the color."

"Mustn't be beaten," the shopkeeper mumbled from the depth of the cupboard. "That's what they said at Trafalgar— and Waterloo, no doubt. Can't have a customer leaving dissatisfied."

"I suppose you know Mr. Treadwell also?" Monk tried the last question.

"Not as I recall. Ah! Here it is! I knew I had some more somewhere. Half a box of it." He backed out and stood up, his shoulders covered in dust, a lidless cardboard box in one hand. He beamed at Monk. "Here you are, sir. How much would you like?"

"Three sticks, thank you," Monk replied, wondering what on earth he could use it for. "Is there a good ostler's yard near here?"

The man leaned over the counter and pointed leftwards, waving his arm. "About half a mile up that way, and one street over. Can't miss it. Up towards Mrs. Anderson's, it is. But you'd know that, knowing Mrs. Gardiner an' all. That'll be tenpence ha'penny altogether, sir, if you please. Oh . . . an' here are the humbugs. That'll be another tuppence, if you please."

Monk took his purchases, thanked him and paid, then set out towards the ostler's yard feeling pleased with himself.

He needed to find Miriam. The details of her youth were of value only inasmuch as they either explained her extraordinary behavior or indicated where she was now.

The ostler's yard was precisely where the shopkeeper had pointed.

"Yes," an old man said, sucking on a straw. He was bow-legged and smelled of the stable yard, horse sweat, hay and leather. " 'E come 'ere often. Right 'andsome pair, they was. Perfick match, pace fer pace."

"Good with horses, was he?" Monk enquired casually.

"Not as I'd say 'good,' " the ostler qualified. " 'Fair,' more like it." He looked at Monk through narrowed eyes, waiting for him to explain himself.

Monk made a grimace of disgust. "Not what he told me. That's why I thought I'd check."

"Don't make no matter now." The ostler spat out the straw, "Dead, poor swine. Not that I'd much time fer 'im. Saucy bastard, 'e were. Always full o' lip. But I wouldn't wish that on 'im. Yer not from 'round 'ere, or yer'd o' know'd 'e were dead. Murdered, 'e were. On Mrs. Anderson's footpath, practically, an' 'er a good woman, an' all. Looked after my Annie, she did, summink wonderful." He shook his head. "Nuffink weren't too much trouble for 'er."

Monk seized the chance. "A very fine woman," he agreed. "Took in Mrs. Gardiner, too, I believe, when she was just a child."

The ostler selected himself another straw and put it in his mouth. "Oh, yeah. Found her wandering around out of 'er wits, they did. Babblin' like a lunatic an' scarce knew 'er own name, poor thing. It were Cleo Anderson wot took 'er in an' cleaned 'er up and raised 'er like she was 'er own. Shame that no-good braggart got 'isself killed on her doorstep. That kind o' trouble nobody needs."

"Can't prevent accidents," Monk said sententiously, but his mind was wondering what could have happened to the young Miriam to cause her such agony of mind. He could imagine it only too vividly, remembering his own fear after the accident, the horrors that lay within himself. Had she experienced something like that? Did she also not know who she was? Was that what terrified her and drove her away from Lucius Stourbridge, who loved her so much?

The ostler spat out his straw. "Weren't no haccident!" He said derisively. "Like I told yer, 'e were murdered! 'It over the 'ead, 'e were."

"He left his horses here quite often," Monk observed, recalling himself to the present.

"I told you that, too, didn't I? 'Course, 'e did. Best place fer miles, this is. In't nuthin' abaht 'orses I don't know as is worth knowin'." He waited for Monk to challenge him.

Monk smiled and glanced at the nearest animal. "I can see that," he said appreciatively. "It shows. And your judgment of Treadwell is probably much what I'd concluded myself. An arrogant piece of work."

The ostler looked satisfied. He nodded. "That's wot I told that policeman wot come 'round 'ere askin'. Treadwell weren't much good, I told 'im. Yer can learn a lot abaht a man by the way 'e 'andles an 'orse, if yer know wot ter look fer. You know, yer a bit pleased wif yerself, an' all!"

Monk smiled ruefully. He knew it was true.

The ostler grinned back, pleased there was no offense.

Monk thanked him and left, digesting the information he had gained, not only about Treadwell's being here but about Miriam's strange early life and the coincidence of Treadwell's being murdered on the doorstep of the woman who had found Miriam and had taken her in years before. And, of course, Robb had had the same idea. Monk must be extremely careful he did not inadvertently lead him right to Miriam.

Out in the street again, he walked slowly. He did not put his hands in his pockets. That would pull his suit out of shape. He was too vain for that. Why was he so fearful of leading Robb to Miriam? The answer was painful. Because he was afraid she was involved in Treadwell's death, even if indirectly. She was hiding from Lucius, but she was hiding from the police as well. Why? What was Treadwell to her beyond the driver of Stourbridge's carriage? What did he know—or suspect?

It was time he went to see Cleo Anderson. He did not want to run into Robb, so he approached cautiously, aware that he was a conspicuous figure with his straight, square shoulders and slightly arrogant walk

He was already on Green Man Hill when he saw Robb crossing the street ahead of him, and he stopped abruptly, bending his head and raising his hands as if to light a cigar, then he turned his back, making a gesture as if to shelter a match from the wind. Without looking up, in spite of the intense temptation, he strolled away again and around the first corner he came to.

He stopped and, to his annoyance, found he was shaking. This was absurd. What had it come to when he was scuttling around street corners to keep from being recognized by the police? And a sergeant at that! A short handful of years before, sergeants all over London knew his name and snapped to attention when they heard it. In rediscovering himself after the accident he had witnessed just how deeply the fear of him was rooted. People cared what he thought of them, they wanted to please him and they dreaded his contempt, earned or not.

How much had changed!

He felt himself ridiculous, standing there on the footpath pretending to light an imaginary cigar so Robb would not see his face. And yet the man he had been then, in hindsight gave him little pleasure. Robb would have feared him, possibly respected his skills, but that fear would have been based in the power he had had and his will to use it—and to exercise the sharp edge of his tongue.

He was still impatient, at times sarcastic. He still despised cowardice, hypocrisy and laziness, and took no trouble to conceal it. But he equally despised a bully and felt a sharp stab of pain to think that he might once have been one.

If Robb had gone to see Cleo Anderson, either with regard to Miriam or simply because Treadwell had been found on her pathway, then there was no point waiting there for him to leave. It might be an hour or two. Better to go and buy himself a decent supper, then return in the early evening, when Robb would have gone back home, probably to minister to his grandfather.

Monk ate well, then filled in a little more of the waiting time asking further questions about Miriam. He pretended he had a sister who had recently married and was considering moving into the area. He learned more than he expected, and Miriam's name cropped up in connection with a botanical society, the friends of a missionary group in Africa, a circle of women who met every other Friday to discuss works of literature they had enjoyed, and the rota of duties at the nearest church. He should have thought of the church. He kicked himself for such an obvious omission. He would repair that tomorrow.

Altogether, by the time he stood on Cleo Anderson's doorstep in the early-evening sunlight, the shadows so long across the street that they nearly engulfed his feet, he was feeling, as the ostler had remarked, pleased with himself.

Considering that Cleo Anderson had already sacrificed a great deal of her evening answering the questions of Sergeant Robb, she opened the door to Monk with remarkable courtesy. It occurred to him that she might have believed him to be a patient. After all, caring for the sick was her profession.

It took her only a moment to see that he was a stranger, and unlikely to belong to the immediate neighborhood. Nevertheless, she did not dismiss him summarily. Her eyes narrowed a trifle.

"Yes, love, what can I do for you?" she asked, keeping her weight where she could slam the door if he tried to force his way.

He stood well back deliberately.

"Good evening, Mrs. Anderson," he replied. He decided in that moment not to lie to her. "My name is William Monk. Mr. Lucius Stourbridge has employed me to find Miriam Gardiner. As you may be aware, she has disappeared from his house, where she was a guest, and he is frantic with concern for her." He stopped, seeing the anxiety in her face, her rapid

98

breathing and a stiffening of her body. But then, considering Treadwell's corpse had been found on her path, she could hardly fail to fear for Miriam, unless she already knew that she was safe, not only from physical harm but from suspicion also. Patently, she did not have any such comfort.

"Can you help me?" he said quietly.

For a moment she stood still, making up her mind, then she stepped back, pulling the door wider. "You'd better come in," she invited him reluctantly.

He followed her into a hallway hardly large enough to accommodate the three doors that led from it. She opened the farthest one into a clean and surprisingly light room with comfortable chairs by the fireplace. A row of cupboards lined one wall, all the doors closed and with brass-bound keyholes. None of the keys were present.

"Mr. Stourbridge sent you?" The thought seemed to offer her no comfort. She was still as tense, her hands held tightly, half hidden by her skirts.

He had walked miles and his feet were burning, but to sit unasked would be rushing her, and ill-mannered. "He is terrified some harm may have come to her," he answered. "Especially in light of what happened to the coachman, Treadwell."

In spite of all her effort of control, she drew in her breath sharply. "I don't know where she is!" Then she steadied herself, deliberately waiting a moment or two. "I haven't seen her since she left to go and stay in Bayswater. She told me all about that, o' course." She looked at him levelly.

He had the strong feeling that she was lying, but he did not know to what extent or why. There was fear in her face, but nothing he recognized as guilt. He tried the gentlest approach he could think of.

"Mr. Stourbridge cares for her profoundly. He would act only in her best interest and for her welfare."

Her voice was suddenly thick with emotion, and she choked back tears. "I know that." She took a shaky breath. "He's a very fine young gentleman." She blinked several times. "But that doesn't alter nothin'. God knows." She seemed about to add something else, then changed her mind and remained silent.

"You were the one who found Miriam the first time, weren't you," he said gently, with respect rather than as a question.

She hesitated. "Yes, but that was years back. She was just a child. Twelve or thirteen, she was." A look of pain and defiance crossed her face. "Bin in an accident. Dunno what 'appened to 'er. 'Ysterical . . . in a state like you never seen. Nobody around to claim 'er or care for 'er. I took 'er in. 'Course I did, poor little thing." Her eyes did not move from Monk's. "Nobody ever asked for 'er nor come lookin'. I expected someone every day, then it were weeks, an' months, an' nobody came. So I just took care of 'er like she were mine."

Perhaps she caught something in his eyes, an understanding. Some of the defiance eased from her. "She were scared 'alf out of 'er wits, poor little thing," she went on. "Didn't remember what happened at all."

Cleo Anderson had taken Miriam in and raised her until she had made a respectable and apparently happy marriage to a local man of honorable reputation. Then Miriam had been widowed, with sufficient means to live quite contentedly . . . until she had met Lucius Stourbridge out walking in the sun on Hampstead Heath.

But it was what had happened one week ago that mattered, and where she was now.

"Did you know James Treadwell?" he asked her.

Her answer was immediate, without a moment's thought. "No."

It was too quick. But he did not want to challenge her. He must leave her room to change her mind without having to defend herself.

"So you were all the family Miriam had after the accident." He allowed his very real admiration to fill his voice.

The tenderness in her eyes, in her mouth, was undeniable. If she had permitted herself, at that moment she would have wept. But she was a strong woman, and well used to all manner of tragedy.

"That's true," she agreed quietly. "And she was the nearest thing to a child I ever had, too. And nobody could want better."

"So you must have been happy when she married a good man like Mr. Gardiner," he concluded.

"O' course. An' 'e were a good man! Bit older than Miriam, but loved 'er, 'e did. An' she were proper fond o' 'im."

"It must have been very pleasant for you to have had her living so close."

She smiled. "O' course. But I don' mind where she lives if she's 'appy. An' she loved Mr. Lucius like nothin' I ever seen. 'Er 'ole face lit up when she jus' spoke 'is name." This time the tears spilled down her cheeks, and it was beyond her power to control them.

"What happened, Mrs. Anderson?" he said, almost in a whisper.

"I dunno."

He had not really expected anything else. This was a woman protecting the only child she had nurtured and loved.

"But you must have seen Treadwell, even in the distance, when Miriam came back to visit you while she was staying in Bayswater," he insisted.

She hesitated only a moment. "I seen a coachman, but that's all."

That might be true. Perhaps Treadwell had crawled here because he had heard Miriam say Cleo was a nurse. It was conceivable it was no more than that. But was it likely?

Who had killed Treadwell . . . and why? Why here?

"What did you tell Sergeant Robb?" he asked.

She relaxed a fraction. Her shoulders eased under the dark fabric of her dress, a plain, almost uniform dress such as he had seen Hester wear on duty. He was surprised at the stab of familiarity it caused inside him.

"Same as I'm tellin' you," she answered. "I 'aven't seen

101

Miriam since she went off to stay with Mr. Lucius an' 'is family. I don't know where she is now, an' I've no idea what happened to the coachman, or 'ow 'e got killed, nor why— except I've known Miriam since she were a girl, an' I've never known 'er to lose 'er temper nor lash out at anyone, an' I'd stake my life on that."

Monk believed her, at least for the last part. He accepted that she thought Miriam innocent. He very much doubted that she had no idea where Miriam was. If all were well with Miriam she would unquestionably not have fled from the Stourbridge house as she had, nor have remained out of touch with Lucius. If she were in trouble, whatever its nature, surely she would have turned to Cleo Anderson, the person who had rescued her, cared for her and loved her since that first time?

"I hope you won't have to do anything so extreme," he said gravely, then he bade her good-night without asking anything further. He knew she would not answer, at least not with the truth.

He bought a sandwich from a peddler about a block away, making conversation with him as he ate it. Then he took an omnibus back towards Fitzroy Street, and was glad to sit down, cramped and lurching as the conveyance was.

He let his thoughts wander. Where could Miriam go? She was frightened. She trusted no one, except perhaps Cleo. Certainly, she did not trust Lucius Stourbridge. She would not want to be in unfamiliar territory, yet she would have to avoid those who were known to be her friends.

A fat woman next to him was perspiring freely. She mopped her face with a large handkerchief. A small boy blew a pennywhistle piercingly, and his mother showed sharp disapproval, to no effect. An elderly man in a bowler hat sucked air through a gap in his teeth. Monk glared at the boy with the whistle, and he stopped in midblow. The man with the gap in his teeth smiled in relief.

Miriam would go to someone she could trust, someone Cleo could trust, perhaps, who owed her a favor for past kindness. Cleo was a nurse. If she was even remotely like Hester, she could count on the trust, and the unquestioning discretion also, of a good many people. That was where to begin, with those Cleo Anderson had nursed. He sat back and relaxed, keeping his eye on the child in case he thought to blow his whistle again.

It was already warm and still by five minutes before nine, when Monk began the next day. The rag and bone man's voice echoed as he drove slowly away from the Heath towards the south. The dew was still deep in the shade of the larger trees, but the open grass was dusty and the dawn chorus of the birds had been over for hours.

Monk did not bother to pursue those patients with large families and, naturally, those whose illness had ended in death. He learned of all manner of misfortune and of kindness. Cleo Anderson's reputation was high. Few had a harsh word to say of her. Miriam also had earned a share of approval. It seemed often enough she had been willing to help in the duties of care, especially after she had been widowed and no longer had her time filled with seeing to the wellbeing of Mr. Gardiner.

Monk followed every trail that seemed likely to lead to where Miriam might be now. By late morning he had crossed Sergeant Robb's path twice and was wondering if Robb was equally aware of him. Surely he must be, by deduction even if he had not actually seen Monk.

A little after midday he came around the corner of Prince Arthur Road and stopped abruptly. Ten yards ahead of him, Robb was glancing at his watch anxiously, and in reading the time he looked reluctantly, once, at a house on the farther side, then, biting his lip, set off at a very rapid pace the opposite way.

For a moment Monk was confused, then he realized Robb was going in the direction of his home. His grandfather would have been alone since early in the morning, almost helpless, certainly needing food and, in this warm weather above all, fresh water to drink and assistance with his personal needs. Robb would never forget that, whatever the urgencies or the requirements of his job.

Monk was moved with an acute pity for him, and also for the sick old man sitting alone day after day, dependent on a young man desperate to do his job and torn between two duties.

But Monk's first duty was towards Miriam Gardiner, because that was what Lucius Stourbridge had hired him for and what he had given his word to do. Robb had far more resources than he had, in information given to the police, his own local knowledge, and in his power to command cooperation. They wished the same thing, to find Miriam Gardiner, Monk because it was his final goal, Robb to learn from her what she knew of Treadwell's murder, perhaps even to charge her with complicity in it. It was imperative Monk find her first.

He sauntered slowly over towards the house Robb had eyed and had then left with such reluctance. He had no idea who lived there or what Robb had hoped to find, but there was no time to investigate more carefully. This was his only chance to gain the advantage. He knocked on the door and stepped back, waiting for it to be answered.

The maid who peered out at him could not have been more than fourteen or fifteen years old, but she was determined to make a good impression.

"Yes sir?"

He smiled at her. "Good afternoon." Time was short. "Mrs. Gardiner asked me if I could carry a message to your mistress, if she is in." He wished he had some way of knowing the family name. It would have sounded more convincing.

For a moment the girl looked blank, but she obviously wished to be helpful. "Are yer sure yer got the right 'ouse, sir? There's no one but old Mr. 'Ornchurch 'ere."

"Oh." He was confounded. What had Robb wanted with old Mr. Hornchurch?

Her face brightened. "Mebbe she meant the 'ousekeeper?

104

Mrs. Whitbread, as comes in every day an' cooks an' does fer Mr. 'Ornchurch. She was took bad the winter before last, an' it were Mrs. Gardiner wot looked after 'er."

He could feel the sweat of relief prickle on his skin. He swallowed before he could catch his breath. "Yes. Of course. That's what I should have said. Perhaps it would be more convenient if I were to speak to Mrs. Whitbread at her home? Can you tell me how to get there from here?" The people Miriam would turn to would be the ones she had helped in their time of need.

The girl looked dubious. "Mebbe. I'll ask 'er. She don' like nobody callin' on 'er at 'ome. Reckon as when yer orff, yer wanna be private, like."

"Of course," he agreed, still standing well back from the step. "I'm sure you could simply give her the message, if you would be so kind?"

"I'm sure I could do that," she agreed, obviously relieved.

He pulled out a piece of paper from his pocket, and a pencil, and wrote "Tell Sergeant Robb nothing about Miriam," then folded the note twice, turning the ends in, and gave it to the girl. "Be sure to give it to her straightaway," he warned. "And if the police come here, be very careful what you say."

Her eyes widened. "I will," she promised. "Never say nothin' to the rozzers, that's wot one ol' man tol' me. That's the best. Known nothin', seen nothin', 'eard nothin', me."

"Very wise." He nodded, smiling at her again. "Thank you," he said, and stepped back and turned to leave.

He would wait until Mrs. Whitbread finished her duties and then follow her. He had real hope that she might lead him to Miriam. For the meantime, he would find something to eat and stay well out of Robb's way when he returned to see Mrs. Whitbread himself.

He sauntered quite casually along the pavement next to a small space of open grass and bought a beef-and-onion sandwich from a stall. It was fresh, and he ate it with considerable enjoyment. He bought a second and enjoyed that as well. He wondered how Robb had traced Mrs. Whitbread. That was a good piece of detection. It commanded his respect, and he gave it willingly. He liked Robb and admired the young man's care for his grandfather.

He must stay within sight of Mr. Hornchurch's house so he could see when the housekeeper left, but not so close that Robb, when returning, would observe him.

He expected Robb to come back the way he had seen him leave, so he was jolted by considerable surprise when he heard Robb's voice behind him, and he swung around to see him only a yard away, his face grim, his mouth pulled tight.

"Waiting for me, Inspector Monk?" he said coldly.

Monk felt as if he had been slapped. In one sentence, Robb had shown that he had learned Monk's history in the police and his reputation both for skill and for ruthlessness. It was there in Robb's face now as he stood in sunlight dappled by the trees, his eyes guarded, challenging. Monk could see the anger in him—and something else which he thought might be fear.

Was there any point in lying? He did not want to make an enemy of Robb, for practical reasons as well as emotional ones; in fact, he could not afford to. The first concern was Miriam. Her freedom, even her life, might depend upon this. And he had no idea whether she was guilty of anything or not. She might have killed Treadwell. On the other hand she might be in danger herself, terrified and running. He knew no more of the truth now than he had when Lucius Stourbridge had walked into his rooms a few days before.

He shifted his weight to stand a little more casually. He raised his eyebrows. "Actually, I'd really been hoping to avoid you," he said truthfully.

Robb's mouth curled downward. "You thought I'd come back the way I left? I would have if I hadn't seen you, and I admit, that was only chance. But I know this area better than you do. I have the advantage. I wondered if you'd follow me. It would seem the obvious thing to do if you had no ideas yourself." There was a contempt in his voice that stung. "Why did you wait here for me? I suppose you already knew I would be going to my grandfather."

Monk was startled—and surprised to find himself also hurt. He had not earned that from Robb. Certainly, he was trying to beat Robb to Miriam, but that was what Lucius Stourbridge had hired him for. Robb would not have expected him to do less.

"Of course, I knew where you were going," Monk answered, keeping his voice level and almost expressionless. "But the reason I didn't go after you was because I wasn't following you in the first place. Does it surprise you so much that my investigations should bring me to the same place as yours?"

"No," Robb said instantly. "You have a wide reputation, Inspector Monk." He did not elaborate as to its nature, but the expression in his eyes told it well, leaving Monk no room to hope or to delude himself.

Memories of Runcorn flooded back, of his anger always there, thinly suppressed under his veneer of self-control, the fear showing through, the expectation that somehow, whatever he did, Monk would get the better of him, undermine his authority, find the answer first, make him look foolish or inept. The fear had become so deep over the years it was no longer a conscious thought but an instinct, like wincing before you are struck.

After the accident Monk had heard fragments about himself here and there and had pieced them together, learned things he had wished were not true. The cruel thing was that in the last year or so, surely they no longer were. His tongue was still quick, certainly. He was intolerant. He did not suffer fools—gladly or otherwise. But he was not unjust! Robb was judging him on the past.

"Apparently," he said aloud, his voice cold. He also knew his reputation for skill. "Then you should not be surprised that I came to the same conclusion you did and found the same people without having to trail behind you."

Robb dug his hands into his pockets, and his shoulders

hunched forward, his body tightening. There was contempt and dislike in his face, but also the awareness of a superior enemy, and a sadness that it should be so, a disappointment.

"You have an advantage over me, Mr. Monk. You know my one vulnerability. You must do about it whatever you think fit, but I will not be blackmailed into stepping aside from pursuing whoever murdered James Treadwell—whether it is Mrs. Gardiner or not." He looked at Monk unblinkingly, his brown eyes steady.

Monk felt suddenly sick. Surely he had never been a person who would descend to blackmailing a young man because he took time off his professional duty to attend to the far deeper duty of love towards an old man who was sick and alone and utterly dependent upon him? He could not believe he had ever been like that—not to pursue any thief or killer, there were other ways; and certainly not to climb up another step on the ladder of preferment!

He found his mouth dry and words difficult to form. What did he want to say? He would not plead; it would be both demeaning and useless.

"What you tell your superiors is your own business," he replied icily. "If you tell them anything at all. Personally, I never had such a regard for them that I thought it necessary to explain myself. My work spoke for me." He sounded arrogant and he knew it. But what he said was true. He had never explained himself to Runcorn, nor ever intended to.

He saw the flash of recognition in Robb's face, and belief.

"And you'll find plenty of sins I've committed," Monk went on, his voice biting. "But you'll not find anyone who knew me to stoop to blackmail. You'll not find anyone who damned well thought I needed to."

Slowly, Robb's shoulders relaxed. He still regarded Monk carefully, but the hostility faded from his eyes as the fear loosened its grip on him. He licked his lips. "I'm sorry— perhaps I underestimated your ability." That was as far as he would go towards an apology.

It was not ability Monk cared about, it was honor, but there was no point pursuing that now. This was all he was going to get. The question was how to remain within sight of the house so he could follow Mrs. Whitbread when she left, and yet at the same time elude Robb so he did not follow them both. And, of course, that only mattered if the maid at the door did not give Robb the same information she had given to Monk, albeit unwittingly.

He looked at Robb a moment longer, then smiled steadily, bade him farewell, and turned and walked away, in the opposite direction from the house. He would have to circle around and come back, extremely carefully.

Mrs. Whitbread left at a quarter to five. Robb was nowhere to be seen. As Monk followed her at a discreet distance, he felt his weariness suddenly vanish, his senses become keen and a bubble of hope form inside him.

They had not gone far, perhaps a mile and a quarter, before Mrs. Whitbread, a thin, spare woman with a gentle face, turned in at a small house on Kemplay Road and opened the front door with a key.

Monk waited a few moments, looking both ways and seeing no one, then he crossed and went to the door. He knocked.

After a minute or two the door was opened cautiously by Mrs. Whitbread. "Yes?"

He had given much consideration to what he was going to say. It was already apparent Miriam did not wish to be found either by the police or by Lucius Stourbridge. If she had trusted Lucius in this matter she would have contacted him long before. Either she was afraid he would betray her to the police or she wanted to protect him.

"Good evening, Mrs. Whitbread," he said firmly. "I have an urgent message from Mrs. Anderson—for Miriam. I need to see her immediately." Cleo Anderson was the one name both women might trust.

She hesitated only a moment, then pulled the door wider.

"You'd better come in," she said quickly. "You never know
109

who's watching. I had the rozzers 'round where I work just today."

He stepped inside and she closed the door. "I know. It was I who sent them to you. You didn't tell them anything?"

" 'Course not," she replied, giving him a withering look. "Wouldn't trust them an inch. Can't afford to."

He said nothing, but followed her down the passage and around the corner into the kitchen. Standing at the stove, facing them, eyes wide, was the woman he had come to find. He knew immediately it was Miriam Gardiner. She was just as Lucius had described, barely average height, softly rounded figure, a beautifully proportioned, gentle face but with an underlying strength. At first glance she might have seemed a sweet-natured woman, given to obedience and pleasing those she loved, but there was an innate dignity to her that spoke of something far deeper than mere agreeableness, something untouchable by anything except love. Even in those few moments Monk understood why Lucius Stourbridge was prepared to spend so much heartache searching for her, regardless of the truth of James Treadwell's death.

"Mrs. Gardiner," he said quietly. "I am not from the police. But nor am I from Mrs. Anderson. I lied about that because I feared you would leave before I could speak to you if you knew I came from Lucius Stourbridge."

She froze, oblivious of the pots on the stove steaming till their lids rattled in the silence that filled the room. Her terror was almost palpable in the air.

Monk was aware of Mrs. Whitbread beside him. He saw the fury in her eyes, her body stiff, lips drawn into a thin line. He was grateful the skillet was on the far wall beyond her reach, or he believed she might well have struck him with it.

"I haven't come to try to take you back to Bayswater," he said quietly, facing Miriam. "Or to the police. If you would prefer that I did not tell Mr. Stourbridge where you are, then I will not. I shall simply tell him that you are alive and unhurt. He is desperate with fear for you, and that will offer him some comfort, although hardly an explanation."

Miriam stared back, her face almost white, an anguish in it that made him feel guilty for what he was doing, and frightened for what he might discover.

"He does not know what to believe," he said softly. "Except that you could and would do no intentional evil."

She drew in her breath, and her eyes spilled over with tears. She wiped the moisture away impatiently, but it was a moment before she could control herself enough to speak.

"I cannot go back." It was a statement of absolute fact. There was no hope in her voice, no possibility of change.

"I can try to keep the police from you," he replied, as if it were the answer to what she had said. "But I may not succeed. They are not far behind me."

Mrs. Whitbread walked around him and went over to the stove, taking the pans off it before they boiled over. She looked across at Monk with bitter dislike.

Miriam stepped out of her way, farther into the middle of the room.

"What happened?" Monk asked as gently as he could.

She coughed a little, clearing her throat. Her voice was husky. "Is Cleo Mrs. Anderson all right?"

"Yes." There was no purpose in pointing out Cleo Anderson's danger if Robb felt she was concealing information or even that it was not coincidence that had taken Treadwell to her front path.

Miriam seemed to relax a little. A faint tinge of color returned to her cheeks.

"Where did you last see Treadwell?" he asked.

Her lips tightened, and she shook her head a tiny fraction, not so much a denial to him as to herself.

He kept his voice low, patient, as devoid of threat as he could.

"You'll have to answer sometime, if not to me, then to the police. He was murdered, beaten over the head—" He stopped. She had turned so ashen-pale he feared she was going to faint. He lunged forward and caught her by the arms, steadying her, pushing her sideways and backwards into the kitchen chair, for a moment supporting her weight until she sank into it.

"Get out!" Mrs. Whitbread commanded furiously. "You get out of here!" She reached for the rolling pin or the skillet to use on him.

He stood his ground, but wary of her. "Put the kettle on," he ordered. "Sending me away isn't going to answer this. When the police come, and they will, they'll not come in friendship as I do. All they will want will be evidence and justice—or what they believe to be justice."

Miriam closed her eyes. It was all she could do to breathe slowly in and out, or to keep consciousness.

Mrs. Whitbread, reluctantly, turned and filled the kettle, putting it on the hob. She eyed Monk guardedly before she took out cups, a teapot, and the round tin caddy. Then she went to the larder for milk, her heels tapping on the stone floor.

Monk sat down opposite Miriam.

"What happened?" he asked. "Where was Treadwell when you last saw him? Was he alive?"

"Yes . . ." she whispered, opening her eyes, but they were filled with horror so deep the words gave him no comfort at all.

"Were you there when he was killed?"

She shook her head, barely an inch.

"Do you know who killed him or why?"

She said nothing.

Mrs. Whitbread came back with a jug of milk in her hand. She glared at Monk, but she did not interrupt. She crossed the floor and tipped a little boiling water into the pot to warm it.

"Who killed Treadwell?" Monk repeated. "And why?"

Miriam stared at him. "I can't tell you," she whispered. "I can't tell you anything. I can't come with you. Please go away. I can't help—there's nothing—nothing I can do."

There was such a terrible, hopeless pain in her voice the argument died on his lips.

The kettle started to shrill. Mrs. Whitbread lifted it off the stove and turned to Monk.

"Go now," she said levelly, her eyes hard. "There's nothing for you here. Tell Lucius Stourbridge whatever you have to, but go. If you come back, Miriam won't be here. There's plenty others who'll hide her. If Mr. Stourbridge is the friend he says he is, he'll leave well enough alone. You can see yourself out." She still held the kettle, steam pouring out of its spout. It wasn't exactly a threat, but Monk did not misunderstand the determination in her.

He rose to his feet, took a last glance at Miriam, then went to the door. Then he remembered Robb and changed his mind. The back kitchen door probably led to an area for coal or coke and then an alleyway.

"I'll tell Mr. Stourbridge you are alive and well," he said softly. "No more than that. But the police won't be far behind me, I know that for certain. I've been dodging them for the last two days."

Mrs. Whitbread understood his thought. She nodded. "Go left," she ordered. "You'll come to the street again. Watch for the ash cans."

"Was that all she said?" Hester was incredulous when he recounted to her what had happened. They were in the comfortable room where he received clients and which also served as sitting room. The windows were open to the warm evening air drifting in. There was a rustle of leaves from a tree close by, and in the distance the occasional clip of hooves from the traffic on the street.

"Yes," he answered, looking across at her. She was not sewing, as other women might have been. She did needlework only as necessity demanded. She was concentrating entirely upon what he was saying, her back straight, her shoulders square, her eyes intent upon his face. All the confusion and tragedy he was aware of could not stifle the deep well of satisfaction within him that underlay everything else.

113

She infuriated him at times; they still disagreed over countless things. He could have listed her faults using the fingers of both hands. And yet as long as she was there, he would never be alone and nothing was beyond bearing.

"What was she like?" she asked.

He was startled. "Like?"

"Yes," she said impatiently. "She didn't give you any explanations? She didn't tell you why she ran away from the Stourbridges' party? You did ask her, I suppose?"

He had not asked. By that point he already knew she would not tell him.

"You didn't!" Hester's voice rose an octave.

"She refused to tell me anything," he said clearly. "Except that she was not there when Treadwell was killed. I don't think she even knew he was dead. When I told her that, she was so horrified she was almost incapable of speech. She all but fainted."

"So she knows something about it!" Hester said instantly.

That was an unwarranted leap of deduction, and yet he had made exactly the same one. He looked across at her and smiled bleakly.

"So you have learned no new facts," she said.

"There's the fact that Mrs. Whitbread was prepared to fight to defend her, and risk the police coming after her instead," he pointed out. "And the fact that almost certainly Robb will find her, sooner or later." He did not want to tell Hester about Robb's opinion of him. It was painful, a dark thing he preferred she did not know.

"So, what was she like?" she asked again.

He did not make any evasions or comments on the obscurity of feminine logic.

"I've never seen anyone more afraid," he said honestly. "Or more anguished. But I don't believe she will tell me—or anyone else—what happened or why she is running. Certainly, she won't tell Lucius Stourbridge."

"What are you going to do?" Her voice was little more than a whisper, and her eyes were full of pity.

114

He realized he had already made his decision.

"I will tell Stourbridge that I found her and she is alive and well, and that she says she had no part in Treadwell's death, but I will not tell him where she is. I daresay she will not be there by the time I report to him anyway. I warned her that Robb was close behind me." He did not need to add the risk he took in so doing. Hester knew it.

"Poor woman," she said softly. "Poor woman."

5

I T WAS the sixth day of Monk's enquiry into Miriam Gardiner's flight. Hester had gone to sleep thinking about her. She wondered what tragedy had drawn her to such an act that she could not speak of it, even to the man she was to marry.

But it was not that which woke her, shaking and so tense her head throbbed with a stiff, sharp pain. She had an overwhelming sense of fear, of something terrible happening which she was helpless to prevent and inadequate to deal with. It was not a small thing, or personal to herself, but of all-consuming proportions.

Beside her, Monk was asleep, his face relaxed and completely at peace in the clear, early light. He was as oblivious of her as if they had been in separate rooms, different worlds.

It was not the first time she had woken with this feeling of helplessness and exhaustion, and yet she could not remember what she had been dreaming, either now or before.

She wanted to wake Monk, talk to him, hear him say it was all of no importance, unreal, belonging to the world of sleep. But that would be selfish. He expected more strength from her. He would be disappointed, and she could not bear that. She lay staring at the ceiling, feeling utterly alone, because it was how she had woken and she could not cast it away. There was something she longed to escape from, and she knew that was impossible. It was everywhere around her.

The light through the chink in the curtains was broadening across the floor. In another hour or so it would be time to get up and face the day. Fill her mind with that. It was always better to be busy. There were battles worth fighting; there always were. She would speak to Fermin Thorpe again. The man was impossible to reason with because he was afraid of change, afraid of losing control and so becoming less important.

It would probably mean more of the interminable letters, few of which ever received a useful answer. How could anyone write so many words which, when disentangled from their dependent clauses and qualifying additions, actually had no meaning?

Florence Nightingale was confined to her home—some said, even to her bed—and spent nearly all her time writing letters.

Of course, hers were highly effective. In the four years since the end of the war she had changed an enormous number of things, particularly to do with the architecture of hospitals. First, naturally, her attention had been upon military hospitals, but she had won that victory, in spite of a change of government and losing her principal ally. Now she was bending her formidable will towards civilian hospitals and, just as Hester was, to the training of nurses. But it was a battle against stubborn and entrenched interests that held great power. Fermin Thorpe was merely one of many, a typical example of senior medical men throughout the country.

And poor Florence's health had declined ever since her return. Hester found that hard to accept, even to imagine. In Scutari, Florence had seemed inexhaustible—the last sort of woman on earth to succumb to fainting and palpitations, unexplained fevers and general aches and weaknesses. And yet, apparently that was now the case. Several times her life had been despaired of. Her family was no longer permitted to visit her in case the emotion of the occasion should prove too much for her. Devoted friends and admirers gave up their

117

own pursuits to look after her until the end should come, and make her last few months on earth as pleasant as possible.

Time and again this had happened. And lately, if anything, she seemed to be recovered and bursting with new and vigorous ideas. She had proposed a school for training nurses and was systematically attacking the opposition. It was said nothing delighted her as much as a set of statistics which could be used to prove the point that clean water and good ventilation were necessary to the recovery of a patient.

Hester smiled to herself as she remembered Florence in the hot Turkish sun, determinedly ordering an army sergeant to bring her his figures on the dead of the past week, their date of admittance to the hospital and the nature of their injuries and cause of death. The poor man had been so exhausted he had not even argued with her. One pointless task was much like another to him, only his pity for his fellows and his sense of decency had made him reluctant to obey. Florence had tried to explain to him, her pale face alight, eyes brilliant, that she could learn invaluable information from such things. Deductions could be made, lessons learned, mistakes addressed and perhaps corrected. People were dying who did not need to, distress was caused which could have been avoided.

The army, like Fermin Thorpe, did not listen. That was the helplessness which overwhelmed her—injury, disease and death all around, too few people to care for the sick, ignorance defeating so much of even the little they could have done.

What an insane, monstrous waste! What a mockery of all that was good and happy and beautiful in life!

And here she was, lying warm and supremely comfortable in bed with Monk asleep beside her. The future stretched out in front of her with as bright a promise as the day already shining just beyond the curtain. It would be whatever she made of it. Unless she allowed the past to darken it, old memories to cripple her and make her useless.

She still wanted to wake Monk and talk to him—no, that was not true, what she wanted was that he should talk to her.

118

She wanted to hear his voice, hear the assurance in it, the will to fight—and win.

She would have liked to get up and do something to keep herself from thinking, but she would disturb him if she did, and that would be the same thing as having deliberately woken him. So she lay still and stared at the patterns of sunlight on the ceiling until eventually she went back to sleep again.

When she woke the second time it was to find Monk waking her gently. She felt as if she had climbed up from the bottom of a well, and her head still hurt.

She smiled at him and forced herself to be cheerful. If he noticed any artificiality about it, he did not say so. Perhaps he was thinking of Miriam Gardiner already, and still worrying about what he could do to help her and what he would say to Lucius Stourbridge.

It was midmorning, as she was coming down the main corridor, when she encountered Fermin Thorpe.

"Oh, good morning, Miss—Mrs. Monk," he said, coming to a halt so that it was obvious he wished to speak with her. "How are you today?" He continued immediately so that she should not interrupt him by replying. "With regard to your desire that women should be trained in order to nurse, I have obtained a copy of Mr. J. F. South's book, published three years ago, which I am sure will be of interest to you and enlighten you on the subject." He smiled at her, meeting her eyes very directly.

They were passed by a medical student whom he ignored, an indication of the gravity of his intent.

"You may not be familiar with who he is, so I shall tell you, so you may correctly judge the importance of his opinion and give it more weight." He straightened his shoulders slightly and lifted his chin. "He is senior consulting surgeon at Saint Thomas's Hospital, and more than that, he is president of the College of Surgeons and Hunterian Orator." He gave the words careful emphasis so she should not miss any part of

119

their importance. "I quote for you, Miss—Mrs. Monk, he is"—his voice became very distinct—" 'not at all disposed to allow that the nursing establishments of our hospitals are inefficient or that they are likely to be improved by any special Institution for Training.' As he further points out, even sisters in charge of wards do, and can, only learn by experience." He smiled at her with increasing confidence. "Nurses themselves are subordinates, in the position of housemaids, and need only the simplest of instructions."

Two nurses passed them, faces flushed with exertion, sleeves hitched up.

Hester opened her mouth to protest, but he continued, raising his voice very slightly to override her. "I am perfectly aware of Miss Nightingale's fund for training young women," he said loudly. "But I must inform you, madam, that only three surgeons and two physicians are to be found among its supporters. That, surely, is an unfailing mark of the regard in which it is held by professional men who are the most highly qualified and experienced in the country. Now, Mrs. Monk"—he pronounced her name with satisfaction at having remembered it—"I trust you will turn your considerable energies towards the true welfare of both the nurses here and the patients, and attend to their cleanliness, their sobriety and their obedience to do what they are commanded, both punctually and exactly. Good day." And without waiting for her reply, which he seemingly took for granted in the affirmative, he strode away purposefully towards the operating theater, satisfied he had dealt with the subject finally.

Hester was too furious to speak for the first few moments, then, when she could have spoken, no words seemed adequate to express her disgust. She marched in the opposite direction, towards the physicians' waiting room.

There she found Cleo talking to an old man who was obviously frightened and doing his best to conceal it. He had several open ulcers on both his legs which must have been acutely painful and looked as if they had been there for some

120

time. He smiled at Cleo, but his hands were clenched till his knuckles were white and he sat rigidly upright.

"You need them dressed regularly," Cleo said gently. "Gotta keep them clean or they'll never heal up. I'll do it for you, if you come here and ask for me."

"I can't come 'ere every day," he answered, his voice polite but with absolute certainty. "In't possible, miss."

"Isn't it, now." She regarded him thoughtfully, looking down at the worn boots and threadbare jacket. "Well, I suppose I'll have to come to you, then. How far, is it?"

"An' why would you be doing that?" he asked dubiously.

" Because those sores aren't going to get any better otherwise," she replied tartly.

"I in't askin' no favors," he said, bristling. "I don't want no nurse woman comin' into my 'ouse! Wot'll the neighbors think o' me?"

Cleo winced. "That you're damn lucky at your age to be pulling a nice-looking woman like me!" she snapped back at him.

He smiled in spite of himself. "But yer can't come, all the same."

She looked down at him patiently. "Call yourself a soldier, and can't take orders from someone who knows better than you do—and make no mistake, I'm your sergeant w'en it comes ter them sores."

He drew in his breath, then let it out again without answering.

"Well?" Cleo demanded. "You going to tell me where you live, or waste me time having to find out?"

"Church Row," he said reluctantly.

"And I'm going to walk up and down the whole lot asking for you, am I?" Cleo said with raised eyebrows.

"Number twenty-one."

"Good! Like drawin' teeth, it is!"

He was not sure whether she was joking or not. He smiled uncertainly.

121

She smiled back at him, then saw Hester and came over to her, trying to look as if she were not out of composure.

"I'm not going to do it in hospital time," she said in a whisper. "Poor old soul fought at Waterloo, he did, an' look at the state of him." Her expression darkened, and she forgot the appropriate deference to a social superior. Anger filled her eyes. "All for soldiers, we was, when we thought them French was gonna invade us and we could lose. Now, forty-five years on, we forgotten all about how fit we was, and who wants to care for some old man with sores all over his legs who's got no money an' talks about wars we don't know nothing about?"

Hester thought vividly of the men she had known in Scutari and Sebastopol, and the surgeons' tents after that chaotic charge at Balaclava. They had been so young, and in such terrible pain. It was their ashen faces that had filled her dreams the previous night. She could see them sharp in her mind's eye. Those that had survived would be old men in forty years' time. Would people remember them then? Or would a new generation be accustomed to peace, and resentful and bored by old soldiers who carried the scars and the pain of old wars?

"See that he's cared for," Hester said quietly. "That's what matters. Do it whenever you wish."

Cleo stared back at her, eyes widening a little, uncertain for a moment whether to believe her. They barely knew each other. Here they had one purpose, but they went home to different worlds.

"Those debts cannot ever be understood," Hester answered her. "Let alone paid."

Cleo stood still.

"I was at Scutari," Hester explained.

"Oh . . ." It was just a single word, less than a word, but there was understanding in it, and profound respect. Cleo nodded a little and went to the next patient.

Hester left the room again. She was in no mood now to see that moral standards were observed or that any nurse was clean, neat, punctual and sober.

As she went back along the corridor she was passed by a nurse arriving with her shawl still on.

"You're late!" Hester said tartly. "Don't do it again!"

The woman was startled. "No, miss," she said obediently, and hurried on, head down, pulling off the shawl as she went.

Just outside the apothecary's room, Hester passed a young medical student, unshaven and with his jacket flapping open.

"You are untidy, sir," she said with equal tartness. "How do you expect your patients to have confidence in you when you look as if you had slept in your clothes and come in with the first post? If you aspire to be a gentleman, then you had better look like one!"

He was so startled he did not reply to her, but stood motionless as she swept past him and on to the surgeons' waiting room.

She spent the morning attempting to comfort and hearten the men and women awaiting care. She had not forgotten Florence Nightingale's stricture that the mental pain of a patient could be at least equal to the physical and that it was a good nurse's task to dispel doubt and lift spirits wherever possible. A cheerful countenance was invaluable, as were pleasant conversation and a willingness to listen with sympathy and optimism.

At the end of the morning Hester sat down at the staff dining room table with gratitude for an hour's respite. Within fifteen minutes Callandra joined her. For once her hair was safely secured within its pins and her skirt and well-tailored jacket matched each other. Only her expression spoiled the effect. She looked deeply unhappy.

"What is it?" Hester asked as soon as Callandra had made herself reasonably comfortable in the hard-backed chair but had not yet begun her slice of veal pie, which seemed to hold little interest for her.

"There is more medicine gone," Callandra said so quietly she was barely audible. "There is no possible doubt. I hate to think that anyone is systematically stealing the amounts we are dealing with, but there can be no other explanation." Her face tightened, her lips in a thin line. "Just think what Thorpe will make of it, apart from anything else."

"I've already had words with him this morning," Hester replied, ignoring her own plate of cold mutton and new potatoes. "He was quoting Mr. South at me. I didn't even have a chance to reply to him, not that I had anything to say. Now I want to ask him if we couldn't make some sort of particular provision for the men who fought for us in the past and who are now old and ill."

Callandra frowned. "What sort of provision?"

"I don't know." Hester grimaced. "I suppose this is not a fortunate time to suggest we provide their medicine and bandages from the hospital budget?"

"We already do," Callandra said with surprise.

"Only if they come here," Hester pointed out. "Some of them can't come every day. They are too old or ill, or lame, to use an omnibus. And a hansom costs far too much, even if they could climb into one of them."

"Who could give them medicines at home?" Callandra asked, curiosity and the beginning of understanding in her eyes. "Us," Hester replied instantly. "It wouldn't need a doctor, only a nurse with experience and confidence—someone trained."

"And trustworthy," Callandra added purposefully.

Hester sighed. The specter of the stolen medicines would not leave. They could not keep the knowledge of it from Fermin Thorpe much longer. It was ugly, dishonest, an abuse of every kind of trust, both of the establishment of the hospital and of the other nurses, who would all be branded with the same stigma of thieving. It was also a breach of honor towards the patients for whom the medicines were intended.

"It's a circular argument, isn't it?" she said with a thread of despair. "Until we get trained women who are dedicated to an honorable calling and are treated with respect and properly rewarded, we won't be able to stop this sort of thing happening all the time. And as long as it does, people, especially those like Thorpe—and that seems to be most of the

124

medical establishment—will treat nurses as the worst class of housemaid."

Callandra pulled her mouth into a grimace of disgust. "I don't know any housemaid who wouldn't take that as an insult—possibly even give notice—if you compared her with a nurse."

"Which is a complete summary of what we are fighting," Hester replied, taking half a potato and a nice piece of cold mutton.

"The Nightingale School is just about to open." Callandra made a visible effort to look more hopeful. "But I believe they had great trouble finding suitable applicants. A very high moral standard is required, and total dedication, of course. The rules are almost as strict as a nunnery."

"They don't call them 'sisters' for nothing," Hester answered with a flash of humor.

But there were other issues pressing on her mind. She had thought again of Sergeant Robb's grandfather sitting alone, unable to care for himself, dependent upon Robb to take time from his work. It must be a burden of fear and obligation to him.

And how many other old men were there, ill and poor now, who were victims of wars the young did not remember? And old women, too, perhaps widows of men who had not come home, or those who were unmarried because the men who would have been their husbands were dead?

She leaned a little over the table. "Would it not be possible to create a body of some sort who could visit those people . . . at least see to the more obvious troubles, advise when a doctor was needed . . ."

The look in Callandra's face stopped her.

"You are dreaming, my dear," she said gently. "We have not even achieved proper nurses for the poor law infirmaries attached to the workhouses, and you want to have nurses to visit the poor in their homes? You are fifty years before your time. But it's a good dream."

"What about some form of infirmary especially for men

who have lost their health fighting our wars?" Hester asked. "Isn't that something at least honor demands, if nothing else?"

"If honor got all it demanded this would be a very different world." Callandra ate the last of her pie. "Perhaps enlightened self-interest might have a greater chance of success."

"How?" Hester asked instantly.

Callandra looked at her. "The best nursing reforms so far have been within army hospitals, due almost entirely to Miss Nightingale's work." She was thinking as she spoke, her brow furrowed. "New buildings have been designed with cleaner water, better ventilation and far less crowded wards . . ."

"I know." Hester disregarded her plate, waiting the suggestion which would link the two.

"I am sure Mr. Thorpe would like to be thought of as enlightened . . ." Callandra continued.

Hester grimaced but did not interrupt again.

". . . without taking any real risks," Callandra concluded. "A poor law infirmary for old soldiers would seem a good compromise."

"Of course it would. Except that it would have to be called something else. A good many soldiers would rather die than be seen as accepting parish charity. And they shouldn't have to. We owe them that much at least." She pushed her chair back and stood up. "But I shall be very tactful when I speak to Mr. Thorpe."

"Hester!" Callandra called after her urgently, but Hester was already at the door, and if she heard her, she showed no sign of it. A moment later Callandra was staring at the empty room.

"Impossible," Thorpe said without hesitation. "Quite out of the question. There are workhouses to care for the indigent—"

"I am not talking about the indigent, Mr. Thorpe." Hester kept her voice level, but it required effort. "I am thinking of men who obtained their injuries or damage to their health fighting in the Peninsula War or at great battles like Quatre Bras or Waterloo . . ."

He frowned. "Quatre Bras? What are you talking about?" he asked impatiently.

"It was immediately before Waterloo," she explained, knowing she sounded patronizing. "It was not a matter of fighting to extend the Empire then; we were fighting to save ourselves from invasion and becoming a subject people."

"I do not require a history lesson, Mrs. Monk," he said irritably. "They did their duty, as we all do. I am sure that, for a young woman, there is a certain glamour attached to the uniform, and one makes heroes of them—"

"No one makes a hero of someone else, Mr. Thorpe," she corrected him. "I am concerned with the injured and ill who need our help and, I believe, have a right to expect it. I am sure that as a patriot and a Christian, you will agree with that."

A variety of emotions flickered across his face, conflicting with each other, but he would not deny her assessment of him, even if he suspected it contained a powerful element of sarcasm.

"Of course," he agreed reluctantly. "I shall take it under advisement. I am sure it is something we would all wish to do, if it should prove possible." His face set in a mask of finality. He would no longer argue with her, he would simply lie. Certainly, he would consider it—indefinitely.

She knew she was beaten, at least in this skirmish. As many times as she came to him he would smile, agree with her, and say he was exploring avenues of possibility. And she would never prove him wrong. She had an overwhelming insight into the obstruction faced by Florence Nightingale and why she had taken to her bed with exhaustion, fever, difficulties of the digestion, and such a fire of the mind as to consume the strength of her body.

Hester smiled back at Fermin Thorpe. "I am sure you will succeed," she lied as well. "A man who is skilled enough to run a hospital the size of this one so very well will be able to exert the right influence and put forward all the moral and social arguments to persuade others of the rightness of such a cause. If you could not, then you would hardly be the man for Hampstead . . . would you?" She would not have dared say such a thing were she dependent upon his goodwill for earning a roof over her head—but she was not! She was a married woman with a husband to provide for her. She was here as a lady volunteer—like Callandra—not a paid worker. It was a wonderful feeling, almost euphoric. She was free to battle him unhampered . . . as she most certainly would.

The flush in his cheeks deepened. "I am glad you appreciate my position, Mrs. Monk," he said with a tight jaw. "I have not always been so certain that you were fully mindful that I do indeed run this hospital."

"I am sorry for that," she answered. "One has but to look around one to see the standard of efficiency."

He blinked, aware of the double meaning implied. His tone was infinitely condescending. "I am sure you are a good-hearted woman, but I fear your lack of understanding of finance hampers your judgment as to what is possible. For instance, the cost of medicines is far greater than you probably appreciate, and we are unfortunate in suffering a considerable degree of pilfering from morally unworthy staff." He opened his eyes very wide. "If you were to direct your attentions towards the honesty and sobriety of the nurses here, we would lose far less, and consequently then have more to give to the sick who rely upon us. Turn your energies towards that, Mrs. Monk, and you will do the greatest service. Honesty! That will save the sick from their diseases and the morally destitute from the wages of sin, both spiritual and temporal." He smiled. He was well satisfied with that.

Hester made a tactical retreat before he could further pursue the question of missing medicines.

She had already made up her mind to call upon old Mr. Robb to see if there was anything she could do to help him. She could not forget Monk's description of his distress, and that was at least one thing she could accomplish regardless of Fermin Thorpe's power.

It was a fine summer afternoon, and not a long walk to the street where Monk had said Robb lived. She did not know the number, but only one enquiry was necessary to discover the answer.

The houses were all clean and shabby, some with whited steps, others merely well swept. She debated whether to knock or not. From what Monk had said, the old man could not rise to answer, and yet to walk in unannounced was a terrible intrusion into the privacy of a man too ill to defend even his own small space.

She settled for standing in the doorway and calling out his name. She waited a few moments in silence, then called again.

"Who is it?" The voice was a deep, soft rumble.

"My name is Hester . . . Monk." She had so very nearly said "Latterly." She was not used to her new name yet. "My husband called on you the other day." She must not make him feel pitied, a suitable case for charity. It would be so easy to do with a careless phrase. "He spoke of you so well, I wished to call upon you myself."

"Your husband? I don't remember . . ." He started to cough, and it became worse so quickly that she abandoned politeness, pushed the door open and went in.

The room was small and cluttered with furniture, but it was clean and as tidy as possible when it was occupied all the time and the necessities of life had to be kept available.

She went straight over to the sink and found a cup, filled it with water from the ewer standing on the bench, and took it over to him, holding it to his lips. There was little else she could do for him. His body shuddered as he gasped for breath, and she could hear the rattling of phlegm in his chest, but it was too deep for him to bring up.

After a minute or two the coughing subsided, more rapidly than she had expected, and he took the water from her gratefully, sipping it and letting it slide down his throat. He handed her back the cup.

"Sorry, miss," he said huskily. "Touch o' the bronchitis. Silly this time o' the year."

"It can happen any time, if you are subject to it," she answered, smiling at him. "Sometimes in the summer it's worse. Harder to get rid of."

"You're surely right," he agreed, nodding slightly. He was still pale and his cheeks were a little flushed. She guessed he probably had a low fever.

"What can I do for you, miss? If you're looking for my grandson, he isn't here. He's a policeman, and he's at work. Very good he is, too. A sergeant." His pride was obvious, but far more than that, a kind of shining certainty that had nothing to do with the nature of his grandson's work but everything to do with the nature of the man.

"It was you I came to see," she reminded him. She must find a reason he would accept. "My husband said you were a sailor and had seen some great days—some of the most important battles in England's history."

He looked at her sideways. "An' what would a young lady like you want with stories of old battles what was over and won before you were even born?"

"If they were over and lost, I'd be speaking French," she replied, meeting his eyes with a laugh.

"Well . . . I s'pose that's true. Still, you know that without coming all the way here to see me." He was faintly suspicious of her. Young women of educated speech and good manners did not casually call on an old and ill sailor who, from the contents of the room, was having desperate trouble finding sufficient money merely to eat, let alone buy fuel for the winter.

A portion of the truth was the best answer, perhaps not as irrelevant as it first seemed.

"I was an army nurse in the Crimea," she told him. "I know more about war than you may think. I don't imagine I've seen as many battles as you have, but I've seen my share, and

130

closer than I'd wish. I've certainly been part of what happens afterwards." Suddenly she was speaking with urgency, and the absolute and fiercely relevant truth. "And there is no one I know with whom I can discuss it or bring back the miseries that still come into my dreams. No one expects it in a woman. They think it all better forgotten . . . easier. But it isn't always. . . ."

He stared at her, his eyes wide. They were clear, pale blue. They had probably been darker when he was young.

"Well, now . . . did you really? And you such a slip of a thing!" He regarded her rather too slender body and square, thin shoulders, but with admiration, not disapproval. "We found, at sea, sometimes the wiry ones outlasted the great big ones like a side o' beef. I reckon strength, when it comes to it, is all a matter o' spirit."

"You're quite right," she agreed. "Would you like a hot drink now? I can easily make one if you would. It might ease your chest a little." Then, in case he thought she was patronizing him, she added, "I should like very much to talk with you, and I can't if you are taken with coughing again."

He understood very well what she was doing, but she had softened the request sufficiently. "You're a canny one." He smiled at her, pointing to the stove. "Kettle's over there, and tea in the tin. Little milk in the larder, maybe. Could be we're out till Michael comes home again."

"Doesn't matter," she replied, standing up. "It's all right without milk, if it isn't too strong."

She was scalding the pot, ready to make the tea, when the door opened, and she turned to see a young man standing just inside the room. He was of average height, slender, with very handsome dark eyes. At this moment he was obviously angry.

"Who are you?" he demanded, coming farther in. "And what are you doing?" He left the door open behind him, as if for her to leave the more easily.

"Hester Monk," she replied, looking at him squarely. "I called upon Mr. Robb to visit with him. We have much in common, and he was kind enough to listen to me. In order

131

that he might speak with more comfort, he permitted me to make a cup of tea."

The young man looked at her with total disbelief. From the expression in his eyes one might have presumed he thought she was there to steal the meager rations on the shelf behind her.

"What on earth could you have in common with my grandfather?" he said grimly.

"It's all right, Michael," the old man intervened. "I'd fairly like to watch her take you on. Reckon as she might have the best of you—with her tongue, any road. Crimean nurse, she is! Seen more battles than you have—like me. She don't mean no harm."

Michael looked uncertainly at the old man, then back at Hester. She respected his protectiveness of his grandfather and hoped she would have done the same had she been in his place. And she was unquestionably an intruder. But the elder Robb should not be treated like a child, even if he was physically all but helpless. She must refrain from defending his judgment now, though the words were on the end of her tongue.

The old man looked at Hester, a glint in his eye. "Wouldn't mind getting another cup, would you, miss?"

"Of course not," Hester said demurely, lifting the last cup from its hook on the shelf that served as a dresser. She finished scalding the pot, put in a meager portion of leaves, then poured on the boiling water, keeping her back to Michael. She heard the door close and his footsteps across the floor.

He came up behind her, his voice very low. "Did Monk send you here?"

"No." She was about to add that Monk did not "send" her anywhere, but on reflection, that was not true. He had frequently sent her to various places to enquire into one thing or another. "So far as I know, he has no idea I am here. I remembered what he said to me of Mr. Robb, and I felt that I wished to visit him. I have no intention of taking anything that belongs to you, Sergeant Robb, or of doing your grandfather

132

any harm, either by meddling or by patronizing him. Nor am I interested in your police concerns with Mrs. Gardiner."

He blushed painfully, but his eyes remained sharp and steady, and considerable animosity showed in them.

"You are direct to a fault, ma'am."

She smiled suddenly. "Yes—I know. Would you rather I beat around the bush a little more? I can go back and make ten minutes of obscure conversation if you wish. Well—perhaps five . . ."

"No, I would not!" In spite of himself his voice rose. "I—"

Whatever else he had been about to say was cut short by the old man's beginning to cough again. He had struggled forward, half out of his chair, and he was in considerable distress, his face flushed and already beads of sweat on his lip and brow.

Michael swung around and rushed towards him, catching him in his arms and easing him back into the chair. For the moment Hester was completely forgotten.

The old man was fighting for breath, trying desperately to drag the air into his damaged lungs, his whole body racked with violent spasms. He brought up great gobbets of phlegm, dark yellow and spotted with blood.

Hester had already guessed how seriously ill he was, but this was agonizing confirmation. She wished that there was something she could do, but at least until the coughing subsided he was beyond all assistance except the physical support Michael was giving him.

If they had been at the hospital she could have got him a tiny dose of morphine, which would have calmed the wrenching lungs and given him the opportunity to rest. Sherry and water would have been good as a restorative. She looked around the shelves to see what there was, her mind racing to think of a way of giving him what he lacked without hurting his pride. She knew perfectly well that anxiety could make people ill, that fear could destroy the passion to survive. Humiliation and the conviction that one was useless, a burden to those one loved, had precipitated the death of many a person

133

who might well have recovered had he perceived himself as valuable.

She saw bread and cheese, three eggs, a carefully covered piece of cold beef, some raw vegetables and a slice of pie. It was not much to feed two men. Perhaps Michael Robb bought his lunch while on duty. On the other hand, he very possibly sacrificed much of his own welfare to care for his grandfather, but in such a way that the old man was unaware of it.

There was a closed cupboard, and she hesitated, reluctant to intrude any further. Was there some way that she could get Kristian Beck to come and visit Mr. Robb and then prescribe morphine for him? He was too old and his illness too far progressed for treatment to accomplish anything beyond alleviating his distress, but surely that was a side of medicine which was just as important. Many things could not be cured. No nurse worth her calling abandoned such cases.

What was there she could find in the meantime? Even hot tea alone might soothe, as soon as he could master himself enough to drink it. Then she saw a small jar of clear honey.

She poured a cup of tea for him, added the honey and sufficient cold water to make it drinkable, and carried it over, waiting for a moment's ease in his coughing. Then she stepped in front of Michael and held the cup to the old man's lips.

"Take a sip," she told him. "It will help."

Fumblingly he obeyed, and perhaps the honey soothed the spasms of his throat, because his body eased and he began to relax, sipping again, and then again. It seemed as if, for the moment at least, the attack was over.

She took the cup away and set it down, then went back to the sink and found a bowl that would serve for washing, poured the rest of the water from the kettle into it and automatically put more on to heat. She added a little cold, tested it with her hand, and with a cloth and a towel returned to the old man's chair.

He was exhausted and very pale, but far calmer. The fact

134

that he had been, for a while, unable to control himself was obviously an embarrassment to him.

Michael stood anxiously, aware of the older man's emotions, angry and protective. This should have been private, and Hester was an intruder.

Hester wrung out the cloth in the hot water and gently bathed the old man's face, then his neck, then, as he did not protest, unfastened his shirt and took it off, very aware of Michael's eyes on her. Wringing out the cloth every few moments, she bathed the old man's arms and body. All the time she did not speak, and neither did they.

Once Michael had ascertained what she was doing, and that his grandfather was eased by it rather than further discomforted, he went to find a clean shirt and returned carrying it. It was rough-dried, but it smelled fresh and was quite soft to the touch. Hester helped the old man into it, then took away the bowl of water and emptied it outside down the drain.

She came back into the room to find John Robb smiling at her, the hectic color fading from his cheeks, and Michael still guarded but less aggressive.

"Thank you, miss," Robb said a little anxiously. "I'm real sorry to have put you out."

"You didn't." She smiled. "I still hope in time we may talk, and you will tell me tales of things I've only imagined."

"I can that," he agreed with a return of enthusiasm.

"Another day," Michael said sharply. "You're tired—"

"I'm all right," Robb insisted. "Don't you worry yourself, Michael. I told you, this lady here's one o' them Crimean nurses, so I reckon she knows all she needs to about the sick. You go back to your watch, lad. I know there's important things only you can do." He looked at him steadily, his voice getting stronger, a touch of old authority back again. "Don't you be worrying."

Michael looked at Hester, frowning a little, his lips drawn tight.

"I appreciate your kindness, Mrs. Monk." He hesitated, the

135

battle within him clear in his face. "And I'm sure my grand-father will enjoy your company."

"And I his," Hester replied. "I shall look forward to coming by whenever I am able to. I am frequently at the hospital, not far away. It is no journey at all."

"Thank you." He must be sensitive to what a relief it would be to the old man to nave company and assistance he could look forward to without the anxiety of knowing that he was keeping Michael from his job, and that every minute spent there was in some essence a risk for Michael. But the young policeman was still angry beneath the gratitude, for all its sincerity.

"It is not a trouble," Hester repeated.

Michael moved towards the door, indicating that she should go with him.

"Good-bye, Grandpa," he said gently. "I'll try not to be late."

"Don't worry," Robb assured him. "I'll be all right." They were brave words, and he said them as if they could be true, although they all knew they might not be.

Just outside on the step Michael lowered his voice and fixed Hester with an intense stare.

"You're a good nurse, Mrs. Monk, and I surely appreciate the way you look after him, better than I can. And you didn't make him feel like it's charity. You've got a way with you. I suppose that comes from being out at the war, and all that."

"It also comes from liking him," she replied honestly.

There was no indication in his eyes as to whether he believed her.

"But don't be thinking anything you do here will make a difference, because it won't," he went on levelly. "I won't stop looking for Miriam Gardiner. And when I find her, which I will, if she's guilty of killing James Treadwell, I'll arrest her and charge her, whatever you do for my grandfather." His face tightened even more, his voice a little hoarse. "And whether you tell the police station or not." He colored slightly. "And if that insults you, I'm sorry."

"I'm used to being insulted, Sergeant Robb," she replied, surprised at how much the suggestion hurt. "But I admit, this is a totally new manner of saying my work is worthless, incompetent or generally of morally questionable nature."

"I didn't mean . . ." he began, then bit the words back, the pink deepening in his cheeks.

"Yes, you did," she contradicted him, making the most of his embarrassment. "But I suppose I can understand it. You must feel very vulnerable, coming away from your post to care for your grandfather. I swear to you that I have no motive for being here except to offer him some care, according to my profession, and to talk with him over old memories I can share with no one who has not had the experiences from which they spring. You must believe me, or not, as circumstances prove me." And without waiting to see his response, she turned and went back in through the door, leaving it ajar behind her for the warm air to come in. She was only half aware of Michael's footsteps as he walked away.

She remained far longer than she had originally intended. To begin with she had talked comparatively little, answering a few questions about what life had been like for her in the hospital at Scutari, and even describing Florence Nightingale. Robb was interested to hear about her, what she looked like, her demeanor, her voice, even her manner of dress. Such was her reputation that the smallest details held his attention. Hester was happy to answer, feeling memory so sharp she could almost smell the blood and vinegar again, and the sickening odor of gangrene and the other acrid stenches of disease. She could feel the summer heat and hear the buzzing of flies, as if the mild English sun coming in through the windows were the same, and it would be a Turkish street outside.

Halfway through the afternoon he fell asleep, and she was able to stand up and tidy the kitchen space a little, ready to prepare him another cup of tea, should he want it. She would certainly welcome one herself, milk or no milk to go with it. She considered going out to purchase some but decided not to. It would be a slight to his hospitality, a small and needless hurt. Tea was perfectly adequate without.

She tried the closed cupboard, to see if there was anything in it which might help him should he have another attack, any herbal leaves such as camomile to settle the stomach, or feverfew to help headache or even a little quinine to reduce temperatures. She was pleased to find all those things, and also a small packet that suggested morphine to her. A taste on a moistened finger confirmed it. This was quite a respectable medicine cabinet, too accurate to his needs to have been collected by an amateur or by chance, and too expensive to have been purchased out of a police sergeant's pay, except by the most desperate economies elsewhere.

She closed the cupboard silently and stood facing the room, her mind whirling. Morphine was one of the principal medicines missing from the hospital. She had assumed, as everyone else had, that it was being taken for addicts who had been given it for pain and now could not survive without it. But perhaps it was being taken to heal the sick who could not come to the hospital, people like John Robb. Certainly, that was still theft, but she could not find it in herself to disapprove of it.

The questions that burned in her mind were who had brought them and did Michael Robb know. Was that, even in part, the cause of his concern at her being here?

She did not believe it. Intelligence told her it was possible, instinct denied it without consideration.

The old man himself, so peacefully asleep in the afternoon sun, undoubtedly must know who had brought them, but would he know they might be stolen? He might guess, but she thought it unlikely. She would not ask him. There was no decision to make. The question did not arise that she should pursue it. She sat down and waited patiently until he should awaken, then she would make him tea again, with a little more honey. It would be a good idea to bring him a further supply, to make up for what she had drunk herself.

He awoke greatly refreshed and delighted to find her still

138

there. He started to talk straightaway, not even waiting while she served tea and brought it for them both.

"You asked about my sailing days," he said cheerfully. "Well, o' course the greatest o' them was the battle, weren't it!" He looked at her expectantly, his eyes bright.

"The battle?" she asked, turning around to face him.

"C'mon, girl! There's only one battle for a sailor—only one battle for England—really for England, like!"

She smiled at him. "Oh . . . you mean Trafalgar?"

" 'Course, I mean Trafalgar! You're teasin' me, aren't you? You've gotta be."

"You were at Trafalgar! Really?" She was impressed, and she allowed it to show in her voice and her eyes.

"Surely I was. Never forget that if I live to be a hundred—which I won't. Great day that was . . . an' terrible, too. I reckon there's bin none other like it, nor won't be again."

She poured the water onto the tea. "What ship were you on?"

"Why, the *Victory*, o' course." He said it with pride in his voice so sharp and clear that for a moment she could hear in it the young man he had been over half a century before, when England had been on the brink of invasion by Napoleon's armies and nothing stood between them and conquest except the wooden walls of the British fleet—and the skill and bravado of Horatio Nelson and the men who sailed with him. She felt a stirring of the same pride in herself, a shiver of excitement and knowledge of the cost, because she, too, had seen battle and knew its reality as well as its dream.

She brought the tea over to him and offered him a cup. He took it, and his eyes met hers over the rim.

"I was there," he said softly. "I remember that morning like it were yesterday. First signal come in about six. That was on the nineteenth of October. Enemy had their tops'l yards hoisted. Least that's what we heard later. Then they were coming out o' port under sail. Half past nine and bright light over the sea when we heard it on the *Victory*." He shook his head. "All day we tacked and veered around toward Gibraltar, but we never saw 'em. Visibility was poor—you got to understand that. Weather gettin' worse all the time. Under close-reefed topsails, we were, an' too close to Cádiz."

She nodded, sipping her tea, not interrupting.

"Admiral gave the signal to wear and come northwest, back to our first position. Next day, that was, you see?"

"Yes, I see. I know the battle was on the twenty-first."

He nodded again, appreciation in his face. "By dawn o' the twenty-first the admiral had it exactly right. Twenty-one miles north by west o' Cape Trafalgar, we were, and to windward o' the enemy." His eyes were smiling, shining blue, like the sea that historic day. "I can smell the salt in the air," he said softly, screwing up his face as if the glare of the water blinded him still. "Ordered us into two columns and make full sail."

She did not speak.

He was smiling, his tea forgotten. "Made a notch on me gun, I did, like the man next to me. He was an Irishman, I remember. The admiral came around to all of us. He asked what we were doin'. The Irishman told him we were making a mark for another victory, like all the others, just in case he fell in the battle. Nelson laughed an' said as he would make notches enough in the enemy's ships.

"About eleven in the morning the admiral went below to pray, and wrote in his diary, as we learned afterwards. Then he came up to be with us all. That was when he had the signal run up." He smiled and shook his head as if some thought consumed him. "He was going to say 'Nelson confides,' but Lieutenant Pascoe told him that 'expects' was in the Popham code, an' he didn't have to spell it out letter by letter. So what he sent was 'England expects that every man will do his duty.' " He gave a little shrug, looking at her to make sure she knew how those words had become immortal. He saw it in her face, and was satisfied.

"I don't really know what happened in the lee column," he went on, still looking at her, but his eyes already sea blue and far away, his inner vision filled with the great ships, sails bil-

140

lowing in the wind, high up masts that scraped the sky, coming around to face the enemy, men at the ready, muscles taut, silent by their guns, the decks behind them painted red, not to show the blood when the slaughter began.

She could see in his eyes and the curve of his lips the memory of a sharper light than this English summer, the pitch of the deck as the ship hit the waves, the waiting, and then the roar and slam of cannon fire, the smell of saltpeter, the sting of smoke in the eyes and nose.

"You can't imagine the noise," he said so softly it was almost a whisper. "Make them train engines they got now sound like silence. Gunner, I was, an' a good one. Nobody knows how many broadsides we fired that day. But it was about half past one that the admiral was hit. Pacing the quarterdeck, he was. With the captain—Captain Hardy." He screwed up his face. "There was some idiots as says he was paradin' with a chest full o' medals. They haven't been in a sea battle! Anyway, when he was at sea he never dressed like that. Shabby, he was, wore an ordinary blue jacket, like anyone else. He wore sequin copies of his orders, but if you ever spent time at sea, you'd know they tarnish in a matter o' days." He shook his head in denial again. "And you couldn't hardly see anybody to make 'em out clear during a battle. Smoke everywhere. Could miss your own mother not a dozen feet from you." He stopped for a few minutes to catch his breath.

Hester thought of offering him more tea, fresh and hot, but she could see that memory was more important, so she sat and waited.

He resumed his story, telling her of the knowledge of victory and the crushing grief felt by the entire fleet when they knew Nelson was dead. Then of the other losses, the ships and the men gone, the wounded, the securing of the prizes, and then the storm which had arisen and caused even further devastation. He described it in simple, vivid words, and his emotion was as sharp as if it had all happened weeks before, not fifty-five years.

141

He told of putting Nelson's body in a cask of brandy to preserve it so it could be buried in England, as he had wished.

"Just a little man, he was. Up to my chin, no more," he said with a fierce sniff. "Funny that. We won the greatest victory at sea ever—saved our country from invasion—an' we came home with flags lowered, like we lost—because he were dead." He fell silent for some time.

She rose and boiled the kettle again, resetting the tray and making a light supper for him with a piece of pie cut into a thin slice, and hot tea.

After he had eaten with some pleasure, he told her of Nelson's funeral and how all London had turned out to wish him a last farewell.

"Buried in a special coffin, he was," he added with pride. "Plain an' simple, like death, or the sea. Made from wood taken from the wreckage of the French flagship at the Battle of the Nile. Pleased as punch when Hallowell gave it to him way back, he was. Kept it all those years. Laid in the Painted Hall in Greenwich Hospital. First mourners come on January fourth." He smiled with supreme satisfaction. "Prince o' Wales hisself."

He took a deep breath and let it out in a rasping cough, but held up his hand to prevent her from interrupting him. "Laid there four days. While all the world went by to pay their respects. Then we took him up the river, on Wednesday morning. The coffin was placed on one of the royal barges made for King Charles II, an' all covered over in black velvet, with black ostrich plumes, and went in a flotilla up to London. Eleven other barges, there were, all the livery companies with their banners flying. Never seen so much gold and color. Stiff wind that day, too. Fired the guns every minute, all the way up to Whitehall Stairs."

He stopped again, blinking hard, but he could not keep the tears from spilling over and running down his cheeks.

"Next day we took him to Saint Paul's. Great procession, but mostly army. Only navy there was us—from the *Victory* herself." His voice cracked, but it was from pride as well as grief. "I was one of them what carried our battle ensigns. We opened them up now and again so the crowd could see the shot holes in them. They all took their hats off as we passed. It made a sound like the noise of the sea." He rubbed his hand across his cheek. "There isn't anything I'd take this side o' heaven to trade places with any man alive who wasn't there."

"I wouldn't understand it if you did," she answered, smiling at him and unashamed to be weeping, too.

He nodded slowly. "You're a good girl. You know what it means, don't you." That was a statement, not a question. He drew in his breath as if to thank her, then knew it was unnecessary, even inappropriate. It would have implied debt, and there was none.

Before she could say anything in answer the door opened and Michael Robb came in. Only then did she realize how long she had been there. It was early evening. The shadows of the sun were long across the floor and touched with a deeper color. She felt a warmth of self-consciousness wash up her face. Automatically, she stood up.

Michael's disapproval and alarm were too obvious to hide. He saw the tears on the old man's face and turned to glare at Hester.

"I had the best afternoon in years," Robb said gently, looking up at his grandson. "She kept me real company. We talked about all sort o' things. I've got a kind o' peace inside me. Come, sit down and have a cup o' tea. You look like your feet hurt, boy, and you're mortal tired."

Michael hesitated, confusion filling his face. He looked from one to the other of them, then finally accepted that his grandfather was telling the truth about his pleasure and Hester really had given him a rare gift of companionship, unspoiled by duty or the seeking of recompense. A wide smile of relief lit his face, cutting through the weariness and showing for a moment the youth he wanted to be.

"Yes," he agreed vehemently. "Yes, I will." He turned to Hester. "Thank you, Mrs. Monk." His eyes shadowed. "I'm sorry . . . I found Miriam Gardiner."

Hester felt a sudden coldness inside. The sweetness of the moment before was gone.

"I had to arrest her for Treadwell's murder," he finished, watching her to see her reaction.

"Why?" she protested. "Why on earth would Miriam Gardiner murder the coachman? If she wanted to escape from Lucius Stourbridge, for whatever reason, all she had to do was have Treadwell leave her somewhere. He would never have known where she went after that." She drew in her breath. "And if she simply went somewhere near her home, Lucius would know more about that than Treadwell anyway."

Michael looked as if the answer gave him no pleasure, barely even any satisfaction. He would probably dearly like to have taken off his boots, which were no doubt tight and hot after the long day, but her presence prevented him. "The most obvious reason is that Treadwell knew something about her which would have ruined her prospects of marriage into the Stourbridge family," he answered. "I daresay she loved young Mr. Stourbridge, but whether she did or not, there's a great deal of money to it, more than she'll even have seen in her life."

Hester wanted to protest that Miriam had no regard for the money, but she did not know if that was true. She had impressions, feelings, but barely any real knowledge.

She walked over to the kettle, refilled it from the ewer, which was now almost empty, and set it on the stove again.

"I'm sorry," Michael said wearily, sinking into the chair. "It's too plain to ignore. The two of them left the Stourbridge house together. They came as far as Hampstead Heath. His body was found, and she ran away. Surely any innocent person would have stayed, or at least come back and reported what had happened."

She thought quickly. "What if they were both attacked by someone else, and she was too afraid of that person to tell anyone what happened?"

He looked at her doubtfully. "So afraid that even when we

arrested her she still wouldn't say?" His voice denied his belief in it.

"Do you know this Miriam Gardiner, girl?" Robb asked, looking at Hester sadly.

"No . . . no, I haven't met her." She was surprised that that was true, since she felt so strongly about it. It defied sense. "I . . . I just know a little about her . . . I suppose I put myself in her place . . . a little."

"In her place?" Michael echoed. "What would make you leave a man, beaten, dying, but still alive, and run away, never to come forward until the police hunted you down, and then give no explanation even when you were arrested for killing him?"

"I don't know," she admitted reluctantly. "I . . . can't think of anything . . . but that doesn't mean there couldn't be a reason."

"She's protecting someone," the old man said, shaking his head. "Women'll do all sorts to protect someone they love. I'll lay you odds, girl, if she didn't kill him herself, she knows who did."

Michael glanced at Hester. "Could be she was having an affair with Treadwell," he said, pursing his lips. "Could be he tried to force her to keep it going, and she wanted to end it because of Stourbridge."

Hester did not argue anymore. Reason was all on his side, and she had nothing to marshal against it. She turned her attention to the kettle.

When she arrived home Monk was already there, and she was startled to see that he had prepared cold game pie and vegetables for dinner and it was set out on the table. She realized how late it was, and apologized with considerable feeling. She was also deeply grateful. She was hot and tired, and her boots felt at least a size too tight.

"What is it?" he asked, seeing the droop in her shoulders and reading her too well to think it was only weariness.

145

"They've found Miriam," she replied, looking up at him from where she had sat down to unlace her boots.

He stood still in the doorway, staring at her.

"They arrested her," she finished quietly. "Michael Robb thinks she killed Treadwell, either because he knew something about her which would have ended her chance of marrying Lucius or because she was having an affair with him and wanted to end it."

His face was grave, the lines harder. "How do you know that?"

She realized the necessity for explanation, a little late. "I was visiting his grandfather, because he is seriously ill, when Sergeant Robb came home."

"And Robb just told you this?" His eyes were wide and steady.

"He knew I was your wife."

"Oh." He hesitated. "And do you think Miriam killed Treadwell?" He was watching her, trying to read not only her words but her feelings. He looked strangely defeated, as if he had felt the same unreasoning hope that Miriam could be innocent.

It was very sweet not to be alone in her sense of disappointment, even disillusion.

She took her boots off and wriggled her feet, then stood up and walked over to him. She smiled and kissed him lightly on the cheek. "Thank you for the dinner."

He grinned with satisfaction. "Don't make a habit of it," he said smugly.

She knew better than to reply. She walked a step behind him to the table.

6

MONK WAS UNABLE to rid his mind of the thought of Miriam Gardiner's arrest. He slept deeply, but when he awoke the memory of her distress twisted his thoughts until he had no choice but to determine to see her.

In case there might be any difficulty with the prison authorities, he lied without compunction, meeting the jailer's gaze with candor and saying he was her legal adviser, with whom, of course, she was entitled to consult.

Monk found her sitting alone in a cell, her hands folded in her lap, her face pale but so composed as to be in a way frightening. There was no anger in her, no will to fight, no outrage at injustice. She seemed neither pleased nor displeased to see him, as if his presence made no difference with regard to anything that mattered.

The cell door clanged behind him, and he heard the heavy bolt shoot home. The floor was perhaps five paces by five, black stone, the walls whitewashed. A single high aperture was heavily glassed, letting in light but not color. The sky beyond could have been blue or gray. The air was stuffy, smelling of decades, perhaps centuries, of anger and despair.

"Mrs. Gardiner . . ." he began. He had rehearsed what to say to her, but now it seemed inadequate. Intelligence was needed, even brilliance, if he was to help her in this dreadful situation of confusion and pain, and yet all that seemed natural or remotely appropriate was emotion. "I hoped Robb would not find you, but since he has, please allow me to do what I can to help."

She looked at him blankly, her face almost expressionless. "You cannot help, Mr. Monk. I mean that as no reflection upon your abilities, simply that my situation does not allow it."

He sat down facing her. "What happened?" he asked urgently. "Do you know who killed Treadwell?"

She kept her eyes averted, staring into some dark space that only she could see.

"Do you know?" he repeated more sharply.

"There is nothing I can tell you which will help, Mr. Monk." There was finality in her voice, no lift of hope, not even of argument. She had no will to fight.

"Did you kill him?" he demanded.

She lifted her head slowly, her eyes wide. Before she spoke, he knew what she was going to say.

"No."

"Then who did?"

She looked away again.

His mind raced. The only reason for her silence must be to protect someone. Had she any conception of what it was going to cost her?

"Did Treadwell threaten you?" he asked.

"No." But there was no surprise in her voice or in the profile of her face. Whom was she protecting? Cleo Anderson, who had been almost a mother to her? Some other lover from the past, or a relative of her first husband?

"Was he threatening someone else? Blackmailing you?" he persisted. All sorts of arguments sprang to his lips about not being able to help her if she would not help herself, but they died unspoken because it was too painfully apparent she had no belief that help was possible. "Was Treadwell blackmailing you about something in your life here in Hampstead?"

"No." She lifted her head again. "There was nothing to blackmail me about." Tears filled her eyes. Emotion had

148

broken through the ice of despair for a few moments, then it withered again. The stark cell with its wooden cot and straw mattress, the bare walls and stifling air were hardly real to her. Her world was within herself and her own pain. Surely, she had not yet even imagined what would follow if she did not present some defense. Either she had some reason for attacking Treadwell or else it was simply someone else who had killed him. The only other alternative was that she had not even been present and had no idea what had happened. Then why did she not say so?

He looked at her hunched figure where she sat, half turned away from him, unresponsive.

"Miriam!" He put out his hand and touched her. Her body was rigid. "Miriam! What happened? Why did you leave the Stourbridge house? Was it something to do with Treadwell?"

"No . . ." There was a driving core of emotion in her voice. "No," she repeated. "It had nothing to do with Treadwell. He was merely good enough to drive me."

"You simply asked him, and he agreed?" he said with surprise. "Did he not require some reason?"

"Not reason. Recompense."

"You paid him?"

"My locket. It doesn't matter."

That she would part so easily with a personal item of jewelry was a measure of how desperate she had been. He wondered what had become of the locket. It had not been with Treadwell's clothes. Had his murderer taken it?

"Where is it now?" he asked. "Did you take it back?"

She frowned. "Where is it? Isn't it with him . . . with his body?"

"No."

She lifted her shoulders very slightly, less than a shrug. "Then I don't know. But it doesn't matter. Don't waste your effort on it, Mr. Monk. Maybe it will find its way to someone who will like it. I would rather it were not lost down some drain, but if it is, I can't help it now."

149

"What should I put my effort into, Miriam?"

She did not answer for so long he was about to repeat himself when at last she spoke.

"Comfort Lucius . . ." Without warning, her composure broke and she bent her head and covered her face, sobs shaking her body.

He longed to be able to help her. She was alone, vulnerable, facing trial and almost certainly one of the ugliest of deaths.

Impulse overcame judgment. He reached out and took hold of her arm.

"Words won't comfort him when you are in the dock, or when the judge puts on his cap and sentences you to hang! Tell me the truth while I can do something about it! Why did you leave the Stourbridge house? Or if you won't tell me that, at least tell me what happened in Hampstead. Who killed Treadwell? Where were you? Why did you run away? Who are you afraid of?"

It took her several moments to master herself again. She blew her nose, then, still avoiding meeting his eyes, she answered in a low, choked voice.

"I can't tell you why I left, only that I had to. What happened in Hampstead is that Treadwell was attacked and murdered. I think perhaps it was my fault, but I did not do it, that I swear. I never injured anyone with intent." She looked at him, her eyes red-rimmed. "Please tell Lucius that, Mr. Monk. I never willfully harmed anyone. I want him to believe that . . ." Her voice trailed off into a sob.

"He already believes that," he said more gently. "It is not Lucius you have to be concerned about. I doubt he will ever think ill of you. It is the rest of the world, especially Sergeant Robb, and then whatever jury he brings you before. And he will! Unless you give some better account. Did you see who attacked Treadwell? At least answer me yes or no."

"Yes. But no one would believe me, even if I would say . . . and I will not." She spoke with finality. There was no room to

150

imagine she hoped to be dissuaded. She did not care what Monk thought, and he knew it from everything about her, from the slump of the body to the lifelessness of her voice.

"Try me!" he urged desperately. "Tell me the truth and let me decide whether I believe it or not. If you are innocent, then someone else is guilty, and he must be found. If he isn't, you will hang!"

"I know. Did you think I didn't understand that?"

He had wondered fleetingly if she was of mental competence, if perhaps she was far more frail than Lucius had had any idea, but the thought had lasted only moments.

"Will you see Lucius? Or Major Stourbridge?" he asked.

"No!" She pulled away from him sharply, for the first time real fear in her voice. "No . . . I won't. If you have any desire to help me, then do not ask me again."

"I won't," he promised.

"You give me your word?" She stared at him, her eyes wide and intense.

"I do. But I warn you again that no one can help you until you tell the truth. If not to me, would you tell a lawyer, someone who is bound to keep in confidence whatever you say, regardless of what it is?"

A smile flickered over her face and vanished. "It would make no difference whatever. It is the truth itself that wounds, Mr. Monk, not what you may do with it. Thank you for coming. I am sure your intention was generous, but you cannot help. Please leave me to myself." She turned away again, dismissing him.

He had no alternative but to accept. He stood up, hesitated a moment longer, without purpose, then called the jailer to let him out.

Just outside the gates he encountered Michael Robb. Robb looked tired, and it was obscurely pleasing to Monk that there was no air of triumph in him.

They stood facing each other on the hot, dusty footpath.

"You've been to see her," Robb said, stating what was obvious between them.

151

"She won't tell you anything," Monk said, not in answer but as a statement of fact. "She won't speak to anyone. She won't even see Stourbridge."

Robb looked him up and down, from his neat cravat and the shoulders of the well-cut jacket to the tips of his polished boots. "Do you know what happened?" he asked, raising his eyebrows.

"No," Monk replied.

Robb put his hands in his pockets, deliberately casual, even sloppy by contrast. "I shall find out," he promised. "No matter how long it takes me, I will know what happened to Treadwell—or enough to make a prosecution. There's something in his past, or hers, that made this happen." He was watching Monk's face as he spoke, weighing his reaction, trying to read what he knew.

"You will have to," Monk agreed wryly. "All you have at the moment is suspicion—not enough to hang anyone on."

Robb winced almost imperceptibly, just a stiffening of his body. It was an ugly word, an ugly reality. "I will." His voice was very soft. "Treadwell may have been an evil man, for all I know deserving some kind of retribution, but the day we allow the man in the street to decide that for himself, without trial, without answering to anyone, then we lose the right to call ourselves civilized. Then law belongs to the quickest and the strongest, not to justice. We aren't a society anymore." He was self-conscious as he said it, daring Monk to laugh at him, but he was proud of it also.

Monk hoped he had never done anything in the past which made Robb imagine he would mock that decision. He would probably never know. A dray rumbled noisily past them.

"I won't stand in your way," he answered levelly. "None of us could afford private vengeance." He wondered if Robb had any idea how true that was.

"She'd be better if she told us." Robb frowned. "Can't you persuade her of that? Otherwise I'll have to dig for it, go through all her life, all her friends, her first husband . . . everything."

"That's one of the things about murder." Monk nodded and lifted his shoulders very slightly. "You have to learn more about everybody than you want to know, all the secrets that have nothing to do with the crime, as well as those that do. Innocent people are stripped of their masks of pretense, sometimes of decently covered mistakes they've long since mended. You have to know everything the victim ever did that could make someone take the last, terrible step of killing him, creep as close as his skin till you see every blemish and can read the hatred that destroyed him. Of course, you'll know Treadwell . . . and you'll come to pity him—and probably hate him as well."

People passed by, and they ignored them.

"Have you solved a lot of murders?" Robb asked. It was not a challenge; there was respect and curiosity in his face.

"Yes," Monk answered him. "Some I understood, and might have done the same myself. Others were so cold-blooded, so consumed in self, it frightened me that another human being I had talked with, stood beside, could have hidden that evil behind a face which looked to me like any other."

Robb stared at him. For several seconds neither of them moved, oblivious of the noisy street around them.

"I think this is going to be one of the first," Robb said at last. "I wish it weren't. I wish I weren't going to find some private shame in Mrs. Gardiner's life that Treadwell was blackmailing her about, threatening to ruin the happiness she'd found. But I have to look. And if I find it, I have to bring it to evidence." That was a challenge.

Monk thought how young he was. And he wondered what evidence he had found—or lost—when he was that age. And for that matter, what he would do now if he were in Robb's place.

But he was not. He had no further interest in the case. His task was over, not very satisfactorily.

"Of course you do," he answered. "There are hundreds of
153

judgments to make. You have to check which are yours and which aren't. Good day, Sergeant Robb."

Robb stood facing him in the sun. "Good day, Mr. Monk. It's been an interesting experience to meet you." He looked as if he was about to add something more, then changed his mind and went on past Monk towards the prison gate.

Monk had no duties in the case now. Even moral obligation took him no further. Miriam had refused to explain anything, either of her flight from Cleveland Square or what had happened in Hampstead. There was nothing more he could do.

Hester was still at the hospital, although it was now late.

Monk sat at his desk writing letters, his mind only half on them, and was delighted when the doorbell rang. Only when he answered it, and saw Lucius Stourbridge, did his heart sink. Should he express some condolence for the situation? Lucius had hired him to find Miriam, and he had done so. The result had been catastrophic, even though it was none of his doing.

Lucius looked haggard, his eyes dark-ringed, his cheeks pale beneath his olive skin, giving him a sallow, almost gray appearance. He was a man walking through a nightmare. "I know you have already done all that I asked of you, Mr. Monk," he began even before Monk could invite him inside. "And that you endeavored to help Mrs. Gardiner, even concealing her whereabouts from the police, but they found her nevertheless, and arrested her . . ." The words were so hard for him to say that his voice cracked, and he was obliged to clear his throat before he could continue. "For the murder of Treadwell." He swallowed. "I know she cannot have done such a thing. Please, Mr. Monk, at any cost at all, up to everything I have, please help me prove that!" He stood still on the front doorstep, his body rigid, hands clenched, eyes filled with his inner agony.

"It is not the cost, Mr. Stourbridge," Monk answered slowly, fighting his common sense and everything his intelligence told him. "Please come in.

154

"It is a matter of what is possible. I have already spoken to her," he continued as Lucius followed him into the sitting room. "She will not tell me anything of what occurred. All she would say was that she did not kill Treadwell."

"Of course she didn't," Lucius protested, still standing. "We must save her from . . ." He could not bear to use the word. "We must defend her. I . . . I don't know how, or . . ." He trailed off. "But I know your reputation, Mr. Monk. If any man in London can help, it is you."

"If you know my reputation, then you know I will not conceal the truth if I find it," Monk warned. "Even if it is not what you wish to hear."

Lucius lifted his chin. "It may not be what I wish to hear, Mr. Monk, but it will not be that Miriam killed Treadwell in any unlawful way. I believe it was someone else, but she dares not say so because she is afraid of him, either for herself or for someone else." His voice shook a little. "But if she brought about his death herself, then it was either an accident or she was defending herself from some threat which was too immediate and too gross to endure."

Monk held very little hope of such a comfortable solution. If that was the case, why had Miriam not simply said so? She would not be blamed for defending her virtue. More sharply etched in his mind were the images of Treadwell's head and his scarred knees, but no other injury at all. He had not been involved in a struggle with anyone. He had been hit one mighty blow which had caused him to bleed to death within his skull in a very short while. During that time he had crawled from wherever the attack had taken place, probably seeking help. He knew the area. Perhaps he even knew Cleo Anderson was a nurse and had tried to reach her. Had Miriam simply watched him crawl away without making any attempt to help? Why had she not at least reported the incident, if she was in any way justified? Hiding was not the action of an honorable woman, the victim of an attack herself.

Further, and perhaps even more damning, what could she

possibly have had at hand with which to inflict such a blow, and how had Treadwell, if he had been threatening her, had his back to her?

"Mr. Stourbridge," he said grimly, "I have no idea whether I can find the truth of what happened. If you wish, I can try. But I hold far less hope than you do that it will be anything you can bear to believe. The facts so far do not indicate her innocence."

Lucius was very pale. "Then find more facts, Mr. Monk. By the time you have them all, they will prove her honor. I know her." It was a blind statement of belief, and his face allowed no argument, no appeal to a lesser thing like reason.

Monk would like to have asked him to wait and thus give himself time to consider all the consequences, but there was no time. Robb would be looking already. The Crown would prosecute as soon as it had sufficient evidence, whether it was the whole story or not. There was nothing on which to mount any defense.

"Are you quite sure?" he tried one more time, useless as he knew it.

"Yes," Lucius replied instantly. "I have twenty guineas here, and will give you more as you need it. Anything at all, just ask me." He held out a soft leather pouch of coins, thrusting it at Monk.

Monk did not immediately take the money. "The first thing will be your practical help. If Treadwell's death was not caused by Miriam, then it is either a chance attack, which I cannot believe, or it is to do with his own life and character. I will begin by learning all I can about that. It will also keep me from following Sergeant Robb's footsteps and perhaps appearing to him to be obstructing his path. Additionally, if I do learn anything, I have a better chance of keeping the option of either telling him or not, as seems to our best advantage."

"Yes . . . yes," Lucius agreed, obviously relieved to have some course of action at last. "What can I do?" He gave a tiny

156

shrug. "I tried to think of what manner of man Treadwell was, and could answer nothing. I saw him almost every day. He's dead, killed by God knows whom, and I can't give an intelligent answer."

"I didn't expect you to tell me from your observation," Monk assured him. "I would like to speak to the other servants, then discover what I can of Treadwell's life outside Bayswater. I would rather learn that before the police, if I can."

"Of course," Lucius agreed. "Thank you, Mr. Monk. I shall be forever in your debt. If there is anything—"

Monk stopped him. "Please don't thank me until I have earned it. I may find nothing further, or worse still, what I find may be something you would have been happier not to know."

"I have to know," Lucius said simply. "Until tomorrow morning, Mr. Monk."

"Good day, Mr. Stourbridge," Monk replied, walking towards the door to open it for him.

Monk was in the house in Cleveland Square by ten o'clock the next morning, and with Lucius's help he questioned the servants, both indoor and outdoor, about James Treadwell. They were reluctant to speak of him at all, let alone to speak ill, but he read in their faces, and in the awkwardness of their phrases, that Treadwell had not been greatly liked—but he had been respected because he did his job well.

A picture emerged of a man who gave little of himself, whose sense of humor was more founded in cruelty than goodwill, but who was sufficiently sensible of the hierarchy within the household not to overstep his place or wound too many feelings. He knew how to charm, and was occasionally generous when he won at gambling, which was not infrequently.

No maid reported any unwelcome attentions. Nothing had gone missing. He never blamed anyone else for his very few errors.

Monk searched his room, which was still empty as no re-placement for him had yet been employed. All his possessions were there as he had left them. It was neat, but there was a book on horse racing open on the bedside table, a half-open box of matches beside the candle on the window-sill, and a smart waistcoat hung over the back of the up-right chair. It was the room of a man who had expected to return.

Monk examined the clothes and boots carefully. He was surprised how expensive they were—in some cases, as good as his own. Treadwell certainly had not paid for them on a coachman's earnings. If the money had come from his gambling, then he must have spent a great deal of time at it—and been consistently successful. It seemed unpleasantly more and more likely that he had had another source of income, one a good deal more lucrative.

Monk did enquire, without any hope, if perhaps the clothes were hand-me-downs from either Lucius or Harry Stour-bridge. He was not surprised to learn that they were not. Such things went to servants of longer standing and remained with them.

As far as Miriam Gardiner was concerned, he learned nothing beyond what he had already been told: she was un-used to servants and therefore had not treated the coachman with the distance that was appropriate, but that was equally true for all the other household staff. No one had observed anything different with regard to Treadwell. Without exception, they all spoke well of her and seemed confused and grieved by her current misfortune.

Monk spent the following day in Hampstead and Kentish Town, as he had told Lucius he would. He walked miles, asked questions till his mouth was dry and his throat hoarse. He arrived home after nine o'clock, when it was still daylight but the heat of the afternoon was tempered by an evening breeze.

158

The first thing he wanted to do was to take his boots off and soak his burning feet, but Hootor's presence stopped him. It was not an attractive thing to do, and he was too conscious of her to indulge himself so. Instead, after accepting her welcome with great pleasure, he sat in the coolness of the office which doubled as a sitting room, a glass of cold lemonade at his elbow, his boots still firmly laced, and answered her questions.

"Expensive tastes, far more than Stourbridge paid him. At least three times as much."

Hester frowned. "Gambling?"

"Gamblers win and lose. He seems to have had his money pretty regularly. But more than that, he only had one day off a fortnight. Gambling to that extent needs time."

She was watching him closely, her eyes anxious. Unexpectedly, she did not prompt him.

He was surprised. "I considered a mistress with the means to give him expensive gifts," he continued. "But in going around the places where he spent his time off, he seems to have had money and purchased the things himself. He enjoyed spending money. He wasn't especially discreet about it."

"So you think it was come by honestly?" Her eyes widened.

"No . . . I think he was not afraid of anyone discovering the dishonesty in it," he corrected. "It wasn't stolen. There are other dishonest means—"

"Available to a coachman? What?"

The answer was obvious. Why was she deliberately not saying it? He looked back at her, trying to fathom the emotion behind her eyes. He thought he saw reluctance and fear, but it was closed in. She was not going to share it with him.

He felt excluded. It was startlingly unpleasant, a sense of loneliness he had not experienced since the extraordinary night she had accepted his proposal of marriage. He was uncertain how to deal with it. Candor was too instinctive to him; the words were the only ones to his tongue.

159

"Blackmail," he replied.

"Oh." She looked at him so steadily he was now doubly sure she was concealing her thoughts, and that they were relevant to what they were discussing. Yet how could she know anything about Treadwell? She had been working at the hospital in Hampstead—hadn't she?

"It seems the obvious possibility," he said, trying to keep his voice even. "That or theft, which he had little time for. He lived in at the Stourbridges', and they have nothing missing. He liked to live well on his time off, eat expensively, drink as much as he pleased, go out to music halls and pick up any woman that took his fancy."

She did not look surprised, only sad and, if anything, more distressed.

"I see."

"Do you?"

"No . . . I meant that I follow your reasoning. It does look as if he might have been blackmailing someone."

He could not bear the barrier. He broke it abruptly, aware that he might be hurt by the answer. "What is wrong, Hester?"

Her back stiffened a little and her chin came up. "I don't know who he was blackmailing, or even that he was, but I fear I might guess. It is something I have learned in the course of caring for the sick, therefore I cannot tell you. I'm sorry." It was very plain in her face that indeed she was sorry, and equally plain that she would not change her position.

He hurt for her. He ached to be able to help. Being shut out was almost like a physical coldness. He must protect her from being damaged by it herself. That was a greater danger than she might understand.

"Hester—are you aware of any crime committed?"

"Not morally," she answered instantly. "Nothing has been done that would offend the sensibilities of any Christian person."

"Except a policeman," he concluded without hesitation.

Her eyes widened. "Are you a policeman?"

"No . . ."

"That's what I thought. Not that it makes any difference. It would be dishonorable to tell you, even if you were. I can't."

He said nothing. It was infuriating. She might hold the missing piece which would make sense of the confusion. She knew it also, and yet she would not tell him. She set her belief in trust, in her own concept of honor, before even her love for him. It was a hard thing, and beautiful, like clean light. It did not really hurt. He was quite sure he wanted it to be so. He was almost tempted to press her, to be absolutely certain she would not yield. But that would embarrass her. She might not understand his reason, or be quite sure he was not disappointed or, worse, childishly selfish.

"William?"

"Yes?"

"Do you know something anyway?"

"No. Why?"

"You are smiling."

"Oh!" He was surprised. "Am I? No, I don't know anything. I suppose I am just . . . happy . . ." He leaned forward and much to her surprise, kissed her long and slowly, with increasing passion.

The following day was the eleventh since Monk had first been approached by Lucius Stourbridge to find his fiancée. Now she was in prison charged with murder, and Monk had very little further idea what had happened the day of her flight. He had still less idea what had occasioned it, unless it was some threat of disclosure of a portion of her past which she believed would ruin either her or someone she loved. And it seemed she would tell no one. Even trial and execution appeared preferable.

What secret could be so fearful?

He could not imagine any, even though as he took a hansom to the Hampstead police station, his mind would not leave it alone.

He arrived still short of nine o'clock to be told that Sergeant Robb had been working until dark the previous evening and was not yet in. Monk thanked the desk sergeant and left, walking briskly in the sun towards Robb's home. He had no time to waste, even though he feared his discoveries, if he made them, would all be those he preferred not to know. Perhaps that was why he hurried. Good news could be savored, bad should be bolted like evil-tasting medicine. The anticipation at least could be cut short, and hope was painful.

There was little he wanted to tell Robb, only his discoveries about Treadwell's extravagant spending habits. He had debated whether to mention the subject or not. It gave Miriam a powerful motive, if she were being blackmailed. But a man who would blackmail one person might blackmail others, therefore there would be other suspects. Perhaps one of them had lain in wait for him, and Miriam had fled the scene not because she was guilty but because she could not prove her innocence.

It was a slender hope, and he did not believe it himself. What if there was an illegitimate child somewhere, Miriam's and Treadwell's? Or simply that he knew of one? That would be enough to ruin her marriage to Lucius Stourbridge.

But was any blackmail worth the rope?

Or had she simply panicked, and now believed all was lost? That was only too credible.

He could not alone pursue all the other possible victims Treadwell might have had. That required the numbers of the police, and their authority.

He reached Robb's home and knocked on the door. It was opened after several minutes by Robb himself, looking tired and harassed. He greeted Monk civilly but with a further tightening of the tension inside him.

"What is it? Be as brief as you may, please. I am late and I have not yet given my grandfather his breakfast."

Monk would like to have helped, but he had no skills that were of use. He felt the lack of them sharply.

162

"I have learned rather more about James Treadwell, and I thought I should share it with you. Let me tell you while you get breakfast," Monk offered.

Robb accepted reluctantly.

Monk excused himself to the old man, then, sitting down, recounted what he had discovered over the previous two days. As he did so, and Michael prepared bread and tea and assisted his grandfather, Monk's eyes wandered around the room. He noticed the cupboard door open and the small stack of medicines, still well replenished, and that there were eggs in a bowl on the table by the sink and a bottle of sherry on the floor. Michael did very well by his grandfather. It must cost him every halfpenny of his sergeant's wages. Monk knew what they were and how far they went. It was little enough for two, especially when one of them needed constant care and expensive medicines.

Michael cleared away the plate and cup and washed them in the pan by the sink, his back to the room.

The old man looked at Monk. "Good woman, your wife," he said gently. "Never makes it seem like a trouble. Comes here and listens to my tales with her eyes like stars. Seen the tears running down her cheeks when I told her about the death o' the admiral an' how we came home to England with the flags lowered after Trafalgar."

"She loved hearing it," Monk said sincerely. He could imagine Hester sitting in this chair, the vision so clear in her mind that the terror and the sorrow of it moved her to tears. "She must have been here some considerable time to hear such a long account."

"Seen a good bit o' battle herself, she has," the old man said with a smile. "Told me about that. Calm and quiet as you like, but I could see in her eyes what she really felt. You can, you know. People who've really seen it don't talk that much. Just sometimes you need to, an' I could see it in her."

Was that true? Hester needed to speak of her experiences in the Crimea, even now. She shared it with this old man she

163

barely knew rather than with him, or even Callandra. But then, they had not seen war. They could not understand, and this man could. Most of the time horror was best forgotten. Occasionally, it broke the surface of the mind and had to be faced. He knew that himself, sensing the ghosts of his past who were no more than shadows to him.

"She must have come several times," he said aloud.

The old man nodded. "Drops by every day, maybe just for half an hour or so, to see how I am. Not many people care about the old and the sick if they're not their own."

"No," Monk agreed with a strangely sinking knowledge that that was true. It had not been said in self-pity but as a simple statement. He could imagine Hester's anger and her pity, not just for John Robb but for all the untold thousands he represented. When he spoke it was from instinct. "Did she ask you about other sailors and soldiers?"

"You mean old men like me? Yes, she did. Didn't she tell you?"

"I'm afraid I wasn't paying as much attention as perhaps I should have been."

Robb smiled and nodded. He, too, had not always listened to women. He understood.

"She would care," Monk continued, hating himself for the thoughts of missing medicines and blackmail that were in his mind and that he could not ignore. "She's a good nurse. Puts her patients before herself, like a good soldier, duty first."

"That's right." The old man nodded, his eyes bright and soft. "She's a real good woman. I seen a few good nurses. Come around now and again to see how you are."

Monk was aware of what he was doing, but he had to do it. "And bring medicines?"

"Of course," Robb agreed. "Can't go an' get 'em myself, and young Michael here wouldn't know what I needed, would he!"

He was unaware of anything wrong. He was speaking of

164

kindness he had received. The darkness was all in Monk's mind.

Michael finished cleaning and tidying everything so he would have as little as possible to do if he managed to slip home in the middle of the day. He left a cup of water where the old man could reach it, and a further slice of bread, and checked once more that he was as comfortable as he could make him. Then he turned to Monk.

"I must go to the police station. I'll consider what you said. There could have been somebody else there when Treadwell was killed, but there's no evidence of it or of who it was. And why did Miriam Gardiner run? Why doesn't she tell us the truth now?"

Monk could think of several answers, but they were none of them convincing, nor did they disprove her guilt. The fear that was forming in his own mind he liked even less, but he could no longer evade it. He rose and took his leave of the old man, wishing him well and feeling a hypocrite, then followed Michael Robb out into the sunny, noisy street.

A hundred yards along they parted, Robb to the left, Monk to the right towards the hospital. He was now almost convinced he knew the cause of Hester's anxiety and why she could not share it with him. Medicines had been disappearing from the hospital. When medicines disappeared in this way they were often stolen either to feed the addiction of the thief or to sell. Hester had been to John Robb's house several times and must have observed the medicine cupboard. The old man had been quite candid in saying that the medicines were brought to him by a nurse. It was so easy from that to conclude that the thefts were not selfishly motivated, far from it. Someone was taking medicines to treat the old and the sick who were too poor to purchase them for themselves.

John Robb had no idea. Apart from the guilt and the danger involved, his pride would never have allowed him to accept help at such a risk. He accepted it because he believed it was already paid for.

165

Hester had been very precise about the words she used in denying knowledge of a crime—"not morally." Legally, it most certainly was.

The question was, could Treadwell have known?

Why not? He came to Hampstead on most of his days off. His body had been found on the path to the house of a nurse—Cleo Anderson. Monk remembered her vividly, her defense of Miriam and her denial of knowing where she was after her flight from Cleveland Square. He hated having to pursue this, but the conclusion was inescapable. It was Cleo Anderson whom Treadwell had been blackmailing, and it was anything but chance that he had been found on her path. Perhaps he had crawled there deliberately, knowing he was dying, determined to the last to incriminate her and find some kind of both justice for himself and revenge. His body would inevitably lead the police to her.

Perhaps, after all, Miriam had had nothing to do with the murder, but knowing why Cleo had stolen the medicines, and owing her a debt of gratitude for her past kindness, she could not earn her own release at the cost of Cleo's implication. That would explain her silence. The debt was too great.

Monk found himself increasing his pace, dodging between pedestrians out strolling in the warm midmorning; peddlers offering sandwiches, toffee apples and peppermint drinks; and traders haggling over a good bargain. He barely saw them. The noise muted into an indistinguishable buzz. He wanted to get this over with.

He walked up the hospital steps and in at the wide, front entrance. Almost immediately he was greeted by a young man in a waistcoat and rolled-up shirtsleeves stained with blood.

"Good morning, sir!" he said briskly. "Is it a physician or a surgeon you require? What can we do for you, sir?"

Monk felt a wave of panic and quashed it with a violent effort. Thank God he had need of neither. The stoicism of those

166

whose pain brought them here earned his overwhelming admiration.

"I am in good health, thank you," he said quickly. "I should like to see Lady Callandra Daviot, if she is here."

"I beg your pardon?" The young man looked nonplussed. It had obviously never occurred to him that anyone should wish to see a woman, any woman, rather than a qualified medical man.

"I should like to see Lady Callandra Daviot," Monk repeated very distinctly. "Or, if she is not here, then Mrs. Monk. Where may I wait?" He hated the place. The gray corridors smelled of vinegar and lye and reminded him of other hospitals, the one where he had awoken after the accident, not knowing who he was. The panic of that had long since receded, but it was too easily imagined again.

"Oh, try that way." The young man waved airily in the general direction of the physicians' waiting room, then turned on his heel and continued the way he had been going.

Monk went to the waiting room, where half a dozen people sat around, tense with apprehension, too ill or too anxious to speak to one another. Mercifully, Callandra appeared after only a few moments.

"William! What are you doing here? I presume you wish to see Hester? I am afraid she is out. She has gone"—she hesitated—"to see a patient."

"Old and ill and poor, I imagine," he replied dryly.

She knew him too well. She caught the edge of deeper meaning in his voice. "What is it, William?" she demanded. Although he had naturally risen to his feet, and he was some eight inches taller than she, she still managed to make him feel as if he should respond promptly and truthfully.

"I believe you have been missing certain medicines from the apothecary's rooms." It was a statement.

"Hester never called you in on the matter?" She was amazed and openly disbelieving.

"No, of course not. Why? Have you solved the problem?"

"I don't think you need to concern yourself with it," she answered severely. "At least certainly not yet."

"Why? Because it is a nurse who has taken them?" That was only half intended to be a challenge, but it sounded like one.

"We do not know who it is," she replied. "And since you agree that Hester did not ask you to investigate for us, why are we discussing the matter? You can have no interest in it."

"You are wrong. Unfortunately, I do have." His voice dipped, the previous moment's confrontation suddenly changed to sorrow. "I wish I could leave it alone. It is not the fact that you are missing them that concerns me, it is the chance that whoever took them may have been blackmailed over the thefts, even though I believe she put them to the best possible use."

"Blackmail!" Callandra stared at him in dismay.

"Yes . . . and murder. I'm sorry."

She said nothing, but the gravity in her face showed her fear, and he felt that it also betrayed her guess as to what else lay beyond the thefts, to the steady draining away of supplies over months, perhaps years, to help those she perceived to be in need. It was a judgment no individual had the right to make, and yet if no one did, who would care and who would break the rules in order to show that they should be changed?

"Do you know who it is?" he asked.

She looked him straight in the eye. "I have not the slightest idea," she replied. They both understood it was a lie and that she would not change it. He did not really expect her to, nor would he have been pleased if she had.

"And neither has Hester!" she added firmly.

"No . . . I thought not," he conceded with the ghost of a smile. "But you can give me an estimate as to how much and of which sorts."

She hesitated.

"Surely you would prefer to do that yourself than for me to have to ask someone else?" he said without blinking.

She realized it was a threat, very barely disguised. He would carry it through no matter how much he would dislike it.

"Yes," she capitulated. "Come with me and I will give you a list. It is only a guess, of course."

"Of course," he agreed.

Monk worked the rest of that day, and most of the following one, first with Callandra's list of medicines, then seeing whom Cleo Anderson had visited and what illnesses afflicted them. He did not have to ask many questions among the sick and the poor. They were only too happy to speak well of a woman who seemed to have endless time and patience to care for their needs, and who so often brought them medicines the doctor had sent. No one questioned it or doubted where she had obtained the quinine, the morphine, or the other powders and infusions she brought. They were simply grateful.

The more he learned, the more Monk hated what he was doing. Time and again he stopped short of asking the final question which could have produced proof. He wrote nothing down. He had nothing witnessed and took no evidence of anything with him.

On the afternoon of the second day he turned his attention to Cleo Anderson herself, her home, her expenses, what she purchased and where. It had never occurred to him that she might ask any return for either the care she gave or the medicines she provided. Even so, he was startled to find how very frugal her life was, even more so than he would have expected from her nurse's wages. Her clothes were worn thin and washed of almost all color. They fitted poorly and presumably had been given to her by grateful relatives of a patient who had died. Her food was of the simplest—again, often provided in the homes of those she visited: bread,

169

oatmeal porridge, a little cheese and pickle. It seemed she frequently ate at the hospital and appeared glad of it.

The house was her own, a legacy from better times, but falling into disrepair and badly in need of reroofing.

No one knew her to drink or to gamble.

So where did her money go?

Monk had no doubt it went into the pocket of James Treadwell, at least so long as he had been alive. Since his death just two weeks before, Cleo Anderson had purchased a secondhand kitchen table and a new jug and bowl and two more towels, something she had not been known to do in several years.

Monk was in the street outside her house a little before half past four when he saw Michael Robb coming towards him, walking slowly as if he was tired and his feet were sore. He was obviously hot, and he looked deeply depressed. He stopped in front of Monk. "Were you going to tell me?" he asked.

There was no need for explanation. Monk did not know whether he would have told him or not, but he was quite certain he hated the fact that Robb knew. Perhaps it was inevitable, and when he had wrestled with it and grieved over it he would have told him, but he was not ready to do that yet.

"I have no proof of anything," he answered. That was uncharacteristically vague for him. Usually he faced a truth honestly, however bitter. This hurt more than he had foreseen.

"I have," Robb said wearily. "Enough to arrest her. Please don't stand in my way. At least we will release Miriam Gardiner. You can tell Mr. Stourbridge. He'll be relieved . . . not that he ever thought her guilty."

"Yes . . ." Monk knew Lucius would be happy, but it would be short-lived, because Miriam had chosen to face trial herself rather than implicate Cleo Anderson. Her grief would be deep, and probably abiding.

170

The police believed Miriam was a material witness to the crime who had not offered them the truth, even when pressed. She was a woman apparently not guilty of murder but quite plainly in a state close to hysteria, and not fit to be released except into the care of some responsible person who would look after her and also be certain that she was present to appear in court on the witness stand as the law demanded. Lucius and his father were the obvious and willing candidates.

It was passionately against her will. She stood white-faced in the police station, turning from Robb to Monk.

"Please, Mr. Monk, I will give any undertaking you like, pledge anything at all, but do not oblige me to go back to Cleveland Square! I will gladly work in the hospital day and night, if you will allow me to live there."

The police station superintendent looked at her gravely, then at Robb.

"I think . . ." Robb began.

But the superintendent did not wish to hear his opinion. "You are obviously distressed," he said to Miriam, speaking slowly and very clearly. "Mr. Stourbridge is to be your husband. He is the best one to see that you are given the appropriate care and to offer you comfort for the grief you naturally feel upon the arrest of a woman who showed you kindness in the past. You have suffered a great shock. You must rest quietly and restore your strength."

Miriam swung around to gaze at Monk. Her eyes were wild, as if she longed to say something to him but the presence of others prevented her.

He could think of no excuse to speak to her alone. Major Stourbridge and Lucius were just beyond the door waiting to take her back to Cleveland Square. There was a constable on one side of her and the desk sergeant on the other. Their intention was to support her in case she felt faint, but in effect they closed her in as if she were under restraint.

There was nothing he could do. Helplessly, he watched her escorted from the room. The door opened and Lucius Stourbridge stepped forward, his face filled with tenderness and joy. Behind him Harry Stourbridge smiled as if the end of a long nightmare was in sight.

Miriam tripped, staggered forward and had to be all but carried by the constable and the sergeant. She flinched as Lucius touched her.

7

HESTER WAS HOME before Monk, and was looking forward to his coming, but when he came in through the door and she saw his face, she knew instantly that something was very seriously wrong. He looked exhausted. His skin was pale and his dark hair limp and stuck to his brow in the heat.

Alarm welled up inside her. "What is it?" she demanded urgently.

He stood in the middle of the floor. He lifted his hand and touched her cheek very lightly. "I know what it is you couldn't tell me . . . and why. I'm sorry I had to pursue it."

She swallowed. "It?"

"The stolen medicines," he answered. "Who took them and why, and where did they go? It's a far more obvious cause for blackmail."

She tried not to understand, pushing the realization away from her. "The medicines couldn't have anything to do with Miriam Gardiner."

"Not directly, but one leads to the other." His eyes did not waver, and she knew that he was quite certain of what he said.

"What? What connection?" she asked. "What's happened?" There was no purpose in suggesting he sit down or rest in any fashion until he had told her, and neither of them pretended.

"Cleo Anderson stole the medicines to treat the old and the sick," he answered her softly. "Somehow Treadwell knew of it, and he was blackmailing her. Perhaps he followed Miriam.

173

Maybe she unintentionally let something slip, and he pieced together the rest."

"Cleo's involved? Do you know that?" She was confused, her mind whirling. "If Treadwell was blackmailing Cleo Anderson, then why would Miriam kill him? To protect her? It doesn't explain why she left Cleveland Square. What about Lucius Stourbridge? Why didn't she go back to him and explain? Something . . ." She trailed off. None of it really made sense.

"Miriam didn't kill Treadwell," he told her. "The police let her go. She was defending Cleo because of old loyalties, and probably because she believed in her cause as well."

"That isn't enough," she protested. "Why did she leave Cleveland Square in the middle of the party? Why wouldn't she allow Lucius to know where she was?"

"I don't know," he admitted. "She was released into his care, and she looked as if she were going to an execution. She begged not to be, but they wouldn't listen to her." A frown creased his face and there was pain etched more deeply than the weariness. "For a moment I thought she was going to ask me to help her, but then she changed her mind. They all but carried her out."

She heard the edge of pity in his voice. She felt it herself, and she was angered that the police authorities should consider that Miriam needed to be released into anybody's care. She should have been permitted the dignity of going wherever she wished, and with whomever. She was no longer charged with anything.

But far more immediate, and closer to her own emotions, was her concern for Cleo Anderson.

"What are we to do to help her?" She took for granted that he would.

Monk was still standing in the middle of the room, hot, tired, dusty and with aching feet. Remarkably, he kept his temper.

"Nothing. It is a private matter between them now."

"I mean Cleo!" she said. "Miriam has other people to care for her. Anyway, she is not accused of a crime."

"Yes, she is: complicity in concealing Treadwell's murder. Even though she says she did not know he was dead. She is almost certainly a witness to the attack. The police want her to testify."

She waved her hand impatiently. She did not know Miriam Gardiner, but she did know Cleo and what she had done for old John Robb and others like him.

"So she'll have to testify. It won't be pleasant, but she'll survive it. If she's worth anything at all, her first concern will be for Cleo, and ours must be, too. What can we do? Where should we begin?"

His face tightened. "There's nothing we can do," he replied briefly, moving away from her and sitting down in one of the chairs. The way his body sank, the sudden release at the last moment, betrayed his utter weariness. "I found Miriam Gardiner, and she is returned to her fiancé. I wish it were not Cleo Anderson who is guilty, but it is. The best I could do was stop short of finding any proof of it, but Robb will. He's a good policeman. And his father's involved." He was angry with himself for his emotions, and it showed in his face and the sharp edge to his voice.

She stood in the center of the floor, cool and fresh in a printed cotton dress with wide skirts and a small, white collar. It was pretty, and it all seemed terribly irrelevant. It was almost a sin to be comfortable and so happy when Cleo Anderson was in prison and facing . . . the long drop into darkness at the end of a rope.

"There must be something. . . ." She knew she should not argue with him, especially now, when he was exhausted and probably very nearly as distressed about this as she was. But her self-control did not extend to sitting patiently and waiting until a better time. "I don't know what . . . but if we look . . . Maybe he threatened her. Perhaps there was some degree of self-defense." She cast about wildly for a better thought.

"Maybe he tried to coerce her into committing some sort of crime. That could be justified. . . ."

"So she committed murder instead?" he said sarcastically.

She blushed hotly. She wanted to swear at him, use some of the language she had heard in the barracks in Sebastopol, but it would be profoundly unladylike. She would despise herself afterwards, and more important, he would never look at her in the same way again. He would hear her words in his ears every time he looked at her face. Even in moments of tenderness, when she most fiercely desired his respect, the ugliness would intrude.

"All right, it wasn't a very good idea," she conceded. "But it isn't the only one!"

He looked up at her in some surprise, not for her words in themselves but for the meekness of them.

She knew what was in his mind, and blushed the more hotly. This was ridiculous and most irritating.

"I wish I could help her," he said gently. "But I know of no way, and neither do you. Leave it alone, Hester. Don't meddle."

She regarded him steadily, trying to judge how surely he meant what he said. Was it advice or a command?

There was no anger in his face, but neither was there any hint that he would change his mind. It was the first time he had forbidden her anything that mattered to her. She had never before found it other than slightly amusing that he should exercise a certain amount of authority, and she had been quite willing to indulge him. This was different. She could not abandon Cleo, even to please Monk. Or if it came to the worst, and it might, even to avoid a serious quarrel with him. To do so would make it impossible to live with herself. All happiness would be contaminated, and if for her, then for him also. How would she explain that to him? It was the first real difficulty between them, the first gulf which could not be bridged by laughter or a physical closeness.

She saw the shadow in his face. He understood, if not in detail, then at least in essence.

176

"Perhaps you could enquire," he suggested cautiously. "But you will have to be extremely careful or you will make things worse. I don't imagine the hospital authorities will look on her kindly."

It was retreat, made gracefully and so discreetly it was barely perceptible, but very definitely a retreat all the same. The rush of gratitude inside her was so fierce she felt dizzy. A darkness had been avoided. She wanted to throw her arms around him and hold him, feel the warmth and the strength of his body next to hers, the touch of his skin. She almost did, until intelligence warned her that it would be clumsy. It would draw attention to his retreat and that would be small gratitude for it. Instead she lowered her eyes.

"Oh, yes," she said gravely. "I shall have to be very careful indeed—should I make any enquiry. Actually, at the moment I can't think of anything to ask. I shall merely listen and observe . . . for the time being."

He smiled with the beginning of satisfaction. He was aware of her gratitude to him, and she knew he was. It was even a sense of obligation for the immense weight lifted, and he knew that also. She could either be annoyed or see the funny aspect of it. She chose the latter, and looked at him, smiling.

He smiled back, but only for a moment. It was still delicate ground.

She prepared dinner: cold ham and vegetables, and hot apple pie with cream. Sitting at the table and sharing it with considerable pleasure, she asked him a little more about Miriam and the Stourbridge family.

He obviously considered hard before answering, and waited several minutes, eating the last of his pie and accepting a second serving.

"All the facts I know seem to mean nothing," he said at last. "They have made Miriam more welcome than one might have foreseen, considering that she has no money or family connections and she is to marry their only son. Everything I can observe supports their assertion that they are fond of her

177

and accept that she is the one woman who can make him happy. Whether she will give him an heir or not. But she is young enough."

"But she did not have any children in her marriage to Mr. Gardiner," Hester pointed out. "That would make the possibility less likely."

"I am sure they have considered that." He took more cream, pouring it liberally over the pie and eating with unconcealed pleasure.

She watched with relief. She was still an unconfident pastry cook, and she had had no time even to look for a woman to come in during the days. It was something she really must attend to, and soon. A well-ordered domestic life was halfway not only to Monk's happiness but to her own. She did not wish to have to spend either time or emotional energy upon the details of living. She would make enquiries tomorrow—unless, of course, she was too busy with matters at the hospital and with whatever might be done for Cleo Anderson. That was immeasurably more important, even if they ate sandwiches from a peddler!

"Cleo Anderson!" Callandra said. "Are you sure?" It was a protest against the truth rather than a real question. Hester was alone with Dr. Beck and Callandra for a few moments in the surgeons' waiting room.

Kristian stood a yard away from Callandra, but any careful observer would have seen the silent communication between them. There was never a meeting of eyes—almost the opposite, an awareness on a deeper level.

"I had no idea," he said softly. "What risks she was taking . . . all the time. How long have you known?" He was looking at Hester.

"I don't really know." She was still being overcareful, as if Sergeant Robb were just beyond the door. "At least . . . not with evidence."

"Of course not," Kristian said, twisting his lips a little. "No one wishes to find evidence. You were quite right not to tell anyone of it. Poor woman." His hands clenched more tightly by his sides. "It is profoundly wrong that any person should have to take such risks to assist the poor and the sick."

"It's monstrous!" Callandra agreed without looking at him. "But we must help. There has to be a way. What does William say?"

Hester had no intention of repeating the conversation, merely the conclusion, and that slightly altered. "That we should be extremely careful in making any enquiries," she replied.

"More than careful," Kristian agreed. "Thorpe would be delighted to brand all nurses as thieves—"

"He will do!" Callandra cut across him, her face pinched with unhappiness. "He'll know soon enough. No doubt the police will be here to ask questions."

"Is there anything we can conceal?" Hester looked from one to the other of them. She had no idea what good it would do, it was instinctive rather than rational. If they convicted Cleo Anderson of murdering Treadwell, a bottle or two of morphine one way or another was hardly going to make a difference. She knew the moment the words were out that it was foolish.

"What proof do they have that it was she?" Kristian asked more levelly. The first shock was wearing off. "Possibly he was blackmailing her, but then he may have blackmailed others as well. She was hardly on an income to provide him with much."

"Unless she gave him morphine," Callandra said with quiet sadness. "And he sold it. That would be worth a great deal more."

Hester had not even thought of that. She did not believe Cleo would sell morphine herself, but she could understand the necessity if Treadwell had been pressing her for money. But what had made the difference that suddenly, on that particular night, that she had resorted to murder? Desperation . . . or simply opportunity?

Why was she accepting Cleo's guilt, even in her own mind?

"But what evidence?" Kristian repeated. "Did anyone see her? Did she leave anything behind at the scene? Is there anything which excludes another person?"

"No . . . simply that his body was found on the path near her house, and he had crawled there from wherever he was attacked." Hester could see the reasoning all too clearly. "It was assumed at first that he had been trying to get help. Now they will be thinking it was no coincidence, but he was deliberately pointing towards her."

Kristian frowned. "You mean they met somewhere close by, she attacked him, left believing him dead, but, still conscious, he crawled after her?"

Callandra's face pulled tight with distress.

"Why not?" Hester loathed saying it, but it was there in the air between them. "He came to blackmail her, and she had reached the point of desperation—perhaps she had nothing more to pay him—and either she intended it before she went to kill him, or it happened on the spur of the moment."

"And where was Miriam?" Callandra asked. Then her expression quickened. "Or did he drop Miriam wherever she wished to be and go back to Cleo Anderson? That would explain why Miriam did not know he was dead."

Hester shook her head. "Whatever the answer is, it does not help Cleo now."

They looked at each other grimly, and none could think of anything hopeful to say.

Matters only seemed worse when, an hour or so later, Hester and Callandra were summoned to the office of an extremely angry Fermin Thorpe and were ordered by him to assist Sergeant Robb in his enquiries.

Robb stood uncomfortably to the side of Thorpe's desk, looking first at Thorpe himself, then at Callandra, lastly and unhappily at Hester.

"I'm sorry, ma'am." He seemed to be addressing both of them. "I'd rather not have had to place you in this position, but I need to know more about the medicines Mr. Thorpe here says are missing from your apothecary's room."

"I didn't know about it until this morning," Thorpe said furiously, his face pink. "It should have been reported to me at the very first instance. Somebody will answer for this!"

"I think first we had better see precisely what is provable, Mr. Thorpe," Callandra said coldly. "It does not do to cast accusations around freely before one is certain of the facts. It is too easy to ruin a reputation, and too difficult to mend it again when one discovers mistakes have been made." She stared at him defiantly, daring him to contradict her.

Thorpe was very conscious of his position as a governor of the hospital and of his innate general superiority. However, he also had an acute social awareness, and Callandra had a title, albeit a courtesy one because of her late father's position. He decided upon caution, at least for the meantime.

"Of course, Lady Callandra. We do not yet know the entire situation." He looked sideways at Robb. "I assure you, Sergeant, I shall do all within my power to be of assistance. We must get the facts of the matter and put an end to all dishonesty. I shall assist you myself."

It was what Hester had feared. It would be so much easier to make light of the losses, even to mislead Robb a little, if Thorpe were not there. She had no idea what the apothecary would do, where his loyalties lay, or how frightened he would be for his own position.

Thorpe hesitated, and Hester realized with a lurch of hope that he did not know enough about the medicines to conduct the search and inventory without assistance.

"Perhaps one of us might fetch Mr. Phillips?" she offered. "And perhaps come with you to make notes . . . for our own needs. After all, we shall have to attend to the matter and see that it does not happen again. We need to know the truth of it even more than Sergeant Robb does."

Thorpe grasped the rescue. "Indeed, Mrs. Monk." Suddenly he found he could remember her name without the usual difficulty.

She smiled at it, but did not remark. Before he could change his mind, she glanced at Callandra, then led the way out of the office and along the wide corridor towards the apothecary's room. She knew Callandra would fetch Mr. Phillips, and possibly even have a discreet word with him as to the effects upon all of them of whatever he might say. Presumably, he would not yet know of the charge against Cleo Anderson, far less the motive attributed to her.

She did not dare look at Sergeant Robb. He might too easily guess Callandra's intention. It was not a great leap of foresight.

They walked briskly, one behind the other, and she stopped at the apothecary's door. Naturally, Thorpe had a key, as he had to all doors. He opened the door and stepped in, and they followed behind, crowding into the small space. It was lined with cupboards right up to the ceiling. Each had its brass-bound keyhole, even the drawers beneath the shelf.

"I am afraid I do not have keys to these," Thorpe said reluctantly. "But as you may see, it is all kept with the utmost safety. I do not know what more we can do, except employ a second apothecary so that there is someone on duty at every moment. Obviously, we may require medicines at night as well as during the day, and no one man can be available around the clock, however diligent."

"Who has keys at night now?" Robb asked.

"When Mr. Phillips leaves he passes them to me," Thorpe replied with discomfort, "and I give them to the senior doctor who will remain here at night."

"From your wording I assume that is not always the same person," Robb concluded.

"No. We do not operate during the night. Seldom does one of the surgeons remain. Dr. Beck does, on occasion, if he has a particularly severe case. More often it will be a student doctor." He seemed about to add something, then changed his mind. Perhaps he felt the whole hospital under accusation because one of its nurses had been given the opportunity to

182

steal, which had resulted in murder. He would have liked to distance himself from it, and it was plain in his expression.

"Who gives the medicine during the night?" Robb asked.

Thorpe was further discomfited. "The doctor on duty."

"Not a nurse?" Robb looked surprised.

"Nurses are to keep patients clean and comfortable," Thorpe said a trifle sharply. "They do not have medical training or experience, and are not given responsibilities except to do exactly as they are told." He did not look at Hester.

Robb digested that information thoughtfully and without comment. Before he could formulate any further questions the apothecary entered, closely followed by Callandra, who avoided Hester's eye.

"Ah!" Thorpe said with relief. "Phillips. Sergeant Robb here believes that a considerable amount of medicine has gone missing from our supplies, stolen by one of our nurses, and that this fact has provided the motive and means for her to be blackmailed." He cleared his throat. "We need to ascertain if this is true, and if it is, precisely what amounts are involved, how it was taken, and by whom." He had effectively laid the fault, if not the responsibility, at Phillips's door.

Phillips did not answer immediately. He was a large man, rather overweight, with wild dark hair and a beard severely in need of trimming. Hester had always found him to be most agreeable and to have a pleasing, if somewhat waspish, sense of humor. She hoped he was not going to get the blame for this, and she would be painfully disappointed in him if it were too easy to pass it onto Cleo.

"Have you nothing to say, man?" Thorpe demanded impatiently.

"Not without thinking about it carefully," Phillips replied. "Sir," he added, "if there's medicine really missing, rather than just wastage or a miscount, or somebody's error in writing what they took, then it's a serious matter."

"Of course, it's a serious matter!" Thorpe snapped. "There's blackmail and murder involved."

"Murder?" Phillips said with a slight lift of surprise in his voice, but only slight. "Over our medicines? There's been no theft that size. I know that for sure."

"Over a period of time," Thorpe corrected him. "Or so the sergeant thinks."

Phillips fished for his keys and brought out a large collection on a ring. First he opened one of the drawers and pulled out a ledger. "How far back, sir?" he asked Robb politely.

"I don't know," Robb replied. "Try a year or so. That should be sufficient."

"Don't rightly know how I can tell." Phillips obligingly opened the ledger to the same month the previous year. He scanned the page and the following one. "Everything tallies here, an' there's no way we can know if it was what we had then in the cupboards. Doesn't look like anyone's altered it. Anyway, I'd know if they had, and I'd have told Mr. Thorpe."

Thorpe stepped closer and turned the pages of the ledger himself, examining from that date to the present. There were quite obviously no alterations made to the entries. It told them nothing. The checking in of medicines was all made in the one hand, the withdrawals in several different hands of varying degrees of elegance and literacy. There were a few misspellings.

Robb looked at them. "Are these all doctors?" he asked.

"Of course," Thorpe replied tartly. "You don't imagine we give the keys to the nurses, do you? If the wretched woman has really stolen medicines from this hospital, then it will be sleight of hand while the doctor's back was turned, perhaps attending to a patient taken suddenly ill, or while he was otherwise distracted. It is a perfectly dastardly thing to do. I trust she will be punished to the fullest extent of the law as a deterrent to any other person tempted to enrich herself at the expense of those in her care!"

"Could just be wastage," Phillips observed, his eyes wide, looking from Thorpe to Robb. "Not easy to measure powders exact. Close enough, o' course, but over a couple o' dozen doses yer could be out a bit. Ever considered that, sir?"

"You couldn't blackmail anybody over that," Robb replied,

but his expression indicated that he said it with reluctance. "There must be more. If there is nothing in the past that is provable now, would you check your present stocks exactly against what is in your books?"

"Of course." Phillips had very little choice, nor for that matter, had Robb.

They stood silently while Phillips went through his cupboards, weighing, measuring and counting, watched impatiently by Thorpe, anxiously by Callandra, and with unease by Robb.

Hester wondered if Robb had even a suspicion that his grandfather's suffering had been treated by this very means, with medicine stolen not for gain but out of compassion by Cleo Anderson, whom he now sought to prove guilty of murdering Treadwell. She looked at his earnest face and saw pity in it, but no doubt, no tearing of loyalties . . . not yet.

Was Cleo guilty? If Treadwell was a blackmailer, was it possible she had believed him the lesser victim, rather than the patients she treated?

It was hard to believe, but it was not impossible.

"The quinine seems a bit short," Phillips remarked as if it were of no great moment. "Could be bad measuring, I suppose. Or someone took a few doses in a crisis an' forgot to make a note of it."

"How far short?" Thorpe demanded, his face dark. "Damn it, man, you can be more exact than that! What do you mean, 'a bit'? You're an apothecary. You don't dose a patient with 'a bit.' "

"About five hundred grains, sir," Phillips answered very quietly.

Thorpe flushed deep pink. "Good God! That's enough to dose a dozen men. This is very serious indeed. You'd better see what else is missing. Look at the morphine."

Phillips obeyed. That measurement was even farther short. Hester was not surprised. It was the obvious treatment for pain, as quinine was for fever. Cleo must have administered it, under supervision, often enough over the years to have an excellent idea of how much to give and in what circumstances. Certainly, Hester herself did.

Thorpe turned to Robb. "I regret, Sergeant, but it seems you are perfectly correct. We are missing a substantial amount of medicine, and it is impossible any random thief could have taken it. It has to be one of our nurses."

Hester drew breath to point out that it had only to be someone within the hospital staff over the last few years, but she knew that would be pointless. Thorpe would not entertain the idea of any of the doctors doing such a thing, and she had no desire to try to shift the blame onto Phillips.

Perhaps it had been Cleo Anderson . . . in fact, if Hester was honest, she had no doubt. It was the reason for it they had misunderstood, and she did not wish to draw their attention to that because it would make no difference whatever to the charge.

With Cleo in prison, who would now care for the old and ill she had visited with medicines to give them respite from distress? Specifically, what of John Robb?

Callandra handed Sergeant Robb the note she had made of the missing medicines and the amounts. He took it and put it in his pocket, thanking her. He looked at Phillips again.

"Over what period has this been missed, Mr. Phillips?"

"Can't say, sir," Phillips replied instantly. "Haven't had occasion to check in that detail for some time. Could have been careless measuring. Perhaps even someone spilled something." His black eyes were bland, his voice reasonable. "More likely careless noting down of what was given out proper, but in the heat of a bad night or something of a crisis. Got to make an allowance. Medicine is an art, Mr. Thorpe, not an exact science."

"God damn it, man!" Thorpe exploded. "Don't tell me how to conduct the practice of medicine in my own hospital."

Phillips did not reply, nor did he seem particularly disturbed by Thorpe's anger, which had the effect of both heightening it and confusing Thorpe into momentary silence. He had not expected an apothecary to be indifferent to him.

186

Phillips turned to Robb. "If there is anything else I can do for you, Sergeant, I'm sure Mr. Thorpe would want me to. Just tell me. And before you ask, I've got no suspicions of any o' the nurses . . . not in that way. Some o' them drink a spot too much porter on an empty stomach. But then I daresay half o' London does that from time to time. 'Specially as porter is included in the wages, like. You'll find me 'round an' about most any day except Sunday." And without asking anything further he handed the keys to Thorpe and went out.

"Impertinent oaf," Thorpe swore under his breath.

"But honest?" Robb asked.

Hester saw the abhorrence in Thorpe's face. He would dearly like to have paid Phillips back for his arrogance, and here was an ideal opportunity given him. On the other hand, to admit he had employed an apothecary of whom he had doubts would be a confession of his own gross incompetence.

But just in case temptation should prove too powerful, Hester answered for him.

"Of course, Sergeant," she said with a smile. "Do you imagine Mr. Thorpe would have permitted him to remain in such a responsible position if he were not trustworthy in every way? If a nurse is a little tipsy it is one thing. She may spill a pail of water or leave a floor unswept. If an apothecary is not above reproach people may die."

"Quite," Thorpe agreed hastily with a venomous look at Hester, then, with a considerable effort to alter his expression, he turned to Robb. "Please question anyone you wish to. I doubt you will find any proof that this wretched woman stole the quinine and morphine. If there were any, we should know of it ourselves. I presume you have her in custody?"

"Yes sir, we have. Thank you, sir." Robb bade them good-day and left.

Hester glanced at Callandra, then excused herself also. She had other matters to attend to, and urgently.

Hester had no difficulty in obtaining permission to visit Cleo Anderson in her cell. She simply told the jailer that she was an official from the hospital where Cleo worked and it was necessary to learn certain medical information from her in order for treatments to continue in her absence.

It transpired that the jailer knew Cleo—she had nursed his mother in her final illness—and he was only too pleased to repay the kindness in any way he could. Indeed, he seemed embarrassed by the situation, and Hester could not guess from his manner whether he thought Cleo could be guilty or not. However, word had spread that the charge was that she had killed a blackmailer, and he had a very low regard for such people, possibly sufficiently low that he was not overly concerned by the death of one of them.

The cell door shut with the heavy, echoing sound of metal on metal, sending a shiver of memory through Hester, bringing back her own few hideous days in Edinburgh, when she was where Cleo sat now, alone and facing trial, and perhaps death.

Cleo looked at her in surprise. Her face was pale, and she had the bruised, staring look of someone deeply shocked, but she seemed composed, even resigned. Hester could not recall if she had felt like that. She believed she had always wanted to fight, that inside herself she was screaming out against the injustice. There was too much to live for not to struggle, always far too much.

But then she had not killed Mary Farraline.

Even if Cleo had killed Treadwell because he had been blackmailing her over the medicines, it was a highly understandable action. Not excusable, perhaps, but surely any God worth worshiping would find more pity than blame for her?

Maybe she did not believe that? At least not now . . . at this moment, facing human justice.

"Can I help you?" Hester said aloud. "Is there anything I can bring for you? Clothes, soap, a clean towel, rather better food? What about your own spoon? Or cup?"

Cleo smiled faintly. The very practicality of the suggestions contrasted with what she had expected. She had anticipated anger, blame, pity, curiosity. She looked puzzled.

"I've been in prison," Hester explained. "I hated the soap and the scratchy towels. It's a little thing. And I wanted my own spoon. I remember that."

"But they let you go. . . ." Cleo looked at her with anxiety so sharp it was close to breaking her composure. "And they let Miriam go? Is she all right?"

Hester sat in the chair, leaning forward a little. She liked Cleo more with each encounter. She could not watch her distress with any impartiality at all, or think of her fate with acceptance. "Yes, they let her go."

"Home?" She was watching Hester intently.

"No . . . with Lucius and Major Stourbridge." She searched Cleo's face for anything that would help her understand why Miriam had dreaded it. She saw nothing, no flicker of comprehension, however swiftly concealed.

"Was she all right?" Cleo said fearfully.

It seemed cruel to tell her the truth, but Hester did not know enough to judge which lies would do least harm.

"No," she answered. "I don't think so. Not from what my husband said. She would far rather have gone anywhere else at all—even remained in prison—but she was not given the choice. The police could not hold her because there was no charge anymore, but it was obvious to everyone that she was deeply distressed, and since she is a witness to much of what happened, they have a certain authority over where she should go."

Cleo said nothing. She stared down at her hands, folded in her lap.

Hester watched her closely. "Do you know why she ran away from Cleveland Square and why she had to be all but dragged back there?"

Cleo looked up quickly. "No—no, I don't. She wouldn't tell me."

Hester believed her. The confusion and distress in her eyes were too real. "Don't answer me whether you took the medicines or not," she said quietly. "I know you did, and I know what for."

189

Cleo regarded her thoughtfully for several moments before she spoke. "What's going to happen to them, miss? There's nobody to look after them. The ones with family are better off than those who haven't, but even they can't afford what they need, or they don't know what it is. They get old, and their children move on, leaving them behind. The young don't care about Trafalgar an' Waterloo now. A few years an' they'll forget the Crimea, too. Those soldiers are all the thing now, because they're young and handsome still. We get upset about a young man with no arms or no legs, or insides all to pieces. But when they get old we can't be bothered. We say they're going to die soon anyway. Wot's the point in spending time and money on them?"

There was no argument to make. Of course, it was not true everywhere, but in too many instances it was.

"What about John Robb, sailor from the victory at Trafalgar?" Hester asked. "Consumption, by the sound of him."

Cleo's face tightened, and she nodded. "I don't think he has long. His grandson does everything he can for him, but that isn't much. He can't give him any ease without the morphine." She did not ask, but it was in her eyes, willing Hester to agree.

Hester knew what that would involve. She would have to give him the morphine herself. It would involve her in the theft. But to refuse would compound the old man's suffering and his sense of being abandoned. When he understood, he would also know that his suffering was of less importance to her than keeping herself from risk. Alleviating pain was all right, as long as the cost was small—a little time, even weariness, but not personal danger.

"Yes, of course." The words were out of her mouth before she had time to weigh what she was committing herself to do.

"Thank you," Cleo said softly, a momentary gleam in her eyes, as if she had seen a light in enclosing darkness. "And I would like the soap, and the spoon, if it is not too much trouble."

"Of course." Hester brushed them aside as already done.

190

What she really wanted was to help with some defense, but what was there? She realized with bitterness that she was half convinced that Cleo had killed Treadwell. "Have you got a lawyer to speak for you?"

"A lawyer? What can he say? It won't make no difference." The tone of her voice was flat, as if she had suddenly been jerked back to the harshness of the present and her own reality, not John Robb's. There was a closed air about her, excluding Hester from her emotions till she felt rebuffed, an intruder. Was Cleo still somehow defending Miriam Gardiner? Or was she guilty, and believed she deserved to die?

"Did you kill Treadwell?" Hester said abruptly.

Cleo hesitated, was about to speak, then changed her mind and said nothing. Hester had the powerful impression that she had been going to deny it, but she would never know, and asking again would be useless. The mask was complete.

"Was he blackmailing you?" she asked instead.

Cleo sighed. "Yeah, 'course he was. Do most things for money, that one."

"I see." There did not seem much else to say. She had resolved without question or doubt that she would do all she could to help Cleo, it was a matter of thinking what that would be. Already, Oliver Rathbone's name was in her mind.

Cleo grasped her wrist, holding hard, startling her. "Don't tell the sergeant!" she said fiercely. "It can't change what he does, and . . ."—she blinked, her face bruised with hurt—"and don't tell old Mr. Robb why I'm not there. Tell him something else . . . anything. Perhaps by the time they try me, and . . . well, he may not have to know. He could be gone hisself by then."

"I'll tell him something else," Hester promised. "Probably that you've gone to look after a relative or something."

"Thank you." Cleo's gratitude was so naked, Hester felt guilty. She was on the edge of saying that she intended to do far more, but she had no idea what it could be, and to raise hope she could not fulfill was thoughtlessly cruel.

"I'll come back with the soap," she promised. "And the

191

spoon." Then she went to the door and banged for the jailer to let her out.

The next thing she did she expected to be the most difficult, and it was certainly the one of which she was most afraid. She felt guilty even as she walked up the steps and in through the hospital door. She returned the stare of two young medical students too directly, as if to deny their suspicion of her. Then she felt ridiculous, and was sure she was blushing. She had done nothing yet. She was no different from the person she had been yesterday or this morning, when she had been perfectly happy to confront Fermin Thorpe in his office and rack her brain to defend Cleo Anderson. Would Callandra in turn have to rack her brain tomorrow to defend her?

And yet she could not escape it. Quite apart from her fondness for John Robb, she had given Cleo the promise. She had tried to form a plan, but so much depended upon opportunity. It was impractical to try stealing Phillips's keys, and unfair to him. Added to which, he really was extremely careful with them, and might be the more so now.

How long would she have to wait for a crisis of some sort to present a chance, the apothecary's room open and unattended, or Phillips there but his back turned? She was suddenly furious with herself. She had been alone with Cleo and not had the wits to ask her how she had accomplished it. She had just blithely promised to do the same, without the faintest idea how to go about it. It was very humbling to realize her own stupidity.

She stood in the middle of the passage and was still there when Kristian Beck reached her.

"Hester?" he said with concern. "Are you all right?"

She recalled herself swiftly and began speaking with the idea only half formed in her mind. "I was wondering how Cleo Anderson managed to steal the morphine. Phillips is really very careful. I mean, how do you think it happened, in practical detail?"

He frowned. "Does it matter?"

Why did he ask? Was he indifferent to the thefts? Was he so certain Cleo was guilty that the details did not matter? Or was it even conceivable that he had some sympathy with her?

"I don't want to prove it," she answered steadily, meeting his eyes with complete candor. "I would like above all things to disprove it, but failing that, at least to understand."

"She is charged with murdering Treadwell," he said softly. "The jury cannot excuse that, whatever they privately feel. There is no provision or law for murdering blackmailers or for stealing medicine, even if it is to treat the old and ill for whom there is no other help." The lacerating edge in his voice betrayed his own feelings too clearly.

"I know that," she said in little above a whisper. "I should still like to know exactly how she did it."

He stood in silence for several moments.

She waited. Part of her wanted to leave before it was too late. But escaping would be only physical. Morally and emotionally, she was still trapped. And that was trivial compared with Cleo—or John Robb.

"What do you think she took?" Kristian asked at length.

She swallowed. "Morphine, for an old man who has consumption. It won't cure him, but it gives him a little rest."

"Very understandable," he answered. "I hope she gave him some sherry in water as well?"

"I believe so."

"Good. I need a few things from the apothecary myself. I'll go and get the keys. You can help me, if you would." And without waiting for her answer, he turned sharply and strode off.

He came back a few minutes later with the keys and opened the door. He went inside and left her to follow him. He started to unlock various cupboards and take out leaves for infusions, cordials and various powders. He passed several of them to Hester while he opened bottles and jars, then closed them again. When he had finished he ushered her out, relocked the door, took some of the medicines back from her, then thanked her and left her standing in the corridor with a small bottle of cordial and a week's dosage of morphine, plus several small paper screws of quinine.

She put them quickly into her pockets and went back towards the front door and out of it. She felt as if dozens of eyes were boring holes in her back, but actually she passed only one nurse with a mop and bucket, and Fermin Thorpe himself, striding along with his face set, hardly recognizing her.

John Robb was delighted to see her. He had had a bad night but was a trifle better towards late afternoon, and the loneliness of sitting in his chair in the empty house, even with the sun slanting in through the windows, had made him melancholy. His face lit with a smile when he recognized her step, and even before she entered the room he was tidying the little space around him and making ready for her.

"How are you?" he said the moment she came through the door.

"I'm very well," she answered cheerfully. He must never know about Cleo if there was any way it could be prevented.

She could not warn Michael without explaining to him the reason, and that would place him in an impossible situation. He would then have either to benefit indirectly from the thefts, which he would find intolerable, or else have to testify against Cleo from his own knowledge. That would also be unbearable, for the old man's sake as well as his own. Such disillusion and sense of betrayal might be more than his old and frail body could take. And then Michael's guilt would be crippling.

"I'm very well indeed," she said firmly. "How are you? I hope you are well enough to share a cup of tea with me? I brought some you might like to try, and a few biscuits." She smiled back at him. "Of course, it was all an excuse so you will tell me more stories of your life at sea and the places you have been to. You were going to describe the Indies for me. You said how brilliant the water was, like a cascade of jewels, and that you had seen fishes that could fly."

"Oh, bless you, girl, I have an' all," he agreed with a smile.

194

"An' more than that, too. You put the kettle on an' I'll tell you all you want to know."

"Of course." She walked across the room and pulled the biscuits and tea out of the bag they were in, filled the kettle from the jug and set it on the stove, then, with her back to him, took out the cordial bottle and placed it on the shelf, half behind a blue bag of sugar. Then she slipped the morphine out of her other pocket and set it underneath the two thin papers that were left from Cleo's last visit.

"Was it very hot in the Indies?" she asked.

"You wouldn't believe it, girl," he replied. "Felt as if the sea itself were on the boil, all simmerin' an' steamin'. The air were so thick it clogged up in your throat, like you could drink it."

"I think you could drink it here, too, when it gets cold enough!" she said with a laugh.

"Aye! An' I bin north, too!" he said enthusiastically. "Great walls of ice rising out o' the sea. You never seen anything like it, girl. Beautiful an' terrible, they was. An' they'd freeze your breath like a white fog in front of you."

She turned and smiled at him, then began to make the tea. "Mrs. Anderson had to go away for a little while. Someone in her family ill, I think." She scalded the pot, tipped out the water, then put the fresh leaves in and poured the rest of the water from the kettle. "She asked me to come and see you. I think she knew I'd like that. I hope it's all right with you."

He relaxed, looking at her with undisguised pleasure. "Sure it's all right. Then you can tell me some o' the places you've bin. About them Turks an' the like. Although I'll miss Cleo. Good woman, she is. Nothin' ever too much trouble. An' I seen her so tired she were fit to drop. I hope as her family appreciates her."

A lie was the only thing. "I'm sure they will," she said without a shadow in her voice. "And I'll get a message to her that you're fine."

"You do that, girl. An' tell her I was asking after her."

"I will." Suddenly she found it difficult to master herself. It

195

was ridiculous to want to cry now! Nothing had changed. She sniffed hard and blew her nose, then set out the rest of the things for tea and opened the bag of biscuits. She had bought him the best she could find. They looked pretty on the plate. She was determined this should be a party.

She did not broach the subject with Monk until after they had eaten. They were sitting quietly watching the last of the light fade beyond the windows and wondering if it was time to light the gas or if it would be pleasanter just to allow the dusk to fill the room.

Naturally, she had no intention whatever of even mentioning John Robb, let alone telling Monk that she was taking over his care from Cleo. Apart from the way he would react to such information, the knowledge would compromise him. There was no need for both of them to tell lies.

"What can we do to help Cleo Anderson?" she said, taking it for granted that there was no argument as to whether they would.

He lifted his head sharply.

She waited.

"Everything we've done so far has made it worse," he said unhappily. "The best service we can do the poor woman is to leave the case alone."

"If we do that she may well be hanged," Hester argued. "And that would be very wrong. Treadwell was a blackmailer. She is guilty of a crime in law, maybe, but no sin. We have to do something. Humanity requires it."

"I discover facts, Hester," he said quietly. "Everything I've found so far indicates that Cleo killed him. I may sympathize with her—in fact, I do. God knows, in her situation I might have done the same."

She could see memory of the past sharp in his face, and knew what he was thinking. She remembered Joscelin Grey also, and the apartment in Mecklenburgh Square, and how close Monk had come to murder then.

"But that would not excuse me in law," he continued. "Nor

196

would it alter anything the judge or jury could do. If she did kill him, there may be some mitigation, but she will have to say what it is. Then I could look for proof of it, if there is any."

She was hesitant to ask him about Oliver Rathbone. There was too much emotion involved, old friendship, old love, and perhaps pain. She did not know how much. She had not seen Rathbone since her marriage, but she remembered— with a vividness so sharp she could see the candlelight in her mind's eye and smell the warmth of the inn dining room—the night Rathbone had very nearly asked her to marry him. He had stopped only because she had allowed him to know, obliquely, that she could not accept, not yet. And he had let the moment pass.

"It's not only what happened," she began almost tentatively. "It's the interpretation, the argument, if you like."

Monk regarded her gravely before replying. There was no criticism in his face, but an acute sadness. "Some plea of mitigation? Don't you think you are holding out a false hope to her?"

That could be true.

"But we must try . . . mustn't we? We can't just give in without a fight."

"What do you want to do?"

She said what he expected. "We could ask Oliver . . ." She took a breath. "We could at least set it before him, for his opinion?" She made it a question.

She could see no change in his expression, no anger, no stiffening.

"Of course," he agreed. "But don't expect too much."

She smiled. "No . . . just to try."

Hester woke in the dark, feeling the movement as Monk got out of bed. Downstairs, there was a banging on the front door, not loud, just sharp and insistent, as of someone who would not give up.

Monk pulled his jacket on over his nightshirt, and Hester

sat up, watching him go out of the bedroom in bare feet. She heard the door open and a moment later close again.

She saw the reflection of the hall light on the landing ceiling as the gas was lit.

She could bear it no longer. She slipped out of bed and put on a robe. She met Monk coming up the stairs, a piece of paper in his hand. His face was bleak with shock, his eyes dark.

"What is it?" she said with a catch in her breath.

"Verona Stourbridge." His voice shook a little. "She's been murdered! Just the same way as Treadwell. A single, powerful blow to the head . . . with a croquet mallet." His fist closed over the white paper. "Robb asked me to go."

8

I T TOOK MONK nearly a quarter of an hour to find a hansom, first striding down Fitzroy Street to the Tottenham Court Road, then walking south towards Oxford Street.

He had left Hester furious at being excluded, but it would be in every way inappropriate for him to have taken her. She could serve no purpose except to satisfy her own curiosity, and she would quite obviously be intrusive. She had not argued, just seethed inside because she felt helpless and as confused as he was.

It was a fine night. A thin film of cloud scudded over a bright moon. The air was warm, the pavements still holding the heat of the day. His footsteps were loud in the near silence. A carriage rumbled by out of Percy Street and crossed towards Bedford Square, the moonlight shining for a moment on gleaming doors and the horses' polished flanks. Whoever had murdered Verona Stourbridge, it had not been Cleo Anderson. She was safely locked up in the Hampstead police station.

What could this new and terrible event have to do with the death of James Treadwell?

He could see pedestrians on the footpath at the corner of Oxford Street, two men and a woman, laughing.

He tried to picture Mrs. Stourbridge on the one occasion he had met her. He could not bring back her features, or even the color of her eyes, only the overriding impression he had had of a kind of vulnerability. Underneath the poised manner and the lovely clothes was a woman who was acquainted with fear. Or perhaps that was only hindsight, now that she was dead . . . murdered.

It had to be one of her own family, or a servant—or Miriam. But why would Miriam kill her, unless she truly was insane?

He turned the corner and walked along the edge of the footpath on Oxford Street, watching the road all the time for sight of a cab. He could recall Miriam only too easily, the wide eyes, the sweep of her hair, the strength in her mouth. She had behaved without any apparent reason, but he had never met anyone who had given him more of a sense of inner sanity, of a wholeness no outside force could destroy.

Maybe that was what madness was . . . something inside you which the reality of the world did not touch?

A hansom slowed down and he hailed it, giving the Stourbridge address in Cleveland Square. The driver grumbled about going so far, and Monk ignored him, climbing inside and sitting down, engulfed in silence and thought again.

He reached the Stourbridge house, paid the driver and went up the steps. It was after one o'clock in the morning. All the surrounding houses were in darkness, but here the hall and at least four other rooms blazed with light between the edges of imperfectly drawn curtains. There was another carriage outside, waiting. Presumably, it was the doctor's.

The butler answered the door the moment after Monk knocked, and invited him in with a voice rasping with tension. The man was white-faced, and his body beneath his black suit was rigid and very slightly shaking. He must have been told to expect Monk, because without seeking any instruction he showed him into the withdrawing room.

Three minutes later Robb came in, closing the door behind him. He looked almost as if he had been bereaved himself. The sight of Monk seemed to cheer him a little.

"Thank you," he said simply. "It's . . . it's the last thing I expected. Why should anybody attack Mrs. Stourbridge?" His voice rose with desperate incomprehension. He looked exhausted, and there was a stiffness about him that Monk recognized as fear. This was not the sort of crime he understood or the kind of people he had ever dealt with before. He knew he was out of his depth.

"Begin with the facts," Monk said calmly, more confidence in his manner than he felt. "Tell me exactly what you know. Who called you? What time? What did they say?"

Robb looked slightly startled, as if he had expected to begin with the body and accounts of where everyone was.

"A little before midnight," he began, steadying himself but still standing. "Maybe quarter to. A constable banged on my door to say there'd been a murder in Bayswater that was part of my case and the local police said I should come straightaway. They had a cab waiting. I was on my way in not more than five minutes." He started moving about restlessly, looking at Monk, then away again. "He told me it was Mrs. Stourbridge, and as soon as I knew that, I sent the beat constable around to get you." He shook his head. "I don't understand it. It can't be Cleo Anderson this time." He faced Monk. "Was I wrong about Mrs. Gardiner, and she's done this, too? Why? It makes no sense."

"If the local police were called," Monk said thoughtfully, "and they sent for you, then the body must have been found about eleven o'clock. That's over two hours ago. Who found her and where was she?"

"Major Stourbridge found her," Robb answered. "She was in her bedroom. It was only chance that he went in to say something to her after he'd said good-night and all the family had retired. He said he'd forgotten to mention something about a cousin coming to visit and just wanted to remind her. Poor man went into the bedroom and saw her crumpled on the floor and blood on the carpet."

"Did he move her?" Monk asked. It would have been a natural enough thing to do.

"He says he half picked her up." Robb's voice tightened as if his throat was too stiff to let him speak properly. "Sort of

201

cradled her in his arms. I suppose for a moment he half hoped she wasn't dead." He swallowed. "But it's a pretty terrible wound. Looks like one very hard blow. The croquet mallet's still there, lying on the floor beside her. At least, that's what they told me it was. I've never seen one before."

Monk tried not to visualize it, and failed. His mind created the crumpled figure and the broken bone and the blood.

"He says he laid her back where she was," Robb added miserably.

"What was she wearing?" Monk asked.

"Er . . ."

"A nightgown or a dress?" Monk pressed.

Robb colored faintly. "A long, whitish sort of robe. I think it could be a nightgown." He was transparently uncomfortable discussing such things. They belonged in the realms where he felt a trespasser.

"Where was she lying, exactly?" Monk asked. "What do you think she was doing when she was struck? Was it from behind or in front?"

Robb thought for a moment. "She was lying half on her side about six feet away from the bed. Looked as if she had been talking to someone and turned away from them, and they struck her from behind. At least that's what I would guess. It fits."

"She had her back to them? You're sure?"

"If the major didn't move her too much, yes. The wound is at the back on one side a bit. Couldn't hit someone like that from the front." His eyes widened a little. "So considering it was in her bedroom, she would hardly turn her back on anyone she was frightened of." His lips pulled tight. "Not that I ever held out hope it was a burglar. There's no sign of anyone forcing their way in. Nothing broken. Too early for burglars anyway. Nobody breaks into a house when half the household is still up and about. It was one of them, wasn't it?" That was less than half a question.

"Looks as if the local police worked that out," Monk said

202

dryly. "Not surprised they wanted to be rid of this. Have you asked where everyone in the house was yet?"

"Only Major Stourbridge. He seems to have a good command of himself, but he's as white as a ghost and looks pretty poorly to me. He said he was in bed. He'd dismissed his man for the night and was about to put out the light when he remembered this cousin who's coming. Seems Mrs. Stourbridge wasn't very fond of him. He was wondering whether to write tomorrow morning and say it wasn't convenient."

"What time was Mrs. Stourbridge last seen alive?"

"I don't know. Her maid is being looked after by the housekeeper, and I haven't spoken with her yet." He glanced around the spacious room where they were talking. Even in the dim light of one lamp there was a warmth to it. The glow reflected on silver frames and winked in the faceted crystal of a row of decanters. "I'm not used to this kind of people having to do with violence," he said miserably. "Questioning them. It's more often a matter of burglary, and asking the servants about strangers being by, and not locking up properly."

"This kind of thing doesn't happen very often in anybody's house," Monk replied. "But it's best to ask now, before they have time to forget—or talk to each other and think up any lies."

"Only one of them's going to lie . . ." Robb began.

Monk snorted. "People lie for all sorts of reasons, and about things they think have nothing to do with the case. You'd better see the maid, hysterics or not. You need to know what time Mrs. Stourbridge was left alone and alive, or if she was expecting anyone. What she said, how she seemed, anything the woman can tell you."

"Will you stay?"

"If you want."

The maid was sent for, and came, supported by the butler and looking as if she might buckle at the knees any moment. Her eyes were red-rimmed, and she kept dabbing her face with a handkerchief, which was now little more than a twisted rag.

203

She had been guided to one of the armchairs, and the butler was permitted to remain. Robb began his questions. He was very gentle with her, as if he himself was embarrassed.

"Yes sir." She gulped. "Mrs. Stourbridge went to bed about ten o'clock, or a little after. I laid out 'er clothes for tomorrow. A green-an'-white dress for the morning. She was going to visit a picture gallery." Her eyes filled with tears.

"What time did you leave her?" Robb asked.

She sniffed fiercely and made an attempt to dab her cheeks with the wet handkerchief. "About quarter to eleven."

"Was she already in bed?" Monk interrupted.

She looked at him with surprise.

"I'm sure you'll remember, if you think for a moment," he encouraged. "It's rather important."

"Is it?"

"Yes. It matters whether she was expecting someone to call on her or not."

"Oh. Yes. I see. No, I don't. She wouldn't hardly expect a thief who'd break in an' kill her!"

"No one broke in, Pearl."

"What are you saying?" She was aghast. Her hands tightened in her lap till the handkerchief tore.

Robb took charge of the situation again.

"We are saying it was someone already in the house who killed Mrs. Stourbridge."

"It . . . it never is!" She shook her head. "No one 'ere would do such a thing! We in't murderers!" Now she was both frightened and affronted.

"Yes, it was," Robb insisted. "The local police and your own butler and footman have made a thorough search. No one broke in. Now, tell me all you know of everyone's comings and goings from the time you left the dinner table until now."

She replied dutifully, but nothing she had to say either incriminated anyone or cleared them.

The maid assigned to Miriam was of no greater help. She had seen Miriam to her bed even earlier, and had no idea whether she had remained there or not. She had been excused and gone up to her own room in the attic. Mrs. Gardiner was extremely easy to work for, and she could not believe any ill of her, no matter what anyone said. People who couldn't speak well shouldn't speak at all.

Nor could any of the other servants swear to the movements of any of the family. However, the maids knew the time of each other's retiring. The cook, whose room was nearest the stairs down, was a light sleeper, and the second stair creaked. She was certain no one had passed after she had gone up at a quarter to eleven.

At last Monk forced himself to go and look at the body. A local constable was on duty on the landing outside the door. He was tired and unhappy. He showed them in without looking past them.

Verona Stourbridge lay as if eased gently onto her back, halfway between the chest of drawers and the bed. It must have been where her husband had laid her when he realized he could do nothing more for her and at last let her go. The carpet was soaked dark with blood about a foot away from her head. It was easy to see where she had originally fallen.

Her hands were limp, and there was nothing in either of them. She was wearing a robe over her nightgown. It looked like silk, and when Monk bent to touch it he knew instantly that it was: soft, expensive and beautiful. He wondered if he would ever be able to buy Hester anything like that. This one would be thrown away after the case was closed. No one would ever want to wear it again.

He stood up and turned to Robb.

"Member of the family?" Robb said hoarsely.

"Yes," Monk agreed.

"Why?" Robb was bewildered. "Why would any of them kill her? Her husband, do you think? Or Lucius?" He took a deep breath. "Or Miriam Gardiner? But why would she?"

"We'll look for the reason afterwards," Monk answered. "Let's go and speak to Major Stourbridge."

Robb turned reluctantly and allowed Monk to lead the way.

Harry Stourbridge met them in the library. He was fully dressed in a dark suit. His fair hair was poking up in tufts, and his eyes were sunken into the bones of his head as if the flesh no longer had life or firmness. He did not speak, but looked from Robb to Monk and then back again.

"Please sit down, Major Stourbridge," Robb said awkwardly. He did not know whether the man was a bereaved husband with whom he should sympathize, or a suspect who deserved his hostility and contempt.

Stourbridge obeyed. His legs seemed to fold under him, and he hit the seat rather too hard.

Robb sat opposite him, and Monk took the third chair in the group.

In a low, husky voice, Stourbridge retold the story of the forgotten message, of leaving his own room and going along the corridor, seeing and hearing no one else, of knocking on his wife's door and going in.

Monk stopped him. "Was the light on, sir?"

"No . . . not the main light, just the bracket on the wall." He turned to look at him with a lift of interest. "Does that mean something? She sleeps with it like that. Doesn't like the dark. Just enough to see by, a glow, no more."

"But enough if she were speaking with someone?" Monk persisted.

"Yes, I suppose so. If it were . . . someone she knew well. One would not receive—" He stopped, uncertainty filling his face again.

"We have already ascertained that it was not any of the servants," Robb said quietly. "That leaves only the family and Mrs. Gardiner."

Stourbridge looked as if he had been struck again.

"That is not p-possible," he stammered. "No one would—" He stopped. He was a man experienced in war, the violence and pain of battle and the horror of its aftermath. There was little that could shock or astound him, but this had cut deep into his emotion in a way the honesty of battle never could. He turned to Monk.

There was nothing Monk could alter, but he could ease the manner of dealing with it. Reality was a kind of healing—and the beginning of exerting some control over the chaos.

"We need to speak to everyone," he said, looking at Stourbridge and meeting his eyes. "Once we have eliminated the impossible, we will have a better idea of what happened."

"What? Oh, yes, I see. I don't think I can be of much help." He seemed to focus a little more clearly. "I believe Aiden retired quite early to his room. He had a number of letters to write. He has been away from his home for a while. Verona . . . Verona relied on him rather a lot. They have always been close. I . . ." He took a deep breath and mastered himself with difficulty. "I was away a great deal during the early years of our marriage. Military duties." He looked beyond Monk into some distance within his memory. "A young army wife does not have an easy time. I was often posted to places where it was unsuitable for her to accompany me. No facilities for women, you see? We were fighting, moving about. She didn't lack courage, but she hadn't the physical strength. She . . ."—he blinked fiercely—"she lost several babies . . . early stages. Lucius was . . . long waited for. She was thirty-five. We had all but given up." His voice cracked. "She longed for a child so much."

Monk was loath to interrupt him, even though he was wandering far from the point. He had known and loved her. Perhaps it was necessary to him to bring her back even in words, to try to make others see her as he had.

"When I was in Egypt and the Sudan," he went on, "which I was quite a lot, Aiden would be with her."

"Mrs. Gardiner . . ." Robb asked.

Stourbridge jerked up his head. "No! No—I cannot believe it of her."

Monk could not either, and yet the alternatives were little easier. Of course, it was possible Stourbridge himself was lying, but then anyone might be.

"What time did she retire?" he asked. "Perhaps you had

207

better tell me the pattern of the whole evening, from sitting down to dinner."

Again Stourbridge looked not at either of his listeners but into the distance between them. "Miriam did not dine with us. She said she felt unwell and would have a tray sent up to her room. I don't think she cared whether she ate or not; she did it to oblige us, and perhaps to avoid discussing the subject or causing Lucius to try to persuade her. In fact, she would not speak to him except in company."

"They had quarreled?" Robb asked quickly.

"No." He shook his head. "That is the thing I do not understand. Nor does he. There has been no quarrel at all. She speaks to him in the gentlest manner but will not explain why she left, nor what happened to Treadwell. And since the Anderson woman has been arrested, that question is no longer at issue." He frowned, creasing up his face. "She merely sits in her room and refuses to do or say anything beyond the barest civility."

"She is deeply distressed over Mrs. Anderson," Monk interposed. "She was in every sense except the literal a mother to her, perhaps the only one she knows."

Stourbridge looked down at the floor. "I forgot. Of course, she must be distressed beyond words. But I wish she would turn to us for comfort and not grieve by herself. We are at our wits' end to know how to help her."

"No one can help," Monk replied. "It must simply be borne. Please describe what happened during dinner, any conversation of importance, especially any differences of opinion, however trivial."

Stourbridge looked up at him. "That's just it, there were no differences. It was most agreeable. There was no shadow upon our lives except Miriam's silence."

"What did you discuss?"

Robb was watching him, then looking at Monk.

Stourbridge shrugged very slightly, with no more than half a gesture.

"Egypt, as I recall. Verona came out there to see me once.

It was marvelous. We saw such sights together. She loved it, even the heat, and the food she was unaccustomed to, and the strange ways of the native people." He smiled. "She kept a diary of it all, especially of the voyage back down the Nile. She allowed me to read some of it when I came here again. She shared it with Lucius, too. Had she been able to remain, he would have been born in Egypt. I think it was that knowledge which made him so keen to go there himself. It was almost as if he could remember it through her eyes." He stopped abruptly, the color rising in his cheeks. "I'm sorry. I'm sure that is far more detail than you require. I just remembered . . . how close we were . . . it was all so . . . normal . . ."

"Is that all?" Monk pressed, seeking for something which could have precipitated the terrible violence he had seen. Egypt sounded such a harmless subject, something impersonal which any cultured family might have discussed pleasantly around the table.

"As far as I recall, Aiden said something about the political news, but it was a mere observation on the Foreign Secretary and his own feelings about the question of the unification of Germany. It was all . . ." He shook his head. ". . . of no importance. Verona retired to bed, Aiden to write letters. Lucius walked in the garden for a while. I don't know when he came in, but doubtless the footman would."

They questioned him further, but he could add nothing which explained the emotions that had exploded in his wife's bedroom, nor any fact which implicated anyone or precluded them.

Robb did not put words to his question, but it was clear in his face that he was struggling with the issue of whether Stourbridge himself could have killed his wife.

Monk was torn with the same indecision. He profoundly believed that he had not, but he was afraid it was his loyalty to a client and his personal liking for the man which were forming his judgment. There was nothing he had seen or heard that night which proved him innocent.

There was a knock on the door.

Robb rose and opened it.

Aiden Campbell came in. He was very pale, and his hands shook a little. His eyes were unnaturally bright and his body stiff. He moved clumsily.

"Surely, Harry didn't call you into this?" he asked, looking at Monk with surprise.

"No. Sergeant Robb asked me to come, since I am already acquainted with some of the circumstances concerning the household," Monk replied.

"Oh—I see. Well, I suppose that is sensible enough," he conceded, coming a little farther into the room. "Anything that can be done to get this over as rapidly as possible. My family is suffering profoundly. First Mrs. Gardiner's inexplicable behavior, and now this—this tragedy to my poor sister. We hardly know which way to turn. Lucius is—" He stopped. "Worsnip tells me you have found no indication of intruders. Is that correct?"

"Yes sir," Robb answered. "And I regret to say all your household staff are also accounted for."

"What?" Aiden turned to Monk.

"That is true, Mr. Campbell," Monk agreed. "Whoever killed Mrs. Stourbridge, it was one of her family. I'm sorry."

"Or it was Mrs. Gardiner," Aiden said quickly. "She is not family, Mr. Monk, not yet, and I fear after the events of the last two weeks, it were better that she not become so. It was a pity that the police saw fit to release her into Lucius's custody. It would have been far better if she had gone back to her own people."

"Mrs. Anderson is the only one she has," Monk pointed out. "And she is presently in the Hampstead jail accused of murdering James Treadwell."

"Then someone else should have been found," Aiden protested. "She lived in Hampstead for twenty years. She must have other friends."

There was a moment's silence.

"I apologize," Aiden said quietly, clenching his jaw and looking down. "That was uncalled for. This has been a terrible

210

night." His voice broke. "I was very close to my sister . . . all my life. Now my brother-in-law and my nephew are in the utmost distress, and there is nothing I can do to help them." He lifted his head again. "Except assist you to deal with this as rapidly as possible and leave us to begin a decent mourning."

Robb looked wretchedly uncomfortable. His rawness at murder showed clearly in his young face. Monk was also sharply aware that Robb could not afford to fail. He needed his job not only for himself but to provide for his grandfather. The shadows of weariness streaked his skin, and it obviously cost him an effort to stand straight-backed.

"We will do everything we can to solve this crime as quickly as we can, sir," he promised. "But we must go according to the law, and we must be right in the end. Now, if you would like to recount the evening as you remember it, sir?"

"Of course. From what time?"

"How about when you all sat down to dinner?"

Aiden sank into the large chair opposite where Robb and Monk were standing, then they also sat. He told them largely what Harry Stourbridge had, varying only in a description here and there. He had been asleep when Harry Stourbridge had awakened him to tell him of the terrible thing that had happened. He fancied that his man, Gibbons, could substantiate most of it.

"Well?" Robb asked when Aiden had gone and closed the door behind him. "Not much help, is it?"

"None at all," Monk agreed. "Can't see any reason why he should lie. According to Stourbridge, he was on the best possible terms with his sister and always had been."

"I can't see any money in it," Robb added disconsolately. "If Mrs. Stourbridge had had any of her own before her marriage, it would belong to her husband since then, and Lucius would inherit it when his father dies . . . along with the title and lands."

Monk did not bother to answer. "And if Mrs. Stourbridge gave Campbell any financial gifts or support that would end at her death. No, I can't see any reason for him to be anything except exactly what he says. We'd better see Lucius."

This was the interview Monk was dreading the most, perhaps because Lucius had been his original client, and so far he had brought him only tragedy, one appalling disaster after another. And now it could appear as if he suspected Lucius of murder as well, or suspected Miriam, which Lucius might feel to be even worse. And yet, what alternative was there? The murderer was someone in the house—and not a servant. Not that he had seriously considered the servants.

When Lucius came he was haggard. His eyes were sunken with shock, staring fixedly from red-rimmed lids, and his dark complexion was bleached of all its natural warmth. He sat down as if he feared his legs might not support him. He did not speak, but waited for Monk, not regarding Robb except for a moment.

Monk had never flinched from duty, no matter how unpleasant. He tended, rather, to attack it more urgently, as if anger at it could overcome whatever pain there might be.

"Can you tell us what happened this evening from the time you sat down to dinner, and anything before that if it was remarkable in any way," he began.

"No." Lucius's voice was a little higher than usual, as if his throat was so tight he could barely force the words through it. "It was the most ordinary dinner imaginable. We talked of trivia, entirely impersonal. It was mostly about Egypt." A ghost of dreadful humor crossed his face. "My father was describing Karnak and the great hall there, how massive it is, beyond our imagining. We speculated a while on what happened to a whole lost civilization capable of creating such beauty and power. Then he spoke of the Valley of the Kings. He described it for us. The depth of the ravines and how insignificant one feels standing on their floor staring up at a tiny slice of sky so vivid blue it seems to burn the eyes. He said it was a place to force one to think of God and eternity, whether one were disposed to or not. All those ancient pharaohs lying there in their huge sarcophagi with their treasures of the world around them—waiting out the millennia for some awakening to heaven, or hell. He knew a little of their beliefs. It was a strange, mystical conversation. My mother had been there to visit him before I was born. She was so lonely in England without him." His voice was so choked with tears he was obliged to stop.

Robb waited a few moments before he spoke. "And there were no disagreements?" he asked at length.

Lucius swallowed. "No, none. What is there to disagree about?"

"And Mrs. Gardiner was not at the table?"

Lucius's face tightened. "No. She was not well. She is terribly distressed about Mrs. Anderson, who was in every way a mother to her for most of her life. How could she not be? I wish there were something we could do to help. Of course, we will find the best lawyer to represent her, but it looks terribly as if she is guilty. I would do anything to protect Miriam from it, but what is there?" He looked back at Monk as if he still hoped Monk might think of something.

"You have already done all you can," Monk agreed, "unless Mrs. Anderson herself can say something in mitigation, and so far she has refused to say anything at all. But tonight we have another issue to deal with, and that will not involve her." He saw Lucius wince. "Please continue. You were all together until your mother retired quite early?"

Lucius braced himself. "Yes. No one wanted to move; there was no point in separating," he said wearily. "We talked a little of politics, I can't remember what. Something to do with Germany. No one was particularly interested. It was just something to say. I went for a walk in the garden. It was peaceful, and I preferred to be alone. I . . . was thinking." He did not need to explain what troubled him.

"Did you see anyone as you came in or went upstairs?" Monk asked him.

"Only the servants . . . and Miriam. I went to her room, but she would not do more than bid me good-night. I didn't see anyone else."

"Did your man assist you to undress, or lay your clothes out for the next day?"

"No. I sent him to bed. I didn't need him, and I preferred to be alone."

"I see. Did you hear anything after that? Any sound, movement, a cry, footsteps?"

"No. At least not that I recall."

Monk thanked him. Lucius seemed about to ask something further, then changed his mind and rose stiffly to his feet.

When he had gone, Robb turned to Monk. They had learned nothing more. No one was implicated nor excluded from suspicion. Robb ran his hand through his hair, his fingers closing so he pulled at it. "One of them killed her! It couldn't have been an accident, and not possibly a suicide!"

"We had better see Miriam Gardiner," Monk said grimly.

Robb shot him a look of helplessness and frustration, then rose and went to the door to send the maid for Miriam.

She looked a shadow of the woman she had been, even when Monk had found her frightened and hiding. Her body was skeletal, as if she had barely eaten since then. Her dress hung on her shoulders so the bones showed through the thin clothes, and her bosom was scarcely rounded. Her skin had no color at all, and her beautiful hair had been dressed with little attention. She looked as if she was a stranger to any kind of rest of mind or body.

She moved jerkily, and refused to be seated when Robb asked her. Her hands were clenched and shaking. She seemed not to blink but to stare fixedly, as though her attention was only partly here.

Robb looked at Monk desperately, then, as Monk said nothing, he began to question her.

She replied in a voice that was unnaturally calm that she knew nothing at all. She had taken dinner in her room and had not left it except to go to the bathroom. She had seen no one other than the servant who had ministered to her personal needs. She had no idea what had happened. She had never quarreled with Mrs. Stourbridge . . . or with anyone else. She refused to say anything further.

And no matter how either Robb or Monk pressed her, she did not yield a word. She walked away stiffly, swaying a little, as if she might lose her balance.

"Did she do it?" Robb asked as soon as the door was closed.

"I have no idea," Monk confessed. He hated the thought, but she appeared to be in a state of suppressed hysteria, almost as if she moved in a trance, a world of her own connected only here and there with reality. He judged that if there was one more pressure, however slight, she would lose control completely.

Was that what had happened? Had she, for some reason or other, gone to see Mrs. Stourbridge in her bedroom, and something, however innocently or well meant, had precipitated an emotional descent into insanity? Had Verona Stourbridge made some remark about Cleo Anderson, suggesting Miriam leave the past and its griefs behind, and Miriam had reacted by releasing all the terror and violence inside her in one fearful blow?

But where had the croquet mallet come from? One did not keep such things in a bedroom. Whoever had killed Verona Stourbridge had brought it, and it could only be as a weapon.

The murder was premeditated. He said as much aloud.

"I know," Robb admitted. "I know. But she still seems the most likely one. We'll have to go farther back than I thought. I'll start again with the servants. It's here, whatever it is, the reason, the jealousy or the fear, or the rage. It's in this house. It has to be."

They worked all night, asking, probing, going back over detail after detail. They were so tired the whole house seemed to be a maze going around and around itself, like a symbol of the confusion within. Monk's throat was dry, and he felt as if there were sand in his eyes. The cook brought them a tray of tea at three o'clock in the morning, and another at a quarter to five, this time with roast beef sandwiches.

They again questioned Mrs. Stourbridge's maid. The woman looked exhausted and terrified, but she spoke quite coherently.

"I don't know nothing to her discredit, not really," she said when Robb asked her about Miriam. "She's always bin very civil, far as I know."

Monk seized on the hesitation, reading the indecision in her face.

"You must be frank," he said gravely. "You owe Mrs. Stourbridge that. What do you mean 'not really'? What were you thinking about when you said that?"

Still, she was reluctant.

Monk looked at her grimly until she flushed and finally answered.

"Well . . . I was thinking of that time I brought back Mrs. Stourbridge's clean petticoats, to hang them up, like, an' I found Mrs. Gardiner sitting at Mrs. Stourbridge's dressing table . . . and she had one of Mrs. Stourbridge's necklaces on. She said as Mrs. Stourbridge had said she could borrow it— but she never said nothing to me as anyone could. And . . . and Mrs. Stourbridge's diary was lying open on her bed, an' that's a thing I've never seen before."

"Did she explain that, too?"

"No . . . I never asked."

"I see."

She looked wretched, and seemed glad to escape when they excused her.

It was half past five. Robb stood facing the window and the brilliant sunlight as the first noises of awakening came in from the street. A horse and cart rolled by. Somewhere on the farther side of the road there were footsteps on the pavement. A door opened and closed. He turned back to the room. His face was pale and he looked exhausted and miserable.

"I've got to arrest her," he said flatly. "Seems she couldn't wait to get her hands on the pretty things . . . or to pry into

Mrs. Stourbridge's affairs. I wish that wasn't so. Money does strange things to some people."

"She didn't have to hurt Verona Stourbridge to have that," Monk pointed out. "No one objected to the marriage."

"Perhaps she did," Robb said, his back stiff, his head high. He was determined to stand up to Monk on the issue, because he believed it. It was a testing ground between them, and he was going to prove his own authority. "Perhaps Mrs. Stourbridge knew whatever it was Treadwell knew, or even that Miriam killed him."

Monk drew in his breath to argue, but each protest died on his lips. They were empty, and he knew it. No one else had any reason or motive to harm Verona Stourbridge, and there was no physical evidence to implicate any of them. Miriam was already deeply involved in the murder of James Treadwell. And strangely enough, she had not defended herself in any coherent way. Any jury would find it easy enough to believe that she had set out deliberately to charm Lucius, a wealthy and naive young man. He was handsome and intelligent enough, but not worldly wise, and might be easily duped by a woman older than he and well practiced in the ways of pleasing.

Then she had seen the luxury of the life she could expect, but through an unforeseeable misfortune, the coachman knew something of her past which was so ugly it would have spoiled her dream. He had blackmailed her.

Her mentor and accomplice, also blackmailed for theft by the same wretched coachman, either helped her kill him or hid her afterwards and obscured the evidence of the crime. He had no choice but to charge her.

The family was shattered. Harry stood white-faced, stammering incoherent assurances that he would do all he could to help her. He looked as if he hardly knew what he was saying or doing. He kept turning to Lucius as if he would protect him, and then realized he was helpless to make any difference at all.

Monk had never felt more pity for any man, but he did not

believe that even Oliver Rathbone could do anything to relieve this tragedy. The most compassionate thing would be to deal with it as quickly as possible. To prolong the suffering was pointless.

Miriam herself seemed the least surprised or distressed. She accepted the situation as if she had expected it, and made no protest or appeal for help. She did not even deny the charge. She thanked Harry Stourbridge for his behavior towards her, then walked uprightly, quite firmly, a step or two ahead of Robb out to the front door. She hesitated as if to speak to Lucius, then changed her mind.

At the doorway, Monk looked back at the three men as they stood in the hall. Harry and Lucius were paralyzed. Aiden Campbell put his arm around Lucius as if to support him.

It was after seven in the morning by the time Monk returned home. It was broad daylight, and the streets were full of traffic, the hiss of wheels, the clatter of hooves and people shouting to each other.

He went in at his own door and closed it behind him. All he wanted to do was wash the heat and grime off himself, then sink into bed and sleep all day.

He was barely across the room when Hester appeared, dressed in blue-and-white muslin and looking as if she had been up for hours.

"What happened?" she said instantly. "You look terrible. The kettle is on. Would you like breakfast, or are you too tired?"

"Just tea," he answered, following her into the kitchen and sitting down. His legs ached and his feet were hot and so tired they hurt. His head throbbed. He wanted somewhere cool and dark and as quiet as possible.

She made the tea and poured it for him before asking any further, and then it was by a look, not words.

"She was struck once, with a croquet mallet," he told her. "There was enough evidence to prove it had to be one of the family . . . or Miriam Gardiner. There was no reason for any of the servants to do it."

She sat across the small table from him, her face very solemn. "And for her?" she asked.

"The obvious. Whatever Treadwell knew of her, Verona Stourbridge knew it as well . . . or else she deduced it from something Miriam said. I'm sorry. The best you can say of her is that she has lost her mind, the worst that she deliberately planned to marry Lucius and assure herself of wealth and social position for the rest of her life . . . and indirectly, of course, for Cleo Anderson as well. When Treadwell threatened that plan, either alone or with Cleo's help, she killed him. And then later when Verona threatened it, she killed her, too. It makes a hideous sense."

"But do you believe it?" she asked, searching his face.

"I don't know. Not easily. But logic forces me to accept it." That was the truth, but he was reluctant to say it. When Miriam had denied it he had more than believed her. He had liked her, and felt compelled to go farther than duty necessitated in order to defend her. But he was not governed by emotion. He must let reason be the last determiner.

Hester sat silently for several minutes, sipping her own tea.

"I don't believe Cleo Anderson was part of killing anyone for gain," she said at last. "I still think we should help her."

"Do you?" He looked at her as closely as his weariness and sense of disillusion would allow. He saw the bewilderment in her, the confusion of thought and feelings, and understood it precisely. "Are you sure you are not looking for a spectacular trial to show people the plight of men like John Robb, old and ill and forgotten, now that the wars they fought are all won and we are safe?"

She drew in her breath to deny it indignantly, then saw in his eyes that he was a step ahead of her.

"Well, I wouldn't mind if something were to draw people's attention to it," she conceded. "But I wasn't using Cleo. I believe she took the medicines to give to those who needed them, not for any profit for herself, and if she killed James Treadwell, at least in part he deserved it."

"And when did it become all right for us to decide that someone deserves to die?"

She glared at him.

He smiled and stood up slowly. It was an effort. He was even more tired than he had thought, and the few moments relaxing had made it worse.

"What are we going to do?" She stood up also, coming towards him almost as if she would block his way to the door. "She hasn't any money. She can't afford a lawyer, never mind a good one. And now Miriam is charged as well, there is no one to help her. You can't expect Lucius Stourbridge to."

He knew what she wanted: that they should go to Oliver Rathbone and try to persuade him to use his professional skill, free of charge, to plead for Cleo Anderson. Because of their past friendship—*love* would not be too strong a word, at least on Rathbone's part—she would also probably rather that Monk asked him, so that it did not appear that she was abusing his affection.

Oliver Rathbone was the last person of whom he wanted to ask any favors, no matter on whose behalf. Was it guilt, because he had asked Hester to marry him before Rathbone had, knowing that Rathbone also loved her?

That was ridiculous. Rathbone had had his opportunity and failed to take it . . . for whatever reason. Monk was not responsible.

Perhaps it was a certain guilt because he had seized a happiness that he knew Rathbone would have treasured, or in some ways would have been more worthy of. There was too often a fear at the back of his mind that Rathbone could have made her happier, given her things Monk never could—not only material possessions and security, or social position, but emotional certainties. He would not have loved her more, but he might have been a better man to share her life with, an easier one, a man who would have caused her less fear or doubt, less anxiety. At the very least, she would have known Rathbone's past. There were no ghosts, no black regions or forgotten holes.

She was waiting for an answer, her brow furrowed, her chin lifted a little because she knew he did not want to, even if she could not guess why.

He would not let Rathbone beat him.

"I think we should ask Rathbone's opinion," he said slowly and quite distinctly. "And if he is willing, his help. He'll take up a lost cause every now and again if the issue is good enough. I'm sure we could persuade him this one is." He smiled with a downward twist of his lips. "And the appearance of Sir Oliver Rathbone in court to defend a nurse accused of theft and murder will ensure that the newspapers give it all the attention we could wish."

She smiled very slowly, her body relaxing.

"Thank you, William. I knew you would say that."

He had not known it, but if she thought so well of him he was certainly not going to argue.

"Now go to sleep," she urged. "I'll waken you in time to go to Vere Street and see Oliver before the end of the day."

He grunted, too tired to argue that tomorrow would do, and climbed slowly up the stairs.

Monk hated presenting himself at Rathbone's chambers on Vere Street without an appointment, and fully expected to be turned away. If he was received, he was certain it would be because Hester was with him. He would rather she had not come, but he could understand her insistence. She wanted to be there not simply to add her own thoughts and words to the story and to try her own persuasion if Monk's should fail, but because she would feel cowardly if she sent Monk and did not go herself. It would seem as if she wanted a favor of Rathbone but had not the courage to face him to ask it.

Therefore they stood in the outer office and explained to the clerk that they had no appointment but they were well acquainted with Sir Oliver (which he knew) and had a matter of some urgency to lay before him. It was the end of the afternoon, and the last client was presently in Sir Oliver's rooms with him. It was a fortunate time.

Some fifteen minutes passed by. Monk found it almost impossible to sit still. He glanced at Hester and read the misgiving in her face, and equally the determination. Cleo Anderson's life was worth a great deal more than a little embarrassment.

At twenty minutes past five the client left and Rathbone came to the door. He looked startled to see them. His eyes flew to Hester, and there was a sudden warmth in them, and the faintest flush on his narrow cheeks. He forced himself to smile, but there was not the usual humor in it. He came forward.

"Hester! How nice to see you. You look extremely well."

"We are sorry to intrude," Hester replied with an equally uncertain smile. "But we have a case that is so desperate we know of no one else who would have even a chance of success in it."

Rathbone half turned to Monk. For the first time since the wedding their eyes met. Then Monk had been the bridegroom. Now he was the husband, the last barrier had been crossed, there was a new kind of intimacy from which Rathbone was forever excluded. Rathbone's eyes were startlingly, magnificently dark in his fair face. Everything that had passed through Monk's mind he read in them. He held out his hand.

Monk shook it, feeling the strength and the coolness of Rathbone's grip.

"Then you had better come in and tell me," Rathbone said calmly. His voice held no trace of emotion. He was supremely courteous. What effort of pride or dignity that had cost him Monk could only guess.

He and Hester followed into Rathbone's familiar office and sat down in the chairs away from the desk. It was a formal visit, but not yet an official one. The late sun poured in through the window, making bright patterns on the floor and shining on the gold lettering on the books in their mahogany case.

Rathbone leaned back and crossed his legs. As always, he

was immaculately dressed, but with an understated elegance and the ease of someone who knows he does not have to try

"What is this case?" he enquired, looking at each of them in turn.

Monk was determined to answer first, before Hester could speak and make it a dialogue between herself and Rathbone, with Monk merely an onlooker.

"A nurse has been stealing medicines from the North London Hospital, where Hester is now assisting Lady Callandra." He had no need to explain that situation; Rathbone knew and admired Callandra. "She doesn't want the medicines for herself, or to sell, but to give to the old and poor that she visits, who are in desperate need, many of them dying."

"Laudable but illegal," Rathbone said with a frown. His interest was already caught, and his concern.

"Precisely," Monk agreed. "Somehow a coachman named James Treadwell learned of her thefts and was blackmailing her. How he learned is immaterial. He comes from an area close by, and possibly he knew someone she was caring for. He was found dead on the path close to her doorway. She has been charged with his murder."

"Physical evidence?" Rathbone said with pressed lips, his face already darker, brows drawn down.

"None, all on motive and opportunity. The weapon has not been found. But that is not all. . . ."

Rathbone's eyes widened incredulously. "There's more?"

"And worse," Monk replied. "Some twenty years ago Mrs. Anderson found in acute distress a girl of about twelve or thirteen years old. She took her in and treated her as her own." He saw Rathbone's guarded expression, and the further spark of interest in his eyes. "Miriam grew up and married comfortably," Monk continued. "She was widowed, and then fell deeply in love with a young man, Lucius Stourbridge, of wealthy and respectable family, who more than returned her feelings. They became engaged to marry with his parents' approval. Then one day, for no known reason, she fled, with the said coachman, back to Hampstead Heath."

"The night of his death, I presume," Rathbone said with a twisted smile.

"Just so," Monk agreed. "At first she was charged with his murder and would say nothing of her flight, its reason, or what happened, except to deny that she killed him."

"And she wasn't charged?" Rathbone was surprised.

"Yes, she was. Then when a far better motive was found for the nurse, she was released."

"And the worse that you have to add?" Rathbone asked.

Monk's shoulders stiffened. "Last night I had a message from the young policeman on the case—incidentally, his grandfather is one of those for whom the nurse stole medicines—to ask me to go to the family home in Cleveland Square, where the mother of the young man had just been found murdered . . . in what seems to be exactly the same manner as the coachman on Hampstead Heath."

Rathbone shut his eyes and let out a long, slow breath. "I hope that is now all?"

"Not quite," Monk replied. "They have arrested Miriam and charged her with the murder of Stourbridge's mother, and Miriam and Cleo as being accomplices in murder for gain. There is considerable money in the family, and lands."

Rathbone opened his eyes and stared at Monk. "Have you completed this tale to date?"

"Yes."

Hester spoke for the first time, leaning forward a little, her voice urgent. "Please help, Oliver. I know Miriam may be beyond anything anybody can do, except perhaps plead that she may be mad, but Cleo Anderson is a good woman. She took medicine to treat the old and ill who have barely enough money to survive. John Robb, the policeman's grandfather, fought at Trafalgar—on the *Victory*! He, and men like him, don't deserve to be left to die in pain that we could alleviate! We asked everything of them when we were in danger. When we thought Napoleon was going to invade and conquer us, we expected them to fight and die for us, or to lose arms or legs or eyes . . ."

224

"I know!" Rathbone held up his slender hand. "I know, my dear. You do not need to persuade me. And a jury might well be moved by such things, but a judge will not. He won't ask them to decide whether a blackmailer is of more or less value than a nurse, or an old soldier, simply did she kill him or not. And what about this other woman, the younger one? What possible reason or excuse did she have for murdering her prospective mother-in-law?"

"We don't know," Hester said helplessly. "She won't say anything."

"Is she aware of her position, that if she is found guilty she will hang?"

"She knows the words," Monk replied. "Whether she comprehends their meaning or not I am uncertain. I was there when she was arrested, and she seemed numb, but she left with the police with more dignity than I have seen in anyone else I can recall." He felt foolish as he said it. It was an emotional response, and he disliked having Rathbone see him in such a light. It made him vulnerable. He was about to add something to qualify it, defend himself, but Rathbone had turned to Hester and was not listening.

"Do you know this nurse?" he asked.

"Yes," she said unhesitatingly. "And I know John Robb. I have been to a few of the patients she visited. I can and will testify that the medicines were used for them and that no return of any kind was asked."

Rathbone forbore from saying that that would be of no legal help. The sympathy of the jury would not alter her guilt and was unlikely to mitigate the sentence. Anyway, was hanging so very much worse than a lifetime spent in the Coldbath Fields, or some other prison like it? He stayed silent for several moments, considering the question, and neither Monk nor Hester prompted him.

"I presume she has no money, this nurse?" Rathbone said at last. "And the family are hardly likely to wish to defend her."

Monk felt anger harsh inside him. So it was all a matter of payment.

"So she is unlikely to have anyone to represent her already," Rathbone concluded. "There will be no professional ethics to break if I were to go and visit her. I can at least offer my services, and then she may accept or decline them as she wishes."

"And who is going to pay you?" Monk asked with a lift of his eyebrows.

Rathbone looked straight back at him. "I have done sufficiently well lately that I can afford to do it without asking payment," he replied levelly. "I imagine she will have no means to pay you either."

Monk felt an unaccustomed heat rise up his cheeks, but he knew the rebuke was fair. He had earned it.

"Thank you!" Hester said quickly, rising to her feet. "Her name is Cleo Anderson, and she is in the Hampstead police station."

Rathbone smiled with a dry twist of humor, as if there were a highly subtle joke which was at least half against himself.

"Don't thank me," he said softly. "It sounds like a challenge which ought to be attempted, and I know no one else fool enough to try it."

9

O*LIVER* R*ATHBONE* *SAT* in his office after Monk and Hester had gone, aware that he had made an utterly impetuous decision, which was most unlike him. He was not a man who acted without consideration, which was part of the reason why he was probably the most brilliant barrister currently practicing in London. It might also be why he had allowed Monk to ask Hester to marry him before he had asked her himself.

No, that was not entirely true. He had been on the verge of asking her, but she had very delicately allowed him to understand that she would not accept. It had been to save his feelings and the awkwardness between them that would have followed.

But then, if he were honest, the reason she would not accept him might easily have been her sense of his uncertainty. Monk would never have allowed his head to rule his heart. That was what Rathbone both admired in him and despised. There was something ungoverned in Monk, something even dark.

And yet he had come with Hester to try to persuade Rathbone to take the hopeless case of defending a nurse certainly guilty of theft, and almost as certainly guilty of murder. That could not have been easy for him. Rathbone leaned back farther in his chair and smiled a little as he remembered the look on Hester's face, the stiffness in her body. He could imagine her thoughts. Monk would have done it for Hester's sake, and he would know that Rathbone knew it also.

He was surprised how sharp the pain was on seeing Hester again, hearing the passion in her voice as she spoke of Cleo Anderson and the old sailor John Robb. That was just like her, full of pity and anger and courage, bound on some hopeless cause, not listening to anyone who told her the impossibility of it.

And he had agreed to help—in fact, to undertake some kind of defense. He would be a fool to pretend it would be less than that. Now he had begun she would not allow him to stop—nor would he allow himself. He would never admit to Monk that he would quit a fight before he had either won it or lost. Monk would understand defeat and forgive it, and respect winner or loser alike. He had tasted bitterness too often himself not to understand. But he would not forgive surrender.

And Rathbone would always want to be all that Hester expected of him.

So now he was committed to a case he could not win and probably could not even fight in any adequate manner. He should have been angry with himself, not analytical, and even in a faraway sense amused. He should have felt hopeless, but already his mind was beginning to explore possibilities, beginning to think, to plan, to wonder about tactics.

Both women had been charged with conspiracy and murder. The penalty would unquestionably be death. Rathbone had a justifiably high opinion of his own abilities, but the obstacles in this case seemed insuperable. It was extremely foolish to have such a will to win. In fact, it was a classic example of a man's allowing his emotions not merely to eliminate his judgment but to sweep it away entirely.

He called his clerk in and enquired about his appointments for the next two days. There was nothing which could not be either postponed or dealt with by someone else. He duly requested that that be done, and left for his home, his mind aboorbod in the issue of Cleo Anderson, Miriam Gardiner and the crimes with which they were charged.

In the morning, he presented himself at the Hampstead police station. He informed them that he was the barrister retained by Cleo Anderson's solicitor and that he wished to speak with her without delay.

"Sir Oliver Rathbone?" the desk sergeant said with amazement, looking at the card Rathbone had given him.

Rathbone did not bother to reply.

The sergeant cleared his throat. "Yes sir. If you'll come this way, I'll take yer ter the cells . . . sir." He was still shaking his head as he led the way back through the narrow passage and down the steps, and finally to the iron door with its huge lock. The key squeaked in the lock as he turned it and swung the door open.

" 'Ere's yer lawyer ter see yer," he said, the lift of disbelief in his voice.

Rathbone thanked him and waited until he had closed the door and gone.

Cleo Anderson was a handsome woman with fine eyes and strong, gentle features, but at the moment she was so weary and ravaged by grief that her skin looked gray and the lines of her face dragged downwards. She regarded Rathbone without comprehension and—what worried him more—without interest.

"My name is Oliver Rathbone," he introduced himself. "I have come to see if I can be of assistance to you in your present difficulty. Anything you say to me is completely confidential, but you must tell me the truth or I cannot be of any use." He saw the beginning of denial in her face. He sat down on the one hard chair, opposite where she was sitting on the cot. "I have been retained by Miss Hester Latterly." Too late he realized he should have said "Mrs. Monk." He felt the heat in his face as he was obliged to correct himself.

"She shouldn't have," Cleo said sadly, her face pinched, emotion raw in her voice. "She's a good woman, but she doesn't have money to spend on the likes o' you. I'm sorry for your trouble, but there's no job for you here."

He was prepared for her answer.

"She told me that you took certain medicines from the hospital and gave them to patients who you knew were in need of them but were unable to pay."

Cleo stared at him.

He had not expected a confession. "If that were so, it would be theft, of course, and illegal," he continued. "But it would be an act which many people would admire, perhaps even wish that they had had the courage to perform themselves."

"Maybe," she agreed with a tiny smile. "But it's still theft, like you said. Do you want me to admit it? Would it help Miriam if I did?"

"That was not my purpose in discussing it, Mrs. Anderson." He held her gaze steadily. "But a person who would do such a thing obviously placed the welfare of other people before her own. As far as I can see, it was an act, a series of acts, for which she expected no profit other than that of having done what she believed to be right and of benefit to others for whose welfare she cared. Possibly she believed in a cause."

She frowned. "Why are you saying all this? You're talking about 'ifs' and 'maybes.' What do you want?"

He smiled in spite of himself. "That you should accept that occasionally people do things without expecting to be paid, because they care. Not only people like you—sometimes people like me, too."

A flush of embarrassment spread up her cheeks, and the line of her mouth softened. "I'm sorry, Mr. Rathbone, I didn't mean to insult you. But with the best will in the world, you can't clear me of thieving those medicines, unless you find a way to blame some other poor soul who's innocent—and if you did that, how would I go to my Maker in peace?"

"That's not how I work, Mrs. Anderson." He did not bother to correct her as to his title. It seemed remarkably unimportant now. "If you took the medicines, I have two options: either to plead mitigating circumstances and hope that they will judge you from the charity of your intent rather than the illegality of your act, or else to try to misdirect their attention from the theft altogether and hope that they concentrate on other matters."

"Other matters?" She shook her head. "They're saying as I killed Treadwell because he was blackmailing me over the medicines. You can't misdirect anybody away from that."

"And was he?"

She hesitated. Something inside her seemed to crumple. She took a deep breath and let it out in a sigh. "Yes."

He waited for her to say more, but she remained silent.

"How did he find out about the medicines?" he asked.

"I suppose it wasn't hard." She stared ahead of her, a shadow of self-mockery in her expression. "Lot o' people could have, if they'd wanted to think about it, and watch. I took stuff to about a score o' the old ones who were really in a bad way. I don't know why I talk about it in the past—they still are, an' here's me sittin' here useless." She looked up at him. "There's nothing you can do, Mr. Rathbone. All the questions in the world aren't going to make any difference. I took the medicines, and it'll be easy enough to prove. Treadwell worked it out. I don't know how."

There was no argument to make. He heard footsteps along the corridor outside, but they continued on and no one disturbed them. He wondered briefly if the jailers here sympathized with her; even were it possible, they might sooner have had the law turn a blind eye to her thefts. Maybe they had little time for a blackmailer.

It was academic, only a wish. The power was not in their hands. Maybe it was a thought each would have had individually and never dared voice.

She was regarding him earnestly, her eyes anxious.

"Mr. Rathbone—don't let them go talking to all the people I took medicines to. It's bad enough they won't get any help now. I don't want them to know they were part of a crime—even though they never understood it."

He wished there was some way he could prevent that from happening, but it would soon enough become common knowledge. The trial would be written up in all the newspapers, told and retold by the running patterers, and in the gossip on every street corner. What should he tell her?

She was waiting, a flicker of hope in her face.

He regarded her almost as if he had not seen her before, not been speaking to her, forming judgments those last ten minutes. She had risked her own freedom, taken her own leap of moral decision in order to help the old and ill who could not help themselves. She had faced the most painful of realities and dealt with it. She did not deserve the condescension of being lied to. She would know the truth eventually anyway.

"I can't stop them, Mrs. Anderson," he said gently, startled by the respect in his own voice. "And they'll know anyway when it comes to trial. That is perhaps the only good thing about this whole affair. All London will hear of the plight of our old people to whom we owe so much—and choose not to pay. We may even hope that a few will take up the fight to have things changed."

She looked at him, hope and denial struggling in her face. She shook her head, pushing the thought away and yet unable to let go completely.

"D'you think so?"

"It is worth fighting for." He smiled very slightly. "But my first battle is for you. How long have you been paying Treadwell, and how much?"

Her voice hardened, and the pity vanished from her eyes. "Five years—an' I paid him all I had, except a couple of shillings to live on."

Rathbone felt a tightening around his heart.

"And he asked you for more the night of his death. How much?"

Her voice sank to a whisper. She hesitated a moment before answering at all. "I never saw him the night he died. That's God's truth."

He asked the question whose answer he did not want to hear and possibly he would not believe.

"Do you know who did?"

She answered instantly, her voice hard. "No, I don't! Miriam told me nothing, except it wasn't her. But she was in a terrible state, frightened half out of her mind an' like the whole world had ended for her." She leaned towards him, half put out her hand, then took it back, not because the emotion or the urgency was any less, simply that she dared not touch him. "Never mind about me, Mr. Rathbone. I took the medicines. You can't help me. But help Miriam, please! That's what I want. If you're my lawyer, like you said, you'll speak up for her. She never killed him. I know her—I raised her since she was thirteen. She's got a good heart an' she never deliberately hurt anyone, but somebody's hurt her so bad she's all but dead inside. Help her—please! I'd go to the rope happy if I knew she was all right. . . ."

He met her eyes and felt his throat choke. He believed her. It was a wild statement. She might have no real conception of what it would be like when the moment came, when the judge put on his black cap, and later when she was alone in the end, walking the short corridor towards the trap in the floor, and the short drop. Then it would be too late. But he still believed her. She had seen much death. There could be little of loneliness or pain that she was not familiar with.

"Mrs. Anderson, I am not sure there is anything I can do, but I promise I will not secure any leniency—or indeed, any defense—for you at Miriam Gardiner's expense. And I will certainly do all I can to secure her acquittal, if she wishes it, and you do—"

"I do!" she said with fierce intensity. "And if she argues with you—for me—tell her that is my wish. I've had a good life with lots of laughter in it and done the things I wanted to. She's very young. It's your profession to convince people of things. You go and convince her of that, will you?"

"I can only work within the facts, but I will try," he promised. "Now, if there is anything more of that night you can tell me, please do."

"I don't know anything else of that night," she protested. "I wish I did, then maybe I could help either one of us. I knew nothing until the police came because someone had reported finding a body on the pathway."

"When was that, what time?" he interrupted her.

"About an hour after dark. I didn't look at the clock. I suppose Miriam must have left the party in late afternoon, and it would be close on dark by the time the carriage got as far as the Heath. I don't know where he was attacked, but I heard say he crawled from there to where they found him."

"And when did you see Miriam Gardiner?"

"Next morning, early. About six, or something like that. She'd been out on the Heath all night and looked like the devil had been after her."

"Like she'd been in a fight?" he asked quickly. "Were her clothes torn, dirty, stained with mud or grass?"

Something inside her closed. She was afraid he was trying to implicate Miriam. "No. Only like she'd been running, p'raps, or frightened."

Was that a lie? He had no way of knowing. He recognized that she was not going to tell him any more. He rose to his feet. The fact that she had withdrawn her trust, at least as far as Miriam was concerned, did not alter his admiration for her or his intent to do all he could to find some way of helping.

"I shall go and speak with Mrs. Gardiner," he told her. "Please do not discuss this with anyone else. I shall return when I have something to tell you or if I need to ask you anything further. You have my word I shall take no steps without your permission."

"Thank you," she answered. "I—I am grateful, Mr. Rathbone. Will you tell Mrs. Monk that, too . . . and . . ."

"Yes?"

"No—nothing else."

He banged on the door, and the jailer let him out. He

walked away along the dim corridor with a fluttering fear inside him as to what else she might have been going to say to Hester. She was a woman prepared to go to any lengths, make any sacrifice, for what she believed to be right and to save those she loved. No wonder Hester was keen in her defense. In the same place she might so easily have done the same things. He could picture Hester with just this blind loyalty, sacrificing herself rather than denying the greater principle. Was that what Cleo had been going to say—some instruction or warning to Hester about the medicines? Was it a request, or was Hester already doing it even now?

He felt sick at the thought. His stomach knotted and sweat broke out on his skin. What could he do to help her if she was caught? He could not even think clearly about Cleo Anderson, whom he had never seen before today.

Start with Miriam Gardiner, that was the only thing. Usually, he would have told himself that the truth was his only ally, always to know the truth before he began. But in this case he was afraid there were truths he might prefer not to know—though he was uncertain which they were. He would have looked the other way, if only he was certain which way that was.

Rathbone was allowed in to see Miriam, but not as easily as when he had been to see Cleo Anderson. The atmosphere was different. Cleo was in police cells, a local woman known to the men—by repute, if not personally—to be undoubtedly a good woman, one whose life they valued far more than that of any blackmailing outsider.

Miriam was in prison, accused of murdering her prospective mother-in-law in order to inherit money the sooner—or possibly because the unfortunate mother-in-law was aware of some scandal in her past which would have prevented the marriage. Greed was an altogether different matter.

Miriam was not at all as he had expected. It was not until he saw her that he realized he had pictured in his mind some rather brashly handsome, bold-eyed woman with accomplished charm, who would quickly try to win him to her cause. Instead he found a small woman, a little too broad of hip, with a fair, tired face full of inner quietness and a strength which startled him. She maintained a deep reserve, even after he had explained to her who he was and the exact circumstances and reasons for his having come.

"It is good of you to take the time, Sir Oliver," she said so softly he had to lean forward to catch her words. "But I don't believe you can help me." She did not meet his eyes, and he was aware that in a sense she had already dismissed him.

If he could not appeal to her mind, he would have to try her emotions. He sat down in the chair opposite her and crossed his legs as if he intended to make himself comfortable.

"Have they told you that you and Mrs. Anderson are to be charged together with conspiracy in the murders of Treadwell and Mrs. Stourbridge?"

She stared at him, her eyes wide and troubled. "That's absurd! How can they possibly think Mrs. Anderson had anything to do with Mrs. Stourbridge's death? She was in their own prison at the time. You must be mistaken."

"I am not mistaken. They know all that. They are saying that they believe you and Mrs. Anderson planned from the beginning that you should marry Lucius Stourbridge, thus gaining access to a very great deal of money, some now, far more later, on Major Stourbridge's death, whenever that might be."

"Why should he die?" she protested. "He is quite young, not more than fifty, and in excellent health. He could have another thirty years, or more."

He sighed. "The mortality rate among those who seem to stand in the way of your plans is very high, Mrs. Gardiner. They would not consider his age or his health to be matters which would deter you."

She closed her eyes. "That is hideous."

Studying the lines of her face, of her mouth, and the way it tightened, the sadness and the momentary surprise and anger in her, he could not believe she had even thought of Harry

Stourbridge's death until this moment, and now that she did, the idea hurt her. But he could not afford to be gentle.

"That is what they are accusing you of—you and Mrs. Anderson together. Unless you accuse each other, which neither of you has done, you will both either stand or fall."

She looked up at him slowly, searching his eyes, his face, trying to read him.

"You mean I am to defend myself if I do not wish Cleo to suffer with me?"

"Yes, exactly that."

"It is completely untrue. I . . . loved Lucius." She swallowed, and he could almost feel the pain in her as if it had been in himself. "I had no thought of anything but marrying him and being happy simply to be with him. Had he been a pauper it would have made not the slightest difference."

He felt she was telling the truth, and yet why had she hesitated? Why had she spoken of her love for Lucius in the past? Was that because the love had died, or simply the hope?

"James Treadwell was blackmailing Mrs. Anderson over the medicines she stole from the hospital to treat her patients. Was he blackmailing you also?"

Her head jerked up, her eyes wide. She seemed about to deny it vehemently, then instead she said nothing.

"Mrs. Gardiner," he said urgently, leaning forward towards her, "if I am to help either of you then I must know as much of the truth as you do. I am bound to act in your interest, and believe me when I say that the outlook could not be worse for either of you than it already is. Whatever you tell me, it cannot harm you now, and it may help. In the end, when it comes to trial, I shall take your instructions, or at the very worst, if I cannot do that, then I shall decline the case. I cannot betray you. If I did so I should be disbarred and lose not only my reputation but my livelihood, both of which are of great value to me. Now—was James Treadwell blackmailing you or not?"

She seemed to reach some decision. "No, he wasn't. He could not know anything which would harm me. Except, I suppose, a connection with Cleo and the medicines, but he never mentioned it. I had no idea he was blackmailing her. If I had, I would have tried to do something about it."

"What could you do?" He tried to keep the edge from his voice.

She gave a tiny, halfhearted shrug. "I don't know. I suppose if I had told Lucius, or Major Stourbridge, they might have dismissed him, without references, and made certain it was very hard for him to find new employment."

"Would that not have driven him to expose Mrs. Anderson in retaliation?" he asked.

"Perhaps." Then she stiffened and twisted around to stare at him, her face bleached with horror. "You think I killed him to protect Cleo?"

"Did you?"

"No! I didn't kill him—for any reason!" The denial was passionate, ringing with anger and hurt. "Neither did Cleo!"

"Then who did?"

Her expression closed again, shutting him out. She averted her eyes.

"Who are you protecting, if it isn't Mrs. Anderson?" he asked very gently. "Is it Lucius?"

She shivered, glanced up at him, then away again.

"Did Treadwell injure you in some way, and Lucius fought with him and it went further than he intended?"

"No." She sounded as if the idea surprised her.

It had seemed to him so likely an answer he was disappointed that she denied it, and startled at himself for believing her for no better reason than the intonation of her voice and the angle and stiffness of her body.

"Do you know who killed him, Mrs. Gardiner?" he demanded with sudden force.

She said nothing. It was as good as an admission. He was frustrated almost beyond bearing. He had never felt more helpless, even though he had certainly dealt with many cases where people accused of fearful crimes had refused to tell him the truth and had in the end proved to be innocent,

238

morally if not legally. Nothing in his experience explained Miriam Gardiner's behavior.

He refused to let it go. If anything, he was even more determined to defend both Miriam and Cleo, not for Hester and certainly not to prove himself to Monk, but for the case itself, for these two extraordinary, devoted and blindly stubborn women, and perhaps because he would not rest until he knew the truth. And maybe also for the principle.

"Did Mrs. Stourbridge know anything about Treadwell or about Cleo Anderson?" he pursued.

Again she was surprised. "No . . . I can't imagine how she could. I didn't tell her, and I can hardly think that Treadwell would tell her himself. He was a—" She stopped. She seemed to be torn by emotions which confused her, pulling one way and then another: anger, pity, horror, despair.

Rathbone tried to read what she was feeling, even to imagine what was in her mind, and failed utterly. There were too many possibilities, and none of them made sense entirely.

"He was a man who did evil things," she said quietly at last, as much to herself as to him. "But he was not without virtue, and he is dead now, poor soul. I don't think Mrs. Stourbridge knew anything about him except that he drove the carriage quite well—and, of course, that he was related to the cook."

"Why was she killed?"

She winced. "I don't know." She did not look at him as she said it. Her voice was flat, the tone of it different.

He knew she was lying.

"Who killed her?"

"I don't know," she repeated.

"Lucius?"

"No!" This time she turned to look at him, eyes dark and angry.

"Were you with him?"

She said nothing.

"You weren't. Then how do you know he did not?"

Again she said nothing.

"It was the same person who killed both people?"

She made a very slight movement. He took it for agreement.

"Has it anything to do with the stolen medicines?"

"No!" Suddenly she was completely frantic again. "No, it has nothing to do with Cleo at all. Please, Sir Oliver, defend her." Now she was pleading with him. "She is the best person I have ever known. The only thing she has done against the law is to take medicines to treat the ill who cannot afford to buy them. She made nothing for herself out of it." Her face was flushed. "How can that be so wrong that she deserves to die for it? If we were the Christian people we pretend to be, she wouldn't have had to take them. We would care for our own old and sick. We would be grateful to those who fought to protect us when we needed it, and we'd be just as keen to protect them now. Please, don't let her suffer for this. It's nothing to do with her. She didn't kill Treadwell and she couldn't possibly have killed Mrs. Stourbridge." Her voice was tight with fear and strain, almost strangled in her throat. "I'll say I killed them both, if it will free her, I swear it!"

He put his hand on her arm. "No—it would only condemn you both. Say nothing. If you will not tell me the truth, at least do not lie to me. I will do anything I can for both of you. I accept that Mrs. Anderson could not have killed Mrs. Stourbridge, and I believe you that you did not kill Treadwell. If there is another answer I shall do everything in my power to find it."

She shook her head fractionally. "You can't," she whispered. "Just don't let them hang Cleo. She only took the medicines—that's all."

Rathbone had a late luncheon at his club, where he knew he would be left in complete solitude, should he wish it—and he did. Then he took a hansom out to the North London Hospital, intending to see Hester. He was not looking forward to it, and yet it was necessary to do so. He had not seen her alone since her marriage, but he had always known that it would be painful to him.

He sat in the cab as it clipped smartly through the streets, unaware of the other passing vehicles, even of where he was as they moved from one neighborhood to another, as they changed eventually from stone-facaded houses to the green stretch of the Heath.

He had changed his mind a dozen times as to what he would say to her, what manner he would adopt. Every decision was in one way or another unsatisfactory.

When he reached the hospital, paid the cabbie and alighted, he walked up the steps and met her without having had time to prepare himself. She was coming along the wide corridor at a brisk, purposeful walk, her head high. She was wearing a very plain blue dress with a small, white, lace collar, almost like a kind of uniform. On anyone else it might have been a little forbidding, but it was how he always visualized her: as a nurse, determined about something, ready to start some battle or other. The familiarity of it almost took his breath away. No amount of imagining this moment could stab like the reality. The sunlight in the corridor, the smell of vinegar, footsteps in the distance, all were printed indelibly in his mind.

"Oliver!" She was startled to see him, and pleased. He could detect none of the roar of emotion in her that he felt himself. But then he should not have expected it. She was happy. He wanted her to be. And part of him could not bear it.

He made himself smile. If he lost his dignity they would both hate it. "I was hoping to see you. I trust I am not interrupting."

"You have news of some sort?" She searched his face.

He must think only of the case. They had a common cause, one that mattered as fiercely as any they had ever fought. The lives of two women depended on it.

"Very little," he replied, moving a step closer to her. He caught a warmth, a faint air of some perfume about her. He ached to move closer still. She was so different now, so much less vulnerable than before. And yet in so many ways she was exactly the same. The will to battle was there, the stubbornness, the unreason, the laughter he had never completely understood, the arbitrariness that exasperated and fascinated him.

There was a very faint flush on her cheeks, as if she guessed some part of his thoughts.

He looked away from her, avoiding her eyes, pretending to be thinking deeply of legal matters.

"I have been to see both Cleo Anderson and Miriam Gardiner. Both deny either conspiracy or murder, but Miriam at least is lying to me about the murders. She knows who committed them, but I believe her when she says it is not she. I have not met Lucius Stourbridge."

Hester was startled. "Do you believe he could be guilty of killing his own mother?"

"I don't think so, but it would seem to have been someone in the family, or else Miriam Gardiner," he reasoned.

She looked up and down the corridor. "Come into the waiting room here. There is no one needing it at the moment. We can speak more easily." She opened the door and led him in.

He closed it, trying to force his emotions out of his consciousness. There were far more important issues between them.

"Major Stourbridge?" he asked. "Or the brother, Aiden Campbell?"

She looked miserable. "I don't know. I can't think of any reason why they would hurt either Mrs. Stourbridge or, still less, Treadwell. But he was a blackmailer. If he would blackmail Cleo, then maybe he would blackmail others as well. William says he seemed to spend more money than he could have had from Cleo, so there will have been other victims."

"Lucius?"

"Perhaps," she said quietly. "That would explain why Miriam is prepared to defend him, even at the price of being condemned for it herself."

It was possible. It would explain Miriam's refusal to tell the truth. But he still found it hard to believe.

"I cannot think of anything we could argue which would convince a jury of that, espccially in the face of Miriam's denial," he said, watching Hester. "And she would not let me try. I have promised not to act against her wishes."

A smile touched the corners of Hester's lips and then vanished. "I would have assumed as much. I would like you to be able to defend Miriam, but I am more concerned with Cleo Anderson. I hope she did not kill Treadwell, but she cannot have killed Mrs. Stourbridge. I am absolutely sure she would not have conspired for Miriam to marry Lucius, or anyone else, for money. That part of it is simply impossible."

"Even to put to a good cause?" he asked gently.

"To put to any cause at all. It would be revolting to her. She loves Miriam. What kind of a woman would have her daughter marry for money? That's prostitution!"

"Hester, my dear! It is the commonest practice in civilization. Or out of it, for that matter. Parents have sold their daughters in marriage, and considered it as doing all parties a service, since time immemorial—longer. Since prehistory."

"Isn't that the same?" she said tartly.

"Actually, no. I believe 'time immemorial' is in the middle of the twelfth century. It hardly matters."

"No, it doesn't. Cleo would not sell her daughter, and she certainly would not conspire to murder someone who got in the way. If you knew her as I do, you wouldn't even have thought of it."

He did not believe it either, but it was what a jury would believe that mattered. He pointed that out to her.

"I know," she said miserably, staring at the floor. "But we've got to do something to help. I refuse to hide behind an intricacy of the law as if it excused one from fighting."

He found himself smiling, but there was no laughter in it, no light at all, except irony. "Murder is not an intricacy of the law, my dear."

She looked at him with utter frankness, all the old friendship warm in her eyes, and suddenly he was short of breath.

The final bit of denial of his emotions slipped away. He forced his mind back to the law and Cleo Anderson.

"How much medicine is missing, and exactly what?"

She looked apologetic. "We don't know, but it's a lot—a few grains a day, I should think. I can't give you precise measurements and I wouldn't if I could. You would rather not know."

"Perhaps you are right," he admitted. "I won't ask again. When the matter comes to court, who is likely to testify on the thefts?"

"Only Fermin Thorpe, willingly—or at least not willingly but for the prosecution," she amended. "He's going to hate having to say that anything went missing from his hospital. He won't know whether to make light of it, and risk being thought trying to cover it up, or to condemn it and be seen on the side of the law, all quivering with outrage at the iniquity of nurses. Either way, he'll be furious at being caught up in it at all."

"Is he not likely to defend one of his staff?"

The look in her face was eloquent dismissal of any such prospect.

"I see," he concluded. "And the apothecary?"

"Phillips? He'll cover all he can—even to risking his own safety, but there's only so much he can do."

"I see. I will speak with a few of the other nurses, if I may, and perhaps Mr. Phillips. Then I shall go and see Sergeant Robb."

It was early evening by the time Rathbone had made as thorough an examination of the hospital routine as he wished to, and had come to the regrettable conclusion that it required considerable forethought and some skill and nerve to steal medicines on a regular basis. The apothecary was very careful, in spite of his unkempt appearance and erratic sense of the absurd. Better opportunities occurred when a junior doctor was hurried, confused by a case he did not understand, or simply a little careless. Rathbone formed the opinion that in all probability Phillips was perfectly aware of what Cleo had been doing, and why, and had either deliberately connived at it, or at the very least had turned a blind eye. Against all his training, he found himself admiring the man for it, and quite intentionally ceased looking for evidence to support his theory.

Consequently, it was after seven o'clock by the time he went looking for Sergeant Robb, and was obliged to ask for his address at home in order to see him.

He found the house quite easily, but in spite of Michael Robb's courtesy, he felt an intruder. A glance told him he had interrupted the care of the old man who sat in the chair in the center of the room, his white hair brushed back off his brow, his broad shoulders hunched forward over a hollow chest. His face was pale except for two spots of color on his cheeks. The sight of him gave a passionate and human reality to the work Cleo Anderson was prepared to risk so much for. Rathbone was startled to find himself filled with anger at the situation, at his own helplessness to affect it, and at the world for not knowing and not caring. It was with difficulty that he answered Michael Robb in a level voice.

"Good evening, Sergeant. I am sorry to intrude into your home, and at such an uncivil hour. If I could have found you at the police station I would have."

"What can I do for you, Sir Oliver?" Michael asked. He was courteous but wary. Rathbone was of both a class and a profession he was unused to dealing with except in court, where the duty of their offices prescribed the behavior for both of them. He was acutely conscious of his grandfather sitting, tired and hungry, waiting to be assisted. But he was by nature, as well as occupation, a gentle-mannered man.

"I have undertaken to defend Mrs. Anderson against the charge of murder," Rathbone replied with a faint, self-deprecating smile. He could not pretend to anyone he hoped for much success, and he did not wish Robb to think him a fool. "The question of theft is another matter."

"I'm sorry," Michael said, and there was sincerity in his

245

face as well as his voice. "I took no pleasure in charging her. But I can't withdraw it."

"I understand that. It provides the motive for the murder of Treadwell."

"Are you talking about Cleo Anderson?" the old man interrupted, looking from one to the other of them.

Michael's face tightened, and he shot Rathbone a look of reproach. "Yes, Grandpapa."

Rathbone had the strong impression that if Michael could have escaped with a lie about it he would have done so to protect the old man from knowledge which could only hurt. Had he any knowledge how much he also was compromised? Did he guess the debt he owed Cleo Anderson?

The old man looked at Rathbone. "And you're going to defend her, young man?" He regarded Rathbone up and down, from his beautifully made boots and tailored trousers to his coat and silk cravat. "And what's an officer-type gentleman, with a title an' all, doing defending a woman like Mrs. Anderson, who in't got two pence to rub together?" He cared about Cleo too much to be in awe of anyone. His faded eyes met Rathbone's without a flicker.

"I don't want payment, Mr. Robb," Rathbone answered. "I undertook it as a favor to a friend, Mrs. Monk. I believe you know her. . . ." He saw the flash of recognition and of pleasure in the old man's face, and felt a warmth within himself. "And I am continuing out of regard for Mrs. Anderson herself, now that I have met her."

Michael was looking at him with anxiety. Rathbone knew what he feared, perhaps better than he did himself. He feared the same thing, and even more keenly. He did not have to look at the cabinet shelf in the far corner to be aware of the medicines that first Cleo had brought, and now he was terrified Hester would continue to bring. There was no point in asking her not to, and he was in no position to forbid her—he doubted even Monk would succeed in that. Altogether, it would be wiser not to try. It would provoke a quarrel and waste time and energy they all needed to address the problem rather than fight each other. The chances of success in dissuading Hester, in his opinion, did not exist.

He preferred, for legal reasons, as well as his own fast-vanishing peace of mind, not to know what was in that cabinet or how it got there.

Michael half glanced at the cabinet, then averted his gaze. If the thought came to his mind, he forced it away. Just now he was too torn by his needs to allow himself to think it.

"So you're going to stand up an' speak for her?" the old man asked Rathbone.

"Yes, I am," Rathbone replied.

The elder Robb screwed up his face. His voice was hoarse, whispering. "What can you do for her, young man? Be honest with me."

Rathbone was candid. "I don't know. I believe she took the medicines. I don't believe she murdered Treadwell, even though he was blackmailing her. I think there is something of great importance that we have not imagined, and I am going to try to find out what it is."

"That why you came to speak to Michael?"

"Yes."

"Then you'd best get on with it. I can wait for me supper." He turned to his grandson. "You help this fellow. We can eat later."

"Thank you," Rathbone acknowledged the gesture. "But I should feel more comfortable if you were to continue as you would have. I think I passed a pie seller on the corner about a hundred yards away. Would you allow me to fetch us one each, and then we can eat and discuss at the same time?"

Michael hesitated only a moment, glancing at the old man and seeing his flash of pleasure at the prospect, then he accepted.

Rathbone returned with the three best pies he could purchase, wrapped in newspaper and kept hot, and they ate together with mugs of tea. Michael was the police officer in charge, and it was his duty to gather evidence and to present it in court. A few years earlier he would also have risked being sued for false arrest had the case failed, not as witness for the Crown but in a personal capacity, and faced jail himself could he not pay the fine. Even so, he seemed as keen as his grandfather to find any mitigating evidence he could for Cleo Anderson.

Old John Robb was convinced that if she had killed Treadwell, then he had thoroughly deserved it, and if the law condemned her, then the law was wrong and should be overturned. His faith that Rathbone could do that was fueled more by hope than realism.

Michael did not argue with his grandfather. His desire to protect him from more pain was so evident Rathbone was greatly moved by it.

Nevertheless, when he left as dusk was falling, he had learned nothing that was of help to him. Everything simply confirmed what he already knew from Hester. He walked briskly along the footpath in the warm evening air, the smells of the day sharp around him: horse manure, dry grass and dust from the Heath, now and then the delicacy of meat and onions or the sharpness of peppermint from one peddler or the other. There was the sound of a barrel organ playing a popular song in the distance, and children shouting.

He hailed the first hansom that passed him and gave the driver his address, then instantly changed his mind and directed him instead to his father's home in Primrose Hill.

It was almost dark when he arrived. He walked up the familiar path with a sense of anticipation, even though he had taken no steps to ensure that his father was home, let alone that it was convenient for him to call.

The sweetness of mown grass and deep shadow engulfed him, and a snare of honeysuckle so sharp it caught in his throat almost like a taste. As he walked around the house and across the lawn to the French doors, he saw that the study light was on. Henry Rathbone had not bothered to draw the curtains and Oliver could see him sitting in the armchair.

Henry was reading and did not hear the silent footsteps or

notice the shadow. His legs were crossed, and he was sucking on his pipestem, though as usual the pipe itself had gone out.

Oliver tapped on the glass.

Henry looked up, then as he recognized his son, his lean face filled with pleasure and he beckoned him in.

Oliver felt the ease of familiarity wash over him like a warmth. Unreasonably, some of his helplessness left him, although he had not even begun to explain the problem, let alone address it. He sat down in the big chair opposite his father's, leaning back comfortably.

For a few moments neither of them spoke. Henry continued to suck on his empty pipe. Outside in the darkness a nightbird called and the branches of the honeysuckle, with its trumpet-shaped flowers, waved in the slight wind. A moth banged against the glass.

"I have a new case," Oliver said at length. "I can't possibly win it."

Henry took his pipe out of his mouth. "Then you must have had a good reason for taking it . . . or at least one that appeared good at the time."

"I don't think it was a good one." Oliver was pedantic, as his nature inclined. He had learned exactness from Henry, and he never measured what he said to him. It was part of the basis of their friendship. "It was compelling. They are not the same."

Henry smiled. "Not in the slightest," he agreed.

"Monk asked me to," Oliver added.

Henry nodded.

"There was a moral imperative," Oliver said, justifying the choice. He did not want his father to think it was because of Monk, still less because of Hester.

"I see. Are you going to tell me what it is?"

"Of course." Oliver moved and crossed his legs comfortably. He gave a succinct outline of the cases against both Cleo Anderson and Miriam Gardiner, then he waited while Henry sat deep in thought for several moments. Outside it was now completely dark except for the patch of luminous moonlight

249

on the grass just short of the old apple tree at the end of the lawn.

"And you assume that this woman Cleo Anderson did not kill the coachman," Henry said at last. "Even in a manner for which there might be some mitigating circumstances—or possibly a struggle in which he died accidentally?"

Oliver thought for a moment before answering. The truth was that that was exactly what he had accepted. Cleo had said she was not present, and he had believed her. He still did.

"Yes. Yes, I am assuming that," he agreed. "She never denied taking the medicines. I have no proof of exactly how she did it, or any of the circumstances. I have deliberately avoided finding them."

Henry made no comment. "How is Monk involved?" he asked instead.

Rathbone explained.

"And Hester?" Henry asked, his voice gentle.

Oliver had not forgotten how fond his father was of Hester, nor his unspoken desire that Oliver should marry her. He sometimes feared Hester's regard for him was at least in part the affection she had for Henry and the desire to belong to a family in which she could know the safety her own had not given her. Her father had shot himself after a financial disgrace visited upon him at the end of the Crimean War by a man who had traded upon their friendship in order to cheat. Hester's mother had died shortly afterwards, largely of grief. Hester had spoken of it only once, unless she had done so more often to Henry when Oliver was not there, perhaps needing to share the burden.

This was a topic of conversation he was dreading. He had deliberately avoided it as long as possible, even to the extent of not coming to Primrose Hill but meeting his father in the City, where private conversations were too liable to interruption. Now it could no longer be deferred.

"Hester seems very well," he answered expressionlessly. At least he thought he had, but judging by Henry's face, perhaps he deluded himself. "Of course, she is deeply concerned for this nurse, both personally and in principle," he added, feeling the warmth rush up his cheeks.

Henry nodded. "I can imagine that she is consumed with her usual fire." He did not say anything about Oliver's motives for accepting what seemed a hopeless case. He was the only person who induced Oliver to make explanations of himself where none had been asked for.

"It matters!" Oliver said urgently, leaning forward a little. He looked at Henry, at his lean and slightly stooped form, his hair very gray, and imagined what he would feel if he had been a soldier or a sailor instead of a mathematician, if he were broken in body, bewildered and alone, unable to afford the care he needed, stripped of the dignity of old age and left only with its helplessness. It was so painful it caught his breath. Now the battle was for John Robb, for Henry, for all those affected by injury and age, or who would be in time to come. "It matters far more than any one person," he said passionately. "More than Cleo Anderson or even than Hester— or winning for its own sake. If we allow this injustice without doing all we can against it, what are we worth?"

Henry regarded him gravely, all the humor gone from his eyes. "Very little," he said quietly. "But emotion will not win for you, Oliver. It is an excellent driving force, the best, and it will keep your courage high. Anger at injustice has righted more wrongs than most other things, and it is one of the great creative forces in a civilized society." He shook his head. "But in order not to replace one enemy with another, albeit innocently intended, you must use your intelligence. You told me that you are certain that both Mrs. Anderson and Mrs. Gardiner are lying to you. You cannot go into court without knowing at least what the lie is—and why they are telling it at the risk of their own deaths. The reason must be a very powerful one indeed."

"I know that," Oliver agreed. "And I have racked my brain to think what it could be."

"Is it the same reason for each?"

"I don't even know that."

Henry sat thoughtfully, elbows on the arms of his chair, fingers steepled together. "I assume that you warned each of them that not only her own life, but the life of the other, rests upon the verdict. Therefore they each have a compelling reason for not telling you the truth. From what you say it seems possible that Mrs. Anderson does not know it, but certainly Mrs. Gardiner does. Why would a woman hang for a crime she did not commit?" He looked very steadily at Oliver. "Only because the alternative to her is worse."

"What could be worse than hanging?" Oliver asked.

"I don't know. That is what you must find out."

"The hanging of someone you love . . ." Oliver said, as much to himself as to Henry.

"Is Lucius Stourbridge guilty?" Henry asked him.

"I don't know," Oliver replied. "I don't know why he could kill either Treadwell or his own mother."

"Treadwell is easier," Henry said thoughtfully. "The man may have threatened Mrs. Gardiner, or threatened the marriage, either through Mrs. Anderson or in some other way. He was a blackmailer. Much is possible. It is far more difficult to think of any motive for Lucius to have killed his mother."

"I've searched for one," Oliver admitted. "I've found nothing."

"It would be extraordinary if the two murders were not connected," Henry pursued, drawing his brows together. "What elements do they have in common?"

"Treadwell himself, and Miriam Gardiner," Oliver replied, "and the nature of the attacks."

"And the unknown," Henry added. "One must always include the possibility of a factor we have not considered, perhaps something outside our knowledge entirely. From what you have told me so far, it seems this may be the case here. Proceed with logic, eliminate what is impossible, and then examine what is left, no matter how ugly it may be. I have a feeling, Oliver, that this case may stretch your compassion to its limits and require more of you than you had thought to give. I am sorry. I appreciate that this is not easy for you, especially considering Hester's involvement in it."

"Her involvement makes no difference!" As soon as the words were on his lips he knew that they were untrue, and quite certainly that Henry knew it also, but it was difficult to withdraw them.

Henry shook his head so minutely it was barely a movement at all.

"It makes no difference to the issues," Oliver amended. What he really meant—the aloneness, the knowledge of having held something precious and having let it slip through his fingers because he would not commit his passions fully enough, the regret—was all there between them, unsaid. Henry knew him well enough that truth was not necessary and lies were not only impossible but damaging. Henry understood as well as he did that Hester made all the difference in the world to the way he felt about it, to know he would continue to fight regardless of what he himself might lose in reputation, self-esteem or money.

Henry was smiling. Oliver knew in that moment that he approved. Much as he revered the law himself, and understood the dedication of a man to his chosen field, to his principles that superseded any individual, he also understood that to do all these things without caring was a kind of death to the heart. He would rather Oliver fought because he cared, and lost, than won with all the rewards but without belief.

They sat in silence for another half hour or so, then Oliver rose and took his leave. Henry strolled with him down the lawn in the darkness, heavy with the scent of wet grass, to look at the moonlight reflected on the leaves in the orchard, then walked back up again towards the road.

It did not need to be said that tomorrow Oliver must begin to prepare a sensible case to defend his clients and to look for whatever alternative was so hideous Miriam Gardiner would rather hang than have it revealed.

253

And if Oliver found it, where did his loyalty lie then? To Miriam or to the truth?

But after they had parted and Oliver walked towards the main thoroughfare he felt a strength restored inside him, a balance returned. He had faced certain lies and no longer allowed them to govern him.

10

$F_{IVE WEEKS LATER,}$ Cleo Anderson and Miriam Gardiner sat in the dock accused of conspiracy and murder. The courtroom was packed to suffocation, people sitting so close to one another that when they moved in discomfort the sound of fabrics rubbing together was audible. The shuffling and squeaking of boots were broken by a cough and the occasional murmur.

When the business of calling to order, reading the charge and pleadings had been accomplished, Robert Tobias opened for the prosecution. He was a man Rathbone had faced several times before and to whom he had lost as often as he had won. Tobias was of a fraction less than average height, slender in his youth, and now, at sixty, still supple and straight-backed. He had never been handsome, strictly speaking, but his intelligence and the power and beauty of his voice made him remarkable—and both intimidating and attractive. More than one society lady had begun by flirting with him for her own entertainment and ended by caring for him more than she wished to, eventually being hurt. He was a widower who intended to retain his freedom to do as he chose.

He smiled at Rathbone and called his first witness, Sergeant Michael Robb.

Rathbone watched as Robb climbed the short staircase to the witness stand and faced the court. He looked unhappy and extraordinarily young. He must have been in his mid-twenties, but he had the scrubbed and brushed look of a child sent off to Sunday school and who would far rather be almost anywhere else.

Tobias sauntered out into the middle of the open space of the floor with the jury on one side, the witness ahead of him, and the judge to his right, high up against the wall in his magnificent seat, surrounded by panels of softly gleaming wood and padded red velvet.

"Sergeant Robb," Tobias began politely, "this whole case is very distressing. No decent man likes to imagine two women, especially when one is young and agreeable to look upon and the other is entrusted with the care of the sick"—he lifted his hand very slightly towards the dock—"would be capable of conspiring together to commit cold-blooded murder for gain. Fortunately, it is not your task, nor mine either, to determine if this is indeed what happened." He turned with a graceful gesture to face the jury and gave a little bow in their direction. "It is the awful duty of these twelve good men and true, and I do not envy them. Justice is a mighty weight. It takes a strong man, a brave man, an honest man, to bear it."

Rathbone was tempted to interrupt this piece of blatant flattery, but he knew Tobias would be only too happy if he did. He remained in his seat, nodding very slightly as if he agreed.

Tobias turned back to Robb. "All we need from you is a simple, exact account of the facts you know. May we begin with the discovery of the body of James Treadwell?"

Robb stood to attention. Rathbone wondered if it was as apparent to the jury as it was to him how much Robb disliked his task. Would they imagine it was repugnance for the crime, or would they know, as he did, that it was a deeper knowledge of complex tragedy, right and wrong so inextricably mixed he could not single out one thread?

How did people judge? On instinct? Intelligence? Previous knowledge and experience? Emotion? How was evidence interpreted? How often he had seen two people describe a single chain of events and draw utterly different conclusions from it.

Robb began by talking with bare, almost schoolboy simplicity of having been called out to see the dead body of a man who had apparently died of a blow to the head.

"So you decided immediately that he was the victim of murder?" Tobias said with surprise and evident satisfaction. He barely glanced at Rathbone, as if he half expected to be interrupted and took it as a sign of Rathbone's foreknowledge of defeat that he was not.

Robb breathed in deeply. "From the kind of marks on his clothes, sir, I didn't think he'd fallen off a coach or carriage, or been struck by one that maybe didn't see him in the dark."

"Very perceptive of you. You judged the matter of great seriousness right from the outset?"

"Death is always serious," Robb answered.

"Of course. But murder has a gravity that accident does not. It is a dark and dreadful thing, a violation of our deepest moral order. Accident is tragic, but it is mischance. Murder is evil!"

Robb's face was pink. "With respect, sir, I thought you said you and I were not here to judge, just to establish the facts. If you don't mind, sir, I'd prefer to stick to that."

There was a murmur around the court.

Rathbone allowed himself to smile; indeed, he could not help it.

Tobias controlled his temper with grace, but it cost him an effort. Rathbone could see it in the angle of his shoulders and the pull of the cloth in his expensive coat.

"I stand corrected," he conceded. "By all means, let us have the bare facts. Will you describe this dead man that you found. Was he young or old? In good health or ill? Let us see him through your eyes, Sergeant Robb. Let us feel as you did when you stood on the pavement and stared down at this man, so lately alive and full of hopes and dreams, and so violently torn from them." He spread his arms wide in invitation. "Take us with you."

Robb stared at him glumly. Never once did he lift his glance towards the two women sitting white-faced and motionless in the dock. Nor did he look beyond Tobias and Rathbone to search the audience for other faces familiar to him: Monk or Hester.

"He was fairly ordinary. It was difficult to tell his height lying down. He had straight hair, strong hands, callused as if he'd held reins often enough."

"Any signs of a fight?" Tobias cut in. "Any bruises or cuts as if he had tried to defend himself?"

"I saw none. Just the grazes on his hands—from crawling."

"I shall naturally ask the surgeon also, but thank you for your observation. Exactly where was this poor man, Sergeant?"

"On the pathway between number five and number six on Green Man Hill, near Hampstead Heath."

"And which way was he facing?"

"Towards number five."

"And is that where he was killed?"

"I don't think so. He looked to have crawled some distance. His trouser knees were all torn and muddy, and his elbows in places."

"How far? Can you tell?"

"No. At least two or three hundred yards, maybe more."

"I see. What did you do then, Sergeant?"

Step by step, Tobias drew from Robb the account of finding the carriage and the horses, and presuming they were connected with the dead man. Then he led him through Monk's arrival, seeking someone answering the dead man's description.

"How very interesting!" Tobias said with triumph. "Presumably, you took this Mr. Monk to look at your corpse?"

"Yes sir."

"And did he identify him?"

"No sir. He couldn't say. But he fetched two gentlemen from Bayswater who said he was James Treadwell, who had been their coachman."

"And the names of these gentlemen?"

"Major Harry Stourbridge and his son, Mr. Lucius Stourbridge."

There was a rustle of movement in the court as people's attention was caught. Several straightened in their seats. "The same Lucius Stourbridge who is the son of Mrs. Verona Stourbridge and who was engaged to marry Mrs. Miriam Gardiner?"

More movement in the gallery. Two women craned forward to stare at the dock.

"Yes sir," Robb answered.

"And when was Treadwell last seen alive, and by whom?"

Reluctantly, Robb told of Miriam's flight from the garden party, Monk's duplicity on the matter, and how first Monk had tracked down Miriam, and then how Robb had himself. There was nothing Rathbone could do to stop him.

"Most interesting," Tobias said sagely. "And did Mrs. Gardiner give you a satisfactory account of her flight from Bayswater and any reason for this most strange behavior?"

"No sir."

"Did she tell you who had killed Treadwell? I assume you did ask her?"

"I did, and no, she did not give me any answer, except to say she did not do it."

"And did you believe her?"

Rathbone half rose to his feet.

The judge glanced at him.

Tobias smiled. "Perhaps that could be better phrased. Sergeant Robb, did you subsequently arrest Mrs. Gardiner for the murder of James Treadwell?"

"Yes, I did."

Tobias raised his eyebrows. "But you have not charged her with it!"

Robb's face was tight and miserable. "She's charged with conspiracy . . ."

"That you should be sad about such a fearful tragedy is very proper, Sergeant," Tobias observed, staring at him. "But you seem more than that, you seem reluctant, as if you do this against your will. Why is that, Sergeant Robb?"

Rathbone's mind raced. Should he object that this was irrelevant, personal? He had intended to use Robb's high opinion of Cleo, his knowledge of her motives, as his only weapon in mitigation. Now Tobias had stolen it. He could hardly object now and then raise it himself later. Even if he did so obliquely, Tobias himself would then object.

There was nothing he could do but sit quietly and try to keep his face from betraying him.

"Sergeant?" Tobias prompted.

Robb lifted his chin a little, glaring back. "I am reluctant, sir. Mrs. Anderson is well known in our community for going around visiting and helping the sick, especially them that's old and poor. Night and day, she did it, as well as working in the hospital. She couldn't have cared for them better if they'd been her own."

"But you arrested her for murder!"

Robb clenched his jaw. "I had to. We found evidence that Treadwell was blackmailing her—"

This time Rathbone did stand up. "My lord . . ."

"Yes, yes," the judge agreed, pursing his lips. "Mr. Tobias, you know better than this. If you have evidence, present it in the proper way."

Tobias bowed, smiling. He had no cause to worry, and he knew it. He turned back to Robb in the witness stand.

"This high regard you have for Mrs. Anderson, Sergeant, is it all upon local hearsay, or can you substantiate it from any knowledge of your own?"

"I have it from knowledge of my own," Robb said wretchedly. "She came regular to see my grandfather, who lives with me."

Tobias nodded slowly. He seemed to be weighing his words, judging what to say and what to leave unsaid. Rathbone looked across at the faces of the jury. There was one man in particular, middle-aged, earnest, who was watching Tobias with what seemed to be understanding. He turned to Robb, and there was pity clear in his face.

Tobias did not ask if Cleo had brought medicines or not. It was not necessary; the jury had perceived it already. They would not want to see the sergeant embarrassed. Tobias was a superb judge of nature.

There was nothing Rathbone could do.

The day proceeded while Tobias drew out all the rest of the evidence, piece by piece, from an unwilling Robb. He told how, at least in part by following Monk, he had learned of the missing medicines, of Cleo's own poverty and that she was being blackmailed by Treadwell. It provided her with a motive for murder that anyone could understand only too well. The jury sat somberly, shaking their heads, and there seemed as much pity in their faces as blame.

That would change when Miriam became involved; Rathbone knew it as well as he knew darkness followed sundown, but there was no protest or argument he could make. Tobias was precisely within all the rules and had laid his plans perfectly. There was nothing for Rathbone to do but endure it . . . and hope.

The second day was no better. Robb finished his testimony, and Rathbone was given the opportunity to question him, but there was nothing for him to ask. If he remained silent he would appear to have surrendered already, without even the semblance of a fight, as if he had no belief in his clients and no hope for them. And yet Tobias had touched on every aspect of Robb's knowledge of the case and there was nothing to challenge. Everything he had said was true, and not open to kinder or more favorable interpretation. To have him repeat it would not only look ineffectual, it would reinforce it in the jury's minds. He rose to his feet.

"Thank you, my lord, but Mr. Tobias has asked of Sergeant

Robb everything that I would have. It would be self-indulgent of me to waste the court's time asking the sergeant to repeat it for me." He sat down again.

Tobias smiled.

The judge nodded to him unhappily. He seemed to find the case distressing, and looked as if he would very much rather have had someone else there in his place, but he would see justice done. He had spent his life in this cause.

Tobias called the minister from the church in Hampstead, a genial man who looked uncomfortable in such surroundings but gave his evidence with conviction. He had known Cleo Anderson for thirty years. He had had no idea she had committed any crime whatsoever and found this news difficult to comprehend. He apologized for expressing such bewilderment. However, human frailty was his field of experience.

Tobias sympathized with him. "And how long have you known Miriam Gardiner?" he asked.

"Since she first came to Hampstead," the vicar replied. Then under Tobias's gentle encouragement he told the story of Miriam's first appearance in acute distress, at about thirteen years old, how Cleo had taken her in and cared for her while seeking her family. This had proved impossible, and Miriam had remained with Cleo until her marriage to Mr. Gardiner.

"A moment," Tobias interrupted him. "Could you describe Mr. Gardiner for us, please. His age, his appearance, his social and financial standing."

The vicar looked a trifle startled.

Rathbone was not. He knew exactly what Tobias was doing: establishing a pattern of Cleo's and Miriam's loyalty to each other, of Miriam's marrying a man with a prosperous business and then sharing her good fortune with her original benefactress, who had become as a mother to her. He did it extremely well, painting a picture of the woman and child struggling in considerable hardship, their closeness to one another, the happiness of Miriam on finding a worthy man, albeit older than herself, but gentle and apparently devoted to her.

It had not been a great romance, but a good, stable marriage—and certainly all that a girl in Miriam's position might have hoped for. A love match with a man her own age and class would not have brought her much material status or security.

Tobias made his point well and delicately. Again there was nothing whatever Rathbone could call into question.

Had Miriam shared her new good fortune with Cleo Anderson?

"Naturally," the vicar replied. "What loving daughter would not?"

"Just so," Tobias agreed, and let the matter rest.

When the court was adjourned for the day Rathbone went immediately to see Miriam. She was alone in the police cells, her face drawn, her eyes dark. She did not ask him why he had not crossexamined, and her silence made it harder for him. He had no idea if she had even hoped for anything, or how much she understood. It was so easy, when he was accustomed to the flow of a trial and its hidden meanings, to assume that others were as aware. He would have liked to allow her the mercy of remaining unaware of how serious her situation was, but he could not afford to.

He drew in his breath to ask her the usual question as to her feelings, or to offer some words of encouragement, true or not, but they would be empty and a waste of precious time and emotion. It would make almost a greater division between them, if that was possible. Honesty, his honesty, was all they had.

"Mrs. Gardiner, you must tell me the truth. I was silent today because I have no weapon to use against Tobias. He knows it, but if I make a show of fighting him, and lose, then the jury will know it as well. Now they think I am merely biding my time. But I am walking blindly. I don't know what he may know that I don't. Or what he may discover—which is worse."

She turned half away from him. "Nothing. There is nothing he can discover."

"He can discover who killed James Treadwell!" he said sharply. The time for any consideration of feeling was past. The rope was already overshadowing not only her but Cleo also.

She turned slowly to look at him. "I doubt that, Sir Oliver. They would not believe it, even if I were to tell them. And I won't. Believe me, it would cause far greater injury than it would ever heal. I have no proof, and all the evidence you have, as you have said, is against me."

The cells were warm, even stuffy, but he felt chilled in spite of it.

"It is my task to make them believe it." He feared even as he said it that she had closed her mind and was not listening to him. "At least allow me to try?" He was sounding desperate. He could hear it in the stridency of his voice.

"I am sorry you don't believe me," she said softly. "But it is true that it would cause more pain than any good it would do. At least accept that I have thought long and very hard about it before I have made this decision. I do understand that I will hang. I have no delusion that some miracle is going to save me. And you have not lied to me or given me any false sense of comfort. For that I thank you."

Her gratitude was like a rebuff, reminding him of how little he had actually done. He was going to be no more than a figurehead, barely fulfilling the requirements of the law that she be represented. The prosecution need not have called in Tobias, the merest junior could have presented this case and beaten him.

He found he was shaking, his hands clenched tight. "It is not only you who will hang—Cleo Anderson will as well!"

Her voice choked. "I know. But what can I do?" She looked at him, her eyes swimming with tears. "I will testify that I was there and that it was not she who killed him, if you want. But who would believe me? They think we are conspirators anyway. They expect me to defend her. I can't prove she wasn't there, and I can't prove he wasn't blackmailing her or that she didn't take the medicines. She did!"

What she said was true.

"Someone killed Treadwell." He picked his words carefully, trying to hurt her enough to make her tell him at last. "If it was not either you or Cleo, the only person I can think of that you would die to defend is Lucius Stourbridge."

Her eyes widened, and the last vestige of color fled from her face. She was too horrified to respond.

"If you will hang for him," he went on, "that is your choice. But is he really worth Cleo Anderson's life as well? Does she deserve that from you?"

She swung around to face him, her eyes blazing, her lips drawn back in a snarl of such ferocity he was almost afraid of her, small as she was, and imprisoned in this police cell.

"Lucius had nothing to do with it. I am not defending Treadwell's murderer! If I could see him hang I would tie the rope with my own hands and pull the trapdoor and watch him drop!" She took a deep, gasping breath. "I can't! God help me, there is nothing—nothing I can do. Now go away and leave me at least to solitude, if not to peace."

Other questions beat in his mind, but his fury and his despair robbed him of the words. He longed to be able to help her, not to increase his own reputation or to defend his honor, but simply to ease the pain he could see, and even feel, as he watched her. She was only a yard away from him, and yet an abyss existed between what she experienced and what he understood. He had no idea at all how he could cross that space. They could have been in separate countries. He did not even know what else he felt: anger; fear that she was guilty; fear that she was not and he would fail her and she would be destroyed by the wheels of the law he was supposed to guide or by pity; even a kind of admiration, because quite without reason, he believed there was something noble in her, something beautiful and strong.

He left, walking out of the cells blind to the heat of the late afternoon and the passersby, the chatter of voices, wheels, hooves, all the clamor of everyday living. He hailed a cab and gave the driver Monk's address in Fitzroy Street. He barely spared thought to how little he wanted to go into the house that Hester shared with Monk. It seemed secondary now, a wound to deal with at another time.

"I pleaded with her," he said, pacing back and forth in the front room where Monk received clients. Monk was standing by the mantelpiece even though the fire was unlit, the evening being far too mild to require one. Hester was sitting upright on the edge of the big armchair, staring at him, her face furrowed in concentration. "But she knows she will hang, and still refuses to tell me who killed Treadwell!" He threw his arms wide, almost banging against the high back of the other chair.

"Lucius Stourbridge," Monk said unhappily. "He is the only one she would hang for—apart from Cleo."

"No, it isn't," Rathbone said quickly. "I assumed that also. She denied it with fury—at me, not at whoever did kill Treadwell. She said she would willingly hang him herself if she could, but no one would believe her, and she would not tell me any more."

Monk stared at him in bewilderment. Rathbone wanted an answer above all things, at this moment, but it was a very small satisfaction to see Monk just as confused as he was.

They both looked at Hester.

"That leaves either Harry Stourbridge or Aiden Campbell," she said thoughtfully. "I suppose Treadwell could have been blackmailing Harry Stourbridge. He had been in the house for several years. He drove the carriage. Maybe Major Stourbridge went somewhere or did something he would pay to hide?"

"What about the brother, Campbell?" Rathbone asked.

Monk shook his head. "Unlikely. He lives in Wiltshire somewhere. Only came up for the engagement party. I did

266

check, and as far as the other servants knew, he barely saw Treadwell. He had his own carriage and driver, and no one ever saw him go anywhere near the mews while he was staying there. And Treadwell never went to Wiltshire in his life. And as for Campbell's killing Mrs. Stourbridge, they were very close, everyone agreed on that, had been ever since they were children."

"Even close siblings can quarrel," Rathbone pointed out.

"Of course," Monk agreed a touch sharply, staring down at the polished fender where his foot was resting. "But no one with enough cold-blooded nerve to murder rather than pay blackmail is going to kill the sister who is his only link with a fortune the size of the Stourbridges'. Now she is dead, he has no claim at all. He is not especially close to either Harry or Lucius. They are friendly enough, but they will not continue Verona's generosity."

Another blind alley.

Hester bit her lip. "Then we must find out if it was Major Stourbridge. However unpleasant, if that is the truth, we should know it."

"It would make sense," Rathbone admitted, pushing his hands into his pockets and taking them out again immediately. He had been taught not to put his hands in his pockets in boyhood, because it looked casual and pulled his clothes out of shape. He turned to Monk.

"Yes," Monk agreed, not to the likelihood but to accepting the task before Rathbone could ask him. "I should have pursued it before. I didn't look at the Stourbridges, either of them."

"I don't know what you can find in a day or two," Rathbone said wretchedly. "I'm going in with nothing! I have no other reasonable suspect to offer the jury, only 'person or persons unknown.' Nobody's going to believe that when Cleo and Miriam have perfect motives and every appearance of guilt."

"They may be guilty," Monk reminded him. "Or one of them may, perhaps in conspiracy with someone else."

"In the Stourbridge household?" Rathbone said with some sarcasm. "That has to be Miriam. And why, for the love of heaven?"

"I don't know," Monk said angrily. "But there is obviously some critical feature about the whole story that we haven't found—even if it is only the reason both women would rather hang than tell the truth. We'd better damned well discover what it is!"

Hester looked from Monk to Rathbone. "How long can you prolong the trial, Oliver?"

"We seem to spend our time asking him to sing songs while we scramble to find something vital," Monk said bitterly. "I'll start tomorrow morning as soon as it's light. But I don't even know where to look!"

"What can I do to help?" Hester asked, more to Rathbone than to Monk.

"I wish I knew," the lawyer confessed. "Cleo admits to taking the medicines. There is nothing we can do to mitigate that except show how she used them, and we already have all the witnesses we need for that. We have dozens of men and women to swear to her diligence, compassion, dedication, sobriety and honesty in all respects except that of stealing medicines from the hospital. We even have people who will swear she was chaste, modest and clean. It will achieve nothing. She was still paying Treadwell blackmail money, and he had all but bled her dry. The only decent meals she ate were those given her either at the hospital or by the people she visited. She even dressed in cast-off clothes left her by the dead!"

Hester sat silently, steeped in misery.

"I must go home," Rathbone said at last. "Perhaps a good night of sleep will clear my mind sufficiently to think of something." He bade them good-night and left, acutely conscious of loneliness. He would lie by himself in his smooth linen sheets. Monk would lie with Hester in his arms. The clear, moonlit night held no magic for him.

Tobias was in an expansive mood when he called his first witness the next day, but he was careful not to exaggerate his manner. He was too clever to alienate a jury by seeming to gloat over his triumph, although Rathbone, sitting at his table, thought his care unnecessary. As things were going at present, and from all future prospect, Tobias could hardly lose, whatever he did.

Neither Hester nor Monk was in the court, nor was Callandra Daviot. All of the Stourbridge family had yet to testify, and therefore were forbidden to be present in case anything they heard should influence what they themselves would say.

Tobias's first witness was the Stourbridges' groom. He took great care to establish his exact position in the household and his so-far blameless reputation. He left no avenue, however small, for Rathbone to call into question either his honesty or his power of observation.

Rathbone was quite satisfied that he should do so. He had no useful argument to make and no desire to try to blacken the man's character. It was always a bad exercise in that it offended the jurors to malign a person who was no more than a witness and in no way involved in a crime. And it had the great advantage—indeed, at the moment the only advantage—in that it took time.

All that he showed by it, unquestionably, was that Treadwell had on a number of occasions driven Miriam from Bayswater back to her home in Hampstead, or had collected her. He had also once or twice delivered messages or gifts from Lucius to her, in the early days of the courtship, before Lucius himself had done so. Undoubtedly, Treadwell knew her home and had spent time in the area.

Next, Tobias called the keeper of the local inn, the Jack Straw's Castle Inn, on the corner of North End Hill and Spaniards Road, who swore that Treadwell had stopped there on more than a few occasions, had a pint of ale and played darts or dominoes, gambled a little, and struck up casual conversation with the locals. Yes, he had seemed to ask a lot of questions. At the time the landlord had taken it for concern for his employer, who was courting a woman who lived in the area.

The landlord of the Bull and Bush, farther up on Golders Hill, said much the same, as did two locals from the Hare and Hounds, a short walk farther along. There he had asked more particularly about Miriam Gardiner and Cleo Anderson. Yes, he was free with his money, as if he knew there would be more where that had come from.

"What sort of questions did he ask?" Tobias enquired innocently.

"About her general reputation," the witness replied. "Was she honest, sober, that kind of thing."

"And chaste?" Tobias asked.

"Yes—that, too."

"Did you not think that impertinent of the coachman?"

"Yes, I did. When I caught him at it I told him in no uncertain terms that Mrs. Gardiner was as good a woman as he'd be likely to find in all Hampstead—and a damn sight too good for the likes of him!" He glanced at the judge. "Beggin' yer pardon, me lud."

"Did he explain why he asked such questions?"

"Never saw him again," the man said with satisfaction. He glanced up at the dock and gave both women a deliberate smile. Miriam attempted to return it, but it was a ghost on her ashen face. Cleo nodded to him very slightly, merely the acknowledgment courtesy demanded. It was a small gesture, but kindly meant.

"You would be glad to see Mrs. Gardiner happily married again, after losing her first husband so young?" Tobias observed conversationally.

"I was glad, and that's the truth! So were everyone else as knew 'er."

"Did you know the late Mr. Gardiner well?"

"Knew 'im in passing, like. A very decent sort o' gent."

"Indeed. But quite a lot older than his wife—his widow?"

The man's face darkened. "What are you tryin' ter say?"

Tobias shrugged. "What did James Treadwell try to say?"

"Nothing!" Now the man was plainly angry.

"You did not like him?" Tobias pressed.

"I did not!"

"No love for blackmailers?"

"No I 'aven't! Nor 'as any man fit ter walk an' breathe God's good air. Filth, they are."

Tobias nodded. "A feeling shared by many." He glanced up at the dock, then back to the witness box.

Rathbone knew perfectly well what he was doing, but he was helpless to stop him.

"Of course." Tobias smiled deprecatingly. "Treadwell may have been asking his questions about Mrs. Gardiner in loyal interest of his employer, Mr. Stourbridge, in order to prevent him from making an unfortunate marriage. Did that possibility occur to you? It may not have been for purposes of blackmail at all."

Rathbone stood up at last. "My lord, the witness is not in a position to know why Treadwell asked questions, and his opinion is surely irrelevant. Unless Mr. Tobias is implying he may have had some part in Treadwell's death?"

There was a sharp stir in the courtroom, and one of the jurors jerked up his head.

"Quite," the judge agreed. "Mr. Tobias, do not imperil your case by wandering too far afield. I am sure your point has already been taken. James Treadwell asked questions in the neighborhood regarding Mrs. Gardiner's character and reputation. Is that all you wish us to know?"

"For the moment, my lord." Tobias thanked his witness and turned invitingly to Rathbone.

Again there was nothing for him to ask. The witness had already made it plain he admired Miriam and was partisan in her favor. As far as he was concerned, Treadwell had met with a fate he deserved. It would not help either Miriam or Cleo to hear him say so again.

"I have nothing to ask this witness," Rathbone said.

Tobias proceeded to call the Stourbridges' servants to tell their account of the day of the party and Miriam's still-unexplained departure with Treadwell. The parlormaid had seen it all and told of it simply and obviously with great unhappiness.

At last Rathbone had something to ask.

"Miss Pembroke," he said with a slight smile, moving into the center of the floor and looking up at her where she stood high in the witness stand. "You have told very clearly what you saw. You must have had a view of Mrs. Gardiner with no one blocking your way."

"Yes sir, I did."

"You said she seemed about to faint, as if she had suffered a great shock, and then after she had recovered herself she turned and ran, even fled, from the garden towards the stables. Is that correct?"

"Yes sir."

The judge frowned.

Rathbone hurried on before he should be cautioned to come to the point.

"Did anyone speak to her, pass her anything?"

"You mean a glass, sir? I didn't see no one."

"No, I meant rather more like a message, something to account for her shock and, from what you describe, even terror."

"No sir, no one came that close to her. And I don't think she had a glass."

"You are not certain about the glass, but you are sure no one spoke to her or passed her anything?"

"Yes, I am."

"Have you any idea what caused her to run away?"

Tobias rose.

"No," the judge said to him bluntly. "Miss Pembroke is an observant girl. She may very well know what happened. It has been my experience that servants frequently know a good deal more than some of us would believe, or wish to believe." He turned to the witness stand. "Do you know what caused Mrs. Gardiner's flight, Miss Pembroke? If you do, this is the appropriate time and place to say so, whether it was a confidence or not."

"No sir, I don't know, an' that's the truth. But I never seen anyone look as dreadful as she did that day. She looked like she'd seen the living dead, she did."

"Do you know where Treadwell was during the party?" Rathbone asked.

"In the stables, sir, same as always."

"So Mrs. Gardiner went to him—he did not come to her?"

"Must be."

"Thank you. That is all I have to ask you."

"But not all I have!" Tobias cut in quickly, striding forward from his table. "You were on the lawn mixing with the guests in your capacity as parlormaid, were you not?"

"Yes sir. I were carrying a tray of lemonade. Parkin had the champagne."

"Is it easy to carry a tray loaded with glasses?"

"It's all right, when you're used to it. Gets heavy."

"And you offered them to those guests whose glasses were empty?"

"Yes sir."

"So you were not watching Mrs. Gardiner all the time?"

"No sir."

"Naturally. Could she have received some message, either in words or on paper, that you were unaware of?"

"I suppose she could."

"Is it possible, Miss Pembroke, that this was the best time for her to catch Treadwell alone, and with no duties or responsibilities which would prevent him from driving her from Cleveland Square? Is it possible, Miss Pembroke, that she knew the working of the household sufficiently well that she was aware she would find Treadwell in the mews, with

273

the carriage available, and had planned in advance to meet him there and drive to a lonely place where she imagined they could do as they pleased together, unobserved, and where she intended—with the help of her foster mother—to get rid, once and for all, of the man who was blackmailing them both?"

Rathbone shot to his feet, but the protest died on his lips.

Tobias shrugged. "I only ask if it's possible," he said reasonably. "Miss Pembroke is an observant young woman. She may know."

"I don't!" she protested. "I don't know what happened, I swear!"

"Your loquacity seems to have ended in confusion," the judge said acidly to Tobias. He turned to the jury. "You will note that the question has gone unanswered, and draw your own conclusions. Sir Oliver, have you anything to add?"

Oliver had not.

Tobias was unstoppable. His rich voice seemed to fill the court, and there was hardly an eye which was not upon him. He called the lady's maid who had seen Miriam in Verona Stourbridge's room, and drew from her a highly damaging account of Miriam's trying on the jewelry and apparently having read the diary.

"Do you know what is in the diary?" Tobias asked.

The girl's eyes widened in horror. "No sir, I do not." Her tone carried bitter resentment that he should suggest such a thing.

"Of course not," he agreed smoothly. "One does not read another person's private writings. I wondered perhaps if Mrs. Stourbridge had confided in you. Ladies can become extremely close to their maids."

She was considerably mollified. "Well . . . well, I know she put in her feelings about things. She used to go back and read again some from years ago, when she was in Egypt. She did that just the day before she . . . died . . . poor lady." She looked tearful, and Tobias gave her a moment or two to compose herself again—and to allow the jury to gather the full import of what had been said—before he continued.

He then went on to elicit a picture of Miriam as gentle, charming, biddable, struggling to fit into a household with a great deal higher social status than she was accustomed to, and unquestionably a great deal more money. It was a portrait quite innocent and touching, until finally he turned to the jury.

"A lovely woman striving to better herself?" he said with a smile. "For the sake of the man she loves—and met by chance out walking on Hampstead Heath." His face darkened, his arms relaxed until his shoulders were almost slumped. "Or a clever, greedy woman blessed with a pretty face, ensnaring a younger man, unworldly-wise, and doing everything she could, suppressing her own temper and will, to charm him into a marriage which would give her, and her foster mother, a life of wealth they could never have attained in their own station?"

He barely paused for breath or to give Rathbone the chance to object. "An innocent woman caught in a dreadful web of circumstances? Or a conniving woman overtaken by an equally cold-blooded and greedy coachman, who saw his chance to profit from her coming fortune but had fatally miscalculated her ruthlessness—and thus met not with payment for his silence as to her past, perhaps their past relationship with each other! Perhaps he was even the means of their meeting—far other than by chance? Instead, he met with violent death in the darkness under the trees of Hampstead Heath."

Rathbone raised his voice, cutting across him scathingly and without reference to the judge.

"Treadwell certainly seems to have been a villain, but neither you nor I have proved him a fool! Why in heaven's name would he threaten to expose Miriam Gardiner's past—which neither you nor I have found lacking in virtue of any kind—*before* she had married into the Stourbridge family?" He spread his hands as if in bewilderment. "She had no money to pay him anything. Surely he would have waited until *after* the wedding—indeed, done everything in his power to make sure it took place?" He became sarcastic. "If, as you suggest, he even helped engineer the meeting between Mr. Stourbridge and Mrs. Gardiner, then it strains the bonds of credibility that he would sabotage his own work just as it was about to come to fruition."

His point was valid, but it did not carry the emotional weight of Tobias's accusation. The damage had been done. The jury's minds were filled with the image of a scheming and duplicitous woman manipulating a discarded lover into a position where she could strike him over the head and leave his murdered body on the Heath.

"Was it chance, or was it Treadwell's dying attempt to implicate his murderers that he used the last of his strength to crawl to the footpath outside Cleo Anderson's door?" Tobias demanded, his voice ringing with outrage and pity. "Gentlemen, I leave it to you!"

The court adjourned with Miriam and Cleo all but convicted already.

Rathbone paced the floor of his rooms, resisting the temptation to call Monk and see if he had made any progress. So many times they had faced together cases that seemed impossible. He could list them all in his mind. But in this one he had no weapons at all, and he did not even know what he believed himself. He still was not prepared to accept that either Cleo or Miriam was guilty, let alone both. But there was very little else that made sense—except Lucius or Harry Stourbridge. And if that were so, no wonder Miriam looked crushed beyond imagining any solution, or that even Rathbone could convince the court of the truth.

It all depended on Monk's finding something—if he even knew where to look—and collecting enough evidence to prove it, and on Rathbone's being able to prolong the case another three days at the very outside. Two days seemed more likely.

He spent the evening thinking of tactics to give Monk more time, every trick of human nature or legal expertise. It was all profoundly unpromising.

Tobias called Harry Stourbridge as his first witness of the morning. He treated him with great deference and sympathy, not only for the loss of his wife but for the disillusion he had suffered in Miriam.

Many seats were empty in the court. The case had lost much of its interest for the public. They believed they knew the answer. It was common garden greed, a pretty woman ambitious to improve herself by the age-old means of marrying well. It was no longer scandalous, simply sordid. It was a beautiful day, the sun was shining, and there were better things to do than sit inside listening to what could be accurately predicted.

Harry Stourbridge looked ten years older than the age Rathbone knew him to be. He was a man walking in a nightmare to which he could see no end.

"I am sorry to force you to endure this," Tobias said gently. "I will keep it as brief as possible, and I am sure Sir Oliver will do the same. Please do not allow loyalty or compassion to direct your answers. This is a time and place when nothing but the truth will serve."

Stourbridge said nothing. He stood like an officer in front of a court-martial, standing stiffly to attention, facing forward, head high.

"We have already heard sufficient about the croquet party from which Mrs. Gardiner fled. I shall not trouble you to repeat it. I turn your attention instead to the tragic death of Mrs. Stourbridge. I need to ask you something about the relationship between your wife and Mrs. Gardiner. Believe me, I would not do it if there were any way in which I could avoid it."

Still, Stourbridge made no reply.

It seemed to unnerve Tobias very slightly. Rathbone saw him shift his weight a little and straighten his jacket.

"How did Mrs. Stourbridge regard Mrs. Gardiner when your son first brought her to Cleveland Square?"

"She thought her a very pleasant young woman."

"And when your son informed you of his intention to marry her?"

"We were both happy that he had found a woman whom he loved and whom we believed to return his feelings wholeheartedly."

Tobias pursed his lips. "You did not regret the fact that she was markedly older than himself and from a somewhat different social background? How did you imagine she would be regarded by your friends? How would she in time manage to be lady of your very considerable properties in Yorkshire? Did those things not concern your wife?"

"Of course," Stourbridge admitted. "But when we had known Mrs. Gardiner for a few weeks we were of the opinion that she would manage very well. She has a natural grace which would carry her through. And she and Lucius so obviously loved each other that that gave us much happiness."

"And the question of grandchildren, an heir to the house and the lands which are, I believe entailed. Without an heir, they pass laterally to your brother and to his heirs, is that not so?"

"It is." He took a deep breath, hands still by his sides as if he were on parade. "Any marriage may fail to provide an heir. One may only hope. I do not believe in governing the choice of wife for my son. I would rather he were happy than produced a dozen children with a woman he could not love and share his heart with as well as his bed."

"And did Mrs. Stourbridge feel the same?" Tobias asked. "Many women care intensely about grandchildren. It is a deep need . . ." He left it hanging in the air, unfinished, for the jury to conclude for themselves.

"I do not believe my wife felt that way," Stourbridge replied wretchedly. Rathbone gained the impression there was far more unsaid behind his words, but he was a private man, loathing this much exposure of his life. He would add nothing he was not forced to.

Step by step, Tobias took him through Miriam's visits to Cleveland Square, her demeanor on each of them, her charm and her eagerness to learn. It was obvious to all that Harry Stourbridge had liked her without shadow of equivocation. He was shattered by her betrayal, not only for his son but for himself. He seemed still unable to grasp it.

Throughout Harry Stourbridge's evidence, Rathbone glanced every now and again up at the dock, and saw the pain in Miriam's face. She was a person enduring torture from which there was no escape. She had to sit still and abide it in silence.

Never once did he catch a member of the jury looking at either Miriam or Cleo. They were completely absorbed in Stourbridge's ordeal. As he studied them he saw in each both pity and respect. Once or twice there was even a sense of identification, as if they could put themselves in his place and would have acted as he had, felt as he had. Rathbone wondered in passing if any of them were widowers themselves, or had sons who had fallen in love or married less than fortunately. He could not choose jurors. They had to be householders of a certain wealth and standing, and of course men. It had never been possible he could have had people who would identify with Miriam or Cleo. So much for a jury of one's peers.

In the afternoon, Tobias quietly and with dignity declined to call Lucius Stourbridge to the stand. It was an ordeal he did not need to inflict upon a young man already wounded almost beyond bearing.

The jury nodded in respect. They would not have forgiven it of him if he had. Rathbone would have done the same, and for the same reasons.

Tobias called the last witness, Aiden Campbell. His evidence was given quietly, with restraint and candor.

"Yes, she had great charm," he said sadly. "I believe everyone in the household liked her."

"Including your sister, Mrs. Stourbridge?"

The question remained unanswered.

Campbell looked very pale. His skin was bleached of color, and there were shadows like bruises under his eyes. He stood straight in the witness stand, but he was shaking very slightly, and every now and again he had to stop and clear his throat. It was apparent to everyone in the courtroom that he was a man laboring under profound emotion and close to losing control of himself.

Tobias apologized again and again for obliging him to relive experiences which had to be deeply distressing for him.

"I understand," Campbell said, biting his lip. "Justice requires that we follow this to its bitter end. I trust you will do it as speedily as you may."

"Of course," Tobias agreed. "May we proceed to the days immediately leading to your sister's death?"

Campbell told them in as few words as possible, without raising his voice, of Miriam's last visit to Cleveland Square after her release from custody and from the charge of having murdered Treadwell. According to him, she was in a state of shock so deep she hardly came out of her room, and when she did she seemed almost to be in a trance. She was civil, but no more. She avoided Lucius as much as possible, not even allowing him to comfort her over her fearful distress on Cleo Anderson's account.

"She was devoted to Mrs. Anderson?" Tobias stressed.

"Yes." There was no expression in Campbell's face except sadness. "It is natural enough. Mrs. Anderson had apparently raised her as a daughter since she was twelve or thirteen. She would be an ungrateful creature not to have been. We respected it in her."

"Of course," Tobias agreed, nodding. "Please continue."

Reluctantly, Campbell did so, describing the dinner that evening, the conversation over the table about Egypt, their returning and each going about their separate pursuits.

"And Mrs. Gardiner did not dine with you?"

"No."

"Tell us, Mr. Campbell, did your sister say anything to you, that evening or earlier, about her feelings regarding the murder of Treadwell and the accusation against Mrs. Gardiner?"

Rathbone rose to object, but he had no legal grounds—indeed, no moral grounds either. He was obliged to sit down again in silence.

Campbell shook his head. "If you are asking if I know what happened, or why, no, I do not. Verona was distressed about something. She was certainly not herself. Any of the servants will testify to that."

Indeed, they already had, although, of course, Campbell had not been in court at the time, since he had not yet appeared himself.

"I believe she had discovered something . . ." His voice grew thick, emotion all but choking him. "It is my personal belief, although I know nothing to support it, that before she died, she knew who had killed Treadwell, and exactly why. I think that is why she returned alone to her room, in order to consider what she should do about it." He closed his eyes. "It was a fatal decision. I wish to God she had not made it."

He had said very little really. He had brought out no new facts, and he had certainly not accused anyone, and yet his testimony was damning. Rathbone could see it in the jurors' faces.

There was no purpose in Rathbone's questioning Campbell. There was nothing for him to say, nothing to elaborate, nothing to challenge. It was Friday evening. He had two days in which to create some kind of defense, and nothing whatever with which to do it—unless Monk found something. And there was no word from him.

When the court rose he considered pleading with Miriam one more time, and abandoned the idea. It would serve no purpose. Whatever the truth was, she had already convinced him that she would go to the gallows rather than tell it.

Instead, he went out into the September afternoon and took

281

a hansom straight to Primrose Hill. He did not expect his father to offer any answers; he went simply for the peace of the quiet garden in which to ease the wounds of a disastrous week, and to prepare his strength for the week to come, which promised to be even worse.

11

W_{HILE} $R_{ATHBONE}$ W_{AS} S_{ITTING} helplessly in the courtroom, Monk began his further investigations into the details of Treadwell's life. He had already asked exhaustively at the Stourbridges' house and generally in the area around Cleveland Square. No one had told him anything remotely helpful. Treadwell had been tediously ordinary.

He began instead in Kentish Town, where Treadwell had grown up. It was a long task, and he held little hope of its proving successful. In time he began to fear that Miriam Gardiner was guilty as charged and that poor Cleo Anderson had been drawn into it because of her love for the girl she had rescued. She had refused to recognize that beneath the charm and apparent vulnerability, Miriam had grown into a greedy and conniving woman who would not stop even at murder in order to get what she wanted. Love could be very blind. No mother wanted to see evil in her child, and the fact that Cleo had not borne Miriam would make no difference to her.

His earlier pity for Miriam hardened to anger when he thought of the grief it would bring to Cleo when she was faced with facts she could no longer deny to herself. Miriam may not have asked to be loved, or to be believed in, but she had accepted it. It carried a moral responsibility, and she had failed it as badly as anyone could. The deception was worse than the violence.

He walked the streets of Kentish Town, going from one

public house to another asking questions as discreetly as the desperately short time allowed. Twice he was too open, too hasty, and earned a sharp rebuff. He left and began again farther along, more carefully.

By sundown he was exhausted, his feet hurt merely to the touch. He took an omnibus home. Monk would earn no further money in this case, but he simply cared passionately to learn the truth. Lucius Stourbridge would have continued to pay him; indeed, he had still implored Monk to help only a week earlier. But Monk had refused to take anything further from him for something he was all but certain he could not accomplish. The young man had lost so much already; to have given him hope he could not justify would be a cruelty for which he would despise himself.

Hester looked at his face as he came in and did not ask what he had learned. Her tact was so uncharacteristic it told him more of his own disappointment, and how visible it was, than he would have admitted.

On the second day he gained considerably more knowledge. He came closer to Hampstead and discovered a public house where they knew Treadwell rather well. From there he was able to trace a man to whom Treadwell had lost at gambling. Since Treadwell was dead, the debt could not be collected.

"Someone ought to be responsible!" the man said angrily, his round eyes sharp and a little bloodshot. "In't there no law? You shouldn't be able to get out of money you owe just by dyin'."

Monk looked knowledgeable. "Well, usually you would go to a man's heirs," he said gravely. "But I don't know if Treadwell had any . . . ?" He left it hanging as a question.

"Nah!" the man said in disgust. "Answer to nob'dy, that one."

"Have a drink?" Monk offered. He might be wasting his time, but he had no better avenue to follow.

"Ta. Don't mind if I do," the man accepted. "Reece." He held out a hand after rubbing it on his trouser leg.

Monk took a moment to realize it was an introduction, then he grasped the hand and shook it. "Monk," he responded.

" 'Ow do," Reece said cheerfully. "I'll 'ave a pint o' mild, ta."

When the pints had been ordered and bought, Monk pursued the conversation. "Did he owe you a lot?"

"I'll say!" Reece took a long draft of his ale before he continued. "Near ten pound."

Monk was startled. It was as much as a housemaid earned in six months.

"That choked yer, eh?" Reece observed with satisfaction. " 'E played big, did Treadwell."

"And lost big," Monk agreed. "He can't have lost like that often. Did he win as well?"

"Sometimes. Liked ter live 'igh on the 'og, 'e did. Wine, women and the 'orses. Must 'a won sometimes, I suppose. But w'ere am I gonna get ten quid, you tell me that?"

"What I'd like to know is where Treadwell got it," Monk said with feeling. "He certainly didn't earn it as a coachman."

"Wouldn't know," Reece said with fading interest. He emptied his glass and looked at Monk hopefully.

Monk obliged.

"Coachman, were 'e?" Reece said thoughtfully. "Well, I guess as 'e 'ad suffink on the side, then. Dunno wot."

A very ugly thought came into Monk's mind concerning Cleo Anderson's theft of medicines, especially morphine. Hester had said a considerable amount might have gone over a period of time. Maybe not all of it had ended in the homes of the old and ill. Anyone addicted to such a drug would pay a high price to obtain it. It would be only too easy to understand how Cleo could have sold it to pay Treadwell, or even have given it to him directly for him to sell. The idea gave him no pleasure, but he could not get rid of it.

He spent the rest of the day investigating Treadwell's off-duty hours, which seemed to have been quite liberal, and found he had a considerable taste for self-indulgence. But there appeared to be several hours once every two weeks or so which were unaccounted for, and Monk was driven to the conclusion that this time may have been used either for selling morphine or for further blackmail of other victims.

The last thing Monk did, late in the evening, was to go and visit Cleo herself, telling the jailer that he was Rathbone's clerk. He had no proof of such a position, but the jailer had seen them together earlier, and accepted it. Or possibly his compassion for Cleo made him turn a blind eye. Monk did not care in the slightest what the reason was; he took advantage of it.

Cleo was surprised to see him, but there was no light of hope in her eyes. She looked haggard and exhausted. She was almost unrecognizable from the woman he had met only a month or so before. Her cheeks were hollow, her skin completely without color, and she sat with her shoulders sagging under the plain dark stuff of her dress.

Monk was caught off guard by his emotions on seeing her. She stirred in him an anger and a sense of outrage at futility and injustice, more passionate than he had expected. If he failed in this he was going to carry the wound for a very long time, perhaps always.

There was no time to waste in words of pity or encouragement, and he knew they would be wasted because they could have no meaning.

"Do you know if Treadwell was blackmailing anyone else apart from you?" he asked her, sitting down opposite her so he could speak softly and she could hear him.

"No. Why? Do you think they could've killed him?" There was almost hope in her voice, not quite. She did not dare.

Honesty forbade him to allow it. "Enough possibility to raise a need to know how much you paid him, exactly," he answered. "I have a pretty good record of how much he spent over the last two or three months of his life. If you paid him all of it, then you must have been taking morphine to sell, as well as to give to patients."

Her body stiffened, her eyes wide and angry. "I didn't! And I never gave him any either!"

"We have to prove it," he argued. "Have you got any records of your pay from the hospital, of all the medicine you took and the people to whom you gave it?"

"No—of course I haven't."

"But you know all the patients you visited with medicine," he insisted.

"Yes . . ."

"Then dictate their names to me. Their addresses, too, and what medicine you gave them and for how long."

She stared at him for a moment, then obeyed.

Was this going to be worth anything, or was he simply finding a way of occupying time so he could delude himself he was working to save her? What could he achieve with lists? Who would listen, or care, regardless of what likelihood he could show? Proof was all the court would entertain. In their own minds they believed Cleo and Miriam guilty. They would have to be forced from that conviction, not merely shown that there was another remote possibility.

Cleo finished dictating the list. There were eighteen names on it.

"Thank you." He read it over. "How much do you earn at the hospital?"

"Seven shillings a week." She said it with some pride, as if for a nurse it was a good wage.

He winced. He knew a constable earned three times that.

"How long do you work?" The question was out before he thought.

"Twelve or fifteen hours a day," she replied.

"And how much did you pay Treadwell?"

Her voice was tired, her shoulders slumped again. "Five shillings a week."

The rage inside him was ice-cold, filling his body, sharpening his mind with a will to lash out, to hurt someone so this could be undone, so it would never happen again, not to Cleo and not to anyone. But he had no one to direct the anger towards. The only offender was dead already. Only the victim was still left to pay the price.

"He was spending a lot more than that," he said quietly, his words coming between clenched teeth. "I need to know where it came from."

She shook her head. "I don't know. He just came to me regularly and I paid him. He never mentioned anyone else. But he wouldn't . . ."

It was on the edge of Monk's tongue to ask her again if she had given him any morphine to sell, but he knew the answer would be the same. He rose to his feet and bade her good-bye, hating being able to make no promises, nor even speak any words of hope.

At the door he hesitated, wondering if he should ask her about Miriam, but what was there to say?

She looked up at him, waiting.

In the end he had to ask. "Could it have been Miriam?"

"No," she said immediately. "She never did anything he could have made her pay for!"

"Not even to protect you?" he said quietly.

She sat perfectly still. It was transparent in her face that she did not know the answer to that—believe, possibly, even certainly—but not know.

Monk nodded. "I understand." He knocked for the jailer to let him out.

He arrived home still turning the matter over and over in his mind.

"There was another source," he said to Hester over the dinner table. "But it could have been Miriam, which won't help at all."

"And if it wasn't?" she asked. "If we could show it was someone else? They'd have to consider it!"

"No, they wouldn't," he answered quietly, watching her face show her disappointment. "Not unless we could bring that person to court and prove that he or she was somewhere near the Heath that night, alone. We've got two days before Rathbone has to begin some defense."

"What else have we?" Her voice rose a little in desperation.

288

"Nothing," he admitted.

"Then let's try! I can't bear to sit here not doing anything at all. What do we know?"

They worked until long after midnight, noting every piece of information Monk had gathered about Treadwell's comings and goings over the three months previous to his death. When it was written on paper it was easier to see what appeared to be gaps.

"We need to know exactly what his time off was," Hester said, making further notes. "I'm sure there would be someone in the Stourbridge household who could tell you."

Monk thought it was probably a waste of time, but he did not argue. He had nothing else more useful to do. He might as well follow through with the entire exercise.

"Do you know how much medicine was taken?" he asked, then, before she could deny it, added, "Or could you work it out if you wanted to?"

"No, but I expect Phillips could, if it would help. Do you think it really would?"

"Probably not, but what better idea have we?"

Neither of them answered with the obvious thing: acceptance that the charge was true. Perhaps it had not been with deliberate greed, or for the reasons Tobias was saying, but the end result was all that counted.

"I'll go tomorrow to the hospital and ask Phillips," Hester said briskly, as if it mattered. "And I'll go as well and find all the people on your list and see what medicines they have. You see if you can account for that time of Treadwell's." She stared at him very directly, defying him to tell her it was useless or to give up heart. He knew from the very brittleness of her stare, the anger in her, that she was doing it blindly, against hope, not with it.

In the morning Monk left early to go out to Bayswater and get the precise times that Treadwell was off duty and see if he could find any indication of where else he might have been, who could have paid him the huge difference between what they could account for and what he had spent. He pursued it slowly and carefully, to the minutest detail, because he did not want to come to the end of it and have it proved to him what he already knew: that it would be of no use whatever in trying to save Cleo Anderson—or Miriam Gardiner either.

Hester went straight to the hospital. Fortunately, even though it was a Saturday she knew Phillips would be there. Usually he took only Sundays off, and then quite often just the morning. Still, she had to search for over half an hour before she found him, and then it was only after having asked three different medical students, interrupting them in a long, enthusiastic and detailed discussion of anatomy, which was their present preoccupation.

"Brilliant!" one of them said, his eyes wide. "We're very fortunate to be here. My cousin is studying in Lincoln, and he says they have to wait weeks for a body to dissect, and all the diagrams in the world mean almost nothing compared with the real thing."

"I know," another agreed. "And Thorpe is marvelous. His explanations are always so clear."

"Probably the number of times he's done it," the first retorted.

"Excuse me!" Hester said again sharply. "Do you know where Mr. Phillips is?"

"Phillips? Is he the one with red hair, bit of a stammer?"

"Phillips the apothecary." She kept her temper with difficulty. "I need to speak with him."

The first young man frowned at her, looking at her more closely now. "You shouldn't be looking for medicines; if one of the patients is—"

"I don't want medicines!" she said. "I need to speak with Mr. Phillips. Do you know where he is or not?"

The young man's face hardened. "No, actually, I don't."

One of the other young men relented, for whatever personal reason.

"He's down in the morgue," he answered. "The new assistant got taken a little faint. Gave him a bit of something to help. He's probably still there."

"Thank you," she said quickly. "Thank you very much." And she all but ran along the corridor, out of the side entrance and down the steps to the cold room belowground which served to keep the bodies of the dead until the undertaker should come to perform the formalities.

"Hello, Mrs. Monk. You're looking a little peaked," Phillips said cheerfully. "What can I do for you?"

"I'm glad I found you." She turned and regarded the young man, white-faced, who sat on the floor with his legs splayed out. "Are you all right?" she asked him.

He nodded, embarrassed.

"Just got a scare," Phillips said with a grin. "One o' them corpses moved, and young Jake 'ere near fainted away. Nobody told 'im corpses sometimes passes wind. Gases don't stop, son, just 'cos you're dead."

Jake scrambled to his feet, running his hands through his hair and trying to look as if he was ready for duty again.

Hester looked at the tables. There were two bodies laid out under unbleached sheets.

"Not as many lately," Phillips remarked, following her glance.

"Good!" she said.

"No—not died here, brought in for the students," he corrected. "Old Thorpe's in a rare fury. Can't get 'em."

"Where do they come from?"

"God knows! Resurrectionists!" he said with black humor.

Jake was staring at him, openmouthed. He let out a sigh between his teeth.

"D'yer mean it?" he said hoarsely. "Grave robbers, like?"

"No, of course I don't, you daft ha'porth!" Phillips said, shaking his head. "Get on with your work." He turned to Hester. "What is it, Mrs. Monk?" All the light vanished from his face. "Have you seen Cleo Anderson? Is there anything we can do for 'er, apart from hope for a miracle?"

291

"Work for one," she said bleakly. She turned and led the way back up the stairs.

He followed close behind, and when they were outside in the air he asked what she meant.

"Someone else was being blackmailed as well, we are almost sure," she explained, stopping beside him. "Treadwell spent a lot more money than Cleo gave him or he earned . . ."

Hope lit in his face. "You mean that person could have killed him? How do we find out who it was?" He looked at her confidently, as if he had every faith she would have an answer.

"I don't know. I'll settle at the moment just for proving he has to exist." She looked at him very steadily. "If you had to . . . no, if you wanted to, could you work out exactly how much medicine has gone missing in, say, the four months before Treadwell's death?"

"Perhaps . . . if I had a really good reason to," he said guardedly. "I wouldn't know that unless I understood the need."

"Not knowing isn't going to help," she told him miserably. "Not charging her with theft won't matter if they hang her for murder."

His face blanched as if she had slapped him, but he did not look away. "What good can you do?" he asked very quietly. "I really care about Cleo. She's worth ten of that pompous swine in his oak-paneled office." He did not need to name Thorpe. She shared his feelings, and he knew it. He was watching her for an answer, hoping.

"I don't really know—maybe not a great deal," she admitted. "But if I know how much is missing, and how much reached the patients she treated, if they are pretty well the same, then he got money from someone else."

"Of course they're the same. What do you think she did? Give it to him to sell?" He was indignant, almost angry.

"If I were being blackmailed out of everything I earned except about two shillings a week, I'd be tempted to pay in kind," she answered him.

292

He looked chastened. His lips thinned into a hard line. "I'm glad somebody got that scheming sod," he said harshly. "I just wish we could prove it wasn't poor Cleo. Or come to that, anyone else he was doing the same thing to. How are we going to do that?" He looked at her expectantly.

"Tell me exactly how much medicine went over the few months before his death, as nearly as you can."

"That won't tell us who the other person is— or people!"

"My husband is trying to find out where Treadwell went that might lead us to them."

He looked at her narrowly. "Is he any good at that?"

"Very good indeed. He used to be the best detective in the police force," she said with pride.

"Oh? Who's the best now?"

"I haven't the slightest idea. He left." Then, in case Phillips should think him dishonest, she added, "He resented some of the discipline. He can't abide pomposity either, especially when it is coupled with ignorance."

Phillips grinned, then the grin vanished and he was totally serious again.

"I'll get you a list o' those things. I could tell you pretty exact, if it helps."

"It'll help."

She spent the rest of the day and into the early evening trudging from one house to the next with Monk's list of Cleo's patients and Phillips's list of the missing medicines. She was accustomed to seeing people who were suffering illness or injury. Nursing had been her profession for several years, and she had seen the horror of the battlefield and the disease which had decimated the wounded afterwards. She had shared the exhaustion and the fear herself, and the cold and the hunger.

Nevertheless, to go into these homes, bare of comfort because everything had been sold to pay for food and warmth, to see the pain and too often the loneliness also, was more harrowing than she had expected. These men were older than the ones she had nursed in the Crimea; their wounds were not fresh. They had earned them in different battles, different wars; still, there was so much that was the same it hurled her back those short four years, and old emotions washed over her, almost to drowning.

Time and again she saw a dignity which made her have to swallow back tears as old men struggled to hide their poverty and force their bodies, disabled by age and injury, to rise and offer her some hospitality. She was walking in the footsteps of Cleo Anderson, trying to give some of the same comfort, and failing because she had not the means.

Rage burned inside her also. No one should have to beg for what he had more than earned.

She loathed asking for information about the medicine they had had. Nearly all of them knew that Cleo was being tried for her life. All Hester could do was tell the truth. Every last man was eager to give her any help he could, to open cupboards and show her powders, to give her day-by-day recounting of all he had had.

She would have given any price she could think of to be able to promise them it would save Cleo, but she could only offer hope, and little enough of that.

When she arrived home at quarter past ten, Monk was beginning to worry about her. He was standing up, unable to relax in spite of his own weariness. She did notice that he had taken his boots off.

"Where have you been?" he demanded.

She walked straight to him and put her head on his shoulder. He closed his arms around her, holding her gently, laying his cheek to her brow. He did not need her to explain the emotion she felt; he saw it in her face, and understood.

"It's wrong," she said after a few minutes, still holding on to him. "How can we do it? We turn to our bravest and best when we are in danger, we sacrifice so much—fathers and brothers, husbands and sons—and then a decade, a generation later, we only want to forget! What's the matter with us?"

He did not bother to answer, to talk about guilt or debt, or the desire to be happy without remembering that others have purchased it at a terrible price—even resentment and simple blindness and failure of imagination. They had both said it all before.

"What did you find?" she said at last, straightening up and looking at him.

"I'm not sure," he replied. "Do you want a cup of tea?"

"Yes." She went towards the kitchen, but he moved ahead of her.

"I'll bring it." He smiled. "I wasn't asking you to fetch one for me—even though I've probably walked as far as you have, and to as little purpose."

She sat down and took off her boots as well. It was a particular luxury, something she would only do at home. And it was still very sweet to realize this was her home, she belonged there, and so did he.

When he returned with the tea and she had taken a few sips, she asked him again what he had learned.

"A lot of Treadwell's time is unaccounted for," he replied, trying his own tea and finding it a trifle too hot. "He had a few unusual friends. One of his gambling partners was even an undertaker, and Treadwell did a few odd tasks for him."

"Enough to earn him the kind of money we're looking for?" She did not know whether she wanted the answer to be yes or no.

"Not remotely," he replied. "Just driving a wagon, presumably because he was good with horses, and perhaps knew the roads. He probably did it as a favor because of their friendship. This young man seems to have given him entry to cockfights and dog races when he wouldn't have been allowed in otherwise. They even had a brothel or two in common."

Hester shrugged. "It doesn't get us any further, does it?" She tried to keep the disappointment out of her voice.

Monk frowned thoughtfully. "I was wondering how Treadwell ever discovered about Cleo and the medicines in the first place."

295

She was about to dismiss it as something that hardly mattered now when she realized what he meant.

"Well, not from Miriam," she said with conviction.

"From any of Cleo's patients?" he asked. "How could Treadwell, coachman to Major Stourbridge in Bayswater, and gambler and womanizer in Kentish Town, come to know of thefts of morphine and other medicines from a hospital on Hampstead Heath?"

She stared at him steadily, a first, tiny stirring of excitement inside her. "Because somewhere along the chain of events he crossed it. It has to be—but where?" She held up her fingers, ticking off each step. "Patients fall ill and go to the hospital, where Cleo gets to know of them because she works there as a nurse."

"Which has nothing to do with Treadwell," he answered. "Unless one of them was related to him or to someone he knew well."

"They are all old and live within walking distance of the hospital," she pointed out. "Most of them are alone, the lucky few with a son or daughter, or grandchild, like old John Robb."

"Treadwell's family was all in Kentish Town," Monk said. "That much I ascertained. His father is dead and his mother remarried a man from Hoxton."

"And none of them have anything to do with Miriam Gardiner," she went on. "So he didn't meet them driving her." She held up the next finger. "Cleo visits them in their homes and knows what they need. She steals it from the hospital. By the way, I'm sure the apothecary knew but turned a blind eye. He's a good man, and very fond of her." She smiled slightly. "Very fond indeed. He regards her as something of a saint. I think she is the only person who really impresses Phillips. Fermin Thorpe certainly doesn't." She recalled the scene in the morgue. "He even teased the new young morgue attendant that Thorpe was buying his cadavers for the medical students from resurrectionists! Poor boy was horrified until he realized Phillips was teasing him."

"Resurrectionists?" Monk said slowly.

"Yes—grave robbers who dig up corpses and sell them to medical establishments for . . ."

"I know what resurrectionists are," he said quickly, leaning forward, his eyes bright. "Are you sure it was a joke?"

"Well, it's not very funny," she agreed with a frown. "But Phillips is like that—a bit . . . wry. I like him—actually, I like him very much. He's one of the few people in the hospital I would trust—" Then suddenly she realized what Monk was thinking. "You mean . . . Oh, William! You think he really was buying them from resurrectionists? He was the other person Treadwell was blackmailing. But how could Treadwell know that?"

"Not necessarily that he was blackmailing him," he said, grasping her hand in his urgency. "Treadwell was friendly with this undertaker. What could be simpler than to sell a few bodies? That could have been the extra driving he was doing: delivering corpses for Fermin Thorpe—at a very nice profit to himself!"

"Wonderful!" She breathed out with exquisite relief. It was only a chink of light in the darkness, but it was the very first one. "At least it might be enough for Oliver to raise doubt." She smiled with a twist. "And even if he isn't guilty, I wouldn't mind seeing Thorpe thoroughly frightened and embarrassed—I wouldn't mind in the slightest."

"I'm sure you wouldn't," he agreed with a nod. "Although we mustn't leap too quickly . . ."

"Why not? There's hardly time to waste."

"I know. But Treadwell may not have blackmailed Thorpe. The money may all have come from selling the bodies."

"Then let Thorpe prove it. That should be interesting to watch."

His eyes widened very slightly. "You really do loathe him, don't you?"

"I despise him," she said fiercely. "He puts his own vanity before relieving the pain of those who trust him to help them." She made it almost a challenge, as if Monk had been defending him.

He smiled at her. "I'm not trying to spare him anything, I just want to use it to the best effect. I don't know what that is yet, but we will only get one chance. I want to save my fire for the target that will do the most good for Cleo—or Miriam—not just the one that does the most harm to Thorpe . . . or the one that gives us the most satisfaction."

"I see." She did. She had been indulging in the luxury of anger and she recognized it. "Yes, of course. Just don't leave it too long."

"I won't," he promised. "Believe me—we will use it."

On Sunday, Monk returned to the undertaker to pursue the details of Treadwell's work for him and to find proof if indeed he had taken bodies to the Hampstead hospital and been handsomely paid for it. If he were to use it, either in court or to pressure Thorpe for any other reason, then he must have evidence that could not be denied or explained away.

Hester continued with her visits to the rest of Cleo's patients, just to conclude the list of medicines. She was uncertain if it would be any use, but she felt compelled to do it, and regardless of anything else, she wanted to go and see John Robb again. It was over a week since she had last been, and she knew he would be almost out of morphine. He was failing, the pain growing worse, and there was little she could do to help him. She had some morphine left, taken with Phillips's connivance, and she had bought a bottle of sherry herself. It was illogical to give it to him rather than anyone else, but logic had no effect on her feelings.

She found him alone, slumped in his chair almost asleep, but he roused himself when he heard her footsteps. He looked paler than she had ever seen him before, and his eyes more deeply sunken. She had nursed too many dying men to delude herself that he had long left now, and she could guess how it must tear Michael Robb to have to leave him alone.

She forced her voice to be cheerful, but she could not place the barrier between them of pretending that she could not see how ill he was.

"Hello," she said quietly, sitting opposite him. "I'm sorry I've been away so long. I've been trying to find some way of helping Cleo, and I think we may have succeeded." She was aware as she spoke that if she embroidered the truth a little he would probably not live long enough to know.

He smiled and raised his head. "That's the best news you could have brought me, girl. I worry about her. All the good she did, and now this has to happen. Wish I could do something to help—but I think maybe all I could do would make it worse." He was watching her, waiting for her to reply.

"Don't worry, nobody will ask you," she answered him. She was sure the last thing the prosecution would do willingly would be to draw in the men like John Robb who would indeed show that Cleo had handed on the medicines, because they would also show so very effectively why. The sympathies of every decent man in the jury would be with Cleo. Perhaps some of them had been in the army themselves, or had fathers or brothers or sons who had. Their outrage at what had happened to so many old soldiers would perhaps outweigh their sense of immediate justice against the killer of a blackmailing coachman. Tobias would not provoke that if he could help it.

Hester herself would be delighted if it came out into the public hearing, but only if it could be managed other than at Cleo's expense. So far she had thought of no way.

He looked at her closely. "But I was one she took those medicines for—wasn't I?"

"She took them for a lot of people," Hester answered honestly. "Eighteen of you altogether, but you were one of her favorites." She smiled. "Just as you're mine."

He grinned as if she were flirting with him. His pleasure was only too easy to see, in spite of the tragedy of the subject they were discussing. His eyes were misty. "But some o' those medicines she took were for me, weren't they?" he pressed her.

"Yes. You and others."

"And where are you getting them now, girl? I'd sooner go without than have you in trouble, too."

"I know you would, but there's no need to worry. The apothecary gave me these." That was stretching the truth a little, but it hardly mattered. "I'll make you a cup of tea and we'll sit together for a while. I brought a little sherry—not from the hospital, I got it myself." She stood up as she said it. "Don't need milk this time—we'll give it a bit of heart."

"That'd be good," he agreed. "Then we'll talk a bit. You tell me some o' those stories about Florence Nightingale and how she bested those generals and got her own way. You tell a good story, girl."

"I'll do that," she promised, going over to the corner which served as kitchen, pouring water into the kettle, then setting it on the hob. When it was boiled she made the tea, putting the sherry fairly liberally into one mug and leaving the morphine on the shelf so Michael would find it that evening. She returned with the tea and set one mug, the one with the sherry, for him, the one without for herself.

He picked up his mug and began to sip slowly. "So, tell me about how you outwitted those generals then, girl. Tell me the things you're doing better now because o' the war an' what you learned."

She recounted to him all sorts of bits and pieces she could remember, tiny victories over bureaucracy, making it as funny as possible, definitely adding more color than there had been at the time.

He drank the tea, then set down the empty mug. "Go on," he prompted. "I like the sound o' your voice, girl. Takes me back . . ."

She tried to think of other stories to tell, ones that had happy endings, and perhaps she rambled a bit, inventing here and there. Now and then he interrupted to ask a question. It was warm and comfortable in the afternoon sun, and she was not surprised when she looked up and saw his eyes closed. It was just the sort of time to doze off. Certainly, she was in no way offended. He was still smiling at the last little victory she had recounted, much added to in retrospect.

She stood up and went to make sure he was warm enough since the sunlight had moved around and his feet were in shadow. It was only then that she noticed how very still he was. There was no labored breathing, no rasp of air in his damaged lungs.

There were tears already on her cheeks when she put her fingers to his neck and found no pulse. It was ridiculous. She should have been only glad for him, but she was unable to stop herself from sitting down and weeping in wholehearted weariness, in fear, and from the loss of a friend she had come to love.

She had washed her face and was sitting in a chair, still opposite the old man, when Michael Robb came home in the late afternoon.

He walked straight in, not at first sensing anything different.

She stood up quickly, stepping between him and the old man.

Then he saw her face and realized she had been weeping. He went very pale.

"He's gone," she said gently. "I was here—talking to him. We were telling old stories, laughing a little. He just went to sleep." She moved aside so he could see the old man's face, the shadow of a smile still on it, a great peace settled over him.

Michael knelt down beside him, taking his hand. "I should have been here," he said hoarsely. "I'm sorry! I'm so sorry . . ."

"If you had stayed here all the time, who could have earned the money for you both to live on?" she asked. "He knew that—he was so proud of you. He would have felt terribly

301

guilty if he'd thought you were taking time away from your work because of him."

Michael bent forward, the tears spilling over his cheeks, his shoulders shaking.

She did not know whether to go to him, touch him; if it would comfort or only intrude. Instinct told her to take him in her arms, he seemed so young and alone. Her mind told her to let him deal with his grief in private. Instinct won, and she sat on the floor and held him while he wept.

When he had passed through the first shock he stood up and went and washed his face in water from the jug, then boiled the kettle again. Without speaking to her he made more tea.

"Is that your sherry?" he asked.

"Yes. Take what you'd like."

He poured it generously for both of them, and offered her one of the mugs. They did not sit down. There was only one vacant chair, and neither wanted to take it.

"Thank you," he said a little awkwardly. "I know you did it for him, not for me, but I'm still grateful." He stopped, wanting to say something and not knowing how to broach it.

She sipped the tea and waited.

"I'm sorry about Mrs. Anderson," he said abruptly.

"I know," she assured him.

"She took all the medicines for the old and ill, didn't she." It was not a question.

"Yes. I could prove that if I had to."

"Including my grandfather." That, too, was a statement.

"Yes." She met his eyes without flinching. He looked vulnerable and desperately unhappy. "She did it because she wanted to. She believed it was the right thing to do," she went on.

"There's still morphine there now," he said softly.

"Is there? I will take it away."

"In the Lord's name—be careful, Mrs. Monk!" There was real fear for her in his face, no censure.

302

She smiled. "No need anymore. Will you be all right?"

"Yes—I will. Thank you."

She hesitated only a moment longer, then turned and went. Outside, the last of the sun was on the footpath and the street was busy.

12

ON SUNDAY EVENING Rathbone went to Fitzroy Street to see Monk. He could stand the uncertainty no longer, and he wanted to share his anxiety and feel less alone in his sense of helplessness.

"Resurrectionists!" he said incredulously when Hester told him of their beliefs regarding Treadwell's supplementary income.

"Not exactly," Monk corrected him. "Actually, the bodies were never buried, just taken straight from the undertaker's to the hospital." He was sitting in the large chair beside the fire. The September evenings were drawing in. It was not yet cold, but the flames were comforting. Hester sat hunched forward, hugging herself, her face washed out of all color. She had told Monk of John Robb's death quite simply and without regret, knowing it to be a release from the bonds of a failing body, but he could see very clearly in her manner that she felt the loss profoundly.

"Saves effort," Monk said, looking across at Rathbone. "Why bury them and then have to go to the trouble and considerable risk of digging them up again if you can simply bury bricks in the first place?"

"And Treadwell carried them?" Rathbone wanted to assure himself he had understood. "Are you certain?"

"Yes. If I had to I could call enough witnesses to leave no doubt."

"And was he blackmailing Fermin Thorpe?"

Monk looked rueful. "That I don't know. Certainly I've no proof, and I hate to admit it, but it seems unlikely. Why would he? He was making a very nice profit in the business. The last thing he would want would be to get Thorpe prosecuted."

The truth of that was unarguable, and Rathbone conceded it. "Have we learned anything that could furnish a defense? I have nowhere even to begin . . ."

Hester stared at him miserably and shook her head.

"No," Monk said wretchedly. "We could probably get Thorpe to get rid of the charges of theft—at least to drop them—and I would dearly enjoy doing it, but it wouldn't help with the murder. We don't have anything but your skill." He looked at Rathbone honestly, and there was a respect in his eyes which at any other time Rathbone would have found very sweet to savor. As it was, all he could think of was that he would have given most of what he possessed if he could have been sure he was worthy of it.

At seven o'clock on Monday morning Rathbone was at the door of Miriam's cell. A sullen wardress let him in. She had none of the regard or the pity for Miriam that the police jailer had had for Cleo.

The door clanged shut behind him, and Miriam looked up. She was a shadow of her former self. She looked physically bruised, as if her whole body hurt.

There was no time to mince words.

"I am going into battle without weapons," he said simply. "I accept that you would rather sacrifice your own life at the end of a rope than tell me who killed Treadwell and Verona Stourbridge—but are you quite sure you are willing to repay all Cleo Anderson has done for you by sacrificing hers also?"

Miriam looked as if she was going to faint. She had difficulty finding her voice.

"I've told you, Sir Oliver, even if you knew, no one would believe you. I could tell you everything, and it would only do more harm. Don't you think I would do anything on earth to save Cleo if I could? She is the dearest person in the world to me—except perhaps Lucius. And I know how much I owe her. You do not need to remind me as though I were unaware. If I could hang in her place I would! If you can bring that about I will be forever in your debt. I will confess to killing Treadwell—if it will help."

Looking into her wide eyes and ashen face, he believed her. He had no doubt in his mind that she would die with dignity and a quiet heart if she could believe she had saved Cleo. That did not mean Cleo was innocent in fact, only that Miriam loved her, and perhaps that she believed the death sufficiently understandable in the light of Treadwell's own crimes.

"I will do what I can," he said quietly. "I am not sure if that is worth anything."

She said nothing, but gave him a thin wraith of a smile.

The trial resumed in a half-empty court.

Rathbone was already in his seat when he saw Hester come in, push her way past the court usher with a swift word to which he was still replying as she left him, and come to Rathbone's table.

"What is it?" he asked, looking at her pale, tense face. "What's happened?"

"I went to Cleo this morning," she whispered, leaning close to him. "She knows Miriam will hang and there is nothing you can do unless the truth is told. She knows only a part of it, but she cannot bear to lose Miriam, whomever else it hurts—even if it is Lucius and Miriam never forgives her."

"What part?" Rathbone demanded. "What truth does she know? For God's sake, Hester, tell me! I've got nothing!"

"Put Cleo on the witness stand. Ask her how she first met Miriam. She thinks it is something to do with that— something so terrible Miriam can't or won't remember it. But there's nothing to lose now."

"Thank you." Impulsively, he leaned forward and kissed

her on the cheek, not giving a damn that the judge and the entire court were watching him.

Tobias gave a cough and a smile.

The judge banged his gavel.

Hester blushed fiercely, but with a smile returned to her seat.

"Are you ready to proceed, Sir Oliver?" the judge asked courteously.

"Yes, my lord, I am. I call Mrs. Cleo Anderson."

There was a murmur of interest around the gallery, and several of the jurors shifted position, more from emotional discomfort than physical.

Cleo was escorted from the dock to the witness stand. She stood upright, but it was obviously with difficulty, and she did not look across at Miriam even once. In a soft, unsteady voice she swore to her name and where she lived, then waited with palpable anxiety for Rathbone to begin.

Rathbone hated what he was about to do, but it did not deter him.

"Mrs. Anderson, how long have you lived in your present house on Green Man Hill?"

Quite plainly, she understood the relevance of the question, even though Tobias evidently did not, and his impatience was clear as he allowed his face to express exasperation.

"About thirty years," Cleo replied.

"So you were living there when you first met Mrs. Gardiner?" Rathbone asked.

"Yes." It was little more than a whisper.

The judge leaned forward. "Please speak up, Mrs. Anderson. The jury needs to hear you."

"I'm sorry, sir. Yes, I was living there."

"How long ago was that?"

Tobias rose to his feet. "This is old history, my lord. If it will be of any assistance to Sir Oliver, and to saving the court's time and not prolonging what can only be painful, rather than merciful, the Crown concedes that Mrs. Anderson took in Mrs. Gardiner when she was little more than a child and looked after her with devotion from that day forward. We do not contest it, nor require any evidence to that effect."

"Thank you," Rathbone said with elaborate graciousness. "That was not my point. If you are as eager as you suggest not to waste the court's time, then perhaps you would consider not interrupting me until there is some good reason for it?"

There was a titter of nervous laughter around the gallery, and distinct smiles adorned the faces of at least two of the jurors.

A flush of temper lit Tobias's face, but he masked it again almost immediately.

Rathbone turned back to Cleo.

"Mrs. Anderson, would you please tell us the circumstances of that meeting?"

Cleo spoke with a great effort. It was painfully apparent that the memory was distressing to her and she recalled it only as an act of despair.

Rathbone had very little idea why he was asking her, only that Hester had pressed him to, and he had no other weapon to use.

"It was a night in September, the twenty-second, I think. It was windy, but not cold." She swallowed. Her throat was dry and she began to cough.

At the judge's request the usher brought her a glass of water, then she continued.

"Old Josh Wetherall, from two doors down, came beating on my door to say there was a young girl, a child, crying on the road, near in hysterics, he said, an' covered all over in blood. He was beside himself with distress, poor man, and hadn't an idea what to do to help." She took a deep breath.

No one moved or interrupted her. Even Tobias was silent, although his face still reflected impatience.

"Of course, I went to see what I could do," Cleo continued. "Anyone would, but I suppose he thought I might know a bit more, being a nurse and all."

"And the child?" Rathbone prompted.

Cleo's hands gripped the rail in front of her as if she needed its strength to hold her up.

"Josh was right, she was in a terrible state . . ."

"Would you describe her for us?" Rathbone directed her, ignoring Tobias, leaning forward to object. "We need to see it as you saw it, Mrs. Anderson."

She stared at him imploringly, denial in her eyes, in her face, even in the angle of her body.

"We need to see her as you did, Mrs. Anderson. Please believe me, it is important." He was lying. He had no idea whether it meant anything or not, but at least the jury were listening, emotions caught at last.

Cleo was rigid, shaking. "She was hysterical," she said very quietly.

The judge leaned forward to hear, but he did not again request her to raise her voice.

No one in the body of the court moved or made the slightest sound.

Rathbone nodded, indicating she should continue.

"I've never seen anyone so frightened in my life," Cleo said, not to Rathbone or to the court, but as if she were speaking aloud what was indelibly within her. "She was covered in blood; her eyes were staring, but I'm not sure she saw anything at all. She staggered and bumped into things and for hours she was unable to speak. She just gasped and shuddered. I'd have felt better if she could have wept."

Again she stopped and the silence lengthened, but no one moved. Even Tobias knew better than to intrude.

"How was she injured?" Rathbone asked finally.

Cleo seemed to recall her attention and looked at him as if she had just remembered he was there.

"How was she injured?" Rathbone repeated. "You said she was covered in blood, and obviously she had sustained some terrible experience."

Cleo looked embarrassed. "We don't know how it happened, not really. For days she couldn't say anything that made sense, and the poor child was so terrified no one

309

pressed her. She just lay curled over in my big bed, hugging herself and now and then weeping like her heart was broken, and she was so frightened of any man coming near her we didn't even like to send for a doctor."

"But the injuries?" Rathbone asked again. "What about the blood?"

Cleo stared beyond him. "She was only wearing a big cotton nightgown. There was blood everywhere, right from her shoulders down. She was bruised and cut . . ."

"Yes?"

Cleo looked for the first time across at Miriam, and there were tears on her face.

Desperately, Miriam mouthed the word *no*.

"Mrs. Anderson!" Rathbone said sharply. "Where did the blood come from? If you are really innocent, and if you believe Miriam Gardiner to be innocent, only the truth can save you. This is your last chance to tell it. After the verdict is in you will face nothing but the short days and nights in a cell, too short—and then the rope, and at last the judgment of God."

Tobias rose to his feet.

Rathbone turned on him. "Do you quarrel with the truth of that, Mr. Tobias?" he demanded.

Tobias stared at him, his face set and angry.

"Mr. Tobias?" the judge prompted.

"No, of course I don't," Tobias conceded, sitting down again.

Rathbone turned back to Cleo. "I repeat, Mrs. Anderson, where did the blood come from? You are a nurse. You must have some rudimentary knowledge of anatomy. Do not tell us that you did nothing to help this blood-soaked, terrified child except give her a clean nightshirt!"

"Of course I helped her!" Cleo sobbed. "The poor little mite had just given birth—and she was only a child herself. Stillborn, I reckoned it was."

"Is that what she told you?"

"She was rambling. She hardly made any sense. In and out

310

of her wits, she was. She got a terrible fever, and we weren't sure we could even save her. Often enough women die of fever after giving birth, especially if they've had a bad time of it. And she was too young—far too young, poor little thing."

Rathbone was taking a wild guess now. So far this was all tragic, but it had nothing to do with the deaths of either Treadwell or Verona Stourbridge. Unless, of course, Treadwell had blackmailed Miriam over the child. But would Lucius care? Would such a tragedy be enough to stop him from wanting to marry her? Or his family from allowing it?

Rathbone had done her no service yet. He had nothing to lose by pressing the story as far as it could go.

"You must have asked her what happened," he said grimly. "What did she say? If nothing else, the law would require some explanation. What about her own family? What did they do, Mrs. Anderson, with this injured and hysterical child whose story made no sense to you?"

Cleo's face tightened, and she looked at Rathbone more defiantly.

"I didn't tell the police. What was there to tell them? I asked her her name, of course, and if she had family who'd be looking for her. She said there was no one, and who was I to argue with that? She was one of eight, and her family'd placed her in service in a good house."

"And the child?" Rathbone had to ask. "What manner of man gets a twelve-year-old girl with child? She would have been twelve when it was conceived. Did he abandon her?"

Cleo's face was ashen. Rathbone did not dare look at Miriam. He could not even imagine what she must be enduring, having to sit in the dock and listen to this, and see the faces of the court and the jury. He wondered if she would look at Harry or Lucius Stourbridge, or Aiden Campbell, who were sitting together in the front of the body of the court. Perhaps this was worse than anything she had yet endured. But if she were to survive, if Cleo were to survive, it was necessary.

"Mrs. Anderson?"

311

"He never cared for her," Cleo said quietly. "She said he raped her, several times. That was how she got with child."

One of the jurors gasped. Another clenched his fist and banged it short and hard on the rail in front of him. It must have hurt, but he was too outraged even to be conscious of it.

Lucius started to his feet and then subsided again, helpless to know what to do.

"But the child was stillborn," Rathbone said in the silence.

"I reckoned so," Cleo agreed.

"And what was Miriam doing alone on the Heath in such a state?"

Cleo shook her head as if to deny the truth, drive it away.

Tobias was staring at her.

As if aware of him, she looked again at Rathbone imploringly. But it was for Miriam, not for herself. He was absolutely sure of that.

"What did she say?" he asked.

Cleo looked down. When she spoke, her voice was barely audible.

"That she had fled from the house with a woman, and that the woman had tried to protect her, and the woman had been murdered . . . out there on the Heath."

Rathbone was stunned. His imagination had conjured many possibilities, but not this. It took him a moment to collect his wits. He did not mean to look at Miriam, but in spite of himself he did.

She was sitting white-faced with her eyes shut. She must have been aware that every man and woman in the room was staring at her, and felt that her only hiding place was within herself. He saw in her face pain almost beyond her power to bear—but no surprise. She had known what Cleo was going to say. That, more than anything else, made him believe it absolutely. Whether it had happened or not, whether there was any woman, whether it was the illusion of a tormented and hysterical girl in the delirium of fever, Miriam believed it to be the truth.

Rathbone looked at Hester and saw her wide-eyed amazement also. She had known there was something—but not this.

He asked the question the whole court was waiting to hear answered.

"And was this woman's body found, Mrs. Anderson?"

"No . . ."

"You did look?"

"Of course, we did. We all looked. Every man in the street."

"But you never found it?"

"No."

"And Miriam couldn't take you to it? Again—I presume you asked her? It is hardly a matter you could let slip."

She looked at him angrily. "Of course, we didn't let it slip! She said it was by an oak tree, but the Heath is full of oaks. When we couldn't find anything in a week of looking, we took it she was out of her wits with all that had happened to her. People see all sorts of things when they've been ill, let alone in the grief of having a dead child—and her only a child herself." Her contempt for him rang through her words, and he felt the sting of it even though he was doing what he must.

Tobias was sitting at his table shaking his head.

"So you assumed she had imagined at least that part of her experience—her nightmare—and you let it drop?" he pressed.

"Yes, of course we did. It took her months to get better, and when she was, we were all so glad of it we never mentioned it again. Why should we? Nobody else ever did. No one came looking for anybody. The police were asked if anyone was missing."

"And what about Miriam? Did you tell the police you had found her? After all, she was only thirteen herself by then."

"Of course, we told them. She wasn't missing from anywhere, and they were only too pleased that someone was looking after her."

"And she remained with you?"

"Yes. She grew up a beautiful girl." She said it with pride.

Her love for Miriam was so plain in her face and her voice, no words could have spoken as clearly. "When she was nineteen, Mr. Gardiner started courting her. Very slow, very gentle, he was with her. We knew he was a good bit older than she was, but she didn't mind, and that was all that mattered. If he made her happy, that was all I cared."

"And they were married?"

"Yes, a while later. And a very good husband he was to her, too."

"And then he died?"

"Yes. Very sad, that was. Died young, even though he was older than her, of course. Took an attack and was gone in a matter of days. She missed him very badly."

"Until she met Lucius Stourbridge?"

"Yes—but that was three years after."

"But she had no children with Mr. Gardiner?"

"No." Her voice was torn. "That was one blessing she wasn't given. Only the good Lord knows why. It happens, more often than you'd think."

Tobias rose to his feet with exaggerated weariness.

"My lord, we have listened with great indulgence to this life story of Miriam Gardiner, and while we have every sympathy with her early experiences, whatever the truth of them may be, it all has no bearing whatever to the death of James Treadwell, or that of Verona Stourbridge—except as it may, regrettably, have provided the wretched Treadwell with more fuel for his blackmailing schemes. If he knew of this first child of Mrs. Gardiner's, perhaps he felt the Stourbridge family would be less willing to accept her—a victim of rape, or whatever else it may have been."

A look of distaste passed across the judge's face, but Tobias's point was unarguable and he knew it.

"Sir Oliver?" he said questioningly. "It does seem that you have done more to advance Mr. Tobias's case than your own. Have you further points to put to your client?"

Rathbone had no idea what to say. He was desperate.

"Yes, my lord, if you please."

314

"Then proceed, but make it pertinent to the events we are here to try."

"Yes, my lord." He turned to Cleo. "Did you believe that she had been raped, Mrs. Anderson? Or do you perhaps think she was no better than she should be and . . ."

"She was thirteen," Cleo said furiously. "Twelve when it happened. Of course, I believed she had been raped! She was half out of her mind with terror!"

"Of whom? The man who raped her—then, nine months afterwards? Why?"

"Because he tried to kill her!" Cleo shouted.

Rathbone feigned surprise. "She told you that?"

"Yes!"

"And what did you do about it? There was a man somewhere near the Heath who had raped this girl you took in and treated as your own, and then he subsequently tried to murder her—and you never found him? In God's name, why not?"

Cleo was shaking, gasping for breath, and Rathbone was afraid he had driven her too far.

"I believed she'd been raped—or seduced," Cleo said in a whisper. "But God forgive me, I thought the attack was all jumbled up in her mind because of having a dead baby, poor little thing."

"Until . . . ?" Rathbone said urgently, raising his voice. "Until she came running to you again, close to hysteria and terrified. And there was really a dead body on the Heath this time—James Treadwell! Who was she running from, Mrs. Anderson?"

The silence was total.

A juror coughed, and it sounded like an explosion.

"Was it James Treadwell?" Rathbone threw the question down like a challenge.

"No!"

"Then whom?"

Silence.

The judge leaned forward. "If you wish us to believe that it

315

was not James Treadwell, Mrs. Anderson, then you must tell us who it was."

Cleo swallowed convulsively. "Aiden Campbell."

If she had set off a bomb it could not have had more effect.

Rathbone was momentarily paralyzed.

There was a roar from the gallery.

The jurors turned to each other, exclaiming, gasping.

The judge banged his gavel and demanded order.

"My lord!" Rathbone said, raising his voice. "May I ask for the luncheon adjournment so I can speak with my client?"

"You may," the judge agreed, and banged the gavel again. "The court will reconvene at two o'clock."

Rathbone left the courtroom in a daze and walked like a man half blind down to the room where Miriam Gardiner was permitted to speak with him.

She did not even turn her head when the door opened and he came in, the jailer remaining on the outside.

"Was it Aiden Campbell you were running from?" he asked.

She said nothing, sitting motionless, head turned away.

"Why?" he persisted. "What had he done to you?"

Silence.

"Was he the one who attacked you originally?" His voice was growing louder and more shrill in his desperation. "For heaven's sake, answer me! How can I help you if you won't speak to me?" He leaned forward over the small table, but still she did not turn. "You will hang!" he said deliberately.

"I know," she answered at last.

"And Cleo Anderson!" he added.

"No—I will say I killed Treadwell, too. I will swear it on the stand. They'll believe me, because they want to. None of them wants to condemn Cleo."

It was true, and he knew it as well as she did.

"You'll say that on the stand?"

"Yes."

"But it is not true!"

This time she turned and met his eyes fully. "You don't

know that, Sir Oliver. You don't know what happened. If I say it is so, will you contradict your own client? You must be a fool—it is what they want to hear. They will believe it."

He stared back at her, momentarily beaten. He had the feeling that were there any heart left alive in her, she would have smiled at him. He knew that if he did not call her to testify, then she would ask the judge from the dock for permission to speak, and he would grant it. There was no argument to make.

He left, and had a miserable luncheon of bread which tasted to him like sawdust, and claret which could as well have been vinegar.

Rathbone had no choice but to call Aiden Campbell to the stand. If he had not, then most assuredly Tobias would have. At least this way he might retain a modicum of control.

The court was seething with anticipation. Word seemed to have spread during the luncheon adjournment, because now every seat was taken and the ushers had had to ban more people from crowding in.

The judge called them to order, and Rathbone rose to begin.

"I call Aiden Campbell, my lord."

Campbell was white-faced but composed. He must have known that this was inevitable, and he had had almost two hours to prepare himself. He stood now facing Rathbone, a tall, straight figure, tragically resembling both his dead sister and his nephew, Lucius, who was sitting beside his father more like a ghost than a living being. Every now and again he stared up at Miriam, but never once had Rathbone seen Miriam return his look.

"Mr. Campbell," Rathbone began as soon as Campbell had been reminded that he was still under oath. "An extraordinary charge has been laid against you by the last witness. Are you willing to respond to this—"

"I am," Campbell interrupted in his eagerness to reply. "I

317

had hoped profoundly that this would never be necessary. Indeed, I have gone to some lengths to see that it would not, for the sake of my family, and out of a sense of decency and the desire to bury old tragedies and allow them to remain unknown in the present, where they cannot hurt innocent parties." He glanced at Lucius, and away again. His meaning was nakedly apparent.

"Mrs. Anderson has sworn that Miriam Gardiner claimed it was you she was running away from when she fled the party at Cleveland Square. Is that true?" Rathbone asked.

Campbell looked distressed. "Yes," he said quietly. He shook his head a fraction. "I cannot tell you how deeply I had hoped not to have to say this. I knew Miriam Gardiner—Miriam Speake, as she was then—when she was twelve years old. She was a maid in my household when I lived near Hampstead."

There was a rustle of movement and the startled sound of indrawn breath around the room.

Campbell looked across at Harry Stourbridge and Lucius.

"I'm sorry," he said fervently. "I cannot conceal this any longer. Miriam lived in my house for about eighteen months, or something like that. Of course, she recognized me at the garden party, and must have been afraid that I would know her also, and tell you." He was still speaking to Harry Stourbridge, as if this were a private matter between them.

"Obviously, you did not tell them," Rathbone observed, bringing his attention back to the business of the court. "Why would it trouble her so much that she would flee in such a manner, as if terrified rather than merely embarrassed? Surely the Stourbridge family was already aware that she came from a different social background? Was this so terrible?"

Campbell sighed, and hesitated several moments before replying.

Rathbone waited.

There was barely a movement in the courtroom.

"Mr. Campbell . . ." the judge prompted.

Campbell bit his lips. "Yes, my lord. It pains me deeply to
318

say this, but Miriam Speake was a loose woman. Even at the age of twelve she was without moral conscience."

There was a gasp from Harry Stourbridge. Lucius half rose in his seat, but his legs seemed to collapse under him.

"I'm sorry," Campbell said again. "She was very pretty— very comely for one so young . . . and I find it repugnant to have to say so, but very experienced—"

Again he was interrupted by an outcry from the gallery.

Several jurors were shaking their heads. A couple of them glanced towards the dock with grim disappointment. Rathbone knew absolutely that they believed every word. He himself looked up at Miriam and saw her bend her ashen face and cover it with her hands as if she could not endure what she was hearing.

In calling Aiden Campbell, Rathbone had removed what ghost of a defense she had had. He felt as if he had impaled himself on his own sword. Everyone in the room was watching him, waiting for him to go on. Hester must be furious at this result, and pity him for his incompetence. The pity was worse.

Tobias was shaking his head in sympathy for a fellow counsel drowning in a storm of his own making.

Campbell was waiting. Rathbone must say something more. Nothing he could imagine would make it worse. At least he had nothing to lose now and therefore also nothing to fear.

"This is your opinion, Mr. Campbell? And you believe that Mrs. Gardiner, now a very respectable widow in her thirties, was so terrified that you would express this unfortunate view of her childhood and ruin the prospective happiness of your nephew?"

"Hardly unreasonable," Tobias interrupted. "What man would not tell his sister whom he loved that her only son was engaged to marry a maid no better than a whore?"

"But he didn't!" Rathbone exclaimed. "He told no one! In fact, you first heard him apologize to his brother-in-law this moment for saying it now." He swung around. "Why

319

was that, Mr. Campbell? If she was such a woman as you describe—should I say, such a child—why did you not warn your family rather than allow her to marry into it? If what you say is true . . ."

"It is true," Campbell said gravely. "The state she was in that Mrs. Anderson described fits, regrettably, with what I know of her." His hands gripped the rail of the witness box in front of him. He seemed to hold it as if to steady himself from shaking. He had difficulty finding his voice. "She seduced one of my servants, a previously decent man, who fell into temptation too strong for him to resist. I considered dismissing him, but his work was excellent, and he was bitterly ashamed of his lapse from virtue. It would have ruined him at the start of his life." He stopped for a moment.

Rathbone waited.

"I did not know at the time," Campbell went on with obvious difficulty. "But she was with child. She had it aborted."

There was an outcry in the courtroom. A woman shrieked. There was a commotion as someone apparently collapsed.

The judge banged his gavel, but it made little impression.

Miriam made as if to rise to her feet, but the jailers on either side of her pulled her back.

Rathbone looked at the jury. To a man their faces were marked deeply with shock and utter and savage contempt.

The judge banged his gavel again. "I will have order!" he said angrily. "Otherwise the ushers will clear the court!"

Tobias looked across at Rathbone and shook his head.

When the noise subsided, and before Rathbone could speak, Campbell continued. "That must be the reason that she was bleeding when Mrs. Anderson found her wandering around on the Heath." He shook his head as if to deny what he was about to say, somehow reduce the harshness of it. "At first I didn't want to put her out either. She was so young. I thought—one mistake—and it had been a rough abortion—she was still . . ." He shrugged. Then he raised his head and looked at Rathbone. "But she kept on, always tempting the men, flirting with them, setting one against the other. She en-

320

joyed the power she had over them. I had no choice but to put her out."

There was a murmur of sympathy around the court, and a rising tide of anger also. One or two men swore under their breath. Two jurors spoke to each other. They glanced up at the dock. The condemnation in their faces was unmistakable.

A journalist was scribbling furiously.

Tobias looked at Rathbone and smiled sympathetically, but without hiding his knowledge of his own victory. He asked no quarter for himself when he lost, and he gave none.

"I wish I had not had to say that." Campbell was looking at Rathbone. "I hesitated to tell Harry before because at first I was not even totally sure it was the same person. It seemed incredible, and of course, she had aged a great deal in twenty-three years. I didn't want to think it was her . . . you understand that? I suppose I finally acknowledged that it had to be when I saw that she also recognized me."

There was nothing for Rathbone to say, nothing left to ask. It was the last result he could have foreseen, and presumably Hester would feel as disillusioned and as empty as he did himself. He sat down utterly dejected.

Tobias rose and walked into the middle of the floor, swaggering a little. Beating Oliver Rathbone was a victory to be savored, even when it had been ridiculously easy.

"Mr. Campbell, there is very little left for me to ask. You have told us far more than we could have imagined." He looked across at Rathbone. "I think that goes for my learned friend as much as for me. However, I do wish to tidy up any details that there may be . . . in case Mrs. Gardiner decides to take the stand herself and make any charges against you, as suggested by Mrs. Anderson—who may be as unaware of Mrs. Gardiner's youthful exploits as were the rest of us."

Campbell did not reply but waited for Tobias to continue.

"Mrs. Gardiner fled when she realized that you had recognized her—at least that is your assumption?"

"Yes."

"Did you follow her?"

"No, of course not. I had no reason to."

"You remained at the party?"

"Not specifically at the party. I remained at Cleveland Square. I was very upset about the matter. I moved a little farther off in the garden, to be alone and think what to do . . . and what to say when the rest of the family would inevitably discover that she had gone."

"And what did you decide, Mr. Campbell?"

"To say nothing," Campbell answered. "I knew this story would hurt them all profoundly. They were very fond of Miriam. Lucius was in love with her as only a young and idealistic man can be. I believe it was his first love . . ." He left the sentence hanging, allowing each man to remember his own first awakenings of passion, dreams, and perhaps loss.

"I see," Tobias said softly. "Only God can know whether that decision was the right one, but I can well understand why you made it. I am afraid I must press you further on just one issue."

"Yes?"

"The coachman, James Treadwell. Why do you think she left with him?"

"He was the servant in the house she knew the best," Campbell replied. "I gather he had driven her from Hampstead a number of times. I shall not speculate that it was anything more than that."

"Very charitable of you," Tobias observed. "Considering your knowledge of her previous behavior with menservants."

Campbell narrowed his lips, but he did not answer.

"Tell me," Tobias continued, "how did this wretched coachman know of Mrs. Anderson's stealing of hospital supplies?"

"I have no idea." Campbell sounded surprised, then his face fell. He shook his head. "No—I don't believe Miriam told him. She was conniving, manipulative, greedy—but no. Unless it was by accident, not realizing what he would do with the information."

"Would it not be the perfect revenge?" Tobias asked smoothly. "Her marriage to Lucius Stourbridge is now im-

322

possible because she knows you will never allow it. Tread-well is ruining her friend and benefactress, to whom she must now return. In rage and defeat, and even desperation, she strikes out at him! What could be more natural?"

"I suppose so," Campbell conceded.

Tobias turned to the judge. "My lord, this is surely sufficient tragedy for one day. If it pleases the court, I would like to suggest we may adjourn until tomorrow, when Sir Oliver may put forward any other evidence he feels may salvage his case. Personally, I have little more to add."

The judge looked at Rathbone enquiringly, but his gavel was already in his hand.

Rathbone had no weapons and no will to fight any further.

"Certainly, my lord," he said quietly. "By all means."

Rathbone had barely left the courtroom when he was approached by the usher.

He did not wish to speak to anyone. He was tasting the full bitterness of a defeat he knew he had brought upon himself. He dreaded facing Hester and seeing her disillusion. She would not blame him. He was certain she would not be angry. Her kindness would be even harder to bear.

"What is it?" he said brusquely.

"Sorry, Sir Oliver," the usher apologized. "Mrs. Anderson asked if you would speak with her, sir. She said it was most important."

The only thing worse than facing Hester was going to be telling Cleo Anderson that there was nothing more he could attempt on her behalf. He drew in his breath. It could not be evaded. If victory could be accepted and celebrated, then defeat must be dealt with with equal composure, and at the very least without cowardice or excuses.

"Of course," he replied. "Thank you, Morris." He turned and was a dozen yards along the corridor when Hester caught up with him. He had no idea what to say to her. There was no comfort to offer, no next line of attack to suggest.

She fell into step with him and said nothing.

He glanced at her, then away again, grateful for her silence. He had not seen Monk, and assumed he was on some other business.

Cleo was waiting in the small room with the jailer outside. She was standing facing them, and she stepped forward as soon as Rathbone closed the door.

"He's lying," she said, looking from one to the other of them.

He was embarrassed. It was futile to protest now, and he had not the emotional strength to struggle with her. It was over.

He shook his head. "I'm sure you want to believe—"

"It has nothing to do with belief! I saw her then. She wasn't aborted. She'd gone full term." She was angry now with his lack of understanding. "I'm a nurse. I know the difference between a woman who's given birth and one who's lost her child or done away with it in the first few months. That child was born—dead or alive. The size of her—and she had milk, poor little thing." She swallowed. "How she wept for it . . ."

"So Campbell is lying!" Hester said, moving forward to Cleo. "But why?"

"To hide what he did to her," Cleo said furiously. "He must have raped her, and when she was with child he threw her out." She looked from Hester to Rathbone. "Though he didn't even notice her condition. Who looks at housemaids, especially ones who are barely more than children themselves? Perhaps he'd already got tired of her—moved on to someone else? Or if he thought she'd had it aborted, and only then realized she hadn't, to avoid the scandal."

"It wouldn't be much of a scandal," Hester said sadly. "If she was foolish enough to say it was his, he would simply deny it. No one would be likely to believe her . . . or frankly, care that much even if they did. It isn't worth murdering anyone over."

Cleo's face crumpled, but she refused to give in. "What about the body?"

"Which body?" Rathbone was confused. "The baby?"

"No—no, the woman!"

"What woman?"

"The woman Miriam saw murdered the night her baby was born. The woman on the Heath."

Rathbone was still further confused. "Who was she?"

Cleo shook her head. "I don't know. Miriam said she had been murdered. She saw it—that was what she was running away from."

"But who was the woman?"

"I don't know!"

"Was there ever a body found? What happened? Didn't the police ask?"

Cleo waved her hands in denial, her eyes desperate. "No—no body was ever found. He must have hidden it."

It was all pointless, completely futile. Rathbone felt a sense of despair drowning him as if he could hardly struggle for breath, almost a physical suffocation.

"You said yourself that she was hysterical." He tried to sound reasonable, not patronizing or offensive to a woman who must be facing the most bitter disillusion imaginable, and for which she would face disgrace she had not deserved, and a death he could not save her from. "Don't you think the loss of her baby was what she was actually thinking of? Was it a girl?"

"I don't know. She didn't say." Cleo looked as if she had caught his despair. "She seemed so—so sure it was a woman . . . someone she cared for . . . who had helped her, even loved her . . . I—" She stopped, too weary, too hurt, to go on.

"I'm sorry," Rathbone said gently. "You were right to tell me about the baby. If Campbell was lying, at least we may be able to make something of that. Even if we do no more than save Miriam's reputation, I am sure that will matter to her." He was making wild promises and talking nonsense. Would Miriam care about such a thing when she faced death?

He banged on the door to be released again, and as soon as they were outside he turned to Hester.

But before he could begin to say how sorry he was, she spoke.

"If this woman really was killed, then her body must still be there."

"Hester—she was delirious, probably weak from loss of blood and in a state of acute distress from delivering a dead child."

"Maybe. But perhaps she really did see a woman murdered," Hester insisted. "If the body was never found, then it is out there on the Heath."

"For twenty-two years! On Hampstead Heath! For heaven's sake . . ."

"Not in the open! Buried—hidden somewhere."

"Well, if it's buried no one would find it now."

"Perhaps it's not buried." She refused to give up. "Perhaps it's hidden somehow, concealed."

"Hester . . ."

"I'm going to find Sergeant Robb and see if he will help me look."

"You can't. After all this time there'll be nothing . . ."

"I've got to try. What if there really was a woman murdered? What if Miriam was telling the truth all the time?"

"She isn't!"

"But what if she was? She's your client, Oliver! You've got to give her the benefit of every doubt. You must assume that what she says is true until it is completely proved it can't be."

"She was thirteen, she'd just given birth to a dead child, she was alone and hysterical . . ."

"I'm going to find Sergeant Robb. He'll help me look, whatever he believes, for Cleo's sake. He owes her a debt he can never repay, and he knows that."

"And doubtless if he should forget, you will remind him."

"Certainly!" she agreed. "But he won't forget."

"What about Monk?" he challenged her as she turned to leave.

"He's still busy trying to find out more about Treadwell and the corpses," she said over her shoulder.

"Hester, wait!"

But she had walked off, increasing her pace to a run, and short of chasing after her there was nothing he could do—except try to imagine how he was going to face the court the next morning.

Michael Robb was sitting alone in the room where until recently his grandfather had spent his days. The big chair was still there, as if the old man might come back to it one day, and there was a startling emptiness without him.

"Mrs. Monk," Robb said with surprise. "What is it? Is something wrong?"

"Everything is wrong," she answered, remaining standing in spite of his invitation to sit. "Cleo is going to be convicted unless we can find some sort of evidence that Miriam also is innocent, and our only chance of that is to find the body of the woman . . ."

"What woman? Just a minute!" He held up his hand. "What has happened in court? I wasn't there."

With words falling over each other, she told him about Rathbone's calling Cleo to the stand and her story of how she had first met Miriam, and then Aiden Campbell's denial and explanation.

"We've got to find the woman that Miriam said was murdered," she finished desperately. "That would prove what she said was true! At least they would have to investigate."

"She's been out there for twenty-two years," he protested. "If she exists at all!"

"Can you think of anything better?" she demanded.

"No—but . . ."

"Then, help me! We've got to go and look!"

He hesitated only a moment. She could see in his face that he considered it hopeless, but he was feeling lonely and guilty because Cleo had helped him in the way he valued the most and he could do nothing for her. Silently, he picked up his bull's-eye lantern and followed her out into the gathering dusk.

Side by side they walked towards Green Man Hill and the row of cottages where Cleo Anderson had lived until her arrest. They stopped outside, facing the Heath. It was now almost dark; only the heavy outlines of the trees showed black against the sky.

"Where do you think we should start?" Robb asked.

She was grateful he had spoken of them as together, not relegating the search to her idea in which he was merely obliging her.

She had been thinking about it as they had traveled in silence.

"It cannot have been very far," she said, staring across the grass. "She was not in a state to run a distance. If the poor woman really was murdered—beaten to death, as Miriam apparently said—then whoever did so would not have committed such an act close to the road." She pushed away the thought, refusing to allow the pictures into her mind. "Even if it was a single blow—and please God it was—it cannot have been silent. There must have been a quarrel, an accusation or something. Miriam was there; she saw it. She, at least, must have cried out—and then fled."

He was staring at her, and in the light of the lantern she saw him nodding slowly, his face showing his revulsion at what she described.

"Whoever it was could not follow her," she went on relentlessly. "Because he was afraid of being caught. First he had to get rid of the body of the woman—"

"Mrs. Monk . . . are you sure you believe this is possible?" he interrupted.

She was beginning to doubt it herself, but she refused to give up.

"Of course!" she said sharply. "We are going to prove it. If you had just killed someone, and you knew a girl had seen you, and she had run away, perhaps screaming, how would you hide a body so quickly that if anyone heard and came to see, they would not find anything at all?"

His eyes widened. He opened his lips to argue, then began

328

to think. He walked across the grass towards the first trees and stared around him.

"Well, I wouldn't have time to dig a grave," he said slowly. "The ground is hard and full of roots. And anyway, someone would very quickly notice disturbed earth."

He walked a little farther, and she followed after him quickly.

Above them something swooped in the darkness on broad wings. Involuntarily, she gave a little shriek.

"It's only an owl," he said reassuringly.

She swung around. "Where did it go?"

"One of the trees," he replied. He lifted the lantern and began shining it around, lighting the trunks one after another. They looked pale gray against the darkness, and the shadows seemed to move beyond them as the lantern waved.

She was acutely glad she was not alone. She imagined what Miriam must have felt like, her child lost, a woman she loved killed in front of her, and herself pursued and hunted, bleeding, terrified. No wonder she was all but out of her mind when Cleo found her.

"We've got to keep on looking," she said fiercely. "We must exhaust every possibility. If the body is here, we are going to find it!" She strode forward, hitching up her skirts so as not to fall over them. "You said he wouldn't have buried it. He couldn't leave it in plain sight, or it would have been found. And it wasn't. So he hid it so successfully it never was found. Where?"

"In a tree," he replied. "It has to be. There's nowhere else!"

"Up a tree? But someone would find it in time!" she protested. "It would rot. It . . ."

"I know," he said hastily, shaking his head as if to rid himself of the idea. He moved the lantern ahead of them, picking out undergrowth and more trees. A weasel ran across the path, its lean body bright in the beam for a moment, then it disappeared.

"Animals would get rid of it in time, wouldn't they?"

"In time, yes."

329

"Well, it's been over twenty years! What would be left now? Bones? Teeth?"

"Hair," he said. "Perhaps clothes, jewelry, buttons. Boots, maybe."

She shuddered.

He looked at her, shining the light a little below her face not to dazzle her.

"Are you all right, Mrs. Monk?" he said gently. "I can go on my own, if you like. I'll take you back and then come back here again. I promise I will . . ."

She smiled at his earnestness. "I know you would, but I am quite all right, thank you. Let's go forward."

He hesitated for a moment, still uncertain, then as she did not waver, he shone the lantern ahead of them and started.

They walked together for forty or fifty yards, searching to left and right for any place that could be used for concealment. She found herself feeling more and more as if she was wasting her time—and more important, Robb's time as well. She had believed Miriam's story because she wanted to, for Cleo's sake, not because it was really credible.

"Sergeant Robb," she began.

He turned around, the beam of light swinging across the two trees to their right. It caught for a moment on a tangle in the lower branches.

"What's that?" he said quickly.

"An old bird's nest," she replied. "Last year's, by the look of it."

He played the light on it, then moved forward to look more closely.

"What?" she asked, with curiosity more than hope. "Clever how they weave them, isn't it? Especially since they haven't got any hands."

He passed her the lantern. "Hold this onto it, please. I want to take a closer look."

"At a bird's nest?" But she did as he requested, and kept the light steady.

With hands free it was easy enough for him to climb up

330

until he was level with the nest and peer inside where it was caught in a fork in the branches, close to the trunk.

"What is it?" she called up.

He turned around, his face a shadowed mask in the up-turned beam.

"Hair," he answered her. "Long hair, lots of it. The whole nest is lined with hair." His voice was shaking. "I'm going to look for a hollow tree. You just hold the light, and keep your eyes away."

She felt a lurch inside. She had no longer believed it, and now here it was. They were almost there—in the next half hour—more or less . . .

"Yes," she said unsteadily. "Yes, of course."

Actually, it took him only fifteen minutes to find the tree with the hollow core, blasted by some ancient lightning and now rotted. It was closer to the road than the nest, but the spread of branches hid the hole until it was deliberately sought. Perhaps twenty-two years ago it had been more obvious. The entire tree was hollow down the heart.

"It's in there," Robb said huskily, climbing down again, the lantern tied to his belt. His legs were shaking when he reached the ground. "It's only a skeleton, but there's still cloth left . . ." He blinked, and his face looked yellow-gray in the beam. "From the head, she was killed by one terrible blow . . . like Treadwell . . . and Mrs. Stourbridge."

13

R*ATHBONE HAD SLEPT LITTLE.* A messenger had arrived at his rooms after midnight with a note from Hester:

Dear Oliver,

We found the body. Seems to be a woman with gray hair. She was killed by a terrible blow to the head—just like the others. Am in the police station with Sergeant Robb. They do not know who she is. Will tell William, of course. I shall be in court in the morning to testify. You MUST call me!

Yours, Hester

He had found it impossible to rest. An hour later he had made himself a hot drink and was pacing the study floor trying to formulate a strategy for the next day. Eventually, he went back to bed and sank into a deep sleep, when it seemed immediately time to get up.

His head ached and his mouth was dry. His manservant brought him breakfast, but he ate only toast and drank a cup of tea, then left straightaway for the courtroom. He was far too early, and the time he had expected to use in preparing himself he wasted in pointless moving from one place to another, and conversation from which he learned nothing.

Tobias was in excellent spirits. He passed Rathbone in the corridor and wished him well with a wry smile. He would have preferred a little fight of it. Such an easy victory was of little savor.

The gallery was half empty again. The public had already made up their minds, and the few spectators present were there only to see justice done and taste a certain vengeance. The startling exceptions to this were Lucius and Harry Stourbridge, who sat towards the front, side by side, and even at a distance, very obviously supporting each other in silent companionship of anguish.

The judge called the court to order.

"Have you any further witnesses, Sir Oliver?" he asked.

"Yes, my lord. I would like to call Hester Monk."

Tobias looked across curiously.

The judge raised his eyebrows, but with no objection.

Rathbone smiled very slightly.

The usher called for Hester.

She took the stand looking tired and pale-faced, but absolutely confident, and she very deliberately turned and looked up towards the dock and nodded to both Cleo and Miriam. Then she waited for Rathbone to begin.

Rathbone cleared his throat. "Mrs. Monk, were you in court yesterday when Mrs. Anderson testified to the extraordinary story Miriam Gardiner told when she was first found bleeding and hysterical on Hampstead Heath twenty-two years ago?"

"Yes, I was."

"Did you follow any course of action because of that?"

"Yes, I went to look for the body of the woman Miriam said she saw murdered."

Tobias made a sound of derision, halfway between a cough and a snort.

The judge leaned forward enquiringly. "Sir Oliver, is this really relevant at this stage?"

"Yes, my lord, most relevant," Rathbone answered with satisfaction. At last there was a warmth inside him, a sense that he could offer a battle. Assuredly, he could startle the equanimity from Tobias's face.

"Then please make that apparent," the judge directed.

"Yes, my lord. Mrs. Monk, did you find a body?"

The court was silent, but not in anticipation. He barely had the jurors' attention.

"Yes, Sir Oliver, I did."

Tobias started forward, jerking upright from the seat where he had been all but sprawled.

There was a wave of sound and movement from the gallery, a hiss of indrawn breath.

The judge leaned across to Hester. "Do I hear you correctly, madam? You say you found a body?"

"Yes, my lord. Of course, I was not alone. I took Sergeant Michael Robb with me from the beginning. It was actually he who found it."

"This is very serious indeed." He frowned at her, his face pinched and earnest. "Where is the body now and what can you tell me of it?"

"It is in the police morgue in Hampstead, my lord, and my knowledge of it is closely observed, but only as a nurse, not a doctor."

"You are a nurse?" He was astounded.

"Yes, my lord. I served in the Crimea."

"Good gracious." He sat back. "Sir Oliver, you had better proceed. But before you do so, I will have order in this court. The next man or woman to make an unwarranted noise will be removed! Continue."

"Thank you, my lord." Rathbone turned to Hester. "Where did you find the body, Mrs. Monk, precisely?"

"In a hollow tree on Hampstead Heath," she replied. "We started walking from Mrs. Anderson's house on Green Man Hill, looking for the sort of place where a body might be concealed, assuming that Mrs. Gardiner's story was true."

"What led you to look in a hollow tree?"

There was total silence in the court. Not a soul moved.

"A bird's nest with a lot of human hair woven into it, caught in one of the lower branches of a tree near it," Hester answered. "We searched all around until we found the hollow

334

one. Sergeant Robb climbed up and found the hole. Of course, the area will have grown over a great deal in twenty-two years. It could have been easier to see, to get to, then."

"And the body?" Rathbone pursued. "What can you tell us of it?"

She looked distressed; the memory was obviously painful. Her hands tightened on the railing, and she took a deep breath before she began.

"There was only a skeleton. Her clothes had largely rotted away, only buttons were left of her dress, and the bones of her . . . undergarments. Her boots were badly damaged, but there was still more than enough to be recognizable. All the buttons to them were whole and attached to what was left of the leather. They were unusual, and rather good."

She stood motionless, steadying herself before she continued. "To judge by what hair we found, she would have been a woman in her forties or fifties. She had a terrible hole in her skull, as if she had been beaten with some heavy object so hard it killed her."

"Thank you," Rathbone said quietly. "You must be tired and extremely harrowed by the experience."

She nodded.

Rathbone turned to Tobias.

Tobias strode forward, shaking his head a little. When he spoke his voice was soft. He was far too wily to be less than courteous to her. She had the court's sympathy and he knew it.

"Mrs. Monk, may I commend your courage and your single-minded dedication to seeking the truth. It is a very noble cause, and you appear to be tireless in it." There was not a shred of sarcasm in him.

"Thank you," she said guardedly.

"Tell me, Mrs. Monk, was there anything on the body of this unfortunate woman to indicate who she was?"

"Not so far as I know. Sergeant Robb is trying to learn that now."

"Using what? The remnants of cloth and leather that were still upon the bone?"

"You will have to ask him," she replied.

"If he feels that this tragedy has any relevance to this present case, and therefore gives us that opportunity, then I shall," Tobias agreed. "But you seem to feel it has, or you would not now be telling me of it. Why is that, Mrs. Monk, other than that you desire to protect one of your colleagues?"

Spots of color warmed Hester's cheeks. If she had ever imagined he would be gentle with her, she now knew better.

"Because we found her where Miriam Gardiner said she was murdered," she replied a trifle tartly.

"Indeed?" Tobias raised his eyebrows. "I gathered from Mrs. Anderson that Mrs. Gardiner—Miss Speake, as she was then—was completely hysterical and incoherent. Indeed, Mrs. Anderson herself ceased to believe there was any woman, any murder, or any body to find."

"Is that a question?" Hester asked him.

"No—no, it is an observation," he said sharply. "You found this gruesome relic somewhere on Hampstead Heath in an unspecified tree. All we know is that it is within walking distance of Green Man Hill. Is there anything to indicate how long it had been there—except that it is obviously more than ten or eleven years? Could it have been twenty-five? Or, say, thirty? Or even fifty years, Mrs. Monk?"

She stared back at him without flinching. "I am not qualified to say, Mr. Tobias. You will have to ask Sergeant Robb, or even the police surgeon. However, my husband is examining the boots and has an idea that they may be able to prove something. Buttons have a design, you know."

"Your husband is an expert in buttons for ladies' boots?" he asked.

"He is an expert in detection of facts from the evidence," she answered coolly. "He will know whom to ask."

"No doubt. And he may be willing to pursue ladies' boot buttons with tireless endeavor," Tobias said sarcastically. "But we have to deal with the evidence we have, and deduce from it reasonable conclusions. Is there anything in your knowledge, Mrs. Monk, to prove that this unfortunate woman whose body you found has anything to do with the murders of James Treadwell and of Mrs. Verona Stourbridge?"

"Yes! You said Miriam Gardiner was talking nonsense because no body of a woman was ever found on Hampstead Heath such as she described. Well, now it has. She was not lying, nor was she out of her wits. There was a murder. Since she described it, it is the most reasonable thing to suppose that she witnessed it, exactly as she said."

"There is the body of a woman," Tobias corrected her. "We do not know if it was murder, although I accept that it may very well have been. But we do not know who she was, what happened to her, and still less do we know when it happened. Much as you would like to believe it is some support to the past virtue of Miriam Gardiner, Mrs. Monk—and your charity does you credit, and indeed your loyalty—it does not clear her of this charge." He spread his hands in a gesture of finality, smiled at the jury, and returned to his seat.

Rathbone stood up and looked at Hester.

"Mrs. Monk, you were at this tree on the Heath and made this gruesome discovery; therefore you know the place, whereas we can only imagine. Tell us, is there any way whatever that this unfortunate woman could have sustained this appalling blow to her head and then placed herself inside the tree?"

"No, of course not." Her voice derided the idea.

"She was murdered and her body was afterwards hidden, and it happened long enough ago that the flesh has decomposed and most of the fabric of her clothes has rotted?" Rathbone made absolutely certain.

"Yes."

"And she was killed by a violent blow to the head, in apparently exactly the same manner as James Treadwell and poor Mrs. Stourbridge?"

"Yes."

337

"Thank you, Mrs. Monk." He turned to the judge. "I believe, my lord, that this evidence lends a great deal more credibility to Mrs. Gardiner's original account, and that in the interest of justice we need to know who that woman was and if her death is connected with those murders of which Mrs. Gardiner and Mrs. Anderson presently stand charged."

The judge looked across at Tobias.

Tobias was already on his feet. "Yes, my lord, of course. Mr. Campbell has informed me that he is willing to testify again and explain all that he can, if it will assist the court. Indeed, since what has been said may leave in certain people's minds suspicion as to his own role, he wishes to have the opportunity to speak."

"That would be most desirable," the judge agreed. "Please have Mr. Campbell return to the stand."

Aiden Campbell looked tired and strained as he climbed the steps again, but Rathbone, watching, could see no fear in him. He faced the court with sadness but confidence, and his voice was quite steady when he answered Tobias's questions.

"No, I have no idea who the woman is, poor creature, nor how long she has been there. It would seem from the state of the body, and the clothes, that it was at least ten years."

"Have you any idea how she came by her death, Mr. Campbell?" Tobias pressed.

"None at all, except that from Mrs. Monk's description of the wound, it sounds distressingly like those inflicted on Treadwell, and"—he hesitated, and this time his composure nearly cracked—"upon my sister . . ."

"Please," Tobias said gently. "Allow yourself a few moments, Mr. Campbell. Would you like a glass of water?"

"No—no thank you." Campbell straightened up. "I beg your pardon. I was going to say that this woman's death may be connected. Possibly she also was a nurse, and may have become aware of the thefts of medicine from the hospital. Perhaps she either threatened to tell the authorities or maybe she tried her hand at blackmail . . ." He did not need to finish the sentence, his meaning was only too apparent.

"Just so." Tobias inclined his head in thanks, turned to the jury with a little smile, then went back to his table.

There was silence in the gallery. Everyone was looking towards Rathbone, waiting to see what he would do.

He glanced around, playing for time, hoping some shred of an idea would come to him and not look too transparently desperate. He saw Harry Stourbridge's face, colorless and earnest, watching him with hope in his eyes. Beside him, Lucius looked like a ghost.

There was a stir as the outside doors opened, and everyone craned to see who it was.

Monk came in. He nodded very slightly.

Rathbone turned to the front again. "If there is time before the luncheon adjournment, my lord, I would like to call Mr. William Monk. I believe he may have evidence as to the identity of the woman whose body was found last night."

"Then indeed call him," the judge said keenly. "We should all like very much to hear what he has to say. You may step down, Mr. Campbell."

Amid a buzz of excitement, Monk climbed the steps to the stand and was sworn in. Every eye in the room was on him. Even Tobias sat forward in his seat, his face puckered with concern, his hands spread out on the table in front of him, broad and strong, fingers drumming silently.

Rathbone found his voice shaking a little. He was obliged to clear his throat before he began.

"Mr. Monk, have you been engaged in trying to discover whatever information it is possible to find regarding the body of the woman found on Hampstead Heath last night?"

"Since I was informed of it, at about one o'clock this morning," Monk replied. And, in fact, he looked as if he had been up all night. His clothes were immaculate as always, but there was a dark shadow of beard on his cheeks and he was unquestionably tired.

"Have you learned anything?" Rathbone asked. Hearing his own heart beating so violently, he feared he must be shaking visibly.

"Yes. I took the buttons from the boots she was wearing and a little of the leather of the soles, which were scarcely worn. Those particular buttons were individual, manufactured for only a short space of time. It is not absolute proof, but it seems extremely likely she was killed twenty-two years ago. Certainly, it was not longer, and since the boots were almost new, it is unlikely to be less than that. If you call the police surgeon, he will tell you she was a woman of middle age, forty-five or fifty, of medium height and build, with long gray hair. She had at some time in the past had a broken bone in one foot which had healed completely. She was killed by a single, very powerful blow to her head, by someone facing her at the time, and right-handed. Oh . . . and she had perfect teeth—which is unusual in one of her age."

There was tension in the court so palpable that when a man in the gallery sneezed the woman behind him let out a scream, then stifled it immediately.

Every juror in both rows stared at Monk as if unaware of anyone else in the room.

"Was that the same police surgeon who examined the bodies of Treadwell and Mrs. Stourbridge?" Rathbone asked.

"Yes," Monk answered.

"And was he of the opinion that the blows were inflicted by the same person."

Tobias rose to his feet. "My lord, Mr. Monk has no medical expertise . . ."

"Indeed," the judge agreed. "We will not indulge in hearsay, Sir Oliver. If you wish to call this evidence, no doubt the police surgeon will make himself available. Nevertheless, I should very much like to know the answer to that myself."

"I shall most certainly do so," Rathbone agreed. Then, as the usher stood at his elbow, he said, "Excuse me, my lord." He took the note handed to him and read it to himself.

It could not have been a blackmailer of Cleo—she was not stealing medicines then. The apothecary can prove that. Call me to testify. Hester.

340

The court was waiting.

"My lord, may I recall Mrs. Monk to the stand, in the question as to whether Mrs. Anderson could have been blackmailed over the theft of medicines twenty-two years ago?"

"Can she give evidence on the subject?" the judge asked with surprise. "Surely she was a child at the time?"

"She has access to the records of the hospital, my lord."

"Then call her, but I may require to have the records themselves brought and put into evidence."

"With respect, my lord, the court has accepted that medicines were stolen within the last few months without Mr. Tobias having brought the records for the jury to read. Testimony has been sufficient for him in that."

Tobias rose to his feet. "My lord, Mrs. Monk has shown herself an interested party. Her evidence is hardly unbiased."

"I am sure the records can be obtained," Rathbone said reluctantly. He would far rather Cleo's present thefts were left to testimony only, but there was little point in saving her from charges of stealing if she was convicted of murder.

"Thank you, my lord," Tobias said with a smile.

"Nevertheless," the judge added, "we shall see what Mrs. Monk has to say, Sir Oliver. Please call her."

Hester took the stand and was reminded of her earlier oath to tell the truth and only the truth. She had examined the apothecary's records as far back as thirty years, since before Cleo Anderson's time, and there was no discrepancy in medicines purchased and those accounted for as given to patients.

"So at the time of this unfortunate woman's death, there were no grounds for blackmailing Mrs. Anderson, or anyone else, with regard to medicines at the hospital?" Rathbone confirmed.

"That is so," she agreed.

Tobias stood up and walked towards her.

"Mrs. Monk, you seem to be disposed to go to extraordinary lengths to prove Mrs. Anderson not guilty, lengths quite above and beyond the call of any duty you are either invested with or have taken upon yourself. I cannot but suspect you of

341

embarking upon a crusade, either because you have a zeal to reform nursing and the view in which nurses are regarded—and I will call Mr. Fermin Thorpe of the hospital in question to testify to your dedication to this—or less flatteringly, a certain desire to draw attention to yourself, and fulfill your emotions, and perhaps occupy your time and your life in the absence of children to care for."

It was a tactical error. As soon as he said it he was aware of his mistake, but he did not know immediately how to retract it.

"On the contrary, Mr. Tobias," Hester said with a cold smile. "I have merely testified as to facts. It is you who are searching to invest them with some emotional value because it appears you do not like to be proved mistaken, which I cannot understand, since we are all aware you prosecute or defend as you are engaged to, not as a personal vendetta against anyone. At least I believe that to be the case?" She allowed it to be a question.

There was a rustle of movement around the room, a ripple of nervous laughter.

Tobias blushed. "Of course that is the case. But I am vigorous in it!"

"So am I!" she said tartly. "And my emotions are no less honorable than your own, except that law is not my profession . . ." She allowed the sentence to remain unfinished. They could draw their own conclusion as to whether she considered her amateur status to mark her inferiority in the matter or the fact that she did not take money for it and thus had a moral advantage.

"If you have no further questions, Mr. Tobias," the judge said, resuming command, "I shall adjourn the court until such time as this unfortunate woman is identified, then perhaps we shall also examine the hospital apothecary's records and be certain in the matter of what was stolen and when." He banged his gavel sharply and with finality.

* * *

Monk left the court without having heard Hester's second testimony. He went straight back to the Hampstead police station to find Sergeant Robb. It was imperative now that they learn who the dead woman had been. The only place to begin was with the assumption that Miriam had told the truth, and therefore she must have had some connection with Aiden Campbell.

"But why is he lying?" Robb said doubtfully as they set out along the street in the hazy sunlight. "Why? Let us even suppose that he seduced Miriam when she was his maid, or even raped her, it would hardly be the first time that had happened. Let us even say the woman on the Heath was a cook or housekeeper who knew about it, that'd be no reason to kill her."

"Well, somebody killed her," Monk said flatly, setting out across the busy street, disregarding the traffic and obliging a dray to pull up sharply. He was unaware of it and did not even signal his thanks to the driver, who shouted at him his opinion of drunkards and lunatics in general and Monk in particular.

Robb ran to catch up with him, raising a hand to the driver in acknowledgment.

"We've nowhere else to start," Monk went on. "Where did you say Campbell lived—exactly?"

Robb repeated the address. "But he moved to Wiltshire less than a year after that. There won't necessarily be anyone there now who knows him or anything that happened."

"There might be," Monk argued. "Some servants will have left; others prefer to stay in the area and find new positions, even stay in the house with whoever buys it. People belong to their neighborhoods."

"It's the far side of the Heath." Robb was having to hurry to keep up. "Do you want to take a hansom?"

"If one passes us," Monk conceded, not slackening his pace. "If she wasn't part of the household, who could she be? How was she involved? Was she a servant or a social acquaintance?"

"Well, there was nobody reported missing around that time," Robb replied. "She wasn't local, or somebody'd have said."

"So nobody missed her?" Monk swung around to face Robb and all but bumped into a gentleman coming briskly the other way. "Then she wasn't a neighbor or a local servant. This becomes very curious."

They said no more until they reached the house where Aiden Campbell had lived twenty-one years before. It had changed hands twice since then, but the girl who had been the scullery maid was now the housekeeper, and the mistress had no objection to allowing Monk and Robb to speak with her; in fact, she seemed quite eager to be of assistance.

"Yes, I was scullery maid then," the housekeeper agreed. "Miriam was the tweeny. Only a bit of a girl, she was, poor little thing."

"You liked her?" Monk said quickly.

"Yes—yes, I did. We laughed together a lot, shared stories and dreams. Got with child, poor little soul, an' I never knew what happened to her then. Think it may 'ave been born dead, for all that good care was took of 'er. Not surprising, I suppose. Only twelve or so when she got like that."

"Good care was taken of her?" Robb said with surprise.

"Oh, yes. Had the midwife in," she replied.

"How do you know she was a midwife?" Monk interrupted.

"She said so. She lived 'ere for a while, right before the birth. I do know that because I 'elped prepare 'er meals, an' took 'em up, on a tray, like."

"You saw her?" Monk said eagerly.

"Yes. Why? I never saw 'er afterwards."

Monk felt a stab of victory, and one of horror. "What was she like? Think hard, Miss Parkinson, and please be as exact as you can . . . height, hair, age!"

Her eyes widened. "Why? She done something as she shouldn't?"

"No. Please—describe her!"

"Very ordinary, she was, but very pleasant-looking, an' all. Grayish sort of hair, although I don't reckon now as she was over about forty-five or so. Seemed old to me then, but I was only fifteen an' anything over thirty was old."

"How tall?"

She thought for a moment. "About same as me, ordinary, bit less."

"Thank you, Miss Parkinson—thank you very much."

"She all right, then?"

"No, I fear very much that she may be the woman whose body was found on the Heath."

"Cor! Well, I'm real sorry." She said it with feeling, and there was sadness in her face as well as her voice. "Poor creature."

Monk turned as they were about to leave. "You didn't, by chance, ever happen to notice her boots, did you, Miss Parkinson?"

She was startled. "Her boots?"

"Yes. The buttons."

Memory sparked in her eyes. "Yes! She had real smart buttons on them. Never seen no others like 'em. I saw when she was sitting down, her skirts was pulled sideways a bit. Well, I never! I'm real sorry to hear. Mebbe Mrs. Dewar'll let me go to the funeral, since there won't be many others as'll be there now."

"Do you remember her name?" Monk said, almost holding his breath for her answer.

She screwed up her face in the effort to take her mind back to the past. She did not need his urging to understand the importance of it.

"It began with a *D*," she said after a moment or two. "I'll think of it."

They waited in silence.

"Dailey!" she said triumphantly. "Mrs. Bailey. Sorry I thought it were a *D*, but Bailey it was."

They thanked her again and left with a new energy of hope.

"I'll tell Rathbone," Monk said as soon as they were out in the street. "You see if you can find her family. There can't have been so many midwives called Bailey twenty-two years ago. Someone'll know her. Start with the doctors and the hospital. Send messages to all the neighboring areas. He may have brought her in from somewhere else. Probably did, since no one in Hampstead reported her missing."

Robb opened his mouth to protest, then changed his mind. It was not too much to do if it ended in proving Cleo Anderson innocent.

It was early afternoon of the following day when the court reconvened. Rathbone called the police surgeon, who gave expert confirmation of the testimony Hester had given regarding the death of the woman on the Heath. A cobbler swore to recognizing the boot buttons, and said that they had been purchased by one Flora Bailey some twenty-three years ago. Miss Parkinson came and described the woman she had seen, including the buttons.

The court accepted that the body was indeed that of Flora Bailey and that she had met her death by a violent blow in a manner which could only have been murder.

Rathbone called Aiden Campbell once again. He was pale, his face set in lines of grief and anger. He met Rathbone's eyes defiantly.

"I was hoping profoundly not to have to say this." His voice was hard. "I did know Mrs. Bailey. I had no idea that she was dead. I never required her services again. She was not, as my innocent scullery maid supposed, a midwife, but an abortionist."

There was a gasp of horror and outrage around the court. People turned to one another with a hissing of breath.

Rathbone looked up at Miriam in the dock and saw the amazement in her face, and then the anger. He turned to Harry Stourbridge, sitting stiff and silent, and Lucius beside him, stunned almost beyond reaction.

"An abortionist?" Rathbone said slowly, very clearly.

"Yes," Campbell agreed. "I regret to say so."

Rathbone raised his eyebrows very slightly. "You find abortion repugnant?"

"Of course I do! Doesn't every civilized person?"

"Of a healthy child, from a healthy mother, I imagine so,"

346

Rathbone agreed. "Then tell us, Mr. Campbell, why you had the woman staying in your house—so that your scullery maid carried up her meals to her on a tray?"

Campbell hesitated, lifting his hands. "If—if that was done, it was without my knowledge. The servants . . . perhaps they felt . . . I don't know . . . a pity—" He stopped. "If that ever happened," he added.

Tobias took his turn, briefly.

"Was that with your knowledge, or approval, Mr. Campbell?"

"Of course not!"

The court adjourned for luncheon.

The family of Flora Bailey arrived. Rathbone called her brother, a respected physician, as his first witness of the afternoon.

The gallery was packed. Word had spread like fire that something new was afoot. The tide had turned.

"Dr. Forbes," Rathbone began, "your sister spent time in the home of Mr. Aiden Campbell immediately before her disappearance. Were you aware of that?"

"No sir, I was not. I knew she had a case she considered very important but also highly confidential. The mother-to-be was very young, no more than a child herself, and whoever engaged her was most anxious that both she and the child should receive the very best attention. The child was much wanted, in spite of the circumstances. That is all she told me."

Rathbone was startled. "The child was wanted?"

"So my sister told me."

"And was it born healthy?"

"I have no idea. I never heard from my sister again."

"Thank you, Dr. Forbes. May I say how sorry I am for the reason which brings you here."

"Thank you," Forbes said soberly.

"Dr. Forbes, one last question. Did your sister have any feelings regarding the subject of abortion?"

"Very deep feelings," Forbes answered. "She was passionately opposed to it, regardless of the pity she felt for women who already had as many children as they could feed or care

347

for, or for those who were unmarried, or even who had been assaulted or otherwise abused. She could never bring herself to feel it acceptable. It was a matter of religious principle to her."

"So she would not have performed an abortion herself?"

"Never!" Forbes's face was flushed, his emotion naked. "If you doubt me, sir, I can name a dozen professional men who will say the same of her."

"I do not doubt you, Dr. Forbes, I simply wanted you to say it for the court to hear. Thank you for your patience. I have nothing further to ask."

Tobias half rose to his feet, then sat down again. He glanced across at Rathbone, and for the first time there was misgiving in his face, even anxiety.

Again there was silence in the room. No one even noticed Harry Stourbridge stand up. It was not until he spoke that suddenly every eye turned to him.

"My lord . . ." He cleared his throat. "I have listened to the evidence presented here from the beginning. I believe I now understand the truth. It is very terrible, but it must be told or an unbearable injustice will be done. Two women will be hanged who are innocent of any wrong."

The silence prickled like the coming of a storm.

"If you have information pertinent to this trial, then you should most certainly take the stand again, Major Stourbridge," the judge agreed. "Be advised that you are still under oath."

"I am aware of it, my lord," Stourbridge answered, and walked slowly from his seat, across the open space and up the steps of the witness box. He waited until the judge told him to proceed, then in a hoarse, broken voice, with desperate reluctance, he began.

"I come from a family of very considerable wealth, almost all of it in lands and property, with sufficient income to maintain them and some extra to provide a more than comfortable living. However, it is all entailed, and has been so for generations. I inherited it from my father, and it will pass to my son."

He stopped for a few seconds, as if regathering his strength. There was not a sound in the room. Everyone understood that here was a man laboring under terrible emotions as he realized a truth that shattered his life.

"If I had not had a son," he continued with difficulty, his voice trembling, "the property would have passed to my younger brother." Again he paused before gathering the strength to proceed. "My wife found it extremely difficult to carry a child. Time and again she conceived, and then miscarried within the first few months. We had almost given up hope when she came to visit me in Egypt while I was serving in the army there. It was a dangerous posting both because of the fighting and because of the natural hazards of disease. I was anxious for her, but she was determined to come, at all costs."

Now he was speaking, the words poured out. Every man and woman in the room was listening intently. No one moved even a hand.

"She stayed with me for over a month." His voice cracked. "She seemed to enjoy it. Then she returned by boat down the Nile to Alexandria. I have had much time to think over and over on what has happened, to try to understand why my wife was killed. She was a generous woman who never harmed anyone." He looked confused, beaten. "And why Miriam, whom we all cared for so much, should have wished her ill.

"I tried to recall what had been said at the dinner table. Verona had spoken of Egypt and her journey back down the Nile. Lucius asked her about a particular excursion, and she said she had wished to go but had been unable because she had not been very well. She dismissed it as of no importance, only a quite usual complaint for her which had passed."

His face was very white. He looked across at Lucius. "I'm so sorry," he said hoarsely. Then he faced forward again. "Yesterday evening I went and read her diary of the time, and found her reference to that day when she had written of the pain, and her distress, and then she had remembered Aiden's words of reassurance that it would all be well if she kept her courage and told no one. And she had done exactly as he had said." His voice dropped. "Then at last I understood."

Rathbone found himself hardly breathing, he was so intent upon Harry Stourbridge's white face and tight, aching voice.

"When she reached England again," Stourbridge continued, "she wrote and told me that during her stay with me she had become with child, and felt very well, and hoped that this time she would carry it until birth. I was overjoyed, for her even more than for myself."

In the gallery a woman sobbed, her heart touched with pity, maybe with an empathy.

Rathbone glanced up at Miriam. She looked as if she had seen death face-to-face.

Harry Stourbridge did not look at her, or at Lucius, or at Aiden Campbell, but straight ahead of him into a vision of the past only he could see.

"In due time I heard that the child was delivered, a healthy boy, my son Lucius. I was the happiest man alive. Some short time after that I returned to duties in England, and saw him. He was beautiful, and so like my wife." He could not continue. It took him several moments to regain even the barest mastery of his voice. When he spoke it was hoarse and little above a whisper.

"I loved him so much—I still do. The truth has no—has nothing to do with that. That will never change." He took a deep breath and let it out in a choking sigh. "But I now know that he is not my son, nor is he my wife's son."

There was a shock wave around the room as if an earthquake had struck. Jurors sat paralyzed. Even the judge seemed to grasp for his bench as if to hold himself steady.

Rathbone found his lips dry, his heart pounding.

Harry Stourbridge looked across at Lucius. "Forgive me," he whispered. "I have always loved you, and I always will." He faced forward again, at attention. "He is the baby my wife's brother, Aiden Campbell, begot by rape upon his twelve-year-old maid, Miriam Speake, so that I should have an heir and his sister should not lose access to my fortune,

350

should I die in action or from disease while abroad. She was always generous to him."

There was a low rumble of fury around the room.

Aiden Campbell shot to his feet, but he found no words to deny what was written on every face.

Two ushers moved forward simultaneously to restrain him, should it become necessary.

Harry Stourbridge went on as if oblivious to them all. He could not leave his story unfinished. "He murdered the midwife so she would never tell, and he attempted to murder the mother also, but distraught, hysterical, she escaped. Perhaps she never knew if her baby lived or died—until at her own engagement party she saw Aiden wield a croquet mallet, swinging it high in jest, and memory returned to her, and with understanding so fearful she could only run from us all, and keep silence even at the price of her life, rather than have anyone know, but above all Lucius himself, that he had fallen in love with his . . . own . . . mother." He could no longer speak; in spite of all he could do, the tears spilled down his cheeks.

The noise in the court increased like the roar of a rising tide. A wave of pity and anger engulfed the room.

The ushers closed in on Aiden Campbell, perhaps to restrain him, perhaps even to protect him.

Rathbone felt dizzy. Dimly he saw Hester, and just beyond her shoulder, Monk, his face as shocked as hers.

He looked up at Miriam. Not for an instant now did he need to wonder if this was the truth; it was written in her eyes, her mouth, every angle of her body.

He turned back to Harry Stourbridge.

"Thank you," he said quietly. "No one here can presume to know what it must have cost you to say this. I don't know if Mr. Tobias has any questions to ask you, but I have none."

Tobias stood up, began to speak, and then stopped. He glanced at the jury, then back to the judge. "I think, my lord, that in the interests of truth, some further detail is required.

Terrible as this story is, there are . . ." He made a gesture of helplessness and left the rest unsaid.

Rathbone was still on his feet.

"I think now, my lord, that Mrs. Gardiner has nothing left to protect. If I call her to the stand, she may be prepared to tell us the little we do not know."

"By all means," the judge agreed. "If she is willing—and if she is able." He turned to Stourbridge. "Thank you, sir, for your honesty. We need ask nothing further of you."

Like a man walking through water, Harry Stourbridge went down the steps and stood for a moment in the middle of the floor. He looked up at the dock, where Miriam had risen to her feet. There was a gentleness in his face which held the room in silence, a compassion and a gratitude that even in her anguish she could not have failed to recognize.

He waited while she came down, the jailer standing aside as if he understood his duty was over.

Miriam stopped in front of Harry Stourbridge. Haltingly, he reached out and touched her arm, so lightly she could barely have felt it. He smiled at her. She put her hand over his for an instant, then continued on her way to the steps of the witness stand, climbed up and turned to face Rathbone and the court.

"Mrs. Gardiner," Rathbone said quietly, "I understand now why you preferred to face the rope for a crime you did not commit rather than have Lucius Stourbridge learn the truth of his birth. But that is not now possible. Nor can Aiden Campbell any longer hide from his acts—or blame you for any part of them. I do not require you to relive a past which must be painful beyond our imagining, but justice necessitates that you tell the jury what you know of the deaths of James Treadwell and Verona Stourbridge."

Miriam nodded very slightly, with just the barest acknowledgment, then in a quiet, drained voice she began.

"I ran from the croquet lawn. At first I did not care where I went, anywhere to be away from the house, alone—to try to realize what had happened, what it was I had remembered—

if it could really be true. More than anything on earth, I did not want it to be." She stopped for a moment.

"Of course—it was, but I did not fully accept it then. I ran to the stables and begged Treadwell to take me anywhere. I gave him my locket as payment. He was greedy, but not entirely a bad man. I asked him to drive me to Hampstead Heath. I didn't tell him why. I wanted to go back to where poor Mrs. Bailey was killed, to remember what really happened—if the flash of recollection I had on the croquet lawn was even some kind of madness."

Someone coughed, and the noise made people start in the tingling silence.

"Aiden Campbell must have seen my recognition," she went on. "He also remembered, and perhaps knew where I would go. He followed us, and found us near the tree where Mrs. Bailey's body was hidden. He had to kill Treadwell if he was going to kill me, or he'd have been blackmailed for the rest of his life. He struck Treadwell first. He caught him completely by surprise.

"I ran. I know the area better than he because I lived near the Heath for years. Perhaps desperation lent me speed. It was getting dark. I escaped him. After that I had no idea where to go or what to do. At last, in the morning, I went to Cleo Anderson . . . again. But this time I could not bear to tell even her what I knew."

"And the death of Verona Stourbridge, after you were released back into the Stourbridges' custody," Rathbone prompted her.

She looked at him. "I couldn't tell anyone . . ."

"We understand. What do you know about Verona Stourbridge's death?"

"I believe she always thought Lucius was . . . an abandoned baby. She hid the truth from Major Stourbridge, but she had no knowledge of any crime, only her own deception, made from her despair that she would never bear a child for her husband. I know now that she knew it was Aiden's child, but not about me or how he was concerned. She must have asked Aiden about it—and although he loved her, he could not afford to let her know the truth." Her voice dropped. "No matter how close they were, and they truly were, she might one day have told someone—she would have had to—to explain—" In spite of herself her eyes went to Lucius, sitting on the front bench, the tears running down his cheeks.

"I'm so sorry," Miriam whispered. "I'm so, so sorry . . ."

Rathbone turned to the judge.

"My lord, is it necessary to protract this any longer? May we adjourn for an hour or so before we conclude? I have nothing further to ask, and I cannot believe Mr. Tobias will pursue this anymore."

Tobias rose to his feet. "I am quite willing, my lord. What little remains can be dealt with after an adjournment. Major Stourbridge and his family have my deepest sympathy."

"Very good." The judge banged his gavel, and after a moment's heavy stillness, people began to move.

Rathbone felt bruised, exhausted, as if he had made some great physical journey. He turned to Hester and Monk, who were coming towards him from the body of the court. Just behind them was a man with scruffy black hair and a beard that went in every direction. He was beaming with satisfaction, his eyes shining.

Hester smiled.

"You have achieved the impossible," Monk said, holding out his hand to Rathbone.

Rathbone took it and held it hard for a few moments.

"We still have the matter of the medicines," he warned.

"No, we don't!" Hester assured him. "Mr. Phillips here is the apothecary at the hospital. He has persuaded Fermin Thorpe that nothing is missing. It was all a matter of natural wastage and a few rather careless entries in the books. No actual thefts at all. It was a mistake to have mentioned it."

Rathbone was incredulous. "How in heaven's name did you do that?" He regarded Phillips with interest and a growing respect.

"Never enjoyed anything more," Phillips said, grinning

broadly. "A little issue of one favor for another—resurrection, you might say!"

Monk looked at Hester narrowly.

She beamed back at him with complete innocence.

"Well done, Mr. Phillips," Rathbone said gratefully. "I am much obliged."

*If you liked this novel, you won't want
to miss the rest. . . .*

The William Monk Novels
by
Anne Perry

THE FACE OF A STRANGER

A DANGEROUS MOURNING

DEFEND AND BETRAY

A SUDDEN, FEARFUL DEATH

THE SINS OF THE WOLF

CAIN HIS BROTHER

WEIGHED IN THE BALANCE

THE SILENT CRY

A BREACH OF PROMISE

Published by Ballantine Books.
Available wherever books are sold.

Immerse yourself in the mysterious world of
Anne Perry's Victorian London. Look for this
thrilling William Monk novel, now
available in paperback!

A BREACH OF PROMISE
A William Monk Novel

by Anne Perry

Stripping away the pretty masks that conceal society's darkest transgressions, Anne
Perry unflinchingly exposes the human
heart's deepest hiding places—and creates
the most mesmerizing courtroom drama of
her distinguished career.

*And don't miss the newest
Charlotte and Thomas Pitt novel
in paperback:*

BEDFORD SQUARE
by
ANNE PERRY

Another matchless Victorian mystery of men
and women who embrace the best and the
worst of human nature, where vicious lies
become weapons of destruction—and dead
men tell no lies.

**And look for the previous
Charlotte and Thomas Pitt novel:**

ASHWORTH HALL
by Anne Perry

The gathering at the country estate of Charlotte
Pitt's wealthy sister has the appearance of a smart
autumn house party. In reality, the guests are Irish
Protestants and Catholics in reluctant parley over
home rule for Ireland, a problem that has plagued
the British Isles since the reign of Elizabeth I.
When the meeting's moderator, a government
bigwig, is found murdered in his bath, the
negotiations seem doomed.

Charlotte and her husband, Superintendent
Thomas Pitt, of Scotland Yard, must root out the
truth before simmering passions above and below
stairs explode again in murder.

If you enjoy the
Charlotte and Thomas Pitt novels,
why not go back to the beginning?

THE CATER STREET HANGMAN

THE FIRST CHARLOTTE AND THOMAS PITT NOVEL

by Anne Perry

While the Ellison girls were out paying calls one afternoon, a maid in their own household was strangled to death. Quiet young Inspector Pitt found no one above suspicion—and his investigation at the staid Ellison home caused many a composed façade to crumble into panic.

But it was not panic beating in the heart of Charlotte Ellison, and something more than brutal murder was on Inspector Pitt's mind. Yet a romance between a society girl and a common policeman was impossible—especially during an investigation of murder . . . .

Published by Ballantine Books.
Available at your local bookstore.